"Enjoy!"

Micah Campbell

BADGER

By Micah Campbell
Book 1 of the Retribution Trilogy

"Teaser"

The worm had no major organs, other than its heart and brain, which were both protected under its head shell, so the bullets caused no damage other then a loss of blood. However, it could very well feel the pain and it did not like it. It was hard to tell which surprised the Chinese more, the Specters that started to fire upon them, or the worm's violent rage.

The worm dug its spades underneath the vehicle, lifted it high above its head and then flung it at the stunned soldiers. The sudden exposure caused both Specters to fire wild at the Chinese. They too were stunned by the worm's rage, it had seemed so gentle.

The vehicle spun as it hurtled towards the soldiers, all but one PDCT managed to leap out of the way and the force of the impact broke his helmet off and his skull was cracked open when he hit the building behind him. One of the light-infantry had managed to avoid being hit, but a bullet from Badger dispatched him.

"Glossary"

"Organizations"

GEN: Galactic Encounter Navy, an extra-terrestrial fighting force.

IPWC: International Progress and Welfare Counsel, a group responsible for the distribution of technology across known space. Founded on November 8, 2232 as a part of ISEN. It's also referred to by some as Inept People Without a Clue.

ISEN: International Space Exploration Navy, a funded organization of frontier soldiers. Founded on March 31, 2223 by the US, UK, and the RSR.

REPEL: Research of Extra-Political Engagement Laws, a US military faction that trains the Specters, who are given the right to do whatever it takes to keep the peace. People given power over every other military amongst the Allies.

RSR: The Renewed States of Russia. After a brutal civil war in 2176, Russia had fallen into a state of chaos and disability. But with the aid of the US and UK, they rebuilt themselves upon a new constitution, pulling themselves up from the wreckage of their ruined homeland, to be called the Renewed States of Russia.

"Technology"

AFT-27: All-Flying Threat, a brand attached to aircraft that can fly into heavy combat situations with heavy payloads.

AI: Artificial Intelligence, computer programs that can either be made to do specified tasks, or think for themselves at a much higher level than humans. Can take on digital forms if it wants to.

EMP: Electromagnetic Pulse, an energy field that shuts down electronic devices.

HUD: head-up display, a computer displayed inside a helmet that analyzes terrain and displays information.

MATO: Mobile All-Terrain Ophthalmic, a machine that is piloted by a man with a neural interface or controls. Can be in various shapes and sizes, with exchangeable parts and weapons.

PDCT: Planetary Drop and Clear Troopers, ISEN Special Forces. They're the first people to be sent onto a planet's surface to clear any major threats to research or reconnaissance teams.

VTOL: Vertical Take-Off and Landing, any vehicle that can lift straight into the air.

"Weapons"

ASP: aerodynamic splinter projector. A military sidearm that can hold a variety of attachment and be quickly used brought into short-range combat for fast cover fire.

BAW5: basic assault weapon, one of several types of standard weapons used in the military. SEAR-firing and capable of semi-auto or full-auto fire, a mid to long-range weapon.

BPR: Biometric Precision Rifle, a high-powered target rifle that uses a living organism (based off of coral) as ammunition. The organism feels no pain and growls to a set size, with a healing factor that allows a soldier to continue firing and never run out of ammo.

GEM: genetic modular, an animal bread and altered for war. Also placed onto their customized weapons to mean it's built for their size as most GEMs are small.

GEM SAR SEC: Genetic Modular Standard Assault Rifle/Short Engaged Contact Rifle. One of the weapons designed for GEMs, but still useable by humans. Also called a GEM Assault Rifle.

HD27: a level 27 High-Destruction bomb. Made with nano harmonizers to adjust the blast radius or radiation release, if any, to fry instruments and people.

SEAR: Systematically Emitted Aluminum Razor(s), standard ammunition. Super-compact aluminum wool that can be nano-enhanced for certain effects such as armor-piercing or explosive properties.

SMG: sub-machine gun, a bullet-firing weapon still used in the military. Typically small, with adjustable grips and folding stocks.

SRW12A: type twelve of a Semi-Recon Weapon, a bullet-firing pistol for medium to short range combat. Popular amongst civilians.

"Preface"

This is the story of a twenty-fifth century soldier from the United States, no one yet knew where he had come from, or exactly what he was. He didn't even know himself, and he didn't care. A decade before he appeared, a war was fought, the first of its kind, a war that sent humanity back two centuries, all their fantastic technology was reduced to a mere shamble of its former glory. But humanity, still spreading throughout space, had survived it all. At least... they thought they had. A new war has arisen, as they always will, and the soldier must face it as he always has. But this time, the foundation of everything he has ever known and put his faith in will be tested, and he will have to choose his every step through the sands of time. Beneath heaven's doorstep the mortals will fight until the King steps down to claim his own, and in this such time the soldier will not be cast away. For though fire may boil his marrow and tear at his mind like a rabid beast, he will stand as the one chosen, his world fall, his heart break, he fights for the Kingdom of God. He stands not alone, and he shall drive away the enemy like chaff in the wind. This is his story, this is his retribution.

"Prologue"

One cloudy spring day, with the twin moons just visible, an older gray truck, a lightweight short-bed with large, wide tires, gravel and grass stuck in them from a long trip and a streamlined windshield, pulled up the long driveway of an old farm.

It approached a curve and the driver turned the steering wheel clockwise. All four wheels turned at once and the truck smoothly navigated the corner, leaving tread marks in the thin layer of mud caused by an earlier rain fall. Its wide body made it very stable around sharp turns.

The truck's dashboard was like an integrated-computer. The driver's side conventional displays were holographic images, while between the driver and the passenger side, was an "intelligence unit" with panel displays.

The driver was a young man in his thirties; with dark black hair and a thick mustache. Henry Mindell was his name. The inside of his truck was a mess of crumpled papers, rags and empty candy wrappers. In his mouth was a pipe, ivory stemmed with a scrimshawed bone bowl from which red embers of tobacco glowed.

With both hands on the steering wheel, he blew puffs of smoke out the window as he glanced at either side of the road. Large greenhouses were on both sides, housing certain crops that the farmers could harvest year-round.

The radio was on and classical music played, a stringed orchestra. He tapped his right index finger on the steering wheel in time with the music. Across Henry's left eye was a short, diagonal scar from a fight long ago. He wore a baseball cap to try to hide it in its shadow. However, it didn't do much good as people still grimaced when they saw it, but he had learned to live with it.

His thick, brown, wool jacket was zipped halfway up. A lump in the jacket was the only giveaway of the concealed weapon. He needed his pistol for both protection and his work. Most people who noticed thought he was a private investigator.

He slowed the truck to a halt in front of the farmhouse. It was a plain, red brick building with a wooden porch graced by potted plants on either side of the steps. What drew him to the farm was a trail of signs ending at the house which read: "Mix-breed puppies to good homes; bargained price, cash, no checks".

There were already several cars out in front of the house and people were looking into a pen. Not to offend anyone, he smothered his pipe and set it on the dashboard. Mindell stepped out of his truck, shut the door and strode into the small crowd to glance into the pen.

The dogs were dark brown with white blotches and bright blue eyes. They had small, rounded ears and whippy tails. They were all crowded against the pen wall, wagging their tails and yipping with energy. While he stood there, the number of puppies dwindled by three. He watched the people who had selected and saw that they took them up to the house's porch where an elderly couple sat and bargained the price.

Now with a clear idea of how the transaction worked, Henry looked down into the mass of wriggling bodies. He was a bit disappointed, they were all cute and energetic, but there weren't any intriguing qualities about them.

He shrugged and was about to leave when he spotted another, different from the others. It was on the far side, wrestling with a piece of knotted rope, disconnected to the revelry of the others. Henry looked at the puppy with immense curiosity. Its fur was short and sleek, cotton white with a black stripe running from between its ears to the tip of its broad muzzle. Its paws were also black and large, and there was something odd about them, but Mindell could not place it. Its ears were tall and erect and its eyes were like amber ice. Its head was slightly large, but that wasn't too noticeable.

The puppy gripped the length of rope in its mouth and rolled about, kicking the air with his paws. He seemed to prefer wrestling with the rope rather then engaging in the distractions that occupied the others. Whenever someone thought that they might be interested in him, he ran out of their reach and continued his little game.

He wagged his tail, growling and play-fighting with the rope as if it was an enemy. He shook it vigorously with his mouth and let go, sending it several inches to his left. He quickly leaped at it again, thrashing at it without mercy.

Henry smiled and leaned forward on the wall of the pen. He stroked his chin thoughtfully with one hand and reached into a coat pocket with the other and felt his wallet thoughtfully. It was then that the dog caught sight of him.

When the amber-eyed pup caught sight of Henry, he froze for a long moment, one of his ears twitched and, after a few more moments, its lips widened into a broad smile, its tail began to wag and it trotted towards Henry. Once at the wall of the pen, he dropped the rope, pressed his forepaws against the wire wall, and barked.

Almost without thinking, Henry removed his hand from his pocket and reached down. Unlike with the others, the puppy let this man lift him from the pen. Not before it grabbed the rope back up into jaws though.

Surprised by its weight, Mindell, with the pup beaming a broad smile at him and wagging its tail, walked over to the table to exchange the cash.

He waited for a moment while a black lady with three young kids handed over several American bills. After they left, he stepped up to the table and asked, "Is this thing even of the same litter as the others?"

The couple seemed stunned, their eyes moved quickly from Henry to the odd puppy. This only lasted a few seconds and then the lady spoke. "How long did it take you to catch 'im?

Henry cocked his eyes. "I didn't catch him, he came to me."

"That doesn't sound like him," she said with a strange look. "There must be something about you he likes."

"Little weirdo," said the elderly man.

Henry didn't know what the man meant and he didn't inquire. "How much do you think is a proper price for a dog like this?"

"Not much, that's all I can say," said the man.

"Quiet, Fred," the lady said.

Henry sighed; this wasn't going as smoothly as he had thought, "how about seventy dollars?"

"In this day and age?" the man scoffed. "You've got to be kidding me."

"Ninety," said Henry.

"Better, but not there yet."

Henry sighed and stroked the puppy's ears, "One-hundred and ten?" Henry didn't know why he said that, but it seemed to be the correct number.

"He's all yours," said the man with a shrewd smile.

Henry set the puppy onto the table and reached into his pocket for his wallet. It was the wrong pocket. He started to reach towards the other pocket, but the dog got there first.

He removed Henry's wallet with his mouth, opened it and cycled through the cash with his nose. After a moment, it pulled out a few bills in its jaws and dropped them on the table. It was the needed amount, all laid atop the table in front of the elderly couple.

Unlike Henry, the elderly couple calmly gathered up the bills and dropped them into a large jar. "Thanks mister," said the lady, as she patted the puppy's head.

"What is he," Henry asked as he lifted the puppy off the table and looked into its face. "Are you independently breeding GEMs?"

The man shook his head, "that one I found outside our shed, a couple days after the litter was born. He's not bred by us, if he is a GEM, you can take him."

"For only one hundred and ten dollars," Henry wondered aloud, curious as to why such a low price.

"You could pay me more then," the man said with a glare.

"No, thank you," said Henry with a smile, "I already bought him. He's mine now, thanks."

"And good riddance to the pestilence," muttered the old

gentleman.

* * *

The driveway exited onto a narrow dirt road with large pines on either side, covered with lichen and moss. The sun was starting to set and now the silhouettes of Mars' twin moons could be seen clear and bright above through a break in the clouds. Phobos and Deimos were part of an orbital-defense grid above Mars, linked up with hundreds of orbital-defense stations that circled the globe. The stations could be seen at night as red blinking lights in the distance.

Henry gripped the wheel of his truck; he still couldn't understand that man's demeanor, but he tried to ignore it. The puppy was on the passenger's side of the truck atop Henry's coat which he had taken off and thrown inside. But, now that he had the dog, he didn't know what to do if it really was a GEM.

A GEM, or genetic modular, was an animal that was specially engineered and bred for military or domestic purposes. There were very few GEM breeds made due to the cost and time it took with the research and engineering. But how could one wind up on a farm?

He leaned back and watched the road. Then he heard a prominent click which made him turn his head. By using a claw that acted like a thumb on his right paw, the dog had removed the magazine from Henry's pistol. Henry almost swerved off the road as he watched it empty the caseless bullets from the magazine.

Henry pressed on the brakes and the truck came to a slow, squeaky stop.

Wondering why the truck had stopped, the puppy looked up at Henry and cocked his head. The odd look in Henry's eyes seemed to please the puppy and its tongue lulled out as it smiled. It laid down the gun's accessories and trotted up to Henry.

To Henry's astonishment, the puppy stood itself onto its hind legs. But being young, the puppy easily lost balance and toppled forward onto Henry's lap. It whined for a moment and then returned to its jubilant mood, smiling up at Henry.

Henry deftly scratched the puppy behind the ears. "So you are a GEM. Why in space and time did God bless me with you? Whatever… why don't you put my gun back together and leave it alone."

Henry meant that as a joke, but the puppy obeyed. Henry was stunned for only a few moments before he started the engine again and drove off down the road. "Whatever modular you are, you're better then any other I've ever seen."

The puppy replaced the pistol inside Henry's coat pocket then picked up the length of rope in his mouth and curled up next to Henry. He chewed slowly as the car hummed and started to lull him to sleep. But before his eyes fully closed, he heard Henry speak.

"I disagree with that man; you're worth quite a lot." Then a thought came to Henry's mind. "Badger… your name is now Badger."

Henry didn't see it, but a large smile formed on the puppy's face and he pressed himself tighter against his master's leg.

The twin moons had now risen to the center of the sky and the sun had pulled back its bright blanket to reveal the stars. A meteor flew across the sky, almost for forever before it disintegrated. What would come of the bond that was being shared between the two? How far will it go?

Chapter 1

"Brief History"

Near the beginning of civilization on Mars, the International Space Research and Habitat Creation Industry (familiarly Enterprise) dug up the remains of an ancient civilization. The remains of the civilization showed a vast array of architecture, transport and combat technology. After learning how to interpret the language of the civilization, Enterprise quickly deciphered the means to create similar devices.

Afterward, many more sites had been dug up from the Martian soil, each site unique in its own way. Several sites that were dug up were full of artwork, images of feasts, great hunts, travels, pleasant scenery, and war. Every picture, painted with an unknown compound that would not deteriorate, had a superb depth of realism and three-dimensionality.

The artwork depicted figures, humans and others strange figures. Some pictures showed what appeared to be the more prosperous of the civilization, showing them wearing fine clothes, jewelry and having enormous collections. Some had collections of weapons, both advanced and primitive. The paintings of the less fortunate were depicted much like Earth's own poor, tattered clothes, rejected, and strong.

The civilization called itself the Settlement. However advanced the Settlement was, they had not reached space, nor flight. This left a few questions, and Enterprise had managed to work with whatever technology that had been found and created an entirely new generation.

Now Mars was covered in vast seas and forests, livable deserts and jungles, tundra and prairies. Diplomacy sectors had been set up for different countries and their governments. Animals had been transported from Earth to their specific environments. Cities had been erected and transportation systems had been built between them.

Also, using the Settlement technology, Enterprise managed to convert Earth's moon, Luna and Mars' twin moons Deimos and Phobos, into livable environments. They also formed a mining and research colony just inside Jupiter's gaseous atmosphere. These mining colonies were also starting to form on the other planets. Weaponry is now based upon magnetic-propulsion ballistics and biometrics.

And, very recently, the International Progress and Welfare Counsel (IPWC) formed the International Space Exploration Navy (ISEN). Using faster then light travel, tunnels formed by artificial black holes that ended at what are known as white holes. But, due to worldwide concern, ISEN had to make slow progress in its movements. They were only allowed to move a certain length when using the wormholes. After two hundred years ISEN hadn't yet covered a fraction of the galaxy.

However, the Navy's progress was amazing; nearly seven planets were found that already sustained life. But the search for extraterrestrial intelligence still went on. The seven planets were named Attain, Discovery, Forerunner, Expedition, Foundling, Grasp and Venture and were full of unintelligent life, both familiar and alien.

Already ISEN had set up bases (and cities on some) on these planets to monitor and research the diverse habitats of these Earth-like planets. Everyday, information was broadcast between the systems. Then one day all contact with Forerunner came to an abrupt end. The first thoughts turned towards some sort of hostile alien force, but the enemy appeared much closer then suspected.

Jealous that they should share information with other countries, Chinese forces took over one of the ships and bombarded Forerunner's colonies. This unprovoked attack caused ISEN and IPWC to return their exploring ships back towards Earth and Mars. These ships now hover above China on both planets, ready to strike back at them for their treachery.

Unwilling to shed more blood than necessary, the United States government has sent in two of their elite operatives. These operatives have been given the right of espionage, theft and assassination to keep the peace between countries. Their mission: to reach the Chinese command computer and call off all attacks on the ISEN fleet. They are alone, they have only each other, but they are the Specters.

Chapter 2

"The Specters"

Henry Mindell was fair-skinned and unshaven. He was average height for his family, about six-two; he was thickly built with large, well toned muscles and sinew. A short diagonal scar cut across his left eye, he let his black hair grow long on that side to try and hide it. He was a Marine veteran that had been asked to join the Specters after he was discharged at age twenty-five. He had now served thirteen years as one of the Specters. He only volunteered for missions he was capable of completing, but then again it was more prayer than talent to him.

The second operativewas only five years old, went by the name of Badger, or "Tall Dwarf", was a dog Genetic-Modular (GEM). A GEM was an animal specially bred and engineered for domestic or military purposes. Badger's origin was a mystery; no one knew what corporation had made him, or where he was really from. Henry had bought him from a farm four years ago and after a few months, had Badger enlisted as a Specter also.

Badger had received the name "Tall Dwarf" because his head seemed slightly larger than it should have been. His name was derived from a stripe that ran between his ears to the tip of his nose. He had tall, erect ears that tapered down to a rounded point. Other than his paws and stripe, he was covered in short, cotton-white fur. His amber eyes could see in the dark and in the same colors as a human. He was the most sophisticated GEM anyone had yet seen.

He was only about three feet nine inches in height, but he was strong and elusive when necessary. Also extremely flexible and a very deadly knife fighter. His design, as most combat GEMs' were, was so that he could easily balance on his hind legs. His weapon preference was a kukri (a long-bladed curved knife) and a compact, bullpup-configured rifle.

Each Specter wore a helmet made out of a laminated, hard-edged fabric, backed with a layer of a deflective gel. Each helmet had an array of hologram projectors inside along the open portion of the helmet to project the heads-up display (HUD). Less advanced systems had a reflector bar that ran over the nose to give third-dimensional images. In front of where the holograms were displayed was a rounded screen to protect their eyes. Along with the helmets they had full body uniforms made of a strong, flexible fabric with hard, laminated fabric plates as extra defense. Underneath the uniform was an exoskeleton that allowed each superior strength and speed as opposed to light militia. The exoskeletons were powered by energy-magnifiers built into the boots of the Specters. The magnifiers took the energy of the boots' impact and amplified it enough to power the exoskeleton and helmet. With all their other equipment added, they were both deadly enemies to be had.

Both Specters stood aboard the *Traveler*, an ISEN ship hovering above New Kunlun Shan, home of the Chinese leader. They were in a small hangar that could only hold two small vertical takeoff and landing vehicles (VTOLs) that were known as Mosquitoes. They were awaiting the arrival of the pilot that would fly them in.

Badger sat on the floor next to Henry, who was standing, scratching his exposed neck with a hind-paw. It always felt good to scratch that area, but he always stopped himself before he got carried away. His kukri was attached to his belt while his rifle was attached to his back.

Henry had a regular single-edged knife which was serrated near the grip. He carried a compact machine-gun; bullpup designed, with an eighty round, 9mm sabot-round, magnetic-propulsion bullet clip, a BAW5. His secondary weapon was a pistol, a simple SRW12A.

VTOL pilots wore a protective fabric armor designed to stop shrapnel, resist extreme heats and absorb impact in case of a crash. They also wore an ophthalmic-helmet that had a full-face screen, designed so that wherever the pilot looked, the VTOL's turrets would turn and they even detected eye movement. Experienced pilots could turn their eyes in two different directions to take on two targets simultaneously. This one was no less then an expert.

Badger stood up on all fours, his eyes moving with the pilot, who saluted Henry before climbing into the VTOL up to the cockpit. Both Specters followed.

Mosquitoes were basically shaped like a blunt cone, with two, thin propulsion wings bent back at an angle behind the cockpit and two stabilizers on either side. At the end of the wings were thick, rotating rings that held the rotary blades which gave the VTOLs lift. The backs of the Mosquitoes were slanted backwards for balance and were the only way in or out. A small, vertical blade was placed on the tail for maneuverability.

The pilot slipped through a narrow doorway to get into the cockpit, while Badger and Henry sat down on one of two benches that were in the rear. The pilot turned on the power and a row of round lights turned on overhead.

"Stay seated," said the pilot with a thick Australian accent. "We have orders that we have to wait for a detachment of PDCTs. They'll be takin' the other VTOL."

Planetary Drop and Clear Troopers were another ISEN military faction. They were volunteer-based soldiers that were used to explore and clear areas for drop-ships. They were trained similarly to Marines and on more then one occasion they had been used in combat with hostile forces that opposed certain options.

The doorway to the hangar opened and the six PDCTs marched

in, following another pilot, towards the second VTOL. One of the soldiers elbowed the PDCT next to him and pointed towards Badger. They both muttered something about a news report and nodded to each other.

The PDCT's uniforms were similar to that of the Specter's save that the plates were large and their helmets provided full coverage for their heads. As a rule, the PDCT's uniforms were completely black with a multicolored galaxy over their hearts. They weren't Marines, but they would do just fine.

The rotary-blades spun by using a series of powerful magnets in the propulsion-funnels, those plus the VTOL was made of lightweight, laminated fabric gave them speed and maneuverability. The Mosquitoes lifted off the hangar floor and passed through the Traveler's habitat shield and down towards New Kunlun Shan.

Chapter 3

"Happy Landings"

Fires rose over the city like nocturnal lights in the night, great pillars of smoke loomed up into the night sky, blotting out the stars. Great was the vastness of the city that ten of ISEN's largest ships had to be spread wide. Because the IPWC was against unnecessary bloodshed, the fleet was ordered not to fire until their shields were reduced to minimum effectiveness. Explosions lit up the sky, tracers zipped through the air and the hot streaks of missiles flashed across the sky.

The Mosquitoes maneuvered their way through the fire, heading towards the city network. The backs of these small VTOLs didn't have coverings; this was a safety regulation so that the occupants could easily bail. The back being open also created a wind tunnel, greatly increasing the VTOL's speed.

The Specter-occupied VTOL swung left to avoid a straight column of tracers. The pilots shifted his eyes and commenced with nasty return fire. Using the VTOL's integrated-computer, the pilot could change the rate of fire and the size of the grouping to what was necessary from Mosquito's two turrets, located underneath the cockpit . A rocket-pod under each wing could fire the same way, although with more precision.

Badger detached his rifle from the holster, which was an

electronically adhesive plate between his shoulders which worked by pressing one of two buttons outside of the trigger guard, one released the rifle and the other activated the adhesive. His rifle was smaller then Henry's, a bullpup design with the handle built into the stock, a double-row clip and a computerized objective-scope; known as the GEM SAR/SEC, or, the GEM Assault Rifle. Badger had always liked the rifle for it weight and efficiency; what it lacked in size was more than made up in its end result.

Henry was slightly worried about Badger, because ever since he got out of combat training, Badger's life seemed to be a void. Nothing was important anymore than to complete the objective and protect Henry with a loyalty yet unseen. Badger had expressed his devotion to Henry on their first mission together, which was something Henry didn't like to think back on; Badger was extremely deadly with his kukri. Henry had owned Badger for four years; he never regretted it, but he was sorry to admit, Badger had a messed up perspective.

"We'll be comin' up on the drop-site any minute," shouted the pilot. "Get ready to get lost."

"That's a new one on me," said Henry as he took his rifle from his holster.

Badger made a noise that affirmed he was ready and turned his rifle on. He set the launch-magnet (the device that launched the bullets) onto a specific spread-fire and growled approvingly. His tall ears and nose twitched and his forehead creased aggressively.

To both Specters it looked as if it would be a long night. There was no telling when or where Chinese forces would show up. They prayed nothing tragic would happen.

*　　*　　*

The PDCT occupied VTOL was close beside the Specter craft. Their platoon, Delta Hunter, was headed by First Sergeant Alexander McClain, a British subject with a taste for victory. The others were: Private John, Corporal Kruger, Private First Class Andy, Specialist Sakuma and Private Douglas. Each of them, except Douglas, had seen human combat, his only battles while a PDCT had been on Grasp and Discovery and then with alien animals only. Everyone called him Rookie.

Alexander gripped the edge of the seat as the VTOL took a sudden, sharp turn. He hated it when that happened. He was from Earth, raised on a tough street in London and one day accidentally walked into an ISEN recruitment center thinking it was a pharmacy. Then, after several years, he was made First Sergeant, well decorated for his achievements on Expedition. Now he was faced by a conflict on Mars, one that he planned on resolving.

"We're nearing the drop-site," said the pilot. "Prepare yourself and… we'll have to delay the drop, aerial-drones have appeared on radar."

"Great," said Kruger as he hefted a large sniper rifle, "I could use the target practice."

"Not if I shoot 'em all first," said John as he unattached a scoped rifle from his holster. Both of them had become good friends since they enlisted and they were very competitive in their fighting.

"It won't be long now before we see some sparks," Sakuma muttered. Sakuma was a Japanese citizen who had been educated in an American university; no one quite knew how he wound up as a PDCT.

"Calm down you two," said Alexander, "Our pilot'll stop them before you even get a... augh!"

The VTOL suddenly bucked, sending everyone onto the floor. Kruger just barely managed to fall inside the VTOL, his legs dangled over the edge. Rookie yelled aloud and covered his head with his arms. Sakuma quickly recovered from the shock and shouted to the pilot.

"We've been hit by a rocket," was the pilot's reply. "Don't worry; our damage status is at minimum."

After the PDCTs had mostly recovered, the pilot commenced firing on the drones. The twin guns and rockets, plus the firepower of the other VTOL were enough to hold the drones at bay.

The rocket had been fired from an infantry unit on the ground, a misfire. The aerial drones that were attacking the VTOLs used simple rotary-guns. The drones were basically shaped like the old helicopters, except that they had VTOL wings, though smaller.

Kruger and John were once again attempting to take down the drones that the VTOLs missed. John had one drone in his crosshairs, but before he could pull the trigger, Kruger had downed it with a single shot. A huge, clean, red-hot hole was placed just between the wings, the drone circled down towards the ground. John cursed and searched for a new target.

Kruger's rifle fired 12.7mm anti-material sabot-rounds; the magnetic propellant was so powerful that it had to launch the bullet in less then one one-thousandth of a second or else attract every piece of metal within six yards. The bullets were fit into a large nonmagnetic clip with an energy-coated inner rim to ensure no extra bullets left the clip after firing. Because the bullet traveled so fast it caused very noticeable shock-waves in the air and a large compensator was attached to the end to cut down on the dangerous recoil. The LPSER90, or Liner, was a deadly tool on any battlefield, although on impact with water the bullets simply exploded, causing casualties within a six meter radius.

John admired Kruger's sniping skills, plus his rifle, but he didn't like the idea of watching body fragments falling all over the place. He fired a quick burst at another drone, the first two bullets glanced off, but the third sank in. Another burst finished it off.

Rookie got up from his seat; he yelped in surprise as several bullets whizzed past his helmet, heard as a buzzing sound over the helmet's sound-enhancer. He shook his head and crouch-walked his way over to where the two competitors were shooting. He grabbed hold of the edge of a seat and leaned forward and watched as the drones flew about, dove, or were eliminated. The next thing Rookie knew was that he was hanging upside down while someone was holding onto his left leg.

What had happened was that another rocket had come up from below and hit the VTOL's underside. That had thrown Rookie off balance, but the sergeant had managed to grab his leg before he fell all the way to the ground.

"Don't let go," Douglas shouted, looking up at the sergeant's blue-tinted screen. "I only have an SMG and an ASP."

"I'm not plannin' on letting go," Alexander shouted at the top of his lungs. "Stop moving, you're going t' take me with you."

"I can't help it," Rookie shouted as he flailed his arms in the rushing air. Then he noticed that Kruger and John weren't helping. "Where'd the other two go?"

"Down," said Alexander, "the blast bucked 'em out. The others are out for the moment; I barely managed to catch you... I said stop moving."

Two red streaks appeared on Rookie's rearview display, these were quickly followed by two crimson flashes. Rookie hollered out loudly as he felt himself falling to the ground below. The ground rushed up at him and then all went black.

*   *   *

Henry and Badger watched as the other VTOL, enveloped in flames and wreathed with smoke, fell like a fire ball into the city. Badger growled as he watched the drones leave off the chase and come after their VTOL. They were already under attack by several drones and these just added to their worries.

The Specters' bullets were having an effect upon the drones, but there were too many. The VTOL pilot had already delayed the landing because of the drones and they were continually circling the drop-site. But, after the elimination of the other VTOL, the pilot would have no choice but to drop the Specters or he might become the next target.

"I'll try to come in as slow as I can," the pilot shouted as he started to lower the altitude. "It's going to be rough."

Assailed by the drones, the VTOL came in low, aiming for a wide, seemingly clear street. Bullets glanced off the fuselage at crazy angles, penetrated in odd ways and skimmed the fabric. The pilot wanted to come in as close as possible and the underside practically scraped against the flexcrete street.

The Specters leapt out, rolled to lessen the impact and then fired on the drones as they passed overhead, still chasing the Mosquito. When the VTOL and drones were out of accurate range, the Specters watched them climb higher into the sky with their zoom-vision. After a few more moments, the VTOL burst into flames and exploded.

Badger growled and stamped a hind-paw on the ground. Now they were alone. There was no way of knowing whether or not any of the PDCT unit had survived and no time to find out.

The Specters quickly reloaded their clips and moved out. The Chinese forces could be anywhere and there was no telling how many. Badger followed Henry, matching his pace and keeping an eye out for hostiles.

They had hadn't gone more then several yards when a noise caused them to freeze. It started out as a hollow groan then slowly grew until it was a deep growl. Both of them looked about cautiously. Neither had ever heard such a noise.

Chapter 4

"History and the Worm"

Slowly and painfully, Rookie pushed himself up off the ground. His armor had absorbed most of the initial impact, but that didn't stop from causing him a headache and multiple bruises. He shakily stood up and looked around; he had fallen in some sort of park. Several gardens of multicolored flowers lined symmetrical pathways, while symmetrically placed fir trees stood at either end of the gardens. Benches made of an exotic red wood were symmetrically placed about the park. But, on the ground, where he had been laying, was a broken pile of branches. He looked up and saw a tall tree; many of its branches were broken.

With a quick look at his armor's health monitor Rookie muttered "no major injuries". He detached his SMG from the holster and examined it carefully. He thought it was fine, until he turned around and scraped the tip of the barrel against the trunk of the tall tree; the SMG bent in half and snapped into two pieces. He dropped the two pieces out of surprise and looked down at them in disgust. He quickly forgot the SMG and removed his ASP from his belt. He held it at a ready position in front of him as he moved to get out of the open park.

The ASP (Aerodynamic Splinter Projector) was a pistol that used electrical currents to break apart and launch small pieces of aluminum wool at lethal speeds. Friction caused the aluminum wool to melt into a solid piece; the aluminum would then expand and cause major splatter-damage on its target. It almost looked like a small, black box with a handle at one end. The aluminum wool (SEAR) was compacted into what appeared to be a solid block that expanded as electricity ran through it. The shooter could fire seemingly indefinitely, before having to reload.

Rookie had barely taken three steps outside the park when he spotted a PDCT up ahead. His HUD projected a red shimmer around the soldier. The shimmer meant it was a hostile Chinese PDCT. The PDCT also saw that Rookie was a hostile on his HUD, they started a quick engagement.

Rookie strafed right, ducking and rolling to try and avoid the return automatic-weapon fire. Rookie returned fire with his ASP, the molten aluminum left red streaks in both PDCTs' vision. The SEAR hit the enemy's armor, glancing at angles and piercing at straight trajectories.

The Chinese PDCT barely felt the SEAR when it glanced off his armor, but when it pierced, he felt an eternal burning deep inside. He grunted as the splinter pierced his leg armor, he felt the warm blood crawl down his leg and the SEAR burn at his bone. He limped in agony.

Rookie had managed to keep the other's bullets from straight impacts, but a couple of bullets had pierced his thigh. He had to end this quickly; he already had the upper hand. He moved his pistol so that the crosshair display on his HUD was around the PDCT's head; he fired four times with rapid succession.

Three of the splinters glanced off the blue-tinted screen of the Chinese PDCT, leaving jagged scratches. The fourth went through the screen, creating a clean hole, the edges red-hot. The PDCT screamed in pain, dropped his rifle and fell to his knees, grabbing unsuccessfully at the helmet's screen. The SEAR had slowed down enough that it only sank into the bone of his forehead.

Rookie, seeing that the PDCT was temporarily incapacitated, pulled a knife with a concave-edge from his belt. He rushed up to the PDCT, knocked his flailing hands aside, pressed back his head and slid the razor-sharp blade across his throat.

Blood splattered across Rookie's screen and onto the road beside them. The PDCT fell backwards without a sound. Rookie's hand went numb as he looked at the dead PDCT; he had actually killed him. It took him a moment to regain and remind himself that it was war; it didn't feel good, but it was the right thing.

* * *

There was a ringing in Kruger's ears as he started to come to; the large black man's vision was a blur as he opened his eyes. There was a large orange blur to his right and to his left was an odd mismatch of colors. He had the oddest sensation that he was being carried. He was being carried.

Whoever was carrying him grunted with pain every second step.

He blinked the weariness from his eyes and groaned. "What happened?"

"We fell out of the VTOL," was the familiar voice of John. "I thought I lost you for a minute back there. Think you can walk?"

Now that he was on foot and his vision had cleared, Kruger saw that they were both on a winding staircase in what appeared to be an old office building. The orange blur was a row of lights built into the railing for safety precautions and the mismatch of colors was an odd red and blue paint job on a wall. John had handed him back his Liner; other than several scratches, it was in perfect working order.

In the fall, John had broken his scope and injured his right leg; his armor had inflated over the injured area to apply the recommended pressure. They had landed on the roof of the building, John was quicker to regain consciousness than Kruger; fearing that more drones were in the area, he picked Kruger up and carried him inside. Now they had both regained their senses and could hold their own in any battle that may come.

A pounding noise from below caused both friends to lean over the edge of the rail and peer down. Red shimmers appeared around hostiles that were climbing the stairs.

Kruger smiled and whispered something to John. John nodded

and crouched below the rail's top and moved slowly down the stairs. Kruger grinned as he placed his crosshairs onto the chest of one hostile and then waited.

Not knowing the demise that was store for them, three Chinese light-infantry placed themselves in line with Kruger's crosshairs. Kruger's first shot blew all three to pieces, a second shot followed quickly, eliminating another threat, a PDCT traitor.

* * *

Badger finished off the last soldier in the patrol with deep-cutting slash from his kukri. They were both moving to investigate the noise when they had run into the patrol made up of light-infantry (without exoskeletons or plate armor) who had taken them by surprise; they suffered no injuries in the quick skirmish.

Badger wiped blood off of his kukri on a dead soldier and then sheathed it while releasing his rifle from the holster. He twitched his right ear, trying to pick up the noise again and his eyelevel HUD showed the motion on his health display (leftmost side). His tail swished across the ground as he concentrated. A heavyset noise caused him to turn swiftly to his right.

Henry looked in the direction that Badger was staring; all he saw was a small fire, shattered flexcrete and a well-worn corner of a building. They both moved forward to investigate. The noise came again, the same haunting tune as they had heard earlier. Now they were against the corner of the building. Henry put his back to the wall and signaled for Badger to check it out.

With a growl and a leap, Badger stood out in the open, ready to fire. What he saw made him freeze. He didn't know whether to fire or not; all he could do was stare.

The creature looked to stand nearly six feet high; it was covered in knotted, dark-blue flesh with four, solid green eyes on either side of its blunt snout. Its head moved about on a stretchable, thick neck, its jaws had no teeth whatsoever and its back was covered in long, hard spikes. It stood on two thick legs that could carry it swiftly over open ground, with two, extremely strong, long arms with an odd formation of gray shell at the ends shaped like spades for digging, and three claws stuck out from the concave sides of the spades, just right for grasping and tearing roots. Another shell formation was atop its head, like a gray helmet.

A visual-ghost display (center of the HUD) of Colonel Warren appeared on Badger's HUD. A visual-ghost display was a mostly-transparent figure for visual contact while in combat, without fully distracting the shooter. Colonel Warren a gray-skinned man with a shaved head and a serpentine smile was in charge of every high-priority mission. Badger was curious as to why he was smiling, rather humorously.

"Do not waste ammo soldier. It's a greater mole-worm, found on both Discovery and Forerunner; completely harmless, unless provoked. This one must have escaped from its cage in the zoo, probably hit by a lower-grade explosive. Don't leave it, this one could be of use to you both, try and get it to follow you. Hold on... Henry, try to get the worm to follow you. Use your ultrasound emitters; they're very curious about those noises." With that, the Colonel disappeared.

"What?"

Henry moved cautiously around the corner, he nearly jumped at the sight of the colossal beast. It turned its head towards Henry and stretched itself up to its full height, nearly nine feet high and as thick as a bull. Henry backed away as it lumbered towards him, using its arms as secondary legs. It stopped a couple feet in front of Henry, contracted itself back to six feet, leaned its face close to Henry's and let out its eerie call. The noise didn't come from its mouth, but from inside, welling up to the rumbling growl.

Henry leaned backwards in horror as the worm's huge face came closer; they were practically nose-to-nose. "Now... what does he think we'll need this tank for?"

Chapter 5

"Still in Action"

With a great heave, First Sergeant Alexander pulled himself up to his feet inside the hot VTOL. The left upper corner of his helmet's screen had been shattered by a bullet that had been fired from a dropped pistol when it hit the ground. The bullet had come in at an angle so it had missed his face entirely and exited out the side of his helmet. A large, sharp fragment of the screen had cut his face from above his left eye to his right cheek, the blood had dried and crusted quickly in the heat.

Alexander took a deep breath and looked about the inside of the VTOL, Sakuma andy and the pilot laid prone on the floor. He bent down and checked the two PDCTs, he already knew the pilot was dead, a long, metal spike protruded from his back. Sadly, he removed each one's helmet and took their dog tags; everyone else had died.

He removed his own helmet, fragments of the broken screen fell onto the floor and he put the others' tags about his own neck. He replaced his helmet and unattached his rifle from the holster, a prototype Biometric Precision Rifle (BPR). The BPR was basically shaped like a rectangular, metal box with an integrated-stock and pistol-grip with thumb-hole. A holographic-sight set near the front in case the HUD lost power. Its ammunition was a genetically-engineered organism, gray in color and made of hard carbon, which was taken apart by an electrical-beam and launched using the same current. The organism didn't have pain cells, so it didn't feel anything as it was being taken apart and it quickly grew back while absorbing excess energy from the gun. However, the unlimited ammo of the BPR was being replaced by the SEAR-firing weapons that had more deadly capabilities.

Swiftly extracting himself from the VTOL, the sergeant ran to the nearest bit of cover, an over turned truck. He remained hidden there until he was sure that it was clear; he quickly tried to contact someone on his radio. After a few unsuccessful moments, he realized that the bullet that had gone through his screen had also destroyed his radio.

As if realizing his predicament, bad fortune added to it. At that moment a sensory-drone, flying ahead of a group of Chinese light-infantry, flew over the truck, heading towards the wrecked VTOL. The drone's movable camera scanned the Mosquito and then turned to look backwards. The last image it was able to send back to the group was of the sergeant shooting with deadly accuracy. Now the group was alerted.

"Rotten son of a…"

Alexander didn't have time to finish his phrase; he could now hear the soldier's pounding footsteps on the flexcrete. He took a small box from one of his pockets, it was wrapped in fabric with a screen and number-keys. He pressed several of the numbers and smiled roguishly.

With a quick glance at the smoldering remains of the drone, he leapt up, looked over the truck, saw the soldiers coming ever closer and threw the box.

One of the soldiers saw the sergeant throw the box; it was a very good throw, the sergeant's exoskeleton allowed him to throw it incredibly far and straight. The soldier kept his eyes on it as it flew through the air not realizing what it was for a moment. Then he saw a little green light on it and then it turned red.

The loud-sound dampening software in Alexander's helmet only allowed him a faint noise of the explosion. The truck tilted a bit, groaning on the flexcrete, then settled back to its original position. The HD27 had done its work, taken out the entire group, but the noise was loud enough to be heard for miles.

Alexander stood up, holstered the BPR, placed both hands underneath the truck and flipped it back up onto its wheels. That was such an easy task with an exoskeleton. Alexander pulled a couple dead civilian bodies out of the truck and then climbed in himself and turned the key in the ignition; the engine started with a light hum.

Alexander ran over the burning bodies of the light-infantry as he sped away from the area. The truck was very maneuverable over the wreckage-strewn streets; it ran over almost every obstacle in its path. Alexander was quickly learning how to work with the Chinese electronic controls. He kept on accelerating.

He had to maneuver around several sharp turns and impassable obstacles; drove through a pile of burning wood and right through a Chinese roadblock. He kept his head down as Chinese forces fired upon the truck. Up ahead, he saw a large bridge over the city that gave the populace direct paths to home and business, a ramp up ahead would allow him to get up there.

Alexander quickly turned onto the ramp; enemy bullets pinged off and penetrated the truck. The bullets didn't just come from behind. Aerial attack-drones and militia were on the ramp leading to the highway ahead of him. The Chinese soldiers dove to the side as the truck raced right past.

The PDCT grinned as he drove up and up the ramp, he would soon be on the highway itself. Suddenly, he was past the Chinese ranks, he shouted out of exuberance and let go of the wheel for a moment. It was a big mistake.

A part of the high way was missing completely, a jagged half-circle had been broken off by an artillery round aiming for one of the ISEN ships. The truck practically flew out into empty space; it seemed to hang there for several long moments and then dropped.

Alexander bellowed out loud as the truck fell towards the city below. The truck, its balance offset because of the PDCT, slowly began to spiral. Alexander swiftly opened his door and climbed out onto the roof of the truck, one hand gripping the doorframe. PDCTs had been trained not to overreact in such situations; if he remained calm he might survive.

The twisting motion of the truck made it hard, but Alexander was confident in his training. But skywalks passing between buildings were not in his thought or training. The truck smashed into a skywalk causing it spin on its side; the PDCT still managed to keep a hold.

As the truck hit another skywalk it spun even faster and Alexander was flung off, up and out into the air in a tangled mass. He started to descend again; he quickly tried to correct his fall pattern. He spread his arms out and positioned himself so his legs would hit the ground first. He bent his legs so that they wouldn't be forced into his chest when he impacted, he wasn't sure it would be enough.

* * *

Rookie watched as three American AFT-27 Warthogs flew over head on a mission to knockout an anti-air battery. He lost sight of them when they flew over another building; he liked those kinds of planes. They were based off the old model A-10 for their efficiency. He had often wondered what it would be like to sit inside a five ton weave of crystallized-titanium fabric and target the enemy with deadly precision.

He turned his attention back to the open road and sighed deeply. There was nothing but obstacles, fires and holes in front of him. If he was in the air he wouldn't have to walk, or run so much. He lifted the Chinese

PDCT's rifle to his shoulder and walked forward slowly.

There was a high-pitched whistle as a rocket, fired from close by, streaked upwards towards the fleet. It exploded a moment later before impacting on its target. The fleet's missile-avoidance systems were working efficiently. The Chinese ground artillery would only be able to make an impact on the fleet by lowering the ships' energy shields. All artillery had to be stopped or else the fleet would fire.

Rookie did not want to be inside the city if or when they fired. None of the PDCTs knew what the Specters' mission was, only that they had to stop all hostilities; the PDCTs were only there to give them some protection on their way. Now that he didn't know where they were, or the rest of his group, things seemed pretty bleak.

A crashing noise above him caused him to lose his train of thought and look up. It was a truck, civilian model and with a well-destroyed black paintjob. Rookie leapt out of the way and the truck smashed into the ground a couple feet from where he was standing a moment before. Rookie stared at the smoldering wreckage; flames came out the engine, working its way hungrily along the rest of the vehicle.

Fearing that if the truck blew up it might attract hostiles, Rookie ran away from it. When he had run a considerable distance, something hit him from above.

Smack!

Rookie fell flat upon the ground and the thing that had hit him was flung forward and it skidded along the flexcrete for several yards. Rookie quickly got back up to his feet and aimed his rifle at the object. A blue shimmer appeared around the object, it was an ally.

"Are you okay?" Rookie asked, bending down to turn the PDCT over. The name Alexander McClain written on the soldier's chest almost caused Rookie to shout for joy. "Sergeant… I thought I was the only one left alive. Are you hurt badly? Can I do something for you?"

The sergeant moaned a little and his head shook slowly as he tried to clear it. "I don't want that truck," he muttered. "Where am I? Who are you?"

Rookie helped the sergeant to his feet and dusted him off. "You're in some kind of city intersection with downed stoplights and I'm Private Douglas, sir, Rookie."

"Oh," said Alexander, still a little dazed. "Glad to hear you're alive."

Rookie looked up expectantly, "Any other survivors?"

Alexander shook his head. "I don't know about John or Kruger, but all the others died in the crash."

"Glad I'm a dropout then," grinned Rookie.

"American humor," muttered Alexander.

"Canadian," corrected Rookie with a nod of his head.

"Whatever," the sergeant said. Suddenly, a thought came to mind. "Rookie, have you contacted anyone on the system-com."

Sheepishly, Rookie shook his head. "It never occurred to me."

"Is it any wonder you're called Rookie? Try and see if you can contact the other two, they can't be more then a couple miles from this position."

"Yes sir," said Rookie, quickly speaking the sys-com's number sequence to activate it. "Two-eight-eight-seven, okay, it's activated. Hello? Kruger, John, this is Private Douglas speaking; I've got the sergeant with me. We're the only two known survivors, tell us there's more."

There was a slight pause before any response.

"Kruger and I are alive, inside some sort of office-building, city coordinates: latitude 24, longitude 67. We're okay, only under fire by eighty or so light-infantry, this shouldn't take long. Uh-oh, that doesn't sound good."

Rookie was having a hard time hearing because of all the gunfire coming over the sys-com, but he heard everything. "What? What doesn't sound good? Hello?"

There was a long pause before John spoke again; his voice was desperate and fearful. "What is that thing? My bullets are only sparking on that armor. Kill it Kruger, kill it... yaaa."

Rookie tried to get some other response, but after several moments of vain trial, he gave up. He turned to the sergeant and spoke urgently, "Something's happened, we have to reach them."

"Where are they," Alexander demanded.

"City coordinates: latitude 24, longitude 67," Rookie said swiftly.

Alexander placed the information into his helmet's GPS and signaled Rookie to follow. "We've already lost two others; I'm not about ready to lose them. Between us I'm sure we can fill Hell a bit more."

Rookie nodded and holstered his rifle and took his ASP from his belt. The sergeant took off at a fast run, Rookie was close behind. Neither PDCT knew what was going on with their other teammates, or the Specters, but they did know that time was running out.

Chapter 6

"Special Delivery"

Henry's ultrasound emitter, which was used to call Badger in case of a HUD malfunction, was working to get the mole-worm to follow. It lumbered casually after them; its arms were held a couple feet above the ground in a ready manner. Henry didn't like the looks of something that large following him, even though he had his back to it. The worm kept on letting out curious rumbles as it followed, giving both Specters a chill.

"It's going to draw every hostile in China if he keeps this up," growled Henry, looking back at the giant worm. "Whatever the colonel thinks it's useful for better be good, I'm not risking my neck for something worthless."

The ultrasound was growing increasingly annoying to Badger. By tilting his head onto his shoulder and putting his free paw up under his helmet over his ear, he found that he could block some of the noise. He growled angrily and shook his rifle at the worm. His tail twitched with agitation and his steps were stiff and awkward.

The worm, however, was having the time of its life. The ultrasound was a kind of music to it, sweet and melodious. The human and the dog that were in front seemed friendly enough that it followed willingly. Although it was supposed to be a forest creature that ate rotten vegetation and dug deep into the ground in search of fat tree roots, it was also a very playful mimicker. Its species was well known to mimic the manners of most anything from humans to birds; and so, after a few more moments, it started to mimic Henry's every move. It wasn't too bad at it.

Neither of the Specters realized what the worm was doing, because they were busy watching for hostiles, but Henry might have been slightly flattered. A NAV-point on each one's HUD gave them the direction and distance of their target, it showed up as a red triangle. Because of this, they would know exactly which direction to take and their target wasn't far away anymore.

The odd feeling that someone was watching him caused Badger to suddenly stop and uncover his ears. Badger's large ears twitched and his eyes rolled about the street. The darkened road and shadowed building seemed lifeless. The alleys and windows were desolate and bleak with no light but small fires caused by explosives and electrical shorts. Still, he could detect the vision of something roving over his body, but no matter where he looked, he could not see it.

Henry, who had stopped just several inches behind and to the right of Badger when he saw him stop, was looking about also; he saw only what Badger was seeing. His right-arm hung limply down at his side, grasping his rifle barrel-down towards the ground.

"What is it, Badger?"

Badger shook his head, grunted once and then started forward again. The sensation quickly disappeared as he moved. He knew it wasn't a drone, he was gifted that way, it was something living, but he couldn't tell what. GEM, human, or just some frightened animal, just as long as it wasn't attacking.

Badger finally managed to ignore the ultrasound and had his ears concentrate on other noises. By doing this he managed to hear the sound of a vehicle up ahead around the bend. It started out as an electric hum, moving slowly and then grew to a grinding noise as whatever it was ran over burnt wood and chunks of flexcrete.

Henry heard it too. He quickly raised his rifle to his shoulder, crouched and moved away to the other side of the street to set up a position. The worm followed him, crouching down in the same manner.

"Will you be leaving soon," muttered Henry with a glance at the mole-worm.

Badger moved to the opposite side of the street, bringing the assault rifle to his shoulder. He watched as the crosshair display on his HUD moved until it was positioned next to the corner where the vehicle would appear. He gave the worm a quick glance; he wasn't that sure about it.

It wasn't long before the vehicle appeared, in fact, in turned the corner and started coming right down the center of the road. It was a light assault vehicle, low-built for speed, no doors and no turrets, room for five passengers with weapons and six wheels that would shift to adjust to the terrain.

The five occupying Chinese soldiers saw the worm before they saw the Specters. They let out shouts of dismay at the sight of the beast and the driver brought the vehicle to a screeching stop. They didn't have time to recover from the shock; the Specters laid them flat in quick succession.

The noise of the soldiers' shouts and the shooting didn't go unnoticed. Soon after hearing gunfire close by, a Chinese PDCT unit and several light-infantry ran to check it out.

Badger had heard the others coming and quickly made Henry aware of this by growling and pointing with a claw. They both turned the vehicle so that it became a barricade and readied themselves for the coming fight. The worm tried to crouch with them, but couldn't hide its huge bulk behind the vehicle.

"Well, at least if it dies it'll give us cover," said Henry.

Badger nodded in silent agreement as he listened to the soldiers come ever closer. He mentally prayed for protection, not for himself, for Henry and breathed deeply. His tail was ridged with expectation, his ears were completely still.

When the first PDCT rounded the corner, he came to a sudden

stop and stared at the worm. After a moment, he shrugged and started to place the crosshairs of his rifle on the worm's head. He took a deep breath, then let it out and pulled the trigger.

The magnetic-impulse launched bullets flew from the barrel and impacted on the worms shell. The bullets pinged off harmlessly, leaving minor scratches that would quickly heal. The worm raised a spade to rub the shell, its long claws scraped over the shell like ice against ice.

Before the PDCT had finished firing his burst of bullets, the others had come around the corner in time to see that no damage had been done. One light-infantry soldier laughed and launched a couple bullets into the worm's neck.

The worm had no major organs, other than its heart and brain, which were both protected under its head shell, so the bullets caused no damage other than a loss of blood. However, it could feel the pain very well, and it did not like it. It was hard to tell which surprised the Chinese more, the Specters that started to fire upon them, or the worm's violent rage.

The worm dug its spades underneath the vehicle, lifted it high above its head and then flung it at the stunned soldiers. The sudden exposure caused both Specters to fire wild at the Chinese. They too were stunned by the worm's rage, it had seemed so gentle.

The vehicle spun as it hurtled towards the soldiers, all but one

PDCT managed to leap out of the way and the force of the impact broke his helmet off and his skull was cracked open when he hit the building behind him. One of the light-infantry had managed to avoid being hit, but a bullet from Badger dispatched him.

The worm ran forward, body turned sideways so it spades could deflect the bullets, it missed all the PDCTs but still scattered them. It whipped about, using one of its arms as a flail to knock a PDCT off his feet. When the PDCT hit the ground the worm spiked his neck with its left spade.

The PDCTs fired as fast as they could into the worm's leathery hide. Though it bled a lot, it just made it angrier. It rushed at another PDCT and brought one of its spades up into the soldier's stomach and flung him over its shoulder. The PDCT crashed into a building, groaned and then fell to the street below. Luckily for the PDCT, the worm forgot about him and started after the remaining three.

The PDCTs tried to keep as much distance between themselves and the worm as possible, but it proved exceedingly worthless. The worm smacked one to the side, he smacked right into another and they both fell in a heap. They both managed to scramble out of the way as the worm brought its right spade down to spike them, instead it cleaved a nice crack in the flexcrete. It swung another spade at the helmet of one PDCT; it hit the screen with the edge, cutting right through the soldier's skull.

The soldier that the worm had thrown into the other PDCT was devoid of a weapon; he ran. A burst from Badger's rifle finished him; four bullets glanced off while two sank in. He dropped with a sigh.

The worm lunged at the last standing PDCT, he leapt backward to void being hit. The worm swung its left spade and knocked the rifle from the soldier's bloodless grip. Now that it wasn't being shot anymore, the worm didn't have reason to be so offensive. It ran at the PDCT as he turned to run; thrust out an arm and closed its claws about the soldier's neck.

The Specters watched in horrified fascination as the worm thrust its free spade through the PDCT's optical-screen multiple times before it was satisfied. They both winced as the limp carcass dropped to the ground with a juicy *thud*.

It was unsettling to them as the worm lumbered back over to them. It let out its haunting sound again and contracted itself back down to its non-aggressive stance. It rumbled a couple of times and scratched its shoulder with its claws. It wasn't hostile towards them.

Both Specters were relieved that it only used its aggression on those that had attacked it. Badger led the way again, moving towards their destination. The worm limped somewhat behind, still following the ultrasound.

Henry looked at the blood that trailed down the worm's body and grimaced. "I'll try to find you a vet as soon as the mission's over."

Chapter 7

"Cat Line"

When Alexander and Rookie had reached the designated area (they ignored the GPS's "you have arrived") they looked about for the office-building that the other two were supposed to be in. There were restaurants, hotels, stores and even a souvenir shop. Rookie was the one to spot it. It was just around the corner from a hotel with a lit-up sign of a rhinoceros with a blue nightcap.

They were both on edge as they got closer to the building, from the noise on the radio it sounded like there should be soldiers all over the area, drawn to the sound of gunfire. But the street was completely deserted. The only living thing they saw was a cat; it ran right past them to the other side of the street.

Rookie stepped up beside the sergeant. "Something's not right. It's too quiet; shouldn't we hear something...like gunfire?"

Alexander didn't even look at Rookie, "only if they're still alive, Rookie."

"They have to be alive," Rookie said with a worried glance about the area.

"Where's it say that in the rule book?"

When they finally reached the main doors of the office-building, they could both sense something was wrong. The doors were huge and thick, made of a sturdy wood, were broken in half and lying on the inside.

"What did this?" Rookie asked as he kicked the edge of one door.

"MATO," said Alexander.

Rookie looked about and shook his head. "I don't think so; we'd see tracks in the flexcrete. And besides, why use a MATO to break open these doors, why not a charge on the lock?"

"I've got a better question," said the sergeant, looking at an electronic panel above the door's lock. "Why not just open them, it was unlocked."

"What?'

"See for yourself. Look at the panel above the lock."

Rookie did; the panel showed the image of a green key. "So?"

Alexander sighed. "In case you don't know, green means its unlocked and red means it's otherwise. Now do you get it?"

Rookie nodded.

"Good. Now let's see if we can't find out what's happened here. Kruger? John?"

As they passed the doorway, it became increasingly apparent that something large had come through before them. Large gouges cut deep into the floor and walls as if an ax had been used. Along one wall were five, parallel, deep scratches that ended at a corner that turned to a spiraling staircase. Blood covered the walls and stairs like an extra coat of paint. Dead bodies lay twisted, dismembered and mutilated all over the place. Many of the bodies were crushed, like snakes that had been partially run over by a car. Both PDCT's were horrified by the grotesque sight.

They both began to mount the stairs, calling out the others' names. There was absolutely no response. The stairs also had the odd gouges in them, through the railing, the wall, doors and the steps. In the distance they could hear the sounds of artillery, planes and streaking missiles; but the building seemed to be completely void of life.

The dead bodies stopped after a point on the stairs, but the gouges did not. The soldiers began to hurry in their assent, taking four steps at a time. The staircase seemed to spiral upwards forever, but they managed to reach the top in a couple of minutes. When they reached the top, they followed the gouges until they came to another staircase, a straight, short one; at the end was a doorway, it was shattered with sharp splinters pointing outwards.

Alexander held up a hand to stop Rookie. "Not so fast, whatever it is, is out there on the roof. I don't see it in front of the doorway, so when we go out there, I'll go right, you go left. 'Ave you got that?"

Rookie nodded and pressed the stock of his rifle hard against his shoulder. When the sergeant went out first to the right, Rookie quickly went out to the left. Out on the roof, Rookie didn't see anything that could be a threat. He scanned the area again and then turned around to look for the sergeant. He froze at what he saw.

The sergeant hadn't made it far outside the doorway when he stopped. Several yards away from him was an enormous mole-worm, lying dead on the ground. Kruger sat upon it, chuckling unstoppably at the sergeant and Rookie. His chuckling woke up John, who had been lying atop the beast; he waved passively at the sergeant.

"What do you think of our trophy?" Kruger asked, while lifting his Liner until the barrel was pointing at the sky.

The worm's shells had been replaced by identical armor plates; the armor plates also covered its chest, arms and shoulders and its legs. The armor was dark-gray in color with ridges and electronic panels covering it in a kind of ceremonial fashion. It was a marvelous thing to look at.

"This is what attacked you," Rookie stepped forward and asked.

John nodded and sat up. "Don't know which one of us killed it, that armor slowed Kruger's bullets enough that it didn't explode. I must've used four cartridges on this thing."

"Absolutely incredible," Alexander remarked.

"So where're the others?" John asked, looking about.

"They didn't survive the crash," said Alexander, solemnly.

Rookie bowed his head and walked around the dead worm to the edge of the roof and looked down. His sad mood disappeared rapidly, being replaced by one of alarm. An army of light-infantry was making its way towards the building.

"Don't look now, but we might be having some company really soon." The PDCTs moved quickly to set up a defensive position, using the worm as cover. Survival was not guaranteed.

After several long moments, the sound of footsteps on the stairs was faintly heard. As soon as the first few light-infantrymen made it through the door, the PDCTs commenced firing.

Chapter 8

"Final Point of Action"

The Specters looked over their target from around a corner, next to a full dumpster. The worm was standing behind them, rubbing at its wounds with its spades. Badger was using his HUD's zoom-vision to check out the defenses up close. Turrets were set up, light-infantry and Chinese PDCTs were all over the place and many barricades had been set up.

Badger growled as he turned off the zoom-vision, it would almost be suicidal to try and get past them. But, he and Henry had gotten past places like this before in the four short years he had been owned by Henry. They had gotten in and out of many similar scrapes.

Henry only gave the area several quick scans before ducking his head back around the corner. He looked down at Badger, watching the dog carefully scan every detail. He smiled and scratched his chin while thinking about their next move.

Curious as to why the dog was looking around the corner, the worm lumbered forward and peered around also. Two things happened. First, the Chinese saw the immense, ugly head of the worm and commenced firing, and the worm, seeing them in the uniforms of those that had attacked it earlier, let out a growl and charged.

Badger ducked back around the corner to avoid being hit. He

heard the cracking noises as bullets and aluminum landed all over the place. Screams tore through the air, there were snapping noises as the worm broke through the barricades, smashed turrets and crushed bone. It was time to move.

Not yet over the shock of the worm's sudden, aggressive behavior, it took Henry a few moments to realize that Badger was running towards the building; he took off after him. He ducked to avoid being hit by a flying light-infantryman and fired at whatever others he could. The worm would keep the Chinese occupied for an uncertain amount of time, valuable time.

Every bullet that hit the worm made it angrier and it made sure to kill every soldier it saw. Cutting, smashing, smacking and ramming, it wrecked havoc everywhere among the ranks. Nothing seemed capable to stop the onslaught of the worm's wrath. Before the night was over there was destined to be deep blood.

Badger shot a PDCT from behind, not doing much because of the armor, the PDCT didn't even notice; his concentration was all on the worm. Badger got closer and fired up at his head, the PDCT didn't have time to notice; four bullets were imbedded in his brain.

A light-infantryman was thrust upwards into the air, impaled on a spade and then thrown far away into the street. Two others followed suit with one smack from the worm. A PDCT leapt over the swinging arm of the worm and fired furiously into its chest, the worm swung another spade and hit the PDCT straight on. He flipped backward with a broken neck.

The high-density doors of the building were locked. To keep them locked were seven, huge, metal bars that were electronically raised to keep them closed until an appointed time. All the windows were barred in the same fashion, so the Specters had to find another means of entry.

Badger found a large vent that they could both crawl through around the corner of the building. The vent cover was bolted down tight and the alloy was hard enough that not even their combined exoskeleton power could pull it off. But, there was still a solution. Badger produced a small box; similar to the one Alexander had used and stuck it onto the grating. He pressed a few buttons and they both moved away to a safe distance.

The box exploded, the grating fragmented and everything within a three-meter radius was burnned. Everyone outside the building was too busy with the worm to pay the explosion any heed; those inside, however, might have been alerted. Hot fumes issued out from the vent, hissing like serpents.

The visual-ghost display of Colonel Warren appeared onto the Specters' heads-up display. "You have to hurry, the fleet is preparing to fire...their shields are just dropping too fast. Get in there now and begin the abort sequence."

Badger brushed several metal fragments off his shoulder and, with a run, dove into the ventilation shaft, followed shortly by Henry. Badger crawled with one paw grasping his rifle and the other grasping his kukri. The space was too small for Henry to leave his rifle on his back, so he gripped it in front of him as he moved.

Their movements were naturally silent, even in the shaft which would echo almost any noise. Each of them had gone through stealth training at the beginning of their enlistment as Specters; they both had received incredibly high marks. What made it more incredible was that Badger had come along almost nine years later and received the same marks in everything that Henry had.

*　　*　　*

The grating at the end of the vent wasn't as strong as the one on the outside, Badger simply pressed outwards and its weaker bolts broke. He crawled out silently, sheathed the kukri and held his rifle protectively as he waited for Henry to extract himself. Once Henry was out and ready, he went first, followed closely by Badger.

They had avoided most of the guards by using the vents, but there was still the Elite Guard. The Elite Guard would most likely be near the mainframe, as many as twelve. However, the Specters had the element of surprise, a worm outside and a bad security system inside. Actually, there was no security system inside; the Chinese hadn't counted on anyone actually finding a way into the vault-like building.

"Please hurry," it was just the colonel's voice, "the fleet is preparing to fire."

Henry stopped at a corner glanced around it. Two PDCTs were standing guard to the door that led to the final hallway to the mainframe. Above the door was an automated-turret that would fire as soon as anyone not bearing the correct beacon came into range. Not a problem. He took his pistol from his belt, switched the magazine to a different type of ammunition and swiveled the pistol around the corner, an optic link showed where the bullet would impact; he fired one silent shot at the turret.

The turret sparked and sputtered as the energy-disruption bullet over charged its internal core. The PDCTs now turned their backs to the Specters and looked up as the turret questioningly. Two well placed shots of lethal ammunition into their spines dropped them like stones.

Badger leapt over one of the bodies after Henry, jaw set and eyes sharpened. The noise-dampening tread on their boots aided in their silent swiftness, but, Badger's senses were tingling with excitement. The objective was ahead.

The hall ran straight, but there was a door at the end, it was black with two intertwining dragons in its center. Both knew that there were two separate factions behind the door, the Elite Guard and the mainframe.

There was a blue panel to the right of the door and pressing it would cause the door to be pulled up. They didn't have any fireflies to blind the soldiers and they couldn't risk damaging the mainframe with a grenade. One of them would have to go in first and Badger most certainly wouldn't allow Henry to.

Henry sighed and pressed the panel. The door lifted open and Badger leapt in, gun ready, fur bristled and growling. There was no one inside the room, just the mainframe. Badger lowered his rifle and glanced about, it was utterly void of life.

Henry stepped quickly in behind Badger and looked about warily, he couldn't see anything either. Where could the Elite Guard be? There didn't appear to be any other way in or out of the room. It might be a trap.

Henry approached the mainframe with caution; it was a large intelligence-projection floating above the floor with a large map of all China, both on Earth and Mars. Tiny red and blue dots covered each map signifying both the Chinese and the Allies. A few inches in front of the mainframe was holographic keyboard, this was rimmed by a large snake. It had all the features of the Chinese mainframe design, all the way down to the finest detail.

"Cover me," said Henry as he holstered his rifle and started on the mainframe. His helmet's HUD translated the Chinese symbols for him as he worked on the abort code.

Badger kept his rifle trained on the door, not even a sound ushered from the outer hall. What was going on? The Chinese couldn't have gotten that arrogant and decided not to protect the most valuable combat asset they had, but nothing appeared to be a deception either.

Henry typed in the final piece of the abort code and watched as all the red dots started to turn blue. The word "abort" appeared on his HUD in bright red capitals, signifying that the conflict was over. The distant sound of artillery stopped and all turned into an eerie silence.

* * *

Rookie had just started pelting a light-infantryman with SEAR from his ASP when the abort signal appeared on his HUD. Immediately all the PDCTs and Chinese stopped firing, they lowered their weapons looked about. It was hard for them to believe that it was over.

Rookie stood up and looked about the city, no more flashes of artillery were seen, the only lights were from buildings and fires. He reattached the ASP to his belt, grabbed Kruger's shoulder and laughed. Kruger laughed with him. It was hard to believe that it stopped so suddenly.

* * *

"That's it?" Henry was taken aback by the swiftness of the code. He had never had to hack a national mainframe before; he had been expecting something else.

"Yep," said the colonel. "That was the entire purpose of the mission and you've succeeded, well done Specters. Get back outside; we'll begin your extraction as soon as we can."

Henry gave the mainframe another look and shrugged before starting to leave the room. "At least it wasn't a trap."

Badger barked concordantly. He began to follow Henry when his fur suddenly stood out straight, like static was pulsing all over him. He turned around to look at the mainframe; it was beginning to turn grainy and jagged. He took a couple steps forward and felt the static grow in its intensity.

"Badger," Henry turned around outside the doorway and watched his teammate.

Badger looked back at Henry and then reached out a paw towards the mainframe's projection. The mainframe turned into swirling mass of projected memory and information, all concentrated on rushing through Badger's entire body, coursing over him and finally up into his head. Badger's amber eyes were wide open, his paw fell limply at his side and, quite slowly, his eyes closed and he collapsed to the ground. The last thing he heard before he lost all his senses was Henry's voice, he was shouting.

"Badger...!"

Chapter 9

"Awakening"

Badger didn't know what he was seeing; it was all too fuzzy for him to make it out. Every time he moved his head remnants of what he was looking at before were carried with his vision to a certain point before vanishing and he picked another bit to drag. Something was holding him, he looked up and saw a fuzzy black shape with what he thought were golden eyes. There was something familiar and comforting about the scene, but, he could not place it anywhere. Then, the black shape appeared to be growing farther away, he was moving away from it. Then he realized something else was carrying him away, but for some reason he couldn't lift his head to see what it was. It was all as if he was under the influence of a powerful anesthetic. Then everything faded to black.

Badger felt so alone now, he wanted to cry out, but no noise would usher forth from his mouth. Then there was an aquamarine light before him, as it grew he saw that it was in the shape of a ring, it came forward until it hovered right in front of his eyes, revolving counterclockwise. Through the ring, he saw a red glow that came forward slowly, it kept coming closer and closer with each passing moment. He couldn't do anything to move closer or farther away, it was as if he was rooted to the spot. It was close enough to make out now; it was a second-dimensional image of a cat-head with slanted eyes and an opened mouth. Then, right when it seemed to be atop him, both the ring and face vanished and were replaced by another image.

The new image was blurred at first, but soon cleared up so he could see that he was standing on a flat surface made of stone and metal and there was a vast view of a large valley before him. He now could see in all directions, but he couldn't move from the spot. All about him were the strange figures from the Settlement artistry, each clad in an identical black suit and carrying a glowing orange rod. They all stood in a circle about Badger, looking up at the sky. Badger looked up and saw a shadowy craft lowering itself down to the ground; but the Settlement never gained the ability to fly. His vision curved so that he was standing with the crowd, sitting where he had been was a thin, cone-shaped pinnacle covered in a kind of energy. Then this too faded.

*   *   *

The dim, red lights of the *Traveler*'s sickbay allowed Badger to open his eyes without being blinded, he was grateful for that. The fact that he was in the sickbay, however, demanded explanation. He wasn't wearing his armor anymore, just his collar, identification-license and headset. The headset was a simple band of stretchy fabric that went around his head and between his ears with a series of sensors connected to a hologram projector that would display the information about objects he was looking at.

He leapt down off the bed, landed on all fours, looked about for a moment and then trotted out of the sickbay without being spotted. The double-sliding doors of the sickbay closed behind him as he turned right down a hall to look for Henry in the ISEN ship. It wouldn't be too hard; he just needed an information console.

The hallway wasn't as full or boisterous as one might think; most of the *Traveler*'s staff was either in their rooms, repairing damages, or had duties elsewhere. The most of anyone else that Badger saw were a few Marines in full combat armor moving opposite his direction.

Finally finding a console built into a wall, and after a moment of designating his owner's name and occupation, the computer showed both a map and a picture of Henry over his location. Badger nodded once and headed in Henry's direction.

*   *   *

Badger's appearance inside Ejection Room 143 had been expected, but his sudden recovery shocked both Henry and the colonel. After Badger's little incident with the mainframe, they hadn't been expecting him until much later. Nevertheless, since he was already there the colonel began speaking about their mission.

"You both did well, our losses weren't as many as we feared and you both completed the objective just in time. However, because Badger here somehow absorbed the mainframe's memory, we were able to link his HUD up to the *Traveler*'s mainframe and download the content. We've found several things that we're very uncertain of. I personally chose this Ejector Room for our meeting for two reasons; it's soundproof and you're both going to be using it soon, after I'm done informing you."

"What?" Henry asked. "Why do we need to use it? I thought we just finished resolving the Chinese conflict."

"You did," said Warren with a tired sigh. "But, during the past eight hours of looking through the HUD's new data, we've found reason to take you both to Forerunner."

That got the Specters' attention. Badger's eyes rolled about, he was mystified. Henry clenched his hands together awkwardly; he didn't know how to react to such a turn of events.

"Yes, Forerunner," the colonel grinned. "Our reasoning is that the mainframe tells us that the Chinese found something, something very old. We don't know what it is exactly at this moment, but when they found it, they became jealous and wanted it for themselves. They left it there; a downloaded map shows the exact location, but it's too heavily guarded for a direct drop. We can't afford to risk destroying the thing with a bomb. And also, it's not too clear, but we believe that the Chinese have formed a new group, the Reach of Nimrod, or the Reach."

"Sounds like a religious group to me," said Henry.

The colonel nodded and turned around to open a gray, metal box that had been lying in front of one of the Ejectors. He reached inside and pulled out a small electronic device, it was almost as thin as paper and nearly translucent. "This is our latest achievement into neural artificial-intelligence. It's far from perfection, but, if certain theories are correct, it should allow Badger communication."

Silent with wonder, Henry watched as the colonel pressed the device against the inside of Badger's right ear and activated the electronic adhesive, locking it to his ear. "Give it a minute to link up," said Warren, standing up and looking down at Badger.

"What are the theories?"

None were more surprised then Henry; the neural AI was actually working. Badger wasn't as surprised, but still surprised, he had never heard himself before. Henry turned his attention towards the colonel, "I'd like to know also, what are the theories?"

"I can't believe it actually works," muttered Warren. "Oh, yes, the theories are that if a properly engineered animal spends enough time around a human it may actually adopt their language. For example, Badger thinks in English, but can't speak it... now. As you can see, those theories were all correct. Don't worry about thinking anything private, the AI knows if you want to say something or not."

"Incredible," projected Badger.

"Have you any other questions about it?" inquired the Colonel.

Badger shook his head.

The colonel turned around and reached into the box again, he pulled out a small, black exoskeleton. "We picked up the survivors of the PDCT unit that was supposed to go with you and they killed something with a very sophisticated external enhancer. With the remains of the external enhancer we managed to make this, only one, sorry, there were just enough pieces to make one big enough for Badger. With some of the left over pieces we managed to modify yours a little, Henry, like in the legs, back, hands and shoulders, but it won't be as powerful as Badger's."

"Just fine," said Henry, admiring the black exoskeleton. "I'm sure he'll need it, his other exoskeleton wasn't as powerful as my larger one and I guess this should give him an edge."

The colonel smiled, "You have no idea how powerful this thing is. But, rather then getting complicated, I'll let you find out for yourselves. It's connected to the neural AI so that if you don't want to break something, it won't allow the exoskeleton to apply more than the required pressure."

"Is there anything else we need to be informed about?" asked Henry as he helped Badger into his new exoskeleton. Exoskeletons split open at the top so the wearers only needed to put their legs through them and them slide their arms into the sleeves and then lock the torso with a series of latches.

"There is actually," said Warren. "Due to the defenses, we won't be able to drop in any extra ammunition, so you're both going to go in with your choice biometric weapons, or SEAR firing weapons. Those should give you the needed ammunition for this job."

"Fine with me," said Henry.

Badger barked in acknowledgment as he tested out the exoskeleton. He had never been able to move so smoothly. It felt so heavy when putting it on, now it seemed as if it was lighter than air.

"Grab hold of something," said Warren. "I'm contacting the bridge now to start our jump."

Henry sat down and grabbed hold of a bar that was used to stabilize equipment during a jump process. Badger did the same, only he held a bar with one paw while the other held onto Henry.

* * *

The artificial black hole was like a gigantic funnel of gravity that yanked the ship inside and then closed up behind it. The remnants of the wormhole quickly vanished like ripples on water after a stone is thrown in. The entire ship was gone like a ghost into the nether.

Chapter 10

"No Violent Actions past This Point"

Light-skinned and brown-haired, Dave was the thirteen year old son of Hagen Hudson, a well known biologist who worked for a major GEM corporation, Program. Program's main occupation was combat modules, with a spreading of domestics; they did, however, have an interest in neural technology. Hagen was trying to biologically create a whole new frontier of modules that needed less human interaction, like the galaxy's most sophisticated GEM. His work was fairly successful.

Dave wasn't alone at home, his dad had, after his mother had been murdered, had created a companion droid for him. The companion droid was almost a necessity; many foreign agencies had requested Hagen to continue his biological research with them, even violently. Dave called it Canine.

Canine didn't look anything like a dog (an insect would be closer); it had a pointed, flat head with a blunt end with a series of sensors that allowed it to recognize and react to objects and actions. Its AI (programmed to act female) allowed it to have emotions and think for itself in any circumstance. Its back had several plates that allowed it to bend over like a contortionist, it arms and legs were designed like human limbs, but flat so they could be folded close to its body and be stored in small spaces. Canine could be very affectionate and her AI loved to play catch.

Dave would sometimes take Canine out to a park and toss around a shock ball. The ball was large with long slits coursing over it and a hollow center so that the ball would fold when it impacted to soften the shock, thus the name. It had little lights all over it that would light up with friction, both Dave and Canine liked to throw it hard to make the lights brighter.

Dave grasped the ball in his right hand and threw it as hard as he could at the insect-like droid. Canine caught in one metal hand and threw it back with a grunt. The little lights flashed brightly and were like bright streaks in the air, the shock ball hit Dave square in the chest. Dave laughed and threw it back; no matter how hard he threw the ball he could never get it as bright as Canine could.

Instead of catching the ball this time, Canine deflected it straight up into the air so that that it fell back to earth at Dave's feet. Canine let out a bark she had been programmed with and awaited Dave's throw. She easily caught the shock ball in one hand and threw it back softly so that the air would buffet it all over the place.

Dave had a harder time catching this one, but he managed to somehow get his fingers inside one of the slits. "Nice try, Canine, catch this one."

Canine watched as the ball went high; it would soar several feet over her head. She leapt into the air to try and catch it, but a wind caused it to fly off to the side. Canine landed back on the ground and watched as the ball rolled a short ways. She strode over to it, picked it up and threw it back, hard.

With its speed, the ball wasn't buffeted by the wind and flew straight. Dave caught it several inches before it hit his face. He dropped it and kicked it at Canine. The folding motion of the ball caused his kick to be way off. Canine gave him a long look and walked after it.

While Dave watched Canine's purposefully slow movement, someone tapped him on the shoulder. He turned around saw that it was a man in a gray casual suit. The man had a pleasant smile, but his eyes betrayed something dark.

"Hello there, I assume that you are young Dave Hudson?"

Dave nodded. "Yes sir."

"Good," said the man. "I was wondering if you could give your father a business proposition."

"What kind of business proposition," Dave asked suspiciously.

"Forgive me; I work for a biological corporation, called Reach. We are trying to create whole new breeds of modules from creatures that we've had caught for us from Forerunner, before the Chinese turned hostile. Your father's research would a valuable aid to our organization.

Will you pass him the message?"

Dave shrugged. "Sure, but I can already tell you his answer. He'll say no."

"Then tell him we'll offer him whatever amount of money he wants, we will pay him." The man was looking desperate now, he wrung his hands together nervously.

"People have offered that before, already," said Dave. "He just wants to work for Program, away from government-operated businesses."

"He will accept our offer if he knows what's good for him… or you." the man growled, grabbing Dave's arms and squeezed hard, Dave cried out in pain. "He's going to give his research to us, he… aaah."

Canine had heard Dave cry out and, when she saw the man handling Dave in such a violent manner, threw the ball as hard as she could. The ball whistled through the air and impacted with such force that the shock-absorbing folding wasn't enough to soften it. The man grabbed the side of his face and danced about, when he removed his hand there was a large red impression of where the ball had hit.

"You haven't heard the last of us, boy," said the man as he ran off.

Dave picked up the ball and called Canine over to his side. "Let's go home, I've a feeling he's not lying."

Chapter 11

"The New World"

The white hole was bright as it grew until it was large enough for *Traveler* to exit and then disappeared like the black hole had. *Traveler* was drifting just a short distance from Forerunner. From space the occupants could see where the forests and jungles gave way to the cold snowy regions of the north and the hot desert regions of the equator. It was very much like Earth and Mars, but Forerunner's oceans and continents were extremely unique. The weather was clearly seen in the areas, sunny, cloudy, rainy and snowy weather could be easily spotted. This was the world from which the Chinese conflict had started. From space, they could see some of the planet's cities; they looked utterly untouched, but reports from survivors had said that the Chinese had bombed them. Something was amiss.

Also around the horizon, seen as shadows, ships drifted above the planet's atmosphere. Colorful structures could be seen down below, but because of the secrecy of their mission, they were not allowed to spy down upon the planet, until the Specters had cleared a safe position. For the moment, the *Traveler* was just observing from space.

* * *

Badger was quicker to recover from the gravitational shock than the other two. He let go of the bar and Henry, stood up on his hind legs and shook himself. "Are you okay Henry?"

Henry nodded and still didn't let go of the bar. The sheer fact that they had just been falling through the gravitational pull of a wormhole for twenty minutes, was enough to momentarily paralyze him. After several minutes, he regained himself and released his pale hands from the bar.

"I suspect that the next time we do this we it shouldn't be as shocking," said the colonel, standing up shakily.

Henry scratched Badger's left ear. "Where's our gear? I want off this ship and onto solid ground."

Warren pointed to another, larger box near the door. "There it is, now remember, we've upgraded your exoskeleton, be very careful around fragile objects. And try not to ruin any rifles."

Henry opened the box and pulled out his thick, green exoskeleton, it did have several new components on the hands, arms, legs and back. He quickly put it on and flexed his hands; he could already tell that they were powerful. Next he put on his over-armor (which changed in coloration with the terrain), helmet, belt and boots. Both of their helmets had been switched out to a full head coverage variety.

Badger waited until Henry was finished with his gear before putting on his own over-armor, helmet and boots. The boots were shaped specially for his hind paws so that they could easily flex and his claws stuck out through little slits in the front. He noticed that his belt had an added feature. The buckle appeared to have an electronic circuit attached, probably a void signature to hide him from detection units. But Henry didn't have one, why just him?

"Your weapon selection will be here soon," said Colonel Warren.

The weapons were brought inside a large box, with a blue grenade painted on top of it, by two ISEN Marines. When it was opened there was an immense array of biometric rifles and pistols along with SEAR firing varieties. Badger chose an ASP and an Assault Rifle, with a backup load of system-linked high-explosive SEAR. Henry chose a biometric Tactical Rifle and a scope for long range precision; he also chose an ASP with an under-slung rocket-launcher. The launcher had five slots for five small, laser-guided missiles, just right for clearing areas.

"Anything else you need?" the colonel asked with a grin. He watched as both specters quickly grabbed three D72 fragmentation grenades and locked them onto their belts. "I was wondering. Now that you're both equipped, do you need anything else?"

"How about some water and food," Henry asked, glancing into the box.

"Already in the Ejectors." the colonel gestured to two Ejectors.

Ejectors were miniature escape pods/fast-attack deployment pods that were used to evacuate ships, sending soldiers out to be rescued later or dropped from outside of a planets atmosphere onto a targeted area. After dropping a mile or so the Ejectors would release what the ISEN military personnel called Friction Anchors. The friction anchors were like rotary-blades, spinning against the direction of descent to slow them down, that, plus the ergonomic shape of the interior would ensure that the occupants would survive. There was one way in or out, a door that would swing up as soon as the Ejector impacted onto the ground, the door had a window that would allow the occupant to see out and be prepared for any possible hostile threats.

"I assume that you're both ready to be deployed," said the colonel, dismissing the Marines. "Once on the ground we'll be relaying the position of the site on your HUD's. If we detect any abnormal hostile movements we'll relay them onto your HUD's also. Anything either of you need to know?"

"What forms of dangerous wildlife can we expect to encounter?" projected Badger's neural AI.

"Nothing either of you have to worry about," Warren remarked, stepping towards a holographic control panel.

The colonel opened the Ejector doors for the Specter and had them place their rifles into holding slots placed on both sides of the pod. Once they were in the doors closed and the colonel checked the systems to make sure everything was in order. He nodded in approval and pressed two buttons that told the computer which Ejectors to drop. He waited a moment for the ship to be over the drop zone before pressing the command switch. The two Ejectors dropped from the *Traveler*.

Badger watched as the metal and fabric plating of the ship disappeared above him and he was thrust into space. He looked out at the uncountable stars and the planet with an expression that had only an edge of interest, his brow was furled seriously and his ears were held stiff and alert. Suddenly, the Ejector burst into the planet's atmosphere. Both pods began to increase their speed of decent, the air whistling past on all sides.

The pods were like red meteors in the day light, leaving behind a trail of vapor in the atmosphere. The steady friction did nothing to heat up the cool interior of the Ejectors. The Friction Anchors were working well to slow the Ejectors; the force of friction would soon be enough to deplete any impact.

The pods broke through a layer of dark clouds, it was raining underneath the canopy, a light drizzle but the steam the pods' incredibly hot outer shell was enough to cloud the windows. It was very hard for the Specters to tell what kind of terrain they would land in; however, green blurs outside their windows suggested a forested landscape. Within seconds there was a great rattling noise as the pods broke through hundreds of tree limbs. The limbs helped slow the impact, however slight; both pods hit the ground with noticeable concussions.

Badger watched as the door opened, revealing a misty forest with a thick layer of undergrowth. He grabbed his Assault Rifle from the holder and stepped out of the Ejector, onto a carpet of broken limbs, leaves and deep mud. Countless leaves were still drifting down towards the ground as he looked about for the other pod.

A humming noise made him turn around. Henry's pod was just opening; several large limbs rested atop the Ejector like tent poles. Henry grumbled and pulled his rifle from the holder. "Basic training had us do it attached to a cable. That doesn't prepare anyone for the actual results."

Badger nodded in agreement and looked up from where they had just come. Through the dense mist he could just make out two large holes and a thick trail of steam that was quickly dissipating. He brushed aside a maple leaf that was about to cover his face and remarked. "It got us here at least."

Just then a large red triangle appeared on their HUD's. They turned about until it was in the center of their screens. That was direction of the targeted area; the estimated distance was over thirty miles. No better time to start than right that moment.

Henry was closest so he gestured towards Badger to follow and started running towards the target. Henry was sprinting as fast as the exoskeleton could react; the new pieces were amazingly agile and he was moving faster then he'd ever seen any exoskeleton travel. He wondered what the pieces had been taken from and then a black and green streak with a white tail rushed by, breaking his train of thought.

Badger felt the wind blow around him as he ran through the forest, dodging through the thick trees. He came to a sudden halt by digging both hind paws into the ground; he left two long gouges in the foliage behind him. He stood stock-still for the longest time; the speed he had been moving was incredible, he had over taken Henry, who had a larger exoskeleton that should have had more programming then a small one. Badger wasn't even worn out in the slightest.

Henry wasn't too amazed, if these few plates that were attached to his exoskeleton could make him move faster then some cars, Badger's full body with neural-link would most certainly move faster. After a few minutes of running, he spotted Badger standing still, looking straight ahead. Henry stopped to see if he was alright.

When he saw Henry, Badger regained himself and told Henry he was alright. They started forward again, this time Badger made sure to keep at Henry's speed; they had slowed to a steady jog, which would cause less noise. They spread out till they were nearly ten yards apart, a regulation distance for fire dispersal. Both Specters wondered what else the new performance-enhancers were capable of.

A wind blew through the forest, rustling through the leaves and under growth; the mist swirled about and began to thicken behind the

Specters. The Ejectors were now completely lost to sight and the only means of direction they had was the NAV-point on their HUD's. Odd creatures raced through the treetops and lichen and bits of moss drifted to the ground below.

Two VTOLs, sent to investigate the two objects that had fallen from the sky, flew over the trees, right over the Specters. Their thrumming gyros blew leaves and branches about wildly like they had them in their arms and were wrenching them about. The VTOLs would be too late to search for the Specters and too late to know which direction they had gone.

Henry and Badger watched the VTOLs fly overhead, Warren told them to stop watching and start moving.

"They're going to find the empty Ejectors you know," said Henry.

"I assume they will," said Warren, "Our presence here won't be secret for long and now you've got a higher priority."

"What about the *Traveler*?" Henry said, looking up to where he thought it might be.

"That's none of your concern, Henry," said Warren. "Our geological map of your area shows a cliff five miles up ahead. Get there. Perhaps you can spot the base then."

"All right," said Henry, "but I trust you've told the captain?"

"Certainly," said Warren, "you're mishap in New Nigeria will not be repeated."

"Thanks for the reminder," Henry muttered.

"Wait Henry," Badger projected, staring off into a space in the trees.

"What is it?" asked Henry, crouching down and walking slowly in the direction Badger was staring.

"A fighter," Badger projected.

"What?" Henry asked, he couldn't see a thing, just trees, undergrowth and dirt.

"Follow me," Badger projected, taking off at a run.

Henry hesitated a moment in thought, but then ran after Badger, knowing it would be impossible to overtake him. The trees were getting thick, but he easily maneuvered through them, all the while keeping Badger in sight and wondering what he saw.

Henry saw Badger suddenly disappear; he raced to where he had last seen Badger and found himself staring down a short dirt bank. Badger was walking along a low stream bed towards a fighter; the fabric body was badly smashed and burnt and some strange residue was clinging to its fuselage.

Badger hadn't exactly seen the fighter; it more or less appeared in his vision. He didn't understand it, but it was as if he was being forced to run towards it. He turned his head to see Henry sliding down the dirt slope and then turned back to the fighter, he felt himself being drawn towards the cockpit.

"How could you spot this?" asked Henry, admiring the practically unrecognizable craft.

"I don't know," Badger projected.

"That mainframe may have done something more than infiltrate just his suit," said Warren. "Keep your eyes open, there may be some other things we'll find out."

Badger had climbed up onto the screen of the cockpit; it was so dirty he couldn't see through it. He searched about for the exterior release latch, upon finding it he pulled, it sounded like crunching gravel. He then dug his claws up under the screen and flipped it up. There was the pilot, mostly rotted and eaten away by insects and mold. Badger was about to shut the screen when he spotted something underneath the pilot's boots. He climbed in and lifted the boots aside. There for all to see was a glowing red ball, with dark blue lines cutting through it.

Badger picked it up and examined it. The ball made a hissing noise and two ends expanded until they were hovering outside the sphere, rotating and humming. A shimmering red halo appeared about the object in Badger's paws and golden symbols appeared all over the halo's rim.

"What is that?" asked Henry, taking a few steps forward to get a better look.

"I don't know said Warren, "but it's not your priority, put it back and we'll retrieve it later. Good work, Badger."

Badger set the object back under the pilot's boots. Upon letting go, Badger saw that the object closed up, returning to its original state. He slowly closed the screen leapt down. He glanced again at the fighter before following Henry along the stream bed. There was something odd about the sphere and he wasn't sure what it was.

Chapter 13

"In Case of Emergency…"

It was nearly midnight when Dave's father got home from work, Canine made a big show of being excited about his return. Dave related the events about the man and his hostile attitude, telling him even about the threat he made. Dave's father remained silent for several moments as he thought over what he son had told him.

Hagen wasn't a large man, but he was relatively strong. His hair was cut very short, his white scalp was almost visible under it and he sported a dusty looking beard. He had lost several of his front teeth due to an incident with a rogue GEM at Program a few years ago and they had been replaced with systematized implants that had a bluish tint to them. The implants were an expensive prototype that gave off a low-pressure shield to protect his skull from minor injury; the US and UK governments had paid for the implants themselves. The friendly countries both shared the same opinion that Hagen's research was far too valuable for any harm to come to him.

"I had hoped that it would never come to this," Hagen said, finally. "Whatever company the Reach is, isn't going to stop after one mishap with Canine. They're going to come back and I can't be here all the time. Son, get a suitcase packed, you're not going anywhere just yet, but I want you to be ready for an emergency. Follow me... I've something to show you."

The Hudson dwelling was on the outskirts of the American city, Forge. It had security features both inside and out, anything coming in or out would be detected. Unauthorized guests would find themselves setting off several alarms. In addition to these security systems, Canine was almost as passionate about protecting the occupants as Badger protected Henry. Though not actually tested, Canine had additional weapon attachments secretly hidden on her by Hagen himself.

Dave followed his father through the house until coming to the storage room where Hagen kept his house tools and supplies. Inside he opened a panel at the very back; it was a fusion panel that controlled power regulation throughout the house. Dave watched in amazement as his father's right-hand went right through the back of the panel, it was a hologram.

There was a low hum that quickly grew and then things started to happen. The doorway into the storage room transformed until it was rimmed by a metallic surface and then a blue force-field was projected in between. A corner of the floor swung up like a trap door and underneath it was a circular tube that ran downwards. After a moment it lit up with little white lights and a magnetic-elevator platform arrived at the top.

"I installed it five years ago," said Hagen. "There's enough room on that elevator for both you and Canine, it leads down to a shaft that you can both crawl through until you reach a ladder heading upwards. When I tell you to leave you are not to hesitate, every second will count. You can leave the house by the door if you want, but you have to bring something that I can contact you with; do not go anywhere without Canine. I am relying on you to obey me. Do you understand?"

Dave nodded wordlessly.

"Good," said Hagen looking at Canine. "Go pack that suitcase; I need to do a little programming on Canine."

As soon as he was sure Dave was out of earshot, Hagen took a tool from his pocket and opened up a part of Canine's arm. He then took a thin disc from his pocket and placed it inside, closing the arm up afterwards. "That disc is too risky for me to carry about anymore; you're the only one that can protect it. I now give you permission to use your weapon systems, use them only when necessary, keep my son safe, don't allow any harm to come to him, understand?"

"Yes, master," said Canine with a nod of her head.

"All right, go see about helping Dave pack. I've got to think. Where's that pitcher of coffee?"

*   *   *

Just a few blocks away from the Hudson household, a black car with darkened windows and false license plates was parked outside of a small café, named: The Stop. It was a low-rider with wide wheels and a chromium bumper; it just sat outside the café with the driver taping the steering wheel and a passenger sitting in the back seat.

The rider was fair-skinned, dressed in a dark suit with gray-leather shoes; he had finely-combed graying hair and a thin, black, tattoo of a rose vine over his right eye. There was a hologram projected in front of him that he used to speak to someone elsewhere. The hologram had only a few multicolored lines that moved up and down when the person it was linked to spoke.

"How's it going?" asked the man with absolutely no expression upon his face.

"It would be a past tense now," said the voice. The voice was slightly high pitched, female.

"What did you find out?"

The voice chuckled a little. "Just that there's an insane amount of security systems; I probably couldn't reach the door without setting off an alarm and bringing the police. There's so many sensors and detectors all over the area, I barely got into the yard. Though, I think it'll be much harder to leave."

"When you said past tense I thought that meant you were out," said the man.

"No-no, it meant I was finished with my examination. I've found just enough to say that you'll need some 'eavy equipment if you want the boy before the Reach gets 'im. You know, those… things, they're fast and extremely strong, the freaks. Although, I'm a little concerned with the boy's bodyguard, it could 'old its own against twelve rhinoceroses."

"It?" the man asked, his eyes were slanted as he waited for an explanation.

"It's a droid of some sort. Looks like a four-legged beetle. Appears to 'ave some sort of emotional bond with the boy, it should be your only concern. Oh, what if the Reach finds out what you're up to?"

The man smiled mockingly. "Don't worry about them, we have an agreement; whoever gets them first, can use them first. Both our… organizations, will profit immensely both ways."

"If you say so," said the voice. "Oh, when I get back to Biotech, can I switch back?"

The man nodded. "Of course. Good work. Get out of that yard, we're still outside of the café. we'll wait."

"Good," said the voice, a sigh of relief mixed in. "It should only take a moment. I could sure go for some ice cream."

"Do hurry, Alder," urged the man. "Every moment counts to our favor."

Chapter 14

"Meeting Score"

Badger and Henry crouched low in the ferns atop the high cliff, peering down and about. Below was a large lake surrounded by trees and clearings. Birds fluttered past below in large groups; in some areas they thought they saw large beasts roaming. But what really drew their attention was the base in the distance. It was circular with the walls leaning outwards and a huge satellite dish situated in the center. Using their zoom-visions, they saw that the base was a maze of low buildings. There were figures walking about, but they weren't able to zoom in far enough to tell any features.

Henry took his ASP from his belt and pointed it down towards the ground below. The distance estimator on his HUD read: 2017.3 feet.

"How far?" projected Badger's desired words.

"Too far," admitted Henry, reattaching the ASP to his belt. Even though Badger hadn't spoken much, Henry had gotten over the shock that Badger thought in English. Even with their new exoskeletons, Henry didn't think they could survive such a fall.

Badger's amber-eyes scanned the area and his ears twitched. Something inside the base glinted and he reactivated his zoom-vision to look about for what could have caused it. As soon as his vision locked with the reflective surface he froze in awe. It looked to be a sort of aircraft, a design of which he had never seen before. Spread out it looked like some sort of mechanical gray whale. The end of the tail was ring-like with a large rotary-blade inside and it had six fins with rotary fixtures near the tips, no cockpit was visible.

Henry was surprised by a little box appearing in the corner of his HUD; the shared information section. He was even more surprised at what Badger was showing him, he scanned the area to see for himself. "What is that?"

"I see it," said Colonel Warren. "I have no idea what it is, neither does anyone else. You need to find a way inside, but from what you saw of the defenses you'll need a discreet way of entry. I'm suggesting an alternate route."

A third-dimensional diagram of a railway system and a small station appeared on the Specters' HUD's. Along the railway system were several odd towers, as big as four story buildings, set upon three legs with rounded shells that covered two long, blue rods that were curved like claws at the ends. The towers were rimmed in a purple shimmer to signify they were unknown entities.

"This is the closest slide-rail system to your location; it should take you both into the base before anyone knows what's happening. Unfortunately it's an extra thirty miles away. We're downloading the position on your HUD's now. Another thing, it's probably heavily guarded, be ready for a fight."

"Right," said Henry. "What were those towers?"

"We don't know," said Warren, "perhaps you can find out for us."

Henry waited until the red triangle switched positions on the HUD before moving again. He removed his biometric rifle from his holster and picked up his pace. He soon passed by Badger, who was eager to take the point.

The Specters moved so smoothly through the forest that they were like wind through the trees. Their green and black camouflage was perfectly suited for the terrain, regardless of how much light there was. Flying insects scattered at their approach and small predators ran away. Birds called to each other overhead and more then once did an inquisitive crow flap close by their helmets.

They were still running along the cliff, and it didn't seem as though it had an end. Badger was weary of his surroundings, the trees were so thick and they could house any number of dangers. He kept his ASP out in front of him in both paws, ready to fire in a moment's notice. He leapt over a small creek, overshooting it by a couple yards and ducked under the fallen trunk of an odd tree.

Henry didn't have as good of hearing as Badger so he had to constantly look about. The undergrowth could house almost anything, it was so thick. This was confirmed when several figures rose up out of the ferns, surrounding the Specters with their rifles trained on them.

"Don't move, there are more of us in the trees," said one of the figures, stepping forward to address Henry. All the figures wore a crude ghillie suit with full-face observation masks (used mainly for scouting) that had detectors arrayed underneath the thin screen; but this one's uniform seemed special. Both Specters could tell that he wore an exoskeleton underneath the ghillie because of his bulky look.

"From the looks of you I'd say you weren't the Chinese, not even the Reach, but how can I be sure? They're both very deceptive. I'm not going to take your weapons, because I want to be sure whether or not you are allies. Have you an explanation?"

"We are United States Specters," said Henry, "it would do you well to point those things somewhere else."

"You're both affirmed," said the figure. "I am Major Tac, leader of the guerrilla forces against these traitors."

Henry was relieved to see that the rifles were lowered and held in a friendlier manner. "I'm Henry Mindell and that's Badger; we've been sent here to locate and secure something that the Chinese discovered. We need to reach a nearby slide-rail station to get into the base."

"Regrettably," said the major, "we can't go with you at this time."

"What do you mean?" Henry asked, looking about at the other

figures.

"One of the reasons why we didn't shoot you both on sight is that we are almost completely out of ammunition. We'll have to go back to our base and get some more. But, if you wait until tomorrow, at almost this same time, we should be able to join you at the station."

"What's the quickest way down?" Henry asked.

"Short of jumping," said the major, "continue on your journey until you reach a platform, don't be surprised by what you see there. Once there you need to activate a centrifugal lift, you'll see it and that should take you right down. On the ground there'll be two paths; take the one on the right."

"Thank you," said Henry, nodding gratefully at the Major.

"Just don't fail," said Tac.

The guerilla team turned and left, leaving the Specters alone again. The treetops rustled slightly as the other soldiers moved away, leaves fell to the ground and birds flapped from their perches. In a few moments there was silence.

"Do what he says," said Colonel Warren. "After you secure the station wait for him to come, you may need him."

"Fine," said Henry. He looked about the forest for a moment.

A large, brown beetle, sitting on a fern, opened its shell and spread its wing to fly, but was grabbed by the calico paw of a predator.

The last noise it made was a startled hiss.

Henry began to move again, Badger moved out in front.

They were more watchful this time; they didn't want to be caught again. Fired by an inner enthusiasm, the Specters moved faster. They passed over several other creeks, rounded large rocks and avoided mole-worm holes. There were a couple of times when they had to leap atop of steep inclines that stretched several yards in the air. But, they both felt that they were making good progress.

Badger stopped suddenly, the hair on the back of his neck stood up straight. Once again he could feel the eyes of the same thing in he had sensed in China. He looked about wearily, searching for even the rustling of a bush to tell him where it was. But it was the same as in China. There was absolutely nothing. He moved forward again.

Henry took notice of Badger's halt, but remained silent as Badger quickly went on his way. Badger was very protective and cautious everywhere they went. Henry dodged a thick, low limb from a pine tree and pushed several other limbs out of the way. The trees seemed to be getting thicker.

Badger pushed through the ever thickening trees, dry limbs merely snapped against his armor as he passed. Just when it was beginning to seem as though they would never reach the specified platform, Badger burst from the trees and onto the platform. He froze and looked it over it;

it was exactly what he had seen in his dream. All the way down to the thin, cone-shaped pinnacle in the center.

Henry came out of the forest shortly after, and he too froze. The platform was nothing that any modern science could have made. The metal and stone floor was very elaborate and let off a small buzz as if it was full of power. The pinnacle was what really drew his attention, he wasn't an expert, but he knew who it was made by.

"Warren? Do you see this," asked Henry, approaching the pinnacle. "Give me some clarification."

"It's Settlement," said Warren, an edge of amazement to his voice.

"That's what I figured," said Henry. "But the Settlement never even discovered how to fly, much less travel to space. Do you have any idea how it got here?"

"No," said Warren. "Look, find the controls to the lift, I'm sending a tag team to retrieve any information locked inside that pinnacle. You don't have time to study ancient history, your only objective is to reach the base and secure whatever it is the Chinese have found."

"Right," said Henry. "Badger, look for the controls."

But Badger wasn't listening, he was being drawn by an unseen force towards the pinnacle. His right paw was outstretched towards the pinnacle, and he spread his claws as he got closer and then pressed his calloused pads against it. From both Specters' vantage points it looked like static was erupting around Badger's paw and was building to a bright concentration of light within a short radius of his paw.

Immediately, he was in his dream again, but he could move this time, except he was unable to remove his paw from the pillar. He tried to pull away, but he was stuck. He growled and looked up, there was the craft he had seen before, it was shaped like a gear, with a red light in its center, and on each tooth was a golden light. The craft began to drop towards the ground, the Settlement figures moved away until there was room for the craft to land. Badger struggled, he didn't know if it was real or not, but he didn't want to find out, the craft would crush him.

It was useless; he closed his eyes and waited. There was a grating noise and then someone was speaking; someone female. He opened his eyes and saw nothing but blue light. The pillar was still there, but he wasn't sure if he was on the ground anymore.

"You will not remember this," said the voice, "until you have completed what I ask, unwittingly of course. You're a little young, but you will serve perfectly, just as the other did."

Badger looked about for the speaker, but there was no one. He tried to use the neural AI, but he couldn't, he couldn't even make a noise.

"Find this one," said the voice.

The blue light shaped and changed color until it formed a

creature. It was as tall as Badger, a weasel and catlike face, a sleek body covered in blue cloth wrappings, with a transparent knife thrust through a belt. It had ears that were split like scissors, a long, flat tail and its throat and the area about its eyes void of fur, exposing dark blue skin. Fused upon the creature's jugular vein was a shimmering blue crystal.

"Find this one," the voice said again. "He does not know his part either, you will both remember once you see each other."

Badger tired to pull away from the pillar again, all the while keeping his eyes on the creature.

"Stop struggling," said the voice, "simply press harder."

Henry stared at Badger with concern. He had remained still for the longest time and after a while he appeared to press harder against the pinnacle. The pinnacle's tip turned bright blue and a beam shot straight up into the air. There was a grinding noise and a large hole opened up near the platform's front.

"Incredible," said Henry. "I believe Badger found it."

"I don't get it," said Warren, "it looked as if he already knew where it was. Keep watching him."

"You really need to be around Badger more often," said Henry with a smile.

Badger backed away from the pillar, he rubbed his neck thoughtfully, he no idea what had just happened. His mind was a complete void. He looked at Henry, who asked him if he was all right, he nodded and stepped to Henry's side to at the hole.

Both Specters approached the hole and looked down; there was absolutely nothing they could stand on, just empty air. "What exactly is a centrifugal lift?" Henry inquired.

"It's a push-pull force that slows your decent downwards," began Warren. "We haven't been able to duplicate it; safely, that is. But the Settlement-built ones are quite safe. Just step into the hole."

Henry took a deep breath and was about to step in when Badger stopped him. Badger pushed him back with a whine, and Henry could see through Badger's visor that he was apprehensive about his master going first. Badger stepped in to test it ahead. It was true. He began to slowly drop. Henry shrugged and stepped in after Badger.

As they fell Henry questioned Badger. "How did you know where the controls were?"

Badger looked at him and shrugged, "I had a dream about it after I had that incident with the Chinese mainframe."

"You dreamed about activating the lift?"

Badger shook his head as he looked at the ground, still far below. "No, I had dreamed I was the pinnacle, the rest came to me when I touched it."

"What GEM production company did you come from?" Henry

asked, mostly to himself. Now that he had actually gotten into a conversation with Badger it was surprising what he knew.

"I do not know," said Badger. "The earliest I can remember is finally opening my eyes and nursing from that farm dog. It doesn't matter."

"What do you mean it doesn't matter?"

Badger sighed; he looked back up at Henry and shrugged. "I may be the most advanced GEM in the known existence, but all that matters to me is to be sure you survive. On that farm I wanted you, you had the look that told me you could count on me and I'm not going to stop because I love you."

"But don't you think there's anything else? Isn't something that's missing?" Henry said as he looked straight back into Badger's unyielding, amber-eyes.

Badger looked away and back towards the ground below. "I will protect you Henry; if I lose you, I will find you."

Henry dropped the subject, it wasn't getting anywhere. Badger's agenda was iron-willed; it would be a great effort to knock it from his mental foundation. It was hard to believe Badger was just a GEM at times, he seemed so much more. Badger had always been there for Henry, even before he was put into training to be a Specter operative.

Henry remembered when he had first brought Badger home; he

had gone immediately to bed with Badger curled up next to him. When he had wakened the following morning he wanted to fix himself a pan of eggs. He had taken the carton out of the fridge and set it on the counter; while he was heating up the stove, Badger had climbed onto a stool and leapt onto the counter. When Henry turned to grab an egg to crack into a pan, Badger deposited one into his hand. This was repeated until Henry had enough for a suitable omelet. But being a puppy, Badger took another egg from the carton, cracked it open with his own paws and devoured the contents for his own breakfast. The training facility had taught Badger much self-control since then.

Badger was the first to touch the ground so he covered the area until Henry touched down beside him. There were indeed two paths, one seemed to head directly towards the slide-rail station, but the one they had been told to take looked as if it lead only farther into the forest.

Henry looked between the two paths, shrugged and nodded towards the marked path. "He told us that that was the right road." He turned to Badger; he was still covering the area with his ASP.

"Come, boy," said Henry.

Badger looked down the sight of his ASP and started to turn in the direction of the right path, when something caught his attention on the other path. It was movement in some bushes, shaking as if something had just left.

"Henry, stop," projected Badger.

"What is it?" Henry asked, raising his rifle to his shoulder and crouching.

Badger pointed with two claws towards where he had seen the bushes move. "Right there, I think we were being watched. It's your call, sir, the station, or find out who it was."

"It might mean the fate of the mission," said Henry. "Let's find out who or what it was."

Chapter 15

"Contact"

Captain Khan of the *Traveler*, a barrel-chested man with grayish skin, silky red hair and thin sideburns, walked rapidly through the ship's halls as the alarm system was going off. Flashing red lights were going off all over the place and holographic maps of the ship's layout appeared below the lights; four red triangles were pointing towards the hangars, located at the stern. Teams of Marines and Navy personnel, well armed and ready, were rushing towards the hangar at full speed. Occasionally, at a corner or curve in the hall, a blinking, static-laced hologram would appear to show an extremely fuzzy image of what was happening in the hangar.

The holograms displayed flashes of light and the swirling of fumes that rose everywhere. Large figures rushed about in pursuit of smaller figures that returned fire with simple handguns. The last image was of a large figure striding up to the camera that was taking it all in and then punching it. The hologram disappeared with a high-pitched beep.

Captain Khan flicked the safety off on his Assault Rifle, put on a crystalline HUD-equipped visor and hastily threw on a hard-edged no-catch breastplate. Soldiers were beginning to set up defensive positions in the halls, keeping in the cover of doorways and around corners. Khan arrived at the entrance to the hangar where several Marines had been waiting for his order to open it.

"We've got some heavy equipment on the way, sir," said one Marine, throwing a hasty salute. "Should we wait until it arrives?"

"No," Khan said hurriedly, "just open the door and we'll find out what's happened."

"Alright," said one Marine pressing a green light in the center of the door.

The light turned red and there was a grating sound, which suddenly stopped as the light turned off. There were exclamations of surprise when the door remained inanimate.

"What?" the Marine shouted, punching the door with an armored fist. "They've locked it from the inside. No fair."

"Can you override it?" Khan asked.

"Sure," said the Marine, focusing a laser, positioned on the back of his hand, onto the light fixture and worked with a holographic keypad on the back of his forearm. "That ought'a do it, sir."

The light came on again and the door lifted up with a crunch.

"Good job," said the captain, signaling them to head in.

Inside the hangar were scores of interstellar and near-atmosphere craft; also there were ground vehicles and VTOLs that could be deployed onto a planet's surface. The vehicles consisted mainly of Technicals, large all-wheel turn truck-like vehicles that could be fixed with multiple armors and weaponry. The armor and weaponry that could be fixed upon the vehicles was placed on large racks along almost every wall, including the parts to create three light tanks. The hangar was filled with the fumes coming from broken pressure pipes. Deep into the fumes could be heard the gunfire and shouts of battle.

"Let's go in slowly," said Khan, stepping into the cloud.

The Marines followed quickly, two punched each others' shoulders before proceeding. They stepped quietly, keeping their breath low, moving around vehicles and equipment. One Marine unwittingly stepped on and passed over the dead body of a Marine, his body pierced with dozens glowing, blue crystals; after a few moments, the crystals disintegrated into a gaseous state.

"We should be getting close," Khan whispered.

"But the sound keeps getting further away," one Marine returned.

"Keep your voice down," Khan hissed.

"Um, sir," a Marine said urgently, "I think you should look at this."

After a quick surveillance around the mist, Khan spotted a Marine, standing near a Technical and waving a hand urgently. He was swiftly at the Marines side, asking what was the matter. The Marine crouched down and pointed to a bloody arm that was sticking out from underneath the truck.

Khan and the Marine quickly pulled the prostrate form of a Navy technician out from under the truck. It was a young man, dead and covered in massive burns with an odd purple residue surrounding the burns like halos. The man's face was a picture of horror, frozen and white like wax. In one hand was a biometric pistol, the barrel severed near the trigger; the lethal blow to the technician had come from a large blade that had cut an enormous gash through his chest.

Khan used two fingers to close the man's eyes and looked about as if he was being watched.

"The Chinese must be here," he said as he stood up.

"But how could they get aboard without being detected?" asked the Marine.

"Advanced void-signatures and the override codes for the hangars to open," said Khan.

"I think your right," said a corporal who was standing a short ways off in the mist. He looked like a ghost. "Look at this."

The Marines advanced towards the corporal. At first the object was a gray silhouette, but when they were close enough they saw it was a strange interstellar or near-atmosphere fighter. Four, long, curved prongs closely surrounding an egg-shaped chassis made it look like the head of a fantasy wizard's staff. The entire craft was a dark purple-red color with blue about the edges and the odd polymer armor looked as if it had scales.

The cockpit was placed near the back, a rounded transparent dome with a green tint to it.

"What is this thing?" asked a Marine, reaching out and touching the craft, it was warm and smooth as still water. "It's beautiful."

"Is there more," Khan asked himself, looking about cautiously.

After a moment, a Marine spoke over the radio link.

"Everyone, I've just found four others and there seems to be... Hold on! What's that? Oh, get away, eat this."

The sound of sonic blasts gave way the position of the Marine and his assailant. The captain and the rest of the Marines quickly rushed to where the shots had come from, weapons ready and eyes searching the mist for anything. Several more blasts were heard and then a distressed groan came from ahead.

"Why did he have to wonder ahead," the corporal growled under his breath.

The Marines nearly jumped when the dead form of a Marine suddenly flew out of the surrounding fumes and landed at the feet of the corporal. Several deep gashes were cut across his face, deep into his brain.

"Spread out," ordered Khan, "I want a comb moving through this mess."

The Marines wordlessly obeyed, disappearing into the fumes as if they had never actually been there.

Khan crept forward, towards from where the Marine had been thrown. The fumes played tricks on his worried eyes; a couple times he even thought a tank was coming towards him. He walked around a small, six-wheeled reconnaissance vehicle, known as a Prowler and stopped when he heard something ahead. About him he could see the four other craft, something was definitely there.

A growl to his right made him turn with a speed only fear could muster. As he stared into the fumes a large silhouette began to walk towards him. At first he thought that it might have been another illusion of the fumes, but then it stepped close enough for him to see color and texture.

It was an enormous beast wearing armor of intertwined polymer cords, wrapped together in such an elegant, ceremonial fashion with inactive light fixtures in the shapes of symbols all around it. The front of the figure's helmet had a symmetrical pattern of dim yellow lights that were designed to look like some majestically horrifying face with a red symbol placed right in the center. In the creature's right hand, which was tipped with even smaller light fixtures, was a weapon that looked like a huge butcher knife with a hook-like handle; all seemingly made from a solid piece of iridescent black polymer. The back of the knife-like weapon resembled a hedgehog with dozens of small, blue crystals, each pointed forward toward the front of the weapon where an integrated, triangular barrel was set.

Khan saw that the beast was easily three times his size, but it seemed afraid as it advanced. Khan was almost too stunned to react as the creature raised the weapon until it was pointed directly at his head. He quickly fired several molten aluminum projectiles into the creature's face.

The cords of the armor seemed to break away and lash out, slapping at the aluminum. The aluminum shattered and still struck the beast square in the face. With a roar, the beast fired several pieces of crystal towards Khan, who dodged to the side and fired several more times at the beast. The armor tried to block the splinters, but the fragmented pieces broke through the armor and into the skull, peppering the brain. With a gurgling noise, it fell like a rag.

Marines suddenly appeared like magic, they all gathered about the beast, looking over it in awe. It lay unmoving, and blood seeped out between the cords. The corporal reached down and removed the beast's weapon, examining it carefully.

"This is what killed Jack," he said feeling the crystals. He let out an exclamation of pain when the razor sharp points cut his finger. "Nice, whatever it is."

"How do you take it apart?" another Marine asked, feeling the smooth polymer. "It looks as if it's one solid piece."

"There's not even a trigger," the corporal remarked, wiping his bleeding finger on his uniform. The weapon was remarkably light and to test a theory, he pointed it in the general direction of the hangar doors and tightened his grip on the handle. Several crystals shot forward into the fumes, seemingly leaving a trail behind.

"Curious," Khan remarked, turning back to where the sounds of combat were still coming. "Corporal, send out an alert. I want everyone aboard to know that we've been boarded. Specify enemy as unknown."

"Yes sir," said the corporal, activating his radio link.

"Private, stay with the corporal."

"Yes sir."

"The rest of you come with me," Khan ordered.

The Marines spread out again, vanishing into the fumes, each now having a clear idea of what they were up against. In each of their minds, they knew that they had found the Reach of Nimrod, an extraterrestrial ally, or perhaps a prototype creature that the Chinese had created. But whatever it was, there were probably more in the hangar.

Suddenly, another large beast appeared out of the mist, but with a more pointed face with green lights that formed a scowl on its helmet, and a thick, armored tail. It wore similar armor, but it's light fixtures were activated, bright florescent pink, its back with covered in thin spikes. All around the creature were hovering lights, the exact same color as those on its armor, probably launched from the spikes on its back, dancing about, causing visual disorientation. It was a tactic where the enemy was actually hidden in the light. It was shorter than the other beast, and its fingers tipped by long claws of hard, purple light. It rushed at one of the Marines, shrieking like a hurricane and slashing madly. It vanished without a sound as quickly as it had appeared, deactivating the light to hide before the Marines could begin firing.

"What was that?" a Marine gulped with a chill. His steps were more hesitant now, as if he expected the very ground to give way.

"Something horrible," said the other Marine, his finger tightening on the trigger to fire again as soon as he saw the beast again. "That thing is smart."

"Whatever it was, it'll be back."

As if to prove the Marine's point, the creature bounded out of nowhere, lights activated and screaming, twirling its claws about in a beautifully deadly fashion. The Marines managed to leap out of the way and fire at the beast. But it employed the same tactic again and vanished.

"Aim for the claws, guys."

"Could it be Settlement? It's shape is similar to guys in their artwork."

"They didn't have space travel."

"I don't think it's Settlement."

"Well, humans are in the Settlement pictures and we're not

Settlement. The Settlement weren't warriors though."

"Probably why they're no longer alive. Based on the shape, what do you think it was?"

"A terrestrial former, or terref for short. This seems to be one of the thick-tailed varieties. I don't like it, it shouldn't exist and it's going to be baaa..."

The terref had come again, but this time it had chosen a different tactic, grabbing the Marine from behind and holding its claws against the man's throat. The terref's claws slid in and out as it growled menacingly at the other Marines that had their weapon trained on it.

"Kill him," shouted the Marine, pulling at the arm.

The other Marine just kept his gun trained on the beast's face, not daring to fire. "I don't have a clear shot, perhaps if you moved a little."

"This is no time for jokes."

"Sorry!"

The terref growled menacingly and advanced towards the other Marine. The cords pulled away, exposing a hard shell, which split in two and slid back over the creature's skull, looking like horns. It was covered in dull black and white fur with two green, sideways feline eyes. Its long snout was covered in what could only be described as holographic tattoos. It seemed to smile, seeing the Marines at an impasse.

"All right ugly," one Marine said, "stay there or I'll make your face look like my breakfast."

The captured Marine, remembering his knife, grabbed it from its sheath and drove into the beast's arm. It let go hurriedly, howling in pain. The Marine than leapt upon the beast and delivered a hard punch to the throat as smacking it between the eyes with the handle of his knife..

The terref threw the Marine off and tried to scramble to its feet, but the other Marine kicked it unconscious with a blow to the side of its head. It exhaled softly and lay still, breathing in a rasp.

"Let's forget the Settlement," said other Marine, standing up and putting away his knife. He pulled out a metal cord with a loop on either end and proceeded to bind the beast's hands behind its back. "These things are nasty."

"Not as nasty as breakfast."

*   *   *

Khan had been concentrating too much on what laid ahead to hear the short combat that had happened to his far left. And it was also hard to distinguish where sounds were coming from in the hangar. Distant shouts echoed everywhere, as if he were surrounded by people.

He kept thinking back to the beast, the odd armor, powerful figure and he could still see that it feared to approach. He passed by another one of the strange craft; laying dead on the deck beside it were the bodies of another one of the beasts and a smaller creature wearing a much different armor.

The smaller creature appeared to stand only three feet tall; but was thick and strong all the same. It had more plate armor than the elegant cords, and four dim pink lights in the shape of an X were set at the front of its helmet. Two large, integrated packs were set on its back, with no apparent purpose. It too had light fixtures all along its arm. Khan reach down and pulled on one of the lights, it detached with a firm tug, underneath it was another fixture, one that couldn't be removed.

Khan turned the creature over and saw that it had been killed from behind by a large rapid-fire weapon. The armor of the creature was stained with violet blood; a large puddle of the blood was on the floor with a footprint from a Marine's boot in it. Also there was its weapon, three solid rods of polymer attached to a hook-shaped handle with a crystal interior. He picked it up and test fired it, a ball of energy shot out, pulling elements from atmosphere, heating them to a super-hot state and splattering on the deck with a ring-shaped pattern. He looked the weapon over a moment and found he could actually take it apart. These weapons were customizable.

Khan got up and walked past the dead bodies. He only took a few steps and then froze. The hairs on the back of his neck stood on end and he turned around to see the most intimidating group of soldiers he had ever laid eyes on. One of which was walking towards him.

Chapter 16

"The Regalia of the Reach"

The figure approaching the captain was like the first beast he had encountered, but it had a different helmet and its lights were a brilliant teal. The helmet had very few cords on it, and the back of it curled back around, coming back up to its face and sticking up like tusks. Upon the tip of each spike was an aquamarine ring and a red cat face. In one hand the creature held a short rod with four curved hooks on one end and in the other hand was a human skull, bleached white and the every opening save the mouth was plugged by a glossy, black substance.

Khan fired at the beast, but the aluminum just glanced off at sharp angles when it met an energy shield. The Beast waved the skull diagonally in a dismissive manner.

"Lay it aside," the beast said in a harmonious voice that was edged with malice. "You shall wish to know what I have to say, an offer that this fool refused."

Khan, never lowering his weapon, watched as the beast tipped the skull so that blood poured from the mouth onto the floor. When the blood was a minor dripping, the beast dropped the skull upon the ground and crushed it underneath a great foot.

"The skulls of those who refuse us are our drinking vessels," said the beast, "do not add yours to the countless."

"You speak the international trade language very well," said Khan, backing away as the beast advanced a step. "China's good at their engineering it seems."

"We of the Reach of Nimrod are bred to learn anything within moments, we found the Chinese, we were not made," the beast said, turning back to the rest of his group. His group consisted of six terrefs in spike-backed armor, two of which had helmets like the speaker, four humans in cord armor with large packs of intertwined spikes on their backs and helmets shaped like grotesque faces with dim yellow lights about where their eyes should be. There were several of the smaller creatures, the duel pack on their backs unfolding and expanding like peacock tails, tipped with bars of blue light. The beast turned back to Khan, his helmet folding back to expose dark red fur with four eyes, two of which were solid violet, a large head with two bottom jaws filled with wicked cutlery. "We have learned much from our new allies; add your voice to our chorus and share in the rewards of eternity."

"You're aliens?" Khan was frozen in place as the creature held out the hand that had held the skull, blood dripped from the fingertips. The sight made his blood boil and he shouted aloud as he shot at the beast's helmet.

"Over here, attack."

The beast roared loudly and a long, maroon battleaxe was projected from the rod, with lines of energy covering his hand like a basket-hilt. He cleaved through the air, cutting the rifle in half and then sending Khan skidding along the floor on his back with a vicious kick.

"You fool," the beast growled, "I offered you a chance, but you refused."

Khan cried out in shock when several white beams shot from the beast's free hand, sounding like cracking stone, wrapped themselves about his body and he was lifted into the air as if gravity didn't exist.

"I am a Militant," the beast shouted, "a holy warrior for Nimrod and the Emperor, a voice of power and justice. Forever, your eternal damnation shall please me; your passing will not be noteworthy. Let me show you the power of the Reach."

"No thanks," said Khan, feeling the odd beams beginning to crush him. He thought that the beams held his entire body like a hand, but when he struggled, he found that the beams were not holding him. It was like gravity, manipulated to the beast's will, slowly crushing him from every angle. He grunted and pulled a pistol from his belt, it was a bullet-firing weapon and he had every confidence that these bullets would have an effect.

The beast roared when the illegal mercury-filled projectile exploded his shield into polyhedral fragments. Khan was dropped to the floor as the beast tried to steady itself. The second bullet hit the beast in the protective armor about its stomach, blood and scraps of tissue flew from its mouth and there was an audible *snap* when its spine shattered.

"I have won," said Khan with a grin, "take your voice to hell."

The Militant's ax deactivated itself and rolled out of the limp hand that had held it. The rest of the Militant's group, who had watched in dumb fascination at their leader's horrible demise, suddenly burst out into incoherent shrieks and advanced towards Khan, activating their hovering lights to disorient and confuse him. The humans showed their power, the packs flew open, sticking out in symmetrical directions as spikes, rimmed with red light, the humans reached back pulled off two spikes each, showing that each spike had a ring-shaped handle. The humans were walking armories. At that very moment, Marines came in from almost every side, cutting down the aliens with their weapons.

The corporal ran up to the captain's side and helped him to his feet, looking at the energy burns on his armor. "You do know how to get into trouble, sir."

"Never mind," said Khan. "The Chinese have allied with them and there's no telling what they could do if they got to any of the other colonies. Send out a full alert, every government must be warned ASAP."

"Yes sir," said the corporal. "PDCT groups are already outside the ship, searching for any other hostiles that we didn't spot. They'll clear them off like barnacles."

Khan didn't have time to reply, another Militant appeared out of the fumes, a human; he held a ring-handled weapon with sickle-shaped blades underneath in either hand. Khan fired one shot; this one hit the Militant's head, fragmenting the shield and bending its head back at such a sharp angle that it ripped the skin about the throat.

"How many of these things are there?" shouted the corporal.

"As many as the Emperor wishes," shouted another Militant that had just appeared, a terref with fan-like device on its back that channeled out a blue energy that allowed it to fly. It activated a maroon spear and from rod with a disc-shaped tip and spiked the corporal to the ground. "This ship is not worthy, all aboard must die."

Khan killed the Militant with two shots. He bent over the screaming corporal and growled angrily, "not my ship."

*   *   *

The Planetary Drop and Clear Troopers (PDCTs) had already met the enemy outside the *Traveler's* hull. ISEN ships had an environmental shield about the exterior so that soldiers and other personnel could actively walk on the outside without any danger. It also had a series of stairways leading to smooth pathways for exercise and quick vehicular movement about the hull. A group of PDCTs were utilizing a couple of lightweight, three-man VTOLs, known as bi-drifts, for an aerial command. They had four thin wings, two above and two below and a cockpit for one pilot along with a two landing-sleds underneath for two others to sit on.

The aliens outside the ship were utilizing their own aircraft as well; irregular single-occupant, purple craft with three anti-gravity extremities fit about a rounded chassis. The extremities could be lowered to allow the crafts to walk about like tripodal creatures. The craft were very fast in the tripod state and many of the soldiers had to dodge aside as they rushed past like crazed spiders. The Reach were practically swarming on the hull now.

The *Traveler*'s exterior defensive systems were inactive as the Reach had somehow disabled them. Large, purple, teardrop-shaped crafts would appear out of nowhere and deploy several more soldiers as the PDCTs manually fixed and operated the exterior defenses, one at a time. The tide began to change when two PDCTs found one of the missile pods and began using the emergency computer-system to launch filter-fletches at the aircraft.

Filter-fletches were a special design of missile, unlike the old version of flaps, filter-fletches had a symmetrical spiderweb-like, metal fletching that created a wind-tunnel for pinpoint accuracy and incredible speed. These missiles were devastating against the alien vehicles, practically disintegrating the tripod crafts.

The missiles being too dangerous to the ship if used against infantry, several PDCTs took up rapid-fire turrets to eliminate the hostiles. Several officers took up a position on an observation tower to view the combat. By using their helmets integrated zoom-vision modification, they were able to spot and route PDCTs to alien concentrations. Then one officer spotted a structure that the aliens were building at the stern, near the engines. Two groups of PDCTs were quickly called to check it out.

Alexander and his group, leaving two turrets they had been using to another group, moved quickly to the location now indicated on their HUDs. The sergeant used his favored biometric weapon to eliminate three terrefs, then used it to fend off a couple of the shielded soldiers with crystal swords and the knife-like weapons.

"I hate these things," growled Rookie, using an SMG to suppress a gray-armored human.

"Why couldn't the Settlement just stay dead?" growled Kruger, using his Liner to pick off a Militant and a golden-armored soldier. "I thought they hadn't discovered flight."

"These aren't Settlement," said Rookie, diving to the side when several purple flashes of energy flew at him. "The Settlement are all dead."

"How are you so sure?" Kruger asked, blowing a large hole through a stomach of a sprik.

"Uh," began Rookie, "we've found no evidence of space travel."

"Cut it," said Alexander, laying suppressive fire upon a hostile position, "we've got work to do."

A couple of the short creatures (spriks) in dark purple armor took up positions on two rapid-fire turrets and began to spray aluminum about the area. They let out incoherent shouts as the turrets vibrated with the recoil.

"Kruger," shouted Alexander, pointing to the turrets.

Kruger quickly snapped the scope of his sniper rifle onto the turrets, with two quick, successive shots, the mutilated spriks landed a short distance away. "Let's go."

Upon reaching the turrets, the PDCTs could see the structure. It was starting to form a conical shape and orange light creased all over it. A large group of aliens were standing about the structure; among them were three Militants, carrying ISEN handheld rocket launchers. A large, dome-shaped, particle shield surrounded the structure and its guardians.

"Kruger," said Alexander, "test that shield and we'll provide cover fire."

Kruger placed two random shots upon the shield; each one glanced off with a drum-like sound. He tried to sight in on the Militants, but the bullet glanced away into eternity. He turned to Alexander, who was shooting at a group of spriks and shook his head.

"It is not working," he said, "they just glance off."

"Great," said Alexander, stomping a foot hard onto the deck. "It's probably a bomb, or even... hold on. I think I've got an idea."

The sergeant quickly radioed for assistance. "We need static emitter weapons up here now."

Three VTOLs loaded with static-pulse lasers soon arrived upon the scene. The pilots hovered close by and focused the white-blue beams onto the shield; the static beams began to spread over the shield like vines. At first nothing seemed to happen; then gradually the shield began to look dull, thin and then it began to blink.

"This is working," said Alexander, "everyone, pick your targets, when the shield goes, kill every hostile in sight."

"Simple plan," said John, "I like it."

*　　*　　*

After the short entanglement, during which one of the VTOLs was hit by two rockets from the Militants, the PDCTs crowded about the structure, searching for a way to deactivate it. After it was apparent that they didn't know enough to disable the structure, they employed the use of some other VTOLs to use cables to lift the structure off the stern and send it drifting away while the *Traveler* ignited its engines to get away.

When the *Traveler* was several miles away, the structure exploded in a flash of blue light and then sent a halo of green residue throughout the area. It lit up the sky for miles, like a star.

"What was that?" asked Kruger.

"Something I don't want to deal with again," said Alexander.

"Calling all available forces, hostiles inside the *Traveler*, all available units converge inside."

John sighed and shouldered his rifle. "Looks like our day's cut out for us."

"Couldn't ask for more," said Alexander.

Chapter 17

"It Was Simple, Then…"

The Specters had been moving along the path for the better part of an hour, following the deemed direction of the one who had been observing them. It was obvious that whoever or whatever it was had come out of the forest, marked by a lot of broken foliage, and was now running up the path, trying to keep ahead of the Specters. They didn't dare run for fear of triggering an alarm system but the time it was taking in tracking the thing was getting dangerous also.

After a few more moments, Henry knew they weren't going to get anywhere fast and time was of the essence. "Badger," he said, nodding up the trail, "fetch."

Badger needed no second bidding; he attached his ASP to his belt, dropped to all fours and took off, leaving behind a cloud of dust. All four of Badger's paws kept a steady beat on the path as he cruised at an insurmountable pace. He narrowed his eyes as he followed the winding path, deeper into the forest ahead of Henry. His body was literally a black, green and white streak. The observer was dead ahead of him.

The observer was just like the short aliens aboard the *Traveler*, only this one wore forest camouflage without any armor, made of a much thinner weave of the polymer cords that could change shape to mimic surrounding foliage. It didn't appear have a weapon, though it probably had one before it started running. It let out garbled gasps as it tried to keep as far ahead of Badger as it could.

With a leap, Badger had pinned the alien to the ground, it wriggled and shrieked pitifully. Badger leaned close to where he figured the neck was and growled menacingly; this quieted the alien very quickly. Badger stood back up on his hind paws and pulled the creature up to its feet; it was only slightly taller than him, twisting it around so they were face-to-face. It's long face was painted with black and greens, but that didn't hide its features, a large nose, six purple eyes and a small mouth, with tough skin.

The creature swung an arm and hit Badger in the chest; he didn't even move. Badger pulled as much of the camouflage as he could into his paw and lifted the creature into the air as if it didn't weigh anything. The creature struggled for a moment in the air and then calmed down when it saw that it couldn't do anything.

Badger began to contact Henry, activating the radio-link and shared-information software. "It's alright, Henry, there are no traps, but what do you think this is?"

"That's a sprik you got there," replied Henry in admiration, "maybe this the Reach of Nimrod?"

"A small part," intruded Warren's voice. "More are aboard the

Traveler; don't worry, we outnumber them and are handling the situation. We've taken some alive, and they're pretty cooperative. So be on the lookout for anything weird and carrying a gun; it's most likely not friendly."

"Why didn't that Major tell us about this?" said Henry, his voice filling with suspicion.

"Probably been out of contact so long that he figures we've already met them," answered Warren. "Even if he is setting you up, it's too late."

Communications ended with Henry telling Badger to stay where he was. Badger spent that time examining the alien. It was most likely some sort of scout, not given a radio to minimize the risk of capture. But what really drew Badger attention was the ring and cat insignia over its right eye. It was exactly like his dream.

When Henry arrived at Badger's location, he found that Badger was still holding the alien in the air. Hilariously, the sprik was humming a tune with its arms crossed in front of its chest. When it saw Henry, it stopped humming, dropped it arms, leaned its head back and sighed as though it was bored.

"You can put him down now," said Henry.

Badger lowered the sprik gently to the ground and let go. The sprik looked down at itself and began to dust its camouflage off. Badger curiously watched the sprik's calm demeanor; before it had been running for its life. Now it just regarded Henry with more interest; the man was twice its size.

"Now what do we do with it?" Henry was at loss, he doubted the alien understood, much less spoke English. They wouldn't get any information out of it. The sprik casually kicked up dust with one leg as it waited for something to happen.

"We can't have it following us," projected badger. He reached slowly for his ASP.

"No, you can't kill it," Henry remarked distastefully. "It's unarmed and is considered a prisoner."

"The thought never crossed my mind." Badger swung the ASP with the desired strength, rendering the sprik unconscious. Its snoring was soon an annoying ruckus.

"Oh," said Henry.

*   *   *

Instead of heading back along the path and traveling the path that the Major had told them to use, the Specters kept moving forward. It was curious to them that he would suggest a road would that curved away from their destination rather then head straight towards it. They were extremely quiet as they moved, like ghosts; they had a feeling about what might be up the road. Their first alien encounter had made them careful; they had a new foe that could not be predicted. Even though the sun shown brightly with a few dark clouds to the east (their left), they felt as though there was a shadow over them.

Henry kept his Tactical Rifle ready, the safety was off as he pointed it at every bush large enough to be holding a waiting sprik. The scope could be switched through a series of options, including: organic-thermal, night, electronic and heartbeat. He used the organic-thermal to examine the brush. The scope had a wireless link to his HUD; the display in the top-center of his screen allowed him to know where hostiles could be concealed.

Badger had already made it a point not to tell Henry about the insignia, he felt it might attract unneeded attention. As every image of that dream came into his mind he felt as if he were only half alive. It was as if half of him lived and breathed, but the other half was a machine; a machine that ran in a continual cycle of persistent and lethal energy. It was as if something had a grip upon him and wouldn't let go. Never since before his eyes opened had he felt such fearfulness.

Ever since he saw the insignia and the platform, he had wondered more deeply about his dream. Who was the black figure that seemed so familiar to him? Two parts of the dream had come to light and he mused over the last part. Reluctantly, for lack of anything else to do, he switched his ASP out for the Assault Rifle.

The path lead on further and further into the forest, the slide-rail station was still far in the distance. A flock of birds too far away to identify, flew in a nondescript pattern, heading away from the dark eastern clouds. A strong wind, blowing westward, picked up sending the rain-heavy clouds towards the Specters' area. Within an hour the entire region would be drenched in rain. A small, catlike predator, bluish-white with black blotches, walked on the tips of its paws across the path, far behind the Specters, it carried a kitten in its mouth, moving its litter to another hideaway.

The operatives began to quicken their pace, hoping to arrive at the station before the storm hit. Already a mist was beginning to drift over the path, it wasn't very thick but it could still hide the Reach of Nimrod or Chinese forces. Forerunner's sun shined dimly through the mist, like a golden lake in the sky. Several oak leaves drifted slowly to the path below, they landed on the ground just in front of Badger and he cautiously stepped over them.

Badger felt it before he saw it; up ahead on the trail were a dozen little lights moving towards the Specters. The little blue lights were aligned in arrow-like patterns pointing upwards and the lights at the tips blinked on and off. Badger noticed that Henry had just caught sight of them with his scope's organic-thermal vision. Quietly, they moved off the path and hid in the tall ferns that were dripping with moisture from the mist.

The lights came from the odd armor of the Reach of Nimrod, they were illuminated simply to be able to see, not using any special tactic. Heading them was a Militant. They were just out on a routine patrol, not really expecting to see anything. Their leader was a terref; he had a thick tail and yellow eyes, and carried an Assault Rifle that it had taken from an ISEN soldier who it had stabbed in the back. Attached to the grip was a gold necklace with writing on it; the terref put it there as an ornament.

As the aliens passed by, Badger couldn't help but noticing the canteens attached to their hips. Each one carried a skull-canteen after its own race; the eyeless sockets seemed to cry out to him, begging for liberation. He suppressed an angry growl and raised his rifle level with the Reach. When the last soldier passed by, Badger pulled the trigger and began to pepper the backs of the Reach with molten aluminum.

Henry, too, had the same idea. The loud, faster-than-sound projectiles tore through the group. Anger against the Reach filled him to the boiling point; the startled Reach didn't stand a chance.

Not knowing where the attackers were, the leader leapt about, yelling out in a strong voice: "Uadbae id uauad uawud… uadbae id uauad uawud!" He shot wildly into the forest with the Assault Rifle; the recoil of the weapon wasn't a problem with his immense strength.

The Specters also had very little recoil, thanks to their new exoskeletons. The small sound-waves of their projectiles were getting so numerous that they were actually seeing them as small, distorted rings. Within just a few moments the Reach lay dead, save the leader.

Upon seeing that everyone else was dead, the Militant raised its arms into the air, still holding the rifle, "Ouai ualarweid!"

Badger stepped out of the brush, rifle aimed directly at the terref's chest. He growled warningly as he approached. His tail was stiff with anger and caution, the tip twitched with every step.

The leader was extremely startled at the sight of Badger. He lowered his rifle and fired a few bursts, "Demaw… fei Demaw, fei." Its fire was halted when Badger and Henry returned fire; the Assault Rifle was hit several times and the Militant dropped it with a cry. It fell to the ground; seven holes in its chest.

Henry came out of the brush and both he and Badger approached the Militant. It lay on the ground, clutching at its chest to try and stop the flow of blood. It looked at the approaching Specters and tried to drag itself away, whimpering and sobbing.

"Stop right there," said Henry, training his Tactical Rifle at the terref's head.

The Militant stopped and kept most of its attention on Badger. It breathed heavily and watched as Badger examined the ISEN Assault Rifle. The last thing it saw, before all vanished, was Badger taking his ASP from his belt and firing one shot.

"Why'd you do that?" Henry demanded, spreading his arms out inquisitively.

"Look," projected Badger, handing Henry the terref's rifle.

Henry noticed the gold chain and read the inscription out loud, "For Sacra, the best daughter a mother could ever have, happy twentieth."

Badger watched as Henry closed his eyes and clenched the rifle tightly, actually beginning to crush it. "I'm sure she died well," projected Badger, scowling at the dead terref.

"Murderer of women," shouted Henry. He gripped the rifle in the middle and stabbed it down with such force that it pierced through the Militant's body. The rifle sank in like a spear and blood splattered across the path.

From the pool of blood building up from underneath the terref, Badger figured the Assault Rifle had gone straight into the ground. He looked back at Henry and softened a little; Henry was in a very distressed state. His head hung slightly and he loosely gripped the Tactical Rifle, his lips were pressed tight together, a sure indication that he was pondering something.

"Don't let it bother you... Henry?"

When Henry didn't reply, Badger sighed and pressed his face into Henry's side. It would have been more comforting to them both if he didn't have a full-coverage helmet on. After a moment, Badger felt Henry pat his neck; he looked up, waiting for what Henry would say.

"Thank you, Badger," said Henry, smiling a little. "I can always count on you to be at my side. We have to hurry. You want to make these aliens sorry, boy?"

Badger smiled, leapt back, then raised his rifle and barked energetically. A broad smile appeared on his face and his eyes brightened. He began to project enthusiastically, "Let's go, that station's begging to be liberated."

As their dubbed name suggested, the Specters vanished into the mist as if they didn't exist, leaving behind their victims. The dark clouds were coming closer and the trees and undergrowth rustled with the increasing wind. The mist twisted and molded into uncountable shapes and patterns, which vanished with every shift of the wind. The little blue lights of the Reach still shined, marking the unburied dead. The skulls lay on the ground, laying at peace for once.

Chapter 18

"The Slide-Rail"

Night had fallen over Forerunner's forest; rain pelted her mercilessly. The mist had grown thicker now and the NAV-point on the Specters' heads-up displays showed they still had ten miles left. They had seen no other hostiles since the group they had eliminated hours ago. Both were wondering about the Major's directions; this trail was still leading straight towards the station and they hadn't encountered any natural hazards.

Badger had expressed his idea that the hostiles were heading back towards their base of operations. It seemed the only logical answer. Every other answer he had come up with didn't make sense. The group couldn't have come from the slid-rail station; at their pace they would have reached it by the following morning.

Henry wiped rainwater from his screen and muttered something about rain and hazards. Henry was feeling much better since their encounter with the Reach; the inscription and the skulls were still clear in his mind though. They had both been running at a brisk jog since they ambushed the Reach of Nimrod and Henry figured they would reach the station in just a few more hours.

The rain was pounding against the ground, creating large puddles and slippery mud that the operatives splashed and stumbled through.

Several dry limbs, becoming soaked with water, made loud snapping noises and fell to the path below, some brought smaller branches with them. The undergrowth was bent low with the weight of the rain and streams of water flowed off of leaves and down stems, making an ominous rushing noise. Every so often there was the rumble of thunder and the flash of lightning in the distance. The wind whistled through the trees, sounding like a mournful howl, as if grieving over a loss.

Badger looked about the forest, no matter where he looked he could only a see a few yards, but he could see far up the trail. He figured it was because the forest on both sides held more water and so the mist was much thicker there. It almost seemed haunted, lonely and desperate to the GEM.

Badger, on more than one occasion, was alarmed at what he thought were eyes, peering back at him from the undergrowth. Each time they had vanished as if they were part of the mist, a couple times they flew off in separate directions. One time Badger caught sight of one of the flying creatures; it looked like a tiny jellyfish, expanding and shrinking to fly through the air. It even landed on his screen for a moment; underneath the umbrella-like top there was a round knob covered in a dozen little black eyes. But Badger knew that these floating creatures weren't what were making all the eyes appear; he heard growls and mewing noises from within the forest, they were being watched.

A flash of lightning lit up the area and reflected off Henry's helmet. Henry looked up at the sky; all he could see was the mist. He looked back down and stopped suddenly. Badger stopped beside him and stared at what was ahead of them. They could scarcely make out the edge of a cliff on both sides of what appeared to be a bridge.

Both Specters looked at each other for a moment and then looked back at the beginning of the bridge. It was very wide so that vehicles could cross it and made of a dark metal with large bolts pressed into every panel. They approached it carefully, not knowing what could be on it. As they both stepped upon it, a metallic clink echoed about, it seemed perfectly safe. But still cautious, they both advanced with weapons ready.

Both Specters walked forward until they saw what the Major had been warning them about. The length ahead was gone, they couldn't even see the other side; it had all been destroyed. Runny looking parts of the metal suggested a hot explosive of some kind had melted it. It almost made Henry scream.

"We came all this way to be stopped here?" he said, shaking his head furiously. "How stupid, why didn't I listen?"

Badger lowered his gun and sighed, he didn't know what to say. He looked about the jagged edge of the bridge; it almost looked as if some giant beast had taken a bite out of it. He turned around to face the way they came; he could see the path and the floating creatures and something else. He cocked his head and stepped up to the object. It was a panel, built into the bridge's railing at such an angle that it could only be seen when someone was walking back.

When he was within touching range of it, a hologram appeared over the panel. It had a blue background with several odd symbols above a green circle. He stretched out his right paw and touched the circle with a claw.

The flash of light startled Henry, and he jumped, looking at the now filled space before him. It was some sort of projection energy; a straight, golden bar of energy ran across the space to the other side. He stepped forward in blind amazement, his foot touching the projected Bridge. It was solid; he guessed that it worked the same way as a starship's shield, as a deflective surface of impulses.

Badger followed Henry onto the energy bridge, looking about in wonder as to how it could be. He looked down and saw bright-white bars of energy fly past, keeping the impulses working. The energy was transparent enough that he could see mist swirling underneath his paws.

"Stupid alien," Warren's voice came over the radio. "Sorry, apparently some of these aliens made it a little further than we thought; we've just finished combating several spriks and a terref. Get across that bridge and make all haste to the slide-rail system, after eliminating any and all hostiles you are to wait for the Major. Due to interception risks, these will be our last instructions to you both. Good luck."

"Alright," said Henry, looking both directions on the bridge, "Now we're alone and we need to hurry."

"Right," projected Badger, "Do you want me to go on ahead? I'll eliminate any dangers in your path."

Henry nodded and flicked his hand in the station's general direction. "I know you will, but don't assault the station until I get there. Go."

* * *

Badger had been waiting on a small rise that overlooked the station. The station was a covered platform that stood nearly forty feet into the air, a cable-operated elevator connected to the outside was the only way up. Two, thick rails stretched out both the front and the back of the platform, these were the magnetic rails that the slides traveled on. The slides, one just pulled out of the station, were simple aluminum boxes with transparent lids that seated a max of seven persons. Henry was just fifteen minutes behind Badger.

Henry gave Badger a quick nod and examined the area surrounding the station. Chinese and Reach of Nimrod soldiers were standing about the area; there was even a Mobile All-Terrain Ophthalmic (MATO). MATOs, nicknamed "walking tanks", were heavily armored combat vehicles that moved about on legs with two movable arms that carried any chosen variety of weapons. The pilots of these tanks wore the same ophthalmic-helmets that the VTOL pilots wore. Some pilots had a movement coordinating neural-AI so they could move the vehicle almost completely by thought.

"Looks like we're in for some real fun," Henry said as he loaded a rocket into his ASP's attachment.

Badger crouched low and growled ferociously, his teeth were bared and his ears were pulled flat against his neck. "Did you notice they are also working on a drone?"

"No I didn't," said Henry, peering about again; he spotted it, mostly hidden in the shadows, its only giveaway were the sparks flying from an integration torch. A Chinese PDCT was working the torch.

"That drone's still working," said Henry, giving the area another quick glance. "I spy two overhead biometric turrets atop of it. This won't be easy."

"Maybe it shall," Badger projected, looking back towards the buckle on his belt, he figured it was time to see what the device did. He extended a claw and pressed the device, his entire body digitalized until there was nothing to be seen of him but a distortion.

Henry nodded and chuckled. "Take out that drone and then I'll take care of the MATO."

The PDCT was looking into an open panel of the drone, it had once been a forest surveillance walker, but the Chinese had refitted it to be a tool of destruction. The drone walked upon four multi-jointed legs and had several sensors placed around its circumference to pick up unregistered signals. But a guerilla sniper had ruined much of the walking mechanism. He merely had to replace a few gears and reversal bits and it would be as good as new.

Badger silently removed his kukri from its sheath and jabbed the knife deep into the soldier's solar plexus. The PDCT was unable to give a single noise; he dropped to the ground, still clutching the integration torch. Badger withdrew the knife, slit the the man's throat and then wiped it on the grass before using it to sabotage the drone completely, by cutting out its internal core.

Instead of tossing the core aside, Badger stabbed it with his kukri and then threw it at the other soldiers. There was some sound of confusion and then the core exploded, a mild explosion, nothing deadly, but that started a great rampage. Badger took out his ASP and, still invisible, stepped around the drone and began to pick off the other soldiers.

The MATO pilot, a terref, was confused; the other soldiers were dropping dead, without any clue of where the projectiles were coming from. He turned the MATO about; searching for something he could see and shoot at. But there was nothing, he couldn't understand it. Suddenly, without warning, the cockpit opened and the pilot was pulled out of his seat.

Henry gripped the frightened terref by the throat, holding him high in the air. The terref swung it's tail instinctively, it smacked against Henry's armor, no affect. Henry broke the alien's neck by squeezing it; and then threw it to the side and dropped into the cockpit. It was an ISEN model MATO; he knew the controls of the craft. Henry subsequently launched a rain of impulse bullets at every hostile.

Badger had retreated back to a tree while Henry peppered the area; he had already gotten his target. He pressed a button on his Assault Rifle, a latch snapped open and the block of SEAR dropped out, it almost looked as if none of the block had been used. Badger set the block into a pocket on his side and pulled out another block, this one was slightly golden-green in color. He pressed it into the cavity and locked the latch; a smile spread across his face and the tip of his tail twitched knowingly.

He aimed the crosshairs over a Chinese soldier that was in too much cover to be hit by an impulse bullet. He switched the rate-of-fire to semiautomatic, "detonate on target." He ordered.

He pulled the trigger and the molten aluminum wool blasted out of the barrel. The glowing projectile flew threw the air and hit the soldier. There was a quick flash of crimson light and the soldier lay dead, several feet from where he was originally hidden, his flesh burnt and blackened.

"You can stop firing now," Badger projected into the radio.

"They're all dead now, although, I think we'll find some more atop the platform itself."

"They're not coming down," said Henry, "Not with a MATO down here."

Badger watched as the MATO turned and tilted so that the cockpit was looking at the edge of the platform.

"Badger," said Henry, "clear that space."

Wordlessly, Badger attached his Assault Rifle to the holster and took his ASP from his belt. He stood up and climbed the tree. Actually he was more leaping upwards from branch to branch. When he reached a high enough branch, he leapt out across the air and landed on the platform. He looked about eagerly.

The platform was full of Reach soldiers, mainly spriks and the humans, but there was a three-jawed Militant. The Militant and three spriks were setting up a large turret; a long, thick barrel, a large drum magazine of huge projectiles and a large holographic sight that ran along the entire length of the weapon. A gauss turret; it would tear the MATO to shreds.

Crates were stacked on the platform, each made of the same polymer as the armor and weapons of the Reach and marked with the ring and cat. spriks were moving the crates about for barricades; these were just like the scout, except they had masks that made then look like grotesque, fanged beasts. But there was one in golden armor, with a hood and a brace around its mouth with a large fan on its back with two transparent circles set into it.

Badger gripped the ASP tightly in his paws and hurried towards the Militant at the turret. Leaping, he punched the Militant in the side of the face and then shoved his ASP into its mouth, pulling the trigger. The Militant fell dead, but it had already fired three shots upon the MATO.

Badger let out a loud bark and looked down at the MATO, it was still moving.

"Don't worry boy," said Henry, "they missed."

Thank you, Badger mentally prayed. He turned around, shot two of humans and a sprik, killing them instantly. But then the remaining spriks returned fire, filling the air with energy and projectiles. Badger fired back, but before he could get to cover, an energy bolt hit the buckle, burning it out of commission.

"Demaw," the spriks began to shout.

The strange sprik let out a grunt and then spread his arms wide, his armor lit up with bright yellow lights. He rushed at Badger, shrieking and possibly even laughing. Badger shot him many times, but something was driving the sprik into a mad dash.

Badger performed a front flip over the crazed sprik, grabbed the fan and then swung the sprik out into nothingness. He finished off two other spriks and then watched as the still-flying sprik's armor exploded in a flash of gold and pink flames. He let out a sound of amazement and then turned back to the other soldiers and decommissioning each one in turn.

After a minute, he exhaled and lightly kicked the prostrate form with a hind paw. They were all dead. He contacted Henry.

"All clear Henry," he projected, "Should we wait for the major?"

"Yes," said Henry, "I'll be up in a minute."

"There are a couple that aren't dead, Henry," Badger projected, looking at a terref and a sprik that were moaning in pain. "Do you want me to kill them?"

"Yes, but don't," said Henry. "They may have a use."

"Fine then, I'll just restrain them." Badger quickly went to work strapping the two survivors to a column, using a length of metal cord he found.

Chapter 19

"In Harm's Way"

Leisure time in Forge was usually in the form of the perspective-theater, jogging, biking, or shreg hunting (which was done only at night). Shregs were jungle-dwelling crustaceans, transported from Grasp's jungles, that traveled in small hives consisting of the Monitor (fertile female), King (fertile male) and a few workers. Shregs weren't normally dangerous, usually digging through dumpsters and trashcans for vegetables and molds, but there were several incidents when people had been killed by a protective Monitor or King. The hunting was only at night because that was when the shregs emerged from their muddy burrows near the waterfront and wandered into the city. Licensed hunters were only permitted the use of blades in the hunting of these large beasts. This was also a good job for those who were out of work, because restaurants would pay a high price for every fresh shreg kill. They made a fine meal.

Dave enjoyed biking and the perspective theater; his father wouldn't let him hunt the shregs. On this mostly sunny afternoon with a few clouds and a steady breeze blowing through the buildings, he had chosen the theater. The perspective-theater was a circular auditorium that dipped down to the refractive projectors that produced an image that would give the viewers different perspectives of the movie, including the background that could only be seen across from the each individual viewer. Like watching one-way mirrors.

Dave, still worried about what his father had told him, had gone to the theater, where he felt that he would be safer. The auditorium was packed with people eagerly watching the movie; surely there was no question to the saying "safety in numbers". Canine was beside him, keeping her protocol and watching.

The movie, titled: *Host of the Galaxies,* was about a plantlike organism that was infecting the galaxy, destroying every warm-blooded creature it found and a group that were searching for a way to destroy it. The movie had started with an image of Earth, and then a ship, misshaped twisted like a hideous lump of ivy, appeared in orbit. After crash-landing on Earth, the ship slowly warmed and unwound to become a towering beast with tentacles that stretched and continued to spread as it roots dug into the soil. From its tentacles sprouted large "seeds" that walked about like octopuses and killed everything that came into their path. Each of the seeds grew into another beast and grew until they had heads that looked like the mouth of a four-jawed barracuda. The group was searching through the galaxies for a legendary weapon, one that supposedly made the beast and could destroy also it. Dave was only half way through it, a part where the group had run into a veritable hive of the seeds; they were trying to fight their way through to find a clue of where the weapon lay.

Dave had a small paper dish full of honeyed pineapple slices, his favorite snack at the theater and also a cup of on-tap root beer. Even though he felt sure that he was safe in the theater, he found himself looking about the auditorium every few minutes. He tried to enjoy the movie, but concern for his father and the executive from the Reach Corporation distracted him immensely.

One of the main characters blew one of the seeds apart with a handheld laser and then smashed another with his foot. Dave sighed wearily, the movie hadn't exactly been as he had expected. Suddenly he felt his Canal vibrate.

A Canal was a simple communications device that fit into an ear and used an electronic conduit to send the wearer's voice to the other side of the link. What was strange was that Dave had turned it off before entering the auditorium.

Dave reached up and pressed the side of the Canal. "Hello?" he whispered softly.

He was shocked to hear his father's voice on the other side, he sounded urgent and worried. "Dave, praise the Lord, where are you?"

"The theater," said Dave, looking about again.

"I would've thought that'd be safe too," said Hagen, there was a stepping noise in the background. "There's little time, get out of there, get home somehow. I've already informed some... friends that you're in danger. Listen, Canine has aaahh! Let go of me. Run Dave, get away."

Dave couldn't reply, all he could do was listen to the struggle going on. He almost cried out as he heard shots. The link then broke and Dave was left without contact.

A simulated growl from Canine drew Dave's attention to one of the four doorways into the auditorium. Three well-dressed men were casually striding in. Dave recognized one as being the man he'd met in the park.

Dave stuffed two slices into his mouth and took one more sip from his cup before starting for another exit. He hoped the men hadn't noticed him and he dared not look back. Canine was crawling low on the ground like a spider missing half its legs. The Auditorium's exit was two soundproof fabric screens separated by a couple yards for quiet passage into and from the auditorium.

"Weren't enjoying the movie?" asked a young woman with dyed, green hair behind a counter, setting candy bars into little trays.

"Actually," said Dave, "the movie was fine, but there's some men in there that are following me."

"Really?" asked the woman, turning a perturbed face towards the doorway. "What do they look like?"

"One had a very noticeable bruise on the side of his face," said Dave. "And they're all nicely dressed with dark blue suits and black ties."

"You just get on out of here kid," said the Woman, pressing a button that was hidden under the counter. "Security will deal with them."

"Thank you," said Dave turning to leave.

"Wait a minute, kid," said the woman, she promptly tossed him three chocolate candy bars, "company policy."

Dave caught two and Canine caught the other. "Thanks!"

"Hey! No problem." The women tapped her nails on the counter as she waited for security. "Chasing kids and their companions, what next?" she muttered.

Outside the theater Dave and Canine watched the thick traffic of semis, which were streamlined with trapezoid trailers to reduce the danger of tipping and multicolored sports cars. Dave immediately sat down on a bench at a bus-stop and pulled the soles off his running shoes. Underneath each sole were three metal rings that promptly popped out to form a pair of magnetic roller-blades, better known as the popular youth sport hover-wheels. Dave put the soles into his pockets and stood up, excellently balanced, began to take off down the sidewalk, Canine matched Dave's speed, running alongside.

Pedestrians leapt aside as the boy and the droid zoomed along the sidewalk. A lady with a small dog and a bag of groceries was almost trampled, but Canine reacted in time by sensibly grabbing Dave's hand and yanking him to the side. Dave closed his mouth tight to stifle a groan growing in his throat; it felt like his arm was torn off.

"Young brat," the lady shouted after them. Her small dog yipped pathetically a couple times.

"Sorry," Dave muttered under his breath, rubbing his shoulder tenderly.

"I am sorry master," Canine projected.

"No, it was my fault; I should've been looking ahead."

The sidewalk dipped and Dave crouched low to the ground to let the wind pass over him. Up ahead the sidewalk curved sharply to the left, at his present speed he wouldn't be able to make the turn.

"Uh oh," Dave cried.

Canine had already formulated a plan, a plate shifted on her back and a handlebar slid out. Dave grabbed the bar and held on tightly. Canine's programs already had the timing down; she blasted ahead dragging the wide-eyed Dave behind her at a breakneck pace. She zigzagged through the traffic, several of the vehicles skidded to a halt and the drivers shouted at them.

"Canine," Dave shouted, "what are you doing?"

"What I have been programmed to do," the droid returned in a bold manner Dave had never heard before.

"I think dad must have been crazy to build a droid," Dave mumbled, "he's a biological engineer, not a mechanic."

"He knew what he was doing," Canine projected.

"Great, now I'm talking to a droid."

"You could have all these years," Canine projected in a smug voice. "You just had to ask."

"What else did dad do that I don't know about," Dave asked, his face a mask of perplexity.

Canine had reached her maximum speed; she was practically leaving behind a trail. She easily avoided the obstacles of benches, trashcans and people that walked on the sidewalk or unpredictably stepped out of stores. A man stepping out of a drugstore leapt at the sudden appearance of the two, he slipped upon a piece of paper and landed hard on his rear.

"Canine," shouted Dave, his body tingling with worry and excitement, "you can't keep this up forever, you're going to hit someone eventually."

"I suppose your right," projected Canine.

"Good," Dave exhaled happily, "glad to hearraaah."

Canine had pulled him off of the sidewalk and into the street. Canine, unrelentingly, weaved through the traffic, outrunning the vehicles and zooming about turns that would eventually lead them home.

Dave now gripped onto the bar with both hands, eyes squinting against the force of the wind. "This isn't what I meant, Canine."

"It doesn't matter," Canine projected. "You're perfectly safe as long as you don't let go."

"Obviously," Dave rolled his eyes as best he could in the wind.

"Please keep down," projected Canine.

"What?"

Instead of answering, Canine projected a hologram in front of Dave. The hologram showed a mirror image of Dave, in the background could be seen a couple of thin wings with two uncovered rotary-blades. Dave released one hand from the handlebar and turned his upper body to look back.

The following VTOL was practically silent in its menacing approach. The nose was bent down like a vulture's beak and the cockpit was circular and red like a Cyclops. The wings seemed to have virtually no part in the craft's maneuverability, instead, a heavy weight on the underside, between the two landing sleds, was shifted from side-to-side to shift its axis. Magnetically latched to each side of the strange VTOL was a heavily-armored motorcycle with a man in a gray, semi-armor uniform and a pair of dark goggles.

"Can you get a signature on it or something?" asked Dave, turning back and reattaching his other hand to the bar.

"I'm not a radio receiver, master," Canine projected.

"Of everything you weren't…" Dave muttered irately.

The two motorcycles were detached from the VTOL and they landed with a springy bounce on the ground. Two panels behind the front wheel of each cycle were pushed out and a small rotary-gun was exposed. The drivers pulled a trigger on the handlebars and the guns began to fire a special kind of biometric bullets, fired by primitive explosive cartridges. The bullets were an ugly black color and splattered on impact with the ground, leaving a sticky tar-like substance.

"Can you go any faster," shouted Dave.

"Sorry," regretted Canine.

Chapter 20

"Gone With the Storm"

The biometric bullets splattered all over the place like unhealthy tree sap and the cyclists looked as though they had an infinite supply. The loud percussions of the rotary-guns sped up until they were an ominous drone. Amazingly, Canine avoided the pathways of the biometric bullets with astounding ease with Dave in tow.

The motorcycles were closing the gap rapidly and, for the moment, had stopped firing. Their uniforms billowing about them, the cyclists split apart to try and get onto either side of Dave and Canine. Using a computer between the handle bars, the two men opened two other panels, just above the guns. Two cylinders stuck out from each side and three red-tipped capsules stuck from each.

Dave looked back just in time to see one cyclist fire one of the capsules, it streaked forward like a rocket, leaving a trail of white fumes behind. Dave let out a short gasp as the rocket seemed to move slowly towards him. But then, he found himself no longer holding onto Canine and the capsule had struck the other bike. The capsule released a black spiderweb of resin that encompassed the cyclist and his bike.

The bike weaved out of control and finally came to a skidding halt into the side of sports car that had turned off to the side of the road to avoid the bikes and the boy. The biker struggled as a man and women got out of the car to try and help him, the web was no longer sticky, but it was stronger than steel.

What had happened was that Canine, sensing the danger to her keep, had quickly managed to detach Dave's hand from the bar and leapt over him and slapped the capsule to the side. The capsule hitting the other biker was merely a lucky bonus. She then turned around to run alongside the shouting Dave.

"I don't know how long I can control this, Canine," Dave shouted as he waved his arms to keep balance as he raced along. His mouth went dry when he saw the street drop to a steep decline up ahead. "Can you help me at all?"

"You'll be fine for the moment," projected Canine, whirling around to face the other biker.

"What?" Dave shouted, his eyes never leaving the decline. A semi passed in front of it. "Dad was insane."

Canine's left arm began to transform, her mechanical fingers moved until they were like two hooks, four formed into one with three slits and the thumb as a shorter one. a sharp point stuck out of her palm and her forearm expanded until it looked like a rounded box. Purple beams of light were projected from each finger tip until they formed a ball of plasma where they all connected. The spike in her palm flew through the ball and instantly became energized; it struck the front tire of the bike and passed through until it stuck in the flexcrete, humming with energy.

Flames and blue smoke issued out from the mechanics of the bike and the underside blew out with a flash of blue sparks and crimson flames. The biker laid down his bike, but it began to roll with him on it.

Canine's armed transformed back to its original shape and she took off after Dave, who was just about to go over the edge. She made sure that Dave grabbed hold of the bar and then took off down the road; the decline giving her more speed.

Dave held on for dear life, knowing that letting go would be disastrous. Every muscle in his body was stiff and rigid as he remained still to keep from toppling over. He looked back to see if the other bike was still following, it was nowhere.

"What did you do Canine," Dave shouted he was weaved around a van and two trucks.

"Nothing, master," Canine projected dismissively.

"Is he dead?"

"I hope so," Canine projected innocently.

Dave remained quiet.

They were going against traffic again, drivers swerved crazily to avoid hitting them and the other traffic. Many of the people rolled down their windows and shouted at them, most of it very illiterate. The path they were making quickly closed up behind them, but there were some minor collisions that resulted in dents ranging from noticeable to ugly.

From the view of the slope there was a wide expanse of Forge's surrounding Martian jungles and great lakes, the cloudy blue sky made it all seem mysterious. Alien and terrestrial birds flew through the air, calling out in their exotic voices. A reptilian creature with four leathery wings, known to the locals as a conwic, flapped wildly after a distraught parrot, mouth open as it closed the gap to its prey. Sparrows flew after insects and started to cross the road after mosquitoes, but quickly dispersed when they met the traffic; the insects had the worst of it.

The companions had just reached the bottom of the slope when two shadows overtook them. Dave looked up to see two more VTOLs, each with two more cyclists. He let out a cry when the VTOLs released the motorcycles and one almost landed atop of him. The cyclist tried to grab him, but he knocked the arm aside punched him in the helmet.

The cyclist was only slightly perturbed by this pitiful assault, he shook his head and reached out again. This time he wouldn't be stopped by this boy's attempt to knock his hand away. His fingertips had just touched the boy's shirt when he felt a sudden pain and his vision darkened; he was no longer strong enough to hold his arm out. He wanted to sleep.

Dave blinked the blood from his eyes; someone had just shot the cyclist right through the stomach. He looked up to see a black and blue Mosquito VTOL, police coloration. There were two flashing red and blue lights along the bottom and a siren was ringing out good and loud. He smiled when he saw two SWAT team members; one was a large feline GEM, taking aim at the other cyclists.

"It would appear we've attracted attention," remarked Canine.

"Needed attention," Dave yelled over the noise.

Another cyclist went down with the GEM's bullet through his skull; the other two took pistols from their waists and started shooting at the VTOL. Their pistols were the standard caseless, impulse design, but had been modified for automatic fire. Their shots went everywhere, one pinged off of the helmet of the human SWAT member and a few others glanced off the chassis.

The GEM dropped onto his stomach to get a steadier position, looking through his holographic scope.

"Careful not to hit the boy, Steaks," said the human, finishing off the other cyclist.

Steaks nodded and then pulled the trigger. The impulse bullet knocked the cyclist out of his seat with the impact and shattered the spine upon exiting.

"Why do I even have to speak?" muttered the other SWAT member.

"What about those?" Dave asked himself, looking at the hostile VTOLs.

As if on cue, a low flying, V-shaped aircraft flew with incredible speed overtook one of the hostile VTOLs and an electronic adhesive plate attached to a cable grabbed the VTOL's cockpit. The VTOL was quickly yanked away with a groaning jerk. The other VTOL followed when another craft flew overhead. The two VTOLS would be forced to land outside of the city and the pilots brought back to the city's prison.

"I guess that'll cover it," said Dave, watching as the Mosquito slowed down and began to drop in altitude.

The SWAT members, when the VTOL was practically skidding along the ground, grabbed hold of the bars that were on the inside and stretched out their free hand and paw.

"C'mon kid," shouted the man. "Your daddy's disappeared and wants us to take you someplace safe."

"He called you?" asked Dave, reaching out a hand, just a little further before he could grab the man's hand.

"Best I can figure," said the man, giving Dave a comforting smile. "But don't worry, we'll find your daddy soon enough."

Their fingertips touched and then the VTOL suddenly gained altitude, the SWAT members were almost thrown out. The man turned around to face the cockpit.

"I'm not that desperate to see hell, thank you," he shouted.

"Sorry," replied the pilot, "we ran out of road."

"Just get after them," shouted the man, waving his arm frantically.

"Can't," apologized the pilot, "that dumb droid just turned down Okapi."

"Well get us down so we can use our bikes," shouted the man.

SWAT bikes, both GEM and human, had one design, armor-plated with two thick wheels in the front and back, pressed tightly together to give them astounding maneuverability and traction on almost any terrain. The bikes were black with lines of white, flashing red and blue lights were between the handlebars and a loud siren was placed lower, almost atop of the front wheels. They were located near the front of the VTOL and they both mounted and zipped out the open rear and landing on the ground with a springy motion. The sirens and lights were activated and they zoomed down the road with gusto, looking for the boy in the heavy traffic of Okapi.

Okapi was a wide street that went underneath the ground as a shortcut between the two large business areas of Forge, Anvil and Tong. The tunnel had six lanes and a series of off-ramps and was reinforced with titanium bars and white flexcrete, a crystal polymer that reflected light to illuminate the tunnel. Okapi was filled with traffic during the daylight hours, but lightened after dark.

Drivers pulled off to the sides as the two bikes roared along the street, sirens sounding off. The bikes had a small windshield on the handlebars and a HUD was projected on it, a GPS, damage register and speed meter, nothing very fancy. The GEM followed the man closely, crouching low to keep out of the wind.

"C'mon," the man groaned, "where are you, kid?"

*   *   *

Still questioning his father's sanity in Canine's construction, Dave felt the blood leaving his hands that were still gripping the bar like vises. He wondered why Canine had lead them down Okapi, if they had gone the other way they could have got into the police VTOL. But he didn't have time to think about that, the sheer terror of traveling at this speed and the crazy turns and weaves that Canine was performing dazzled him.

Unlike in the thin traffic outside, this traffic was so thick that Canine ran between, dodged in front of and weaved around the vehicles like a snake. People slammed on their brakes or just watched in stunned amazement as the two whizzed by. And then the law enforcement bikes came along, many were left pondering an answer. Why would SWAT be chasing a boy and a droid?

The SWAT members were now catching glimpses of the two weaving through the traffic. The man smiled and pulled ahead of a truck and found himself in between lanes, the boy directly ahead of him.

"Kid," he shouted, "slow down and tell your droid to head for the next exit. We'll be right behind you."

Dave looked back and shook his head to show he didn't hear it properly.

The man got closer before shouting again, "Head to the next exit."

Canine had heard the command loud and clear and without Dave having to tell her, she suddenly zoomed off to the right and they burst out a small tunnel, alongside a red sport car and into the sunlight.

"Ow, that's bright," Dave groaned, squinting against the direct sunlight.

He turned around to look for the SWAT team, they were nowhere to be seen; they had missed the exit due to heavy traffic. A sound drew his attention to the roadway built over the exit like a bridge, leaping over the short wall, three other cyclists in the same gray uniforms landed onto the road, one landed atop of a van, crushing in the roof.

"Wonderful," he said between clenched teeth.

"Don't worry, master," Canine said. Two plates on her sides shifted to expose four metal spikes. After a moment, one blasted out and turned red-hot, like SEAR, puncturing the front tires of one bike and stuck.

The back of the spike struck the ground and cyclist was flipped forward while still atop of his bike. The man came to a complete stop on the side of the road, unmoving with blood flowing freely from multiple wounds.

"Wish I'd known about those before," Dave remarked, with a glance at the remaining three spikes.

"That's why you weren't informed," Canine replied. "You're father gave me permission to use them after our incident in the park."

"Maybe he's not so insane," Dave muttered.

The other two bikers began firing the biometric bullets at the two, but Canine was still paying attention and kept her keep out of harm's way. One car had an entire side pasted with the bullets, the driver quickly pulled over to the side of the road.

Dave kept his head down, looking about for familiar landmarks that would tell him where he was. But he was too excited to concentrate on anything. But then he saw that Canine had turned off of the road and down a ramp leading onto a freeway with dry dirt, reddish sand and trees on either side. A large rock alongside the road, covered in moss and lichen and resembling the face of a man, informed him that home was just a minute away.

Canine fired another spike at one of the other bikes, popping the tire and making it spin out. The other pulled quickly up beside the two, took out his pistol and aimed it at Canine. She would have no defense now.

"No!" Dave shouted, grabbing the man's hand yanking it so that the man was thrown off balance, pistol firing wildly. Dave looked behind to see the man stagger to his hands and knees and crawl off to the side of the road.

"Thank you," projected Canine, "but I would have gladly taken the shot for you."

"That doesn't matter now," said Dave, breathing heavily.

* * *

The pilot of the police VTOL had followed the directions of the SWAT team as to where the two had gotten off of Okapi. It had taken him a little while to finally catch sight of the two again, just when Dave had rid himself of the last cyclist.

"They've gotten off at 12," he called into the radio, "the only thing down that road is the professor's house."

"We'll be there in a flash," the man called back over the radio.

"I'll continue aerial observations until you arrive," said the pilot.

"You do that," said the man.

* * *

The Hudson's house was just several yards past a short bridge that passed over a thin river with muddy banks. Dave smiled broadly when he saw it up ahead, surrounded by trees and dirt; the single-story, brown building never looked so good. He looked up when he heard the Mosquito overhead, all he had to do was wait until they came to pick him up.

"Master, duck," Canine projected loudly.

Dave obeyed wordlessly and felt something pointy scrape across his back. "Ah," he cried when he saw what had attacked him.

It was a shreg, four, long, hard-shelled legs, a large crest that covered its face and the back of its head, with a long carapace curved up at the back and completely red with green spots. But what was amazing was that it had come out during the day.

Dave then noticed that there were dozens of the crustaceans converging on him and Canine. "What's going on Canine?"

"It would appear that they've gone mad," Canine projected, coming to a complete stop in front of the house. "Please go on inside, I'll see to these."

Dave pried his stiff fingers from the bar and quickly deactivated his skates. He burst through the door and turned about to watch as Canine's left arm transformed into the weapon he hadn't seen.

Canine sighted on the nearest shreg and fired the spike, it struck the face of the beast, but it didn't go all the through, the glowing back stuck out like a beacon. The shreg let out a bubbly roar and lunged at Canine. Canine drove her right arm into the beast's face; it was only knocked back with a few scratches on its shell.

"Canine," said Dave, "get inside, this isn't natural."

"Go get your father's blade," Canine projected, standing on her hind legs and swinging her arms warningly as she backed into the door.

As soon as Canine was inside, Dave slammed the door shut and locked it. "I hope help comes soon."

Dave ran to his father's room and took the blade from its stand atop the dresser. It was a single-edged katana with intricate inlays of friction energizers. The friction energizers worked much the same as the shock ball, they lit up gold with every swing, but these were meant to do damage with the energy they created.

He gripped the green fabric-wrapped ray-skin handle in his hands and walked back to the door. "I hope that the police get here soon, or I'll just take the elevator. Er, do know where it leads?"

"No, I don't," Canine projected apologetically.

A loud scratching noise signified that the shregs were trying to get in. Dave looked out a window beside the door to see one of the beasts striking at the crystal with its mouth and scratching with its pointed legs. Others soon joined it and it wouldn't be too long before they got in.

"Maybe waiting for the police isn't such a good idea," said Dave, backing away and lowering the katana until the tip dragged along the ground.

Suddenly, gunshots sounded outside and in a couple moments, someone was pounding on the door.

"Open this thing, now. These things are possessed."

Dave unlocked the door and cracked it open. It suddenly flew into him and the human SWAT member fell onto his back, a shreg on his chest. Dave let out a cry as the GEM came in firing at the others that were trying to get in.

The man had his hands gripping either side of the shreg's face and pushing it back as its two mandibles snapped lethally close to his face. He gritted his teeth and butted his head against its face, his helmet taking the full brunt of hitting the rock-hard shell of the shreg.

Dave raised the katana over his head and stuck the shreg on the back. Its carapace wasn't as hard as the crest and the beast let out a shriek. He slashed at it again, this time at an angle; the sword struck the back of the beast's head, tearing off the crest to expose an intricate assortment of tubes and machinery.

The man took this moment, to punch the side of the beast's head; it shrieked in pain and raised its head into the air. The man then grabbed his pistol and shot a bullet through its brain."

"They've got no backbone," the man said sarcastically, standing up and firing at the others that tried to crowd in. "Someone's controlling these things."

Dave took another look at the mechanism that was attached to the creature's brain. "We're never going to get rid of all of these."

"Is there another way out?" asked the man, pressing his foot against the face of one and firing two shots against its bullet-proof crest.

"My dad showed me."

"Then let's get out of here," the man shouted, firing a couple shots at another shreg that that was lunging at him.

Chapter 21

"Bizarre Findings"

The rain had finally come, it pattered off the platform's roof like a thousand drums. The Specters had set their helmets aside while they been taking inventory of the station throughout the night; the crates were piled on the other side of the rail's controls to clear some space. Further examination of the platform proved most useful and informative, they had found and secured several transparent canisters containing a bubbly, green liquid and several datapads of war machines schematics.

One of the datapads was different though, its memory was full of untranslatable symbols and complex diagrams. The diagrams ranged anywhere from molecular bone structures to interior organs. On the first page of memory was the image of a bleached human skull with two strands of DNA crossed underneath it. It was a common symbol, used mainly by GEM corporations; it stood for biological nanotechnology (BINAN).

BINAN was still in its fledgling status, but it was a most promising aspect in research. It was rumored that Professor Hagen Hudson had made a breakthrough and it was rumored that he had even had some success. The professor denied these rumors, even to his employers and many felt that governments were trying to pry into his computers. The

•

datapad was replaced into the container they had taken it from.

"Some of this will do good work for the Day Five project," said Henry, looking at a datapad. The datapad had an odd picture of a spider on it, he cycled through some of the schematics, complex genetic terms and BINAN equations, not his field.

Badger shoved another crate into place and then peering inside to see three large, alien weapons. He pulled one out, it was a little smaller then he was, almost weightless, with a ring shaped-handle and a fin sticking out the back, fitting just over a grown man's wrist. The front was made of two silvery two-point horns that almost touched at the tips. He aimed out an opening and squeezed the handle. Several green energy bolts flew out from between the horns.

"Take it," Henry suggested. Watching as the bolts disappeared in the distance.

Badger attached it to his holster; he was surprised that the electronic adhesive held it there. There wasn't a release button, but all he had to do was tug at it and the adhesive would release it.

Badger wagged his tail as he examined the weapon again; it was a piece of art. Looking up, he saw a swarm of the little jellyfish coming out of the forest where the bolts had disappeared; he figured he must have disturbed a nest of them. The jellyfish were quickly passing through the platform on their way to nowhere in particular.

One of the floating jellyfish landed on the back of Badger's right forepaw. He brushed it away, but it came back, landing in the exact same spot. He brushed it away again, but it still came back. He sighed and left it there, not having the desire to smash it; he kept admiring the weapon and rummaging through the platform's crates.

Henry was the first to see the bright, purple light. He had been carefully examining the slide-rail's controls, figuring out how to work it when he heard a *clank*. He looked up and saw that Badger had knocked over a block of metal, probably SEAR. But when Badger leaned over to pick it up, he saw a bright purple spot on his glove.

Henry drew Badger's attention back towards the jellyfish. It had turned purple. Badger leaned his head close towards it. It had lifted its umbrella shielding to form a cone over its head. Its multiple eyes saw in all directions, but there was something strange about them, the centers seemed to glow.

Henry's ears weren't sharp enough to hear it, but Badger heard the creature shriek with every pulse of its body. He had a bad feeling when he heard an answering shriek. This shriek was lower, Henry could hear it.

Henry lifted his biometric Tactical Rifle to his shoulder and looked about the platform. He noticed that the prisoners were beginning to struggle hard at their restraints, a wild look of fear plastered on both their faces.

"Uarwaua, uarwaua," pleaded the sprik, "buaeirwjifi uarni, uarwaua uarni."

"Whatever you say," Badger projected, flicking the jellyfish off his paw and lifting his Assault Rifle to his shoulder. He didn't like how the prisoners were acting and he especially didn't like the periodic shrieks coming from the forest. Everything suddenly went still, not even the sound of a breeze was heard rustling in the trees. His amber eyes flicked about nervously.

Henry began to walk toward where the noise had come from, the prisoners were still struggling and the sprik was constantly shouting. Badger was readily at Henry's side, approaching the platform's edge cautiously. There was sort of a swishing noise and a sound, like someone walking through mud. Both Specters backed away as the source of the noise came into focus.

It steadily floated up over the rim of the platform. A large, purplish-blue body with bubble-like sacs about it that inflated and deflated with lighter-than-air gas, eight frilly tentacles twisted about and powerful electrical currents pulsed through them to the tips. The creature's snakelike head was upon a long, pale neck with its greenish veins shown boldly underneath the skin. Mounted around the neck of the creature was a U-shaped device with a transparent canister that held the same liquid as was in the containers.

"At least we know what the liquids are for," said Henry as he backed away.

The beast began to drift towards them; Badger aimed at the jellyfish's head and pulled the trigger. The beast's head exploded and its burnt remains collapsed to the floor. "What are they complaining about?" projected Badger, meaning the prisoners, they were still struggling. He shouldered the rifle.

Both Specters were shocked when the beast's burns disappeared and its body regenerated itself. It slowly rose up off of the ground and flared it tentacles up around itself.

"Jelly's angry," remarked Henry, as it came at them again, faster this time.

Badger noticed the canister, it had emptied a little. The liquid acted as a duel purpose chemical, both controlling and regenerating its body. He fired another explosive sliver; it impacted on a tentacle and blew the beast in half. The canister was only slightly fogged and drained a little more to regenerate its host.

This shouldn't be hard, Badger thought to himself as he blasted the creature again. A smile lighted on his face as he blasted it yet again and drained the cylinder again. It seemed so simple at first. But then he noticed an unusually thick swarm of tiny jellyfish, coming from all sides, they all congregated underneath the beast, which ate a number of them.

This cannibalistic action refilled the canister.

"Not good," projected Badger as he began to blast at the canister's general position. Some of the splinters missed altogether, sailing away to impact elsewhere in the forest, but they generally hit the beast, or part of the swarm. But, it seemed, no matter how many hit the canister, or around it, there wasn't even a scratch.

Guns were useless; Badger dropped the Assault Rifle and looked about for something else. The beast was showing a particular interest in Henry. It drifted towards him, its tentacles whipped through the air, sometimes cracking like whips. All of a sudden, Badger let out a growl and lunged at the beast, slamming the top of his helmet right into the bulbous body.

Parts of the beast splattered across the platform and its slimy remains flew out of the station and slammed into a tree. Badger had managed to catch himself right at the edge of the platform; his eyes were fiery and challenging. The creature was coming back again.

This time it went after Badger, tentacles outstretched. Badger opened his mouth to bark in frustration, but instead, he howled. The howl seemed to blast out of his mouth like a gunshot, the jellyfishes started to scatter about, confused and disoriented. The canister began to crack; soon the cracks were like a spiderweb, covering the entire canister.

At this point Badger was out of breath, unable to determine how he had just done it; the beast was writhing about, disoriented. Badger listened as it shrieked and gargled. Suddenly, as if he was coming out of a dream, he realized he had his chance. His kukri seemed to magically appear in his forepaw and he leapt at the beast, sweeping the kukri in a downwards motion.

As if he was cutting butter, the kukri slashed through the soft body and shattered the canister. The liquid flew everywhere and the pieces of the canisters spread over the ground, sounding like thousands of tiny bells. However, Badger hadn't taken the time to judge his velocity; he shot over the edge of the platform. He was just fine when he hit the ground, but, he found that he was too tired to move again.

He slumped onto the ground, eyes slowly closing. His odd howl had drained his energy and his final action had been enough. What was the noise? It sounded like someone calling a name. It didn't matter now, Badger was powerless to do anything; he had to sleep.

*   *   *

Badger heard in his sleep, a female voice, somehow familiar, but his memory wouldn't give him a clue.

"Impressive," said the voice, "manipulative travel increases your power, power you didn't know you had. Feel encouraged, you're getting to a wonderful start. You shall never let go."

"Who are you?"

Badger wasn't sure if he had thought it, projected it, or spoke it. All he knew was that he had asked a question. He couldn't move, all was darkness, but he felt as though his ear was resting against a comforting heartbeat.

"You will know in time, child of my friend. Cling to what is your heart. Without that, we shall never win."

The voice faded and Badger was left alone, the darkness began to take sheen and then this turned into wavy strands and he was upon a soft surface. Something was stroking his neck. The heartbeat was like music, he didn't dare move lest it all change.

* * *

Badger woke some time in the afternoon, the sun shining directly into his eyes, he had completely forgotten about his dream. *Not again*, he thought to himself, this was the second time he fallen unconscious in two days. He rolled over onto his stomach, stretched a little and pushed himself up off the ground to all fours.

After a few moments he had regained enough of his senses to tell what was about the area. Soldiers, dozens of ISEN soldiers were standing about the platform. They were quite a mismatched bunch, their uniforms were torn and ratty, some didn't even have helmets and their weapons didn't consist entirely of anything Badger knew of, though some carried a variety of Reach weapons. A couple of the soldiers were holding strange, metallic crossbows that didn't have any strings and they had quivers full of metal rods on their backs. There were several PDCTs, they looked no better than everyone else; one was missing an entire screen.

Badger soon spotted Henry in the crowd, standing with Major Tac next to a slide-rail car. The major wasn't wearing the ghillie suit anymore; instead he was wearing a black uniform of thick, bonding fabric and a helmet void of a HUD. He had an odd weapon down at his side that was held by two handles, the forward was oblique but the back ran parallel with the weapon's body. The front had three triangular prongs that were connected to several thick, exposed cords. The rear handle had a crude trigger built into its forward section. It was curious that the major's right index finger kept on twitching.

Seeing Badger awake, Henry called for him to come. He leaned down, Badger's helmet was in his left hand and he began to caress Badger's ears with his right.

"Good, boy," he said, a small smile lighting on his face. "You were unconscious again; if you keep this up I might just request a vacation."

Badger twisted his head out from underneath Henry's hand and firmly grasped it with his left forepaw. *Not likely*, he thought to himself, *Warren never runs out of assignments.*

"So this is the Badger I saw on the news last year," said the major, looking down at Badger. Badger could now see his face clearly, his skin and graying hair were stained with dirt and vegetation, his beard was disorderly and had bits of foliage stuck in it. His eyes were jaded but an energetic smile canceled them out. "I didn't recognize you with you're helmet on."

Henry looked up at the major, his smile broadening. "There was a couple last year, which one?"

"That biological attack in New Nigeria," said Major Tac, shuffling his feet a little. "Those African photographers are extremely good, their close ups on the most advanced GEM known in the middle of it all was great."

Unnoticed, Badger shrugged modestly.

Henry nodded. "Fortunately, he managed to clear a large enough path for the Dousers, they managed to take care of it just in time and only about twenty people were hospitalized. One died though, an African police officer that didn't know the threat, he was caught in the main force of it."

"Sad," said the major. "I didn't see that part on the news."

"Oh well," said Henry, setting the helmet onto Badger's head and standing back up.

Badger fit the helmet on the rest of the way and locked it. After the HUD was reactivated, he retrieved his weapons from the top of a crate, although he had to pry his ASP from the stubborn grip of a black-spotted, yellow feline GEM with sharply pointed ears.

Leave it to a cat to have such bad manners, he thought as he watched the feline GEM reluctantly pick back up its battered magna-revolver. Odd though, he liked cats, strange as it may seem. He strode back over to Henry on his hind legs and stood stalk-still as he awaited a command.

There were several crudely made radios stationed about the platform, the operators were constantly calling out the locations of other units that were headed towards the platform. The sound of the radios were full of static, but this was understandable because of the limited resources they had. A crunching noise was heard below, probably a MATO with a nervous pilot. Every few moments a VTOL would come, drop off some soldiers and then head back to where it had come from. These guerrilla soldiers were making sure they were well prepared. But how prepared could anyone be that had to fight the Chinese and aliens?

"We've waited long enough," said Major Tac, "by the time we've disabled all their defenses all the units in the area will be marching at the gates. I've already sent several commandos ahead to take out the Reach of Nimrod's anti-air and space turrets, clearing a path for your colonel. I've also chosen those that'll accompany us on the rail, Specters, so we won't need to waste any time. Get in."

The major lifted the car's lid and sat in the front. The car's seating was just a ledge that ran around the lower portion of the interior. Badger and Henry climbed in seating themselves near to the major. All the cars that were at the station (four) quickly filled up, the transparent lids were subsequently closed and then they began to zip along the rails at an incredible rate of speed.

Badger growled inwardly. Right across from him, lying on the lap of a Hispanic ISEN soldier, was the stubborn feline GEM. It was glaring grudgingly back at Badger, claws slowly extending and retracting. *Why?* Badger thought.

Chapter 22

"Tickets Please"

"So," began the Hispanic, "this is the galaxy's most advanced GEM, eh?"

Henry nodded.

The Hispanic carried an Assault Rifle and his green uniform showed the scars of being stitched back together many times. He wore an eyepiece HUD, attached to his cracked helmet, the patch fit over his right eye. He used his left hand to stroke the feline GEM's ears.

"What corporation did you buy him from, sir?"

"No corporation," said Henry, "I bought him at a farm."

"Oh," the soldier nodded, "an independent creator."

Henry smiled and patted Badger on the back. "I guess."

"How much did he cost," the soldier inquired, leaving off stroking the GEM to scratch his own neck. "Quite a lot, I imagine. I got Sarah for ten thousand ISEN credits, from Program."

"Program," Henry exclaimed. "No wonder; Program is the world's largest supplier. Although, ever since they got Hagen Hudson working for them they've shown an increase in quality and efficiency with their products. He's even made his own varieties of prototype BINAN creatures."

The Hispanic smiled, leaned over and clapped Henry on the

shoulder. "I like talking to you, I'm finding out what's been happening since we've been in hiding. Do you know what the professor is doing?"

It was actually old news, but Henry didn't say anything. He then noticed that everyone was leaning in close, listening intently to everything he said. He smiled and shrugged, "I doubt anything exciting, or, at least I don't know how exciting science is."

"Quiet," said the major, glaring at everyone. "I told the commandos to time the detonations of the turrets for twelve forty-seven; and it is now twelve forty-seven."

Everyone looked about, they could see the turrets; their barrels were sticking out above the trees. The time ticked by and the turrets didn't explode. They remained, rotating about, searching for targets.

"I think your clock's wrong," said a PDCT.

Suddenly, with a great thundering noise, all the turrets exploded in unison. Their shells flipped up into the air and then the barrels simply dropped, the entire tripod collapsed, crushing trees and the enemy, sending up huge clouds of mud, leaves and branches. Each explosion was an exotic pink flash that shifted into a dark purple as it settled.

"To bad it's not Independence Day," said a gangly Marine with a camouflage painted face.

"I'd settle for just night," said the PDCT.

"Those are very nice fireworks," said the Hispanic, stroking

Sarah, who was on her hind legs, watching the diminishing fumes.

"Seems like the Reach has really done a number on this planet," said Henry.

"They've done a lot," said Tac, "first, the Chinese came and bombed our cities, destroying all communication. That was to open a gate for their new friends, who rebuilt the cities and erected their own bases all over the planet. They're building billions of vehicles and weapons per day, numbers that we can't stop without more help."

"We're here to retrieve something," said Henry, "we're not here to save a planet. We only brought one ship; Forerunner's lost, there's nothing we can do."

"There's little anyone could do," said Tac, looking at the floor. "These beasts are in impossible numbers, none that we could defeat. Unless there's an ally somewhere, ISEN has lost."

"Let's not be too hasty," said Henry. He then thought of something he wanted to ask. "Major?"

Yes?"

"Why is there a Settlement centrifugal lift on this planet?"

"Settlement artifacts are all over this planet," said Tac. "We don't know how they got here, but as soon as communications were destroyed, the Chinese and Reach uncovered countless objects all over the place. We've secured numerous portions of these and hid them throughout this continent. We've also found several things that don't make any sense."

"Banshees?" asked Henry.

Banshees were a legend upon Forerunner, no one had ever seen one and few thought they existed. But at night, dark shapes could be seen coming down from the mountains. The Banshees were supposedly a weather condition, but no proof of this had ever been found. The Banshees were not dangerous; in fact many thought they were playful, toying with anything they could be moved.

"We found a coffin," said Tac.

"A what," Henry asked, leaning in close.

"A coffin," said the major, "we opened it and inside were ashes. But, the strangest thing, the ashes were arranged to form an enormous skeleton, hard to describe. We tried to remove some of the ashes from the coffin to study them, but they slipped though our fingers, like they were atoms and returned to their original position."

"So you now believe they exist," said Henry.

Tac nodded. "They've got a different science. There have been no silhouettes spotted since the Reach came. They've all hidden, I think they're afraid."

"I'm not surprised," said Henry. "What are the other objects have you found?"

"Several caves in the desert, we uncovered them while hiding."

As Tac spoke, his voice was growing more and more excited and his eyes lit up. "There were pictures on the walls, nothing as amazing as Settlement work, but these were very vivid. We believe we know what the Banshees look like."

"And?" said Henry. He noticed that Badger has his ears fully focused upon the major.

"They looked like dragon-cats," said Tac, a nervous sound to his voice, as if he expected Henry to laugh.

"What?" Henry asked.

The gangly Marine clarified. "They look something between a cat and a salamander, with bat-like wings and long, flat tails. From the pictures they can breathe fire. It-it could just be a dialogue, like… they're enraged."

"Could these have been done after the Reach attacked?" asked Henry. "That could account for the anger."

"You believe us?" Tac asked, exchanging satisfied nods with the Marine.

"A few days ago I wouldn't have," said Henry, laying a hand on Badger's back and looking out the window.

*　　*　　*

When the base was spotted up ahead, every soldier in the car became quiet and brandished their weapons. Even the feline GEM took its grudging eyes off of Badger and cocked back the hammer on the small revolver. Major Tac placed one hand on the lid's electronic release switch.

The gangly Marine had a biometric rifle, which he raised a little. "I've been surviving in this forest for nearly a month; it'll be nice to sleep in an actual bed again."

"Ten credits says I get fifty," said one ISEN soldier to a PDCT that sat across from him.

"Twenty," said the PDCT, reaching out a hand, "says I beat you."

The soldier took the hand and they both shook on it. "Done."

"First one to clear the kitchens gets whatever he wants for dinner," said Major Tac, a smug expression on his face.

"Too bad Charlie is dead," said the Hispanic. "He was the best cook in the area."

The station inside the base was on the ground, two doors opened and the track extended to connect with the station, which was a simple rounded, transparent structure that covered supplies and the controls. A three-jawed beast, void of fur, was working the controls, flexing its lower jaws thoughtfully. It didn't even look up when the cars came to a smooth stop right in front of it. The track retracted and the gates closed.

Major Tac flipped the switch and the lid swung open to reveal the car's deadly cargo. The beast was mowed down and ISEN soldiers began to leap out of the cars.

"To the guns," he shouted. "Rick, open the gates."

The gangly Marine saluted smartly and rushed to the controls. One foot resting atop the beast's face, he worked with the controls for only a moment and then the gates slid open. He then promptly shot up the controls and smiled happily.

The base had five multipurpose defensive-drones spread equally apart along the wall. They were dome-shaped to keep water from collecting on them, with canopied openings for the twelve, independently-rotating ballistic and missile turrets. The drones were computer operated, the technicians placed inside, which could fire a variety of missile and ballistic weapons that could deliver destruction to anyone outside the base. However, being built only for the purpose of keeping out rebels and perhaps an alien attack, they were only designed to look outwards.

The twenty-eight soldiers, plus the GEMs, ran out of the station and onto the base's lawn. The Reach and traitors were completely taken by surprise by their sudden appearance and as a result, those closest to the station were eliminated. It was then that the Specters witnessed what Tac's weapon did.

The major, because he had an exoskeleton, was among the first to reach the bottom of the ramp and encounter the enemy. He came upon a Chinese soldier, who had a scraggly mustache, and a sprik. Tac pulled the trigger and a bright orange beam shot from the three triangular prongs and impacted on the man.

There was a bubble-like distortion in the air with a noise like a small firecracker and the man and sprik were blown away several yards. Neither moved from where they had landed. The man's eyes were wide open and a blood trickled from his mouth onto the grass.

"That's better then a shotgun," remarked Henry as he slammed the stock of his Tactical Rifle against the side of a stunned terref's neck.

Badger had drawn his kukri and threw it sideways. It sunk into the chest of a bulky, blonde-furred terref. Then he turned and eliminated another with his systematic SEAR as he retrieved the kukri from the first body. He quickly wiped the blade off and sheathed it before seeking more targets.

Sarah, the feline GEM, kept as close as she could to her owner while still getting close enough to the hostiles to accurately fire the magna-revolver. The magna-revolver worked practically the same as any other caseless ammo weapon, only it used the magnified energy from the hammer's impact to launch the bullets. She was fairly lethal with it, although she had to reload it after every six bullets.

A terref burst from a bunker, carrying a large, belt-fed machinegun. The belt was draped over its back and it began to wildly pepper the area with bullets. Most hit those on its own side.

A Marine wearing a boonie and filthy camouflage, raised one of the peculiar crossbows to his shoulder. Though the crossbow had no strings, the bow bent back as he cocked back a long bolt. A large rod popped up onto the crossbow's rail. The Marine let go of the bolt and it slid back into place. Both ends of the bow were large and square, these were the magnets that launched the metal rod. A holographic close-up of the terref appeared on the back of the crossbow, just in front of the Marine's right eye; a little red dot positioned on the alien's chest. The Marine squeezed the trigger.

There was a static-buzz as the magnetic bow launched the metal rod from the rail. The rod zipped through the air, non-deterred by the elements; the tip heated up and turned red halfway to its target. By the time the rod hit its target, causing a thin line of distortion all the way from the crossbow, it was almost all white hot.

The terref was dead on impact, the hot rod piercing its heart. The machinegun fell to the ground with a dull *thud*. The terref fell backwards, landing with half its body inside the bunker.

The base's walls were built in three tiers, which were, for the most part, made from gray sandstone and flexcrete. On the bottom tier, a Chinese soldier and a couple of spriks were setting up a halo-turret. A halo-turret was a three-barreled, unison-firing, SEAR-projecting weapon that used a ring of the compact, aluminum wool as its indefinite ammo-source.

After setting up the tripod, the spriks took up defensive positions on either side of the man while he searched for clear targets among the combatants. The soldier's HUD had a full distinguishing display that showed blue shimmers around allies and red around hostiles. He saw a couple of red shimmers that were a safe distance from any ally and began firing.

The molten splinters molded themselves to the wind, though they were far more easily buffeted about then the rod of a crossbow. The SEAR made a wide spread, tearing up grass and even causing small fires. After a few moments, both red shimmered units fell before the halo-turret.

The spriks laughed and raised fists in the air in triumph. One started to cheer, but it soon changed to strangled gargle. Its companions turned to look and watched as it fell forward off the tier, to the ground below, a hole through its throat.

It had been caused by a stray bullet from a caseless load. The other two returned to their work, seeking targets. But then, movement above them drew their attention. It was a mole-worm, wearing golden armor and two spades that ran along its entire forearm like duel shields, charging along the tier, grunting as it hurried to get to the ground below.

The sprik and the human smiled coldly as they looked back at the combat. What could stand in the way of a mole-worm? Victory would be soon and the guerrillas' attack would end vainly and the digging would still go on.

Craase!

Apparently the Chinese soldier wasn't destined to see the outcome. The sound was caused by a red-hot rod, shattering against the gray sandstone. The soldier had a cauterized hole between his eyes and the back of his head; he fell sideways, sweeping the turret over, pulling the trigger and eliminating the other sprik.

The Marine pulled back the bolt, allowing another rod to pop up onto the rail. "That'll teach you."

He swiveled his view to target the mole-worm. He needed a headshot and that would be difficult, the worm's lumbering pace made it difficult to lead properly. "Hold still you oversized maggot."

When he felt confident that he couldn't miss, he squeezed the trigger. The rod's distorted path was perfectly aligned with the worm's head. The nearly molten rod pierced the armor, bending a little and sank deep into the worm's head, missing the brain, but pricking the heart.

The mole-worm let out an inward shriek, instead of traveling down the stairs, it leapt down to the first tier and then to the ground. It was angry and its wrath had no favoritism.

Chapter 23

"Alternating Views"

Colonel Warren watched a holo-screen attentively; the holo-screen displayed the *Traveler*'s prison sector. He moved the view-screen about as he watched each holding cell carefully, the Reach were unsettling to watch. They all sat in perfect rows near the restriction-field, eyes closed, legs crossed and hands held together in front of them.

The Reach didn't make a noise and the silence was eerie. Occasionally, one would move and twist a little, but other than that, it was like watching statues. The Reach had killed nearly seventy ISEN crewmen, including half of the occupants in a sickbay. They had been stripped of their armor and weapons, but they each carried a regal dignity about them. Warren wanted answers for this attack, but he knew that it wouldn't be for a while.

He turned his attention to another holo-screen beside him; it was displaying a unit of three MATOs firing upon a small town. It was a satellite feed from Earth; the Chinese had begun their war again, trying to make a path for the Reach. The Specters' mission had only been to slow them down, but the Chinese had recovered amazingly fast.

"Brave," mocked Warren angrily as he watched a civilian house go up in flames.

He was about to turn back to the prison footage, when the satellite feed changed to show a Mosquito over jungle terrain. A red square appeared over the vehicle and a picture appeared below it. It was of a boy, possibly fourteen. Underneath the picture was the name Dave Hudson.

The name grabbed Warren's attention. *The son of that biological professor,* he thought. He watched as the image zoomed out to show an aerial view. A straight, red line was drawn between the VTOL and a square patch of clear land with a dome structure and several square buildings. Words appeared over the patch of land in bold, red letters: REPEL.

"What's going on?" he muttered to himself.

He sat down at the holo-screen and typed at the keypad. The information of the data's history appeared on the screen, he mumbled it to himself.

"Dave Hudson, son of the well-known scientist Hagen Hudson, was attempted to be kidnapped (supposedly by a genetics corporation; Reach) as leverage for his father's services. The police and SWAT forces have put a stop to the panic in the city where the attempt was put into action.

"There weren't any civilian casualties, but several of the kidnappers were killed. The corporation used a variety of peculiar, illegal equipment including three unknown VTOLs, two of which have been dragged out of the city and forced to land in a field; they are now being transported to AMRAD for further study. One of the pilots was a disgruntled military airman, Douglas Forte, he is currently being held for questioning in police headquarters.

"A police VTOL, after seeing that the Hudson house was being attacked by crazed shregs, picked up the boy and the SWAT team when they got out of a sewer near Okapi. The police are now transporting Dave to REPEL where he is supposed to meet his father. However, Hagen Hudson has apparently vanished; federal authorities are trying to locate him. The only clue found so far is a piece of partially burnt paper with the name Dr. Nordahl Wild."

Warren's eyes widened with recognition, but he read on.

"Several cyclists using illegal biometric weapons were arrested, some others were killed. Those that had survived have minor concussions. One, however, got away before other law enforcement arrived. Police drones are searching the area for him."

Warren stopped reading and rubbed his shoulder thoughtfully. Something from his past had been brought up in this information; something he had hoped had been buried forever. He glanced about the room to make sure no one was watching. Everyone was busy working at their own, assigned computers.

He quickly got into a search menu and wrote in the name Dr.

Nordahl Wildenvey. Before he affirmed his request, a thought came to mind, he quickly added: Reach. The information appeared on the screen and, as he read, his hands twitched nervously. It completely affirmed his fears.

*　　*　　*

The ravaging addition of the mole-worm was unsettling to both sides as it swung its spades about, killing everything that got in its path. The golden mole-worm's strength seemed to have no bounds and conventional projectiles merely glanced off the armor.

The Marines with crossbows fired as fast as they could, but the rods only penetrated certain lengths and stuck out of the armor. One impacted square in the chest and created an area of thin cracks stretching up towards the neck. This only made it angrier.

A Reach terref, using one of the crystal weapons, was peppering the mole-worm's body with a long trail of the blue crystals. He stumbled about, trying to keep as far away from the juggernaut as possible. The crystals were designed with special points that would stick in at any angle. The worm was beginning to look like a scary hedgehog.

The terref's shoulder pulsed with pain from a bullet wound, a delighted smile lit up his long face. The crystals made a noise like ice against ice as they left the barrel, and, on impact, made a noise like cracking eggs. Dozens of other weapons were being used against the worm, although very few had much effect.

Splat!

An ISEN Marine went flying when he was hit by the back of one of the spades. Next went two spriks, and then a Chinese infantryman was spiked to the ground. Another rod hit the worm; this found a soft spot in the armor and stuck out a short ways in the back.

The worm rumbled in pain and several crystals in its face vaporized, momentarily blinding it. While it was blinded, Major Tac rushed up and used his large weapon (the Distorter). The sonic bubble knocked the worm back a couple yards, it let out a growl and charged the major, taking out a couple Reach soldiers on its way.

Five loud percussions and bright lights stopped it in its tracks. Its armor was blackened and severely cracked and its head looked right up at the sky. With it arms draped loosely at its sides, it fell backwards and hit the ground with a disgusting squishing sound.

Standing on the first tier, Badger reset the rate of fire to semiautomatic. He smiled in acceptance.

"Good, boy," said Henry.

With the worm out of the fight, both sides commenced fighting again. A Marine with a crossbow took out three hostiles that had placed themselves in a row. The major blew away four hostiles with one sonic blast. A sprik used an energy handgun to kill a Marine. Sarah eliminated two hostiles and then leapt up onto the shoulder of her Hispanic owner. A terref grabbed a Marine from behind and began to strangle him, but the Marine unsheathed a knife and drove it into the creature's side and then fired a splinter into its face.

A group of four Marines had already captured one of the defensive-drones and were heading to the second. Another group of Marines had found the armory and were beginning to set up a couple of Halo-turrets. A Firefly went off, temporarily blinding units on both sides. Another golden mole-worm was eliminated by one of the Halo-turrets. And large group of hostiles was taken out by Badger's systematic SEAR.

Biometric ammunition, though almost never-ending, isn't the best for the battlefield. The organic fragments don't have any splatter-effect and it usually takes a great many fragments to kill anything. Henry didn't care though; he liked the feeling of power when he held a biometric weapon.

The enemy seemed to just fall before the Specters. Mainly those that were on the tiers were Chinese, because the Reach seemed to like fighting down below. Henry practically didn't let go of the trigger and the fragments took care of the rest.

Without much warning, other than a shriek and a ferocious bark from Badger, Henry found himself sprawling forward onto the ground. He was still holding the trigger when he whipped about and took aim at what had hit him. What he saw was fascinatingly horrible.

It was a Chinese officer; his uniform was in tatters and his skin was deathly pale. The skin around the officer's mouth and eyes was thin and folded, even his cheeks were sharp and shallow. The eyes were blood shot and yellowed, and his lips were cracked and bloody. The only weapons the officer possessed were two, small, double-bladed knives. The biological fragments tore through the officer, but he didn't even seem to notice.

"Die already," yelled Henry. The officer seemed to have been rendered void of sense and language; the only sounds uttered were shrieks and growls. He fell at Henry, slashing and stabbing wildly.

Badger, not able to safely use his systematic SEAR in such close proximity or switch the ammo fast enough, was using his ASP. The well-controlled splinter placement impacted all over the officer's upper-body, with absolutely no devastating effect.

There was a high-pitched beeping and then Henry's rifle shut off from overheating. Henry let out a groan, dropped the rifle and grabbed the officer's wrists to try and force him to a position he could be restrained. Even with his new exoskeleton, Henry could tell that the officer was extremely strong. There was something very wrong with this entire assault.

The officer sudden let out a gasp and fell forward, head colliding into Henry's chest armor. Badger withdrew his kukri from the back of the man's neck and leapt down to the ground. He wiped the kukri off on a clean part of the man's uniform and sheathed it.

Henry couldn't think of anything to say. He didn't know why the officer attacked like that; it was suicide to attack with only those small knives. He picked up his rifle, looked it over carefully and then attached it to the holster. It was useless now. He stooped down and picked up a weapon that a terref had dropped.

It was the same alien weapon that Badger had picked up at the slide-rail station. As soon as he had grabbed the handle of the weapon, its information was absorbed and displayed upon his HUD. It's crosshairs were exotic, it was a creation of two hooks pointing down and away from each other with a chain-like band running from one concave to the other. The ammo display was shown as a simple figure eight, meaning infinite, but there was a heat level display just below it. "This'll do," he said.

*　　*　　*

That Chinese officer wasn't the only one crazed. Many Chinese and Reach soldiers, with the same paleness and other features had burst from bunkers and the main installation in the base's center. Some of them used ranged weapons with wicked looking blades attached to them, but most used a variety of knives and other odd melee weapons. Though, unlike the officer, each one of these wore a kind of ceremonial, brown leather mask over their mouths and it hung down low with bas-relief in the image of an open mouth full of sharp teeth.

These crazies fell upon the Marines, shrieking and slashing. The crossbows, Halo-turrets and Major Tac's sonic blaster were the only weapons with any noticeable effect upon the insane soldiers. The only major point that seemed to bring a quick kill was the head and that was incredibly hard to hit because the soldiers were startlingly fast.

One group of Marines that was using a captured Halo-turret cut a couple of the crazies in half. One was dead immediately, but the other used its strong arms to drag itself towards the group. They eliminated it with a stream to the head.

"That's just wrong," exclaimed one of the Marines, grimacing at the gruesome sight.

Two other mole-worms had joined the fight, but had been quickly eliminated with grenades and a high-explosive projectile weapon taken from the armory. Their bodies served as excellent cover for the Marines. Though they were few, the battle was leaning against the Reach of Nimrod and their Chinese allies.

Another drone was rendered inoperable by a Marine force and the Specters had finally made it to one. There were only two more left, but they didn't face the gate, the rest of the regions survivors had a clear entrance into the base, there was seemingly nothing the Reach or Chinese could do. Victory was imminent.

And then, as if one body, every hostile, save the crazies, began to run away, towards the remaining drones. None even turned to return fire; they just kept going, tearing up grass and dirt. It was strange; the ISEN aerial craft hadn't even arrived with reinforcements. It was as if they just gave up.

Many of the soldiers stood still in dumb amazement at the sheer sight of it. Why did they just give up? Whatever the reason, the Marines retrieved their sense of duty and began to give chase.

Henry and Badger stood upon the top tier outside the drone they had just taken. Both watched as the last of the crazies were killed and the Marines charging the flanks of the losers. There were only seventeen Marines remaining, something wasn't right.

As they thought over this, a shadow fell over them and within moments, the entire base was encompassed by it. The Specters turned around and looked up towards the sky, their eyes widened and their mouths hung open in sheer amazement. It was a ship.

At first it was just a shadow in the clouds and then it broke through the clouds, inspiring awe in everyone that saw it. Birds that were within three miles of the base flew away to find cover. This was something completely new. Unlike the International Space Exploration Navy's ships, which were very angular, this one was completely smooth with rounded edges and corners and was almost entirely an iridescent white. It had four great, hornlike structures on its bow, bent inwards towards a large, gray bowl, with a blue center. To the ISEN soldiers it looked like an ominous, hellish insect.

All eyes watched the ship as it just hovered in the sky. All sounds of conflict were gone, even the Reach stopped to watch, but there was a look of ease upon their faces. Henry backed up a couple paces, but Badger remained where he stood, he slowly lifted his rifle up to his shoulder.

The Specters could feel it; the air was full of a tenseness which continued to increase in volume. Everything was silent. And then, before the Specters' eyes, objects began to drop towards the ground.

At first Henry thought they were bombs, but then he noticed that they had arms and legs, even tails. His eyes widened with the realization of what was happening and he raised his new weapon to the ready. "They're dropping reinforcements," he said aloud, mainly to himself.

The Reach impacted all over the interior of the base, their armor somehow absorbing most of the impact. Mainly terref and humans with the tusked helmets of the Militants, the hostiles projected their lights and dropped objects on to the ground that projected energy barricades. The Marines were forced to take cover.

Chapter 24

"The Professor"

"Aaah," Hagen Hudson moaned, his head was throbbing in pain. He stroked his scalp with a bruised hand and opened his eyes to look about. He was in a small flexcrete cell with a crystal wall that looked out into a dark hall, lying on an uncomfortable cot with a little table at one end that had a glass of water and a plate of vegetables.

The events that had led to his situation slowly came back to him. He had been working in his office, when a beep from his computer informed him that he had a message. He opened the message to see hand written scrawl saying: checkmate, I have you. Underneath the scrawling had been an image, but he couldn't recall it. He then contacted his son to tell him to run, he also tried to tell him of the information that Canine possessed, but some men came into his office. One of the men must have hit him with something, because there was a large lump on the back of his head.

He sat up on the bed and looked down at the floor, a tiny freshwater crab scuttled past his feet and slipped into a small drainage pipe in the middle of the room. A large crack ran along the floor, moisture had been caught in there, promoting the growth of slimy algae and fungus.

"What a dump," he calmly muttered as he looked back out the

crystal wall. There were some dim lights, a few were flickering and there weren't any other cells to be seen. "Where am I? This can't be the Reach Corporation?"

He stood up stiffly and staggered over to the crystal wall, looking it over for weaknesses. It was covered in scratches, some of which looked like they were done by an enormous beast. After what seemed a dull eternity, he found the door, a slight offset in the grains of the crystal forming a large square. He pushed and even kicked it, but he knew it was hopeless.

He eventually sat back down on the bed and placed the plate of vegetables in his lap. He lifted a piece of broccoli to his lips, but then threw it against the door when he saw a large spider clinging to it. He set the plate back on the table and rested his face into his palms.

"Comfortable?"

Hagen jumped and watched as two figures walked into the room, one was dressed in a dark suit with gray-leather shoes and a thick rose vine was tattooed over one eye. The other was a man with caramel skin and a black, sleeveless jacket and raggedy blue pants; circling his left eye was a tattoo of a snake devouring its own tail.

Hagen's mouth went dry at the sight of the snake tattoo; the Mauritanians had used that same tattoo during the war to show what they would do to their enemies. The tattoo represented their implication; the snake devouring its tail was the symbol for cannibalism.

The well-dressed man had a pleasant smile on his face. "I asked you a question Mr. Hudson. Are you comfortable?"

"Not anymore," said Hagen, staring at the other man.

The well-dressed man sighed contentedly. "I wouldn't worry about Sekou, he may be one of the few remnants of the war, a true Mauritanian, but he's not going to eat you; I have got other... clients. And it is not mealtime yet."

"How comforting," Hagen said, a look of disgust on his face.

"Sekou will be your personal guard," said the well-dressed man, patting the stoic-faced Mauritanian on the shoulder.

"Except in the interrogation room," Sekou pointed out.

"That's right!" the well-dressed man exclaimed, looking at the ceiling. "He doesn't have the stomach for my interrogations."

"Doesn't have the stomach?" Hagen inquired to himself. He began to feel himself grow queasy and he swayed a little.

"Oh," the well-dressed man said dismissively, "stop worrying, just give me what I want and I'll let you go."

"Where... his dinner plate?" demanded Hagen, starting to grow bold.

"You're much too valuable for that," said the man, "and, besides, Sekou can't stand rich food."

Hagen slanted his eyes contemptuously. "You're not going to get a thing from me."

"That's what everybody says," said the man, rolling his eyes. "Now listen, I am Dr. Nordahl Wildenvey, I am the founder and fulltime owner of Biotech, I'll need some information."

"Sorry doctor," smirked Hagen, "but my work is for Program, I don't work for the government, though I did get some dental from them, and my work is already public."

"You can't fool me," said Nordahl, "I've had you watched; there is no possible way that you haven't something I want."

"What good would it do you?" Hagen growled.

With a dry chuckle, Nordahl turned to the Mauritanian. "Please take him to the interrogation room; the scenic route."

"It shall be done," the Mauritanian bowed and literally lifted Hagen with one arm, carrying him out of the cell. The Mauritanian smiled wickedly at the terrified figure of Hagen.

Hagen didn't have much in the way of sight, because the Mauritanian held him by the front of his lab coat so that he could only turn his head. The hallway outside the cell wasn't very large; one end, as he could see, was a dead end, the other had an automated door that opened moments before his back collided with it. After passing through the doorway, it closed and saw that it was trapezoid in shape with an aquamarine tint to it. The next thing he knew was that they were traveling down another hallway with one side being transparent. Outside and down below the transparent wall were throngs of people, a mixture of men and women with various, noticeable, physical disabilities.

"What's going on down there?" Hagen tried to sound bold, but his voice was more of a gasp.

The Mauritanian glared and growled at him. "You keep your mouth closed or I'll eat it."

"No you won't," said Hagen, managing a smile, "your boss says you won't."

The Mauritanian let out a hiss and turned his face away from Hagen.

"Ah, you appear to resent his authority."

"Most certainly," the Mauritanian said, clenching Hagen's lab coat tighter. "He knows this, but he also knows I am powerless to do harm."

"And what fear has he implanted in you?" Hagen inquired, glancing at the throngs of people in the lower room.

"I'm not afraid of him or his allies," the Mauritanian yelled.

The people in the lower room looked about, unable to see where the sound had come from. The wall was only transparent from one direction.

"Who are his allies?"

"Those who are bringing a new order to all things," said Sekou, tossing Hagen onto the ground. He picked him up again with the same hand held him higher. "Don't ask another question or I'll willfully have the doctor take my life."

Hagen watched as the Mauritanian seemed to produce a thin, sickle-shaped, serrated blade out of thin air, pressing it against Hagen's stomach.

"I am very fond of the liver. You understand?"ced the Mauritanian grinned from ear-to-ear with pleasure at the paleness of Hagen's face.

They continued along the hallway until the transparent wall gave way to opaque flexcrete. Straight ahead, Sekou could see another trapezoid door, an exact duplicate as the first, but this one opened up into a small, square elevator with a silvery interior. Inside he pressed an arrow pointing upwards and the elevator rocketed upwards and then began to slow down as it reached its destination. With a distinct beep, the elevator came to a complete stop and the door opened up to another hallway, but this time both sides were transparent.

On both sides of the glass were people working with chemicals and machinery, none of the workers could see the Mauritanian or the professor. Both terrestrial and extraterrestrial wildlife were being examined and tested by workers. Hagen looked through both walls in amazement; it appeared that Dr. Wildenvey's workers were completely ignorant of what their employer was really up to. Test-tubes of chemicals were being carted about and cryogenic canisters were pulled out of portable freezers. Guards stood about the area, each wearing a gasmask and carrying a rifle; nothing strange about the security.

After exiting the transparent hall, they wound up inside another elevator that took them even higher into the building. Hagen hadn't any idea how high they had climbed before the elevator came to its long awaited stop. Sekou stepped out of the elevator and let Hagen fall to his feet.

"Keep walking," the Mauritanian growled, pointing to a square door that was rimmed by blue lights.

"Some scenic route," Hagen muttered, smoothing out the front of his lab coat.

"You saw all that was necessary," Sekou said in a strangely friendly voice.

"Not so tough now, are you?" said Hagen walking towards the door. He was perplexed that he couldn't see anything on either side, the only light was the doorframe up ahead, the rest was thick darkness. From scampering sounds and the smell of hot breath, he knew there was something moving in the darkness, he could feel its eyes on his face.

The door opened immediately and then closed after they entered.

The room the door opened to was brightly lit by a band of light that was fixed halfway up the wall, encircling the room. In the middle of the room was a large chair, hovering above the floor by a bright array of electrical currents. Nordahl was already in the room, standing with his back to the door and with an open box in front of him; he addressed the professor in a serious tone.

"Now, professor, how much suffering are you willing to take before you start shouting the information?"

Sekou lifted Hagen with both hands and set him into the chair. The chair bounced for a moment. Sekou pushed Hagen's arms onto the arms of the chair and energy restraints curled about his arms, holding them firmly in place. Next it was his legs and he was fixed to the spot, staring at the doctor's back.

"I'll never talk," he grunted as he pulled vainly at the restraints.

"As corny as a movie," Nordahl sighed and turned around, in one hand was a needle filled partially with a milky, translucent liquid. "You won't know what this is, but I'll tell you. A friend and I, a long time ago, made this as a medicine that could literally replace blood. I finished the research and left for Mauritania to try to sell it to the Mauritanians and Nazis. Unfortunately my friend tried to have me assassinated."

"Pity he didn't succeed," Hagen spat contemptuously.

"Silence," shouted Sekou slapping Hagen's face.

With a burst of white light, Hagen's energy implants stopped Sekou's strike. The tough African let out a yelp and wrung his hands.

"I might have warned you," said the doctor, glancing pitilessly at the hurt man. "Just might."

Sekou glared at the doctor and turned around, leaving by the door in a huff.

Nordahl smiled happily once the doors closed. "We absolutely hate each other, but, we both need one another. Now, where was I?"

"The needle," said Hagen.

"Oh, yes," said Nordahl. "This is actually a specially engineered bacterium, completely healthy for the body and reproduces quickly when their temporary host is losing blood. It even keeps its host from dieing of pain or shock; it might have saved many lives during the war."

"You monster," Hagen hissed.

"Anyway," continued Nordahl, "it has proven most useful in interrogations. I'm tired of people dieing before I get my information. This bacterium will keep you alive and in perfect health during my little... operation."

Hagen began to struggle at his restraints as the doctor approached with the needle. He groaned as he yanked, pulled twisted, convulsed, but it was hopeless. He felt the needle sink into the skin just above his knee and the bacteria was forced into his blood stream.

Nordahl withdrew the needle, smiling fondly at his work. The area about the puncture began to swell as the bacteria started to move throughout the professor's bloodstream.

"It will only live for twelve hours," said Nordahl, turning back to the box and pulling out a scalpel. He cut open the front of the right leg of Hagen's pants. "I love this part."

*   *   *

Outside the room, crouched near the elevator, the strong Mauritanian covered his ears to the terrible screams issuing from the room. He moaned as the screams could still be heard, he shivered uncontrollably; he even tried to sing to block out the noise. He then took out his knife and opened the front of his jacket, his chest was a mass of scars; he began to add to them, the pain keeping himself from hearing the screams.

Chapter 25

"The Odd Couple"

The elevator had led to a tunnel that led them back into the outer rim of Forge, just alongside the road that led out of Okapi. The Mosquito then picked them up and flew them away from the city, flying long and fast over the jungle; down below aviary creatures scattered before the VTOL until at last they reached REPEL. The pilot landed the VTOL upon one of the square buildings; each one was a landing pad, then took off again after Dave and Canine got off, leaving them in the hands of a Marine squad. He was led down a metal staircase that encircled the building and then into the dome (known as the Beehive because all its rooms, halls and doors were hexagons). Most of the Beehive was underground, stretching down nearly four hundred meters; Dave and Canine were taken to the bottom level, known as the Matrix, where they were taken into an empty office and left alone.

Dave rubbed his arms with his hands as he looked about the room; it was very chilly in there. Along each of the six walls in the room was a large computer screen that displayed diverse, red messages at incredible speeds in a series of languages and dialects, lighting up the room. The only furnishings in the room were hard, ceramic chairs, one of which he was sitting on and a hexagon table made of an uncomfortable hard black wood. Dave also noticed that across from him was a small blue bowl with the name Samuel painted in black letters. All in all, the room was very depressing and dark.

"I never expected it to be this cheery," Dave said sarcastically, he had wondered what REPEL was like.

"Colonel Warren has simple taste, master," Canine projected.

"Who's Colonel Warren?" Dave asked.

"His name is upon the plaque above the door, master."

Dave looked above the hexagon door, a circular platinum tablet above the door read: Office of Colonel Warren. He shrugged and turned back around, leaning back so that only the back two legs of the chair were on the ground as he sighed. "Well I hope the colonel gets here soon with some good news."

"Sadly, neither are possibilities."

Dave nearly fell backwards. He quickly stood up and turned around to see a bald-headed man stroking the chin of a hairless cat with symmetrical black skin and gray blotches that was perched on his shoulder. The man was dressed in a crimson suit with a black tie and white gloves, he looked very uncertain about what to say next, in fact he seemed uncertain whether or not to take another step.

The cat, with a shakiness rarely found in felines, twisted his body and looked as if it was whispering into the man's right ear. The man, with a deep breath, walked into the room, bid Dave to sit down and then sat down directly across from him. The door closed automatically.

The cat shakily walked off of the man and onto the table; movement still shaky.

The man watched the cat for a moment until it turned and looked him directly in the eye, its large silver eyes staring unblinkingly. The man then looked directly at Dave and took another deep breath.

"You are certainly Dave Hudson." He spoke slow and gave a queer smile.

"Y-yes sir," Dave stammered unable to tell which of the two was more strange.

"There's no need to be afraid of me and little Samuel," said the man; the cat turned and looked at Dave.

A chill ran up Dave's spine when he noticed that the both the cat's and man's expressions were exactly the same.

"I'm not scared."

"Then you would be the first," said the man, his expression changed along with the cat. "But we can see different."

"Who are you?" Dave asked, looking down at his side to make sure that Canine was still there.

The man stood up and started pacing, the cat and him in exact timing. "I am Victor; I am the colonel's replacement while he is away.

And I do not have good news for you."

Dave felt like his heart was being pulled. "Do you know where my dad is?"

Both Victor and Samuel sat down at the same time. "I was given a message of possibility. So in a way, yes, I do."

"Then where?" Dave asked, blinking back tears.

Samuel and Victor gave him a sympathetic look. "Please believe us that we are extremely sorry, but we cannot divulge this information to you yet. The colonel is very specific when he wants to tell others himself."

"Please," Dave pleaded, openly weeping tears now, he lowered his head until his chin was resting upon his chest. "Can you at least tell me if he's alive?"

A strong hand squeezed his shoulder and something rubbed against his left ear. The man had gotten up out of his chair to comfort him and the cat was rubbing its forehead against his ear.

"Would you be here if he was dead?" the man asked.

Without looking up, Dave shook his head. "No."

"Well, with us in charge without the colonel, you might have," said Victor, trying to cheer up Dave.

Dave managed a smile and whipped a tear from his cheek; the cat licked up the others with its sandpaper tongue.

"Believe us," said Victor, "Your father is alive, though…"

The cat gave Victor a withering glare.

"…we don't know his condition," Victor put out, glad that he had been stopped from saying something wrong.

The cat returned to licking away the salty tears until it was satisfied at its work and sat down silently, looking from the boy to Victor. Samuel curled his tail shakily about his legs and twitched the end about patiently.

Victor walked back over to his seat and he and the cat resumed their similar appearances. "Please rest with confidence that we are doing all we can."

Dave had looked up halfway through the man's sentence and was shocked when he saw that the cat's mouth was also moving in exact context with the man's. His eyes went wide and he subconsciously pressed himself against the back of the chair.

"In the meantime, I see you have a suitcase, you'll have to remain in Matrix until the colonel returns, and maybe some after. I understand that he is having a few difficulties."

"Like what?" Dave asked, starting to feel better.

"That's classified," said Victor, reaching into a pocket on his jacket and pulling out a small can of tuna.

Samuel staggered quickly over to the bowl and sat down, patiently watching as Victor pressed the back of the can with his thumb until the lid broke open. Samuel waited until the last of the tuna was dropped into the bowl. He then watched as Victor took a tiny spoon from another pocket.

Dave watched in odd fascination as Victor started to actually spoon-feed the tuna to the cat. In fact he was even using the spoon to open and close cat's mouth. *This is weird,* he thought.

Victor saw Dave staring and stroked Samuel's chin with his right index finger. "I know this looks strange, but Samuel doesn't have the brain capacity to eat normally."

"How's that," Dave asked, leaning forward to listen.

Victor began to spoon another bit of tuna into the cat's mouth.

"During the Mauritanian war," he began with a sigh, "I was a vet, still am, for a very unusual patient, but I could fight just like any other Marine. Regulars and GEMs, I was very good with it all, I loved the animals I worked on. In fact, I was so good that I never lost a single patient. But maybe I got arrogant, gave myself all the glory, left God out, I can't remember, but one day I got caught in a crossfire."

Dave listened intently, not wanting to miss a word of the story.

"Our commanding officer had spotted smoke up ahead. When we arrived on the spot, we found it was a discarded campsite with human bones scattered about the area. Several skulls were placed about the fire in a semicircle." Victor's face began to grow red with anger and his eyes narrowed as he tried to concentrate on the story. "Each one had a dog tag wreathed around it; I read every single one, the last one I read was my only surviving family member's name, Samuel Ray, my brother." His voice almost rose to a yell. "They had eaten him."

Dave felt his heart go out to Victor, but he still wondered what the cat had to do with any of this.

"Then there was the noise of motors, an ISEN Technical and a Nazi Rover were running side-by-side, shooting at each other." Victor's voice calmed down. "I don't know which side hit me, but the next thing I knew was waking up inside a field hospital with our commanding officer, Colonel Warren, standing over me. I didn't know what to do. Warren soon gave me the answer. The frontal lobe of my brain had been shot and I'd lost a chunk of it; that's the part that allows you to make decisions."

Dave nodded, that explained a lot.

"However, he had managed to convince the doctors to save that chunk in a preservative container. I didn't know why he had done that and I didn't care at the moment. Because of this misfortune, I was given a medical discharge. When REPEL took me on, I saw what they had done with that piece of my brain."

Dave leaned in closer.

"Little Samuel here was grown around it, an experiment that the government had wanted to try for a long time. Because of this, I had to go through a surgery that applied neural implants that allows me and Samuel to take on each other. As you have observed, I can become his mouth and motivation for decisions, he's very good with them and he can become my movement and intelligence. But this requires a lot of concentration."

Dave stared wide-eyed from the smiling Samuel and the serious Victor. It was quite a sad tale. He didn't know what do or say.

"God shined through this though," said Victor, spooning another bit of tuna into Samuel's open mouth and then using a finger to make him chew. "It takes a lot of prayer and faith to work with someone who can't live without you and vise versa. Though he's made from my brain, he really is someone else entirely. And he sure loves his tuna... something I don't."

"I'm sorry," said Dave.

"No!" said Victor. Samuel gave Dave a confident look. "Be glad."

"I-I mean... about your brother," said Dave.

Victor looked down at the tuna inside the small bowl. "That was nearly ten years ago, just two weeks before Big Old 5. That campsite, I can see it now as if I was still there."

Samuel purred encouragingly.

"Maybe I shouldn't have mentioned it," Dave apologized.

"That would have been very nice," said Victor.

Dave sighed wearily. He wanted to talk with this man, but he couldn't think of anything. And then, to completely change the subject, he said, "Where's the bathroom?"

Victor looked up from making Samuel chew, his face showed that he'd completely forgot about what Dave had said. "Hold on, Samuel will be done soon and I'll take you there."

Dave smiled and gave a mental prayer of thanks.

Chapter 26

"Higher Power"

The Militants that had just dropped in were unconcerned by the sight of their dead, each only seeing the enemies they had to fight now. About their shoulders was draped what was once a white fur, held tightly to their bodies by strong polymer cords, they were stained and stiff from countless, bloody fights. They each carried an ISEN Assault Rifle on one hip and another weapon of their choosing on the other. There was not a noise from them.

"Personally, I'd have thought they'd be using something more spectacular," Badger remarked.

Henry gave Badger an odd look, "was that sarcasm?"

Badger shrugged, "I guess."

Now that everyone knew why the enemy had retreated, there was the problem of the reinforcements. Silence seemed to fill the air like a fog and for what seemed an eternity, no one moved. The seventeen remaining Marines seemed rooted to the spot as they watched the new hostiles. And then, with a lunge, a terref started the battle.

The terref had used its left hand-paw to grab a short rod from a band about its waist. Either end of the rod was wide and silvery, with a ring of purple light in the centers. The terref had squeezed the rod and two, broad, purple blades were projected from the ends, curving around his knuckles and fusing together at the tip, looking like some terrible scimitar. He lunged forward, and lifted a Marine high into the air on the blade.

The Marine let out a groan as the blade was withdrawn, he fell down to his knees and looked up at the sky. He did this for what seemed a long time. Then he dropped his gaze towards the alien, a grin spread across his face as he lifted his crossbow to his shoulder. "I win."

The terref fell to the ground with a painful gargle, right at the Marine's knees. The Marine crumpled backward and his eyes closed as he slipped away, seeking the darkness that would take him.

The aliens began to shriek and shout, the battle was on. One of the terrefs grabbed its dead comrade's rifle and began to fire both weapons at the same time. The Marines began to scatter before the onslaught of the enemy.

The Reach were taken by surprise when Badger began to fire explosives all over the area. From this range the splinters made groupings of about ten feet, but that didn't matter. Badger's Assault Rifle had been switched to automatic and the wild fire was making all the difference.

Barely five of the Marines remained, one being Major Tac and they had managed to find shelter in a bunker. The gangly Marine and the Hispanic were also among the survivors, they crouched beside the doorway while bullets hit everywhere. One splinter ricocheted off the back wall and stuck into the wall in front of the Hispanic's face.

"Ah," he shouted, "that was close."

The major used an ASP to fire around the doorway. "I didn't count on this."

"Dumb Special Forces," the Hispanic cried over the noise.

"No, they're not really Special Forces," said the gangly Marine. "They're really just normal soldiers, but their armor is modified for these short attack drops. After this battle they'll return to their original design. I know this because Sacra and I, may she rest in peace, observed this in Whisper Valley; they were taking over the wind farms.

"Temporary Special Forces?" said the major, shooting another three rounds out the doorway, "thats something new."

Sarah let out a yowl and fired two bullets into the face of a human. She purred contentedly at her work. The humans were odd, their weapons were placed onto heir backs like spikes, but they were, for some reason, using the weapons from heir hips.

* * *

One of the terrefs, with half his armor burnt from a few close explosions, saw Badger firing the deadly splinters from the top tier. The terref let out a growl and cringed as the side of his face was set on fire by the burns. He dropped the Assault Rifle and took another weapon from his other thigh.

There was no way to hold the weapon upside-down, the basic

pattern was a long triangle with the back curled inward like a couple of hooks towards the handle. The weapon's handle was a steely socket that the shooter would fit his hand into and grab a bar that would launch metal spikes every time it was squeezed. The spikes were double-pointed projectiles that hummed with an internal energy; they were inserted into slots on the hooked portion of the weapon. The Reach called it the Sticker.

The Militant terref raised it up and used the close-up hologram system to place the crosshairs over the dog that was causing the havoc. He pulled the trigger and several of the metal spikes were sucked into the weapon and projected out the barrel.

The terref rushed to the cover of a barricade after firing his barrage.

"Fei Demaw," it growled.

*   *   *

Though he knew it wouldn't do too much, Henry assisted Badger with his captured energy weapon. He had long since found out that it worked like a shotgun, it fired several blue balls of static out at once, each spreading with the exact proportions of the exotic crosshairs. Every shot made a distinct cracking noise, like the snapping of a dry twig.

Badger tried his best to position shots so that they would hit behind the enemy's cover, but that was nearly impossible with the weapon he was using. These soldiers' armor was stronger, even when they were in the open it took a direct hit to kill them. He figured the ship might have something to do with it. As Badger was admiring the Reach's armor, he hadn't noticed the terref come out of cover and fire the Sticker.

Five spikes stuck into Badger's Assault Rifle and four others stuck into his armor. He let out a bark of surprise and dropped his rifle. He could feel the points of the spikes pricking his flesh and he also felt them start to vibrate.

Badger immediately knew why the spikes were vibrating. He kicked his rifle away and began to yank the spikes out of his armor and exoskeleton. After he threw the last spike away, they all began to explode into red-hot fragments.

"Praise the Lord," said Henry as he watched the fragments fall to the ground. Those that landed on the tiers sounded like tiny bells. "They almost had you there, Badger."

"That only counts with high-yield explosives," projected Badger. "Speaking of which, I'm out."

"Same here," Henry remarked, firing a couple more blasts at the blackened ground. "We're not bound to do much damage just sitting here."

"Nope," Badger said as he detached his ASP from his belt. "There's only one way to get some more action in."

At that moment, the sounds of rotary blades could be heard in the general direction the gate. The Reach even stopped firing to listen. And then, over the walls came VTOLs by the dozens, their turrets and occupants firing down upon the hostiles. Halo-turrets and Assault Rifles began to rain SEAR all over the buildings and barricades.

Noticing how the VTOLs tore up everything with the turrets, Badger reattached his ASP to his belt. "Actually, I might just sit this one out."

Henry gave Badger an odd look, it was strange to him; Badger was developing a sense of humor. The Chinese and Reach were easily cut down by the VTOLs, but the Militants were a different story. As Henry observed, the Militants' armor could resist more damage then the others and also gave greater performance.

The remaining Reach soldiers began to retreat for the main installation, running backwards in an attempt to inflict as much damage as they could on their lethal pursuers. Several of them were cut down before they reached the main building. As soon as they were inside, the two and a half scores of remaining hostiles began to rush towards the entrance to the storage room to secure something inside it.

* * *

"Specters," shouted Warren over the radio.

"Colonel?" exclaimed Henry, "You're breaking radio silence."

"It doesn't matter if they intercept now or not," said Warren, his voice was urgent.

"What's so important?" Badger asked.

"We've just received a radio signal from someone. The Reach is trying to retrieve an object from a digging inside the storage room. Get into the main installation now and make sure that they don't get it. Stop them by any means possible."

"I don't know what good that'll do," Henry said, looking up at the ship. "We've got a vessel above us and it may just wipe us all out to get the object."

"Already been informed," said Warren, "The *Traveler* has altered its position to scare it away."

"Hurry," urged Henry, "we'll do our best; just make sure that thing's out of the sky before we make contact."

"Far ahead of you," said Warren.

A rumbling noise in the sky made everyone's head turn to the watch the sky far off the starboard side of the Reach vessel. A dark shape pierced the clouds, the great ISEN flagship bursting through as it beared down on the alien ship.

ISEN ships were generally made with rifle-like designs, but the Traveler's older design was somewhat broader, with the bow looking like two barrels. Actually, the rifle-like design of the ship was very meaningful, situated on both barrel-like apertures were two barrels that used magnetism to fire high-explosive shells. Simply named comet-guns, the weapons had an undetermined range and were strictly prohibited for atmospheric use. The shock waves were also undetermined.

The Specters were already running at full speed towards the main installation, dazzling the eyes of the few Marines that actually noticed them. The Reach ship was already firing upon the *Traveler* with projectile canons of its own, but they were only slowly weakening the flagship's shields. Before the Specters reached the door, they felt the shock wave created by the comet-guns and saw the cracks form in the flexcrete and sandstone.

Whump! Whump!

The shells smacked alien vessel with a tooth-rattling percussion. The Reach had nothing strong enough to withstand such a weapon; the two explosives had knocked the vessel sideways a very noticeable distance. Two humongous holes, spanning nearly four-hundred yards in diameter each, were motivation enough for the Reach to retreat. Fires burned brightly inside the vessel and electrical circuitry sent sparks in every direction. Smoke and a dark blue vapor billowed out of the holes like a great cloud.

"They won't be back for a while," Warren shouted energetically. "Good shot captain."

"I have never missed," said the captain, this was a kind of joke since he'd never had reason to fire them at all before.

The forces on the ground cheered wildly as they saw the Reach vessel run before the flagship. The flagship did not give chase however; it slowed down and hovered above the base. The captain and the colonel both agreed that the hostile ship would prove more useful in fewer pieces.

Chapter 27

"The Object"

Badger and Henry had entered the main installation alone; the interior walls were made of wood and old cement bricks. The floor was made of an exotic looking wood, though they were sure that it was probably something common on Forerunner. Ahead were several doors, three of which were open, one was a staircase leading up and the others were bunkrooms.

"This may take a moment," Henry muttered.

"The storage room is a door that opens to catwalks that leads nearly forty feet down," said Warren, the sound of pounding feet in the background.

"What do they have stored down there?" inquired Henry, kicking a door open.

"Specimens, food, weapons and heavy equipment," said Warren.

Badger used the palm of his right forepaw to break a door open. *Not this one,* he thought. "Where do you think we'll find the object," he projected as he moved onto another door.

"Our mysterious informant places it directly opposite the entrance, behind a large door. The door's bolted, but I guess that there must be some way to enter. There are also four mole-worms guarding the door, those may be your main concern."

"Found it," Badger projected, he was pointing with his ASP into an open doorway.

"Four worms and about fifty aliens that have armor that can resist anything but a direct hit," said Henry, "I don't think that the worms will be our main concern."

"Our informant is very imperative," said Warren.

"Whatever you say," remarked Henry as he stepped into the doorway.

The entrance was in the very corner of the catwalk spiral, and neither of the Specters had expected the immensity of the storage room. Henry gave the comment, "you could place a baseball field in here". Wooden and metal crates were stacked high, almost to the ceiling in perfect rows with large pathways between. The crates were marked with various pictures and multi-language manifests. The ceiling lights reflected off the dull, metal walls, illuminating everything.

"You could hide just about anything in here," Badger remarked.

As if to prove this statement, a terref Militant leapt from behind one of the higher crates, holding one of the energy swords. The terref viciously kicked Henry to the side, tackled Badger, stabbing the weapon at Badger's chest.

Badger watched in dumb fascination as the blade only pierced his armor a short way with each location of impact. And then, the terref stabbed it downward and held it, pressing it hard so that it started to sink in slowly. Badger quickly regained his senses and counteracted the beast's attack.

The terref fell onto its side when Badger used its own weight against it. But, before Badger could scramble to his feet, Henry had already shot two bursts of energy into its body. The second one had been unnecessary, the first one killed it.

Henry took the weapon from the dead alien and examined the purple blade. The energy seemed to move, in several areas it swirled about as bright energy met darker. He squeezed the rod and the blade vanished with a low hum. "I think I'll take this."

Henry attached the rod to his holster, next to the Tactical Rifle.

"And I think I'll take this," projected Badger, yanking a Sticker from the beast's thigh. It weighed almost nothing to him and his paw could curl around the handle in the slot. He removed the spikes that he deemed were the ammunition; they were stuck together around the alien's waist like a belt and it almost wrapped about his waist three times.

"Looks a little big for you," Henry remarked, noting that Badger was probably just a head taller than the Sticker.

"Weighs nothing," said Badger. He suddenly twisted around when he heard a sound further along the catwalk, he twitched his ears cautiously. "We need backup."

"You have it then," said Warren. "I'm sending four platoons of PDCTs into the storage room now."

"Overkill," said Henry.

"No chances," said Warren, "I want you two alive; I've a couple of missions of the highest priority. And those PDCTs don't include the survivors that'll be helping you too."

"We're going to suffocate," muttered Henry.

The Specters moved at a hurried, yet cautious pace along the catwalk. Badger could both hear and feel the aliens, they were everywhere, but he didn't know the exact locations. He felt certain they were on the crates, but they never gave away their position by anything but breathing. It made him shiver.

And then he heard it, an almost indistinguishable clinking sound. Anyone with ears that were less sensitive wouldn't have been able to distinguish it. It was from behind, getting closer with ever step. Badger raised the Sticker and whispered to Henry, "turn and fire."

Henry whipped around and fired the energy shotgun full into the chest of a tri-jaw beast. The beast dropped its Assault Rifle and clenched at its chest, feeling the hot burns. Henry raised the weapons angle and fired another blast into its face. It fell backwards with a cry and began to writhe on the floor, grasping its ruined face.

Almost instantaneously, others began dropping from the crates above and leaping up from below. In just a few moments, the Specters were pressed between two groups of the aliens, neither of which were attacking, they only held their ground, yelling and gesturing menacingly at the Specters.

"You two have done it again," Warren complained, "REPEL's best operatives."

"Old habits are hard to break," Henry shrugged.

"Lucky for you they think you're the only ones."

"Even if we were the only ones coming in here," began Henry, "they still wouldn't have a chance."

To emphasize this, Badger squeezed the handle and three spikes pierced the face of a terref who was in the middle of a screech. The terref grabbed at its face, changing its screech to one of pain. The other Militants tried hold him still to remove the spikes, but there wasn't time. Three militants were killed by the explosion.

Henry began to fire the energy shotgun and the aliens began to return fire.

"We may have to leave this party," said Henry, a splinter glancing off his screen.

"You first," said Badger, "I'll cover you."

Henry fired twice more and then leapt over the railing. He landed upon a terref that was standing below, snapping its neck with the collision.

Badger followed suit after emptying the caddie. "I believe we've got their attention."

"All the better for the others," said Henry, a smile on his face.

The Militants were taken completely off guard by the PDCT units and Marines that came flooding along the catwalk. Sergeant Alexander and his group led the charge. The Militants fell before the brutal onslaught, their disadvantage cost them dearly. They could expect no mercy.

A deep rumbling noise to their right caused the Specters to turn and step back a pace. A mole-worm in white armor began to approach them, its inward rumble increasing to a haunting note. Then another such noise came from behind the Specters. Another one was starting to flank them.

Henry grabbed the rod and handed it out to Badger, "I'll trade you."

Wordlessly, Badger took the rod and handed over the Sticker and ammo after inserting more spikes; the slots actually sucked the spikes into place. *The brain and heart are in the head,* he remembered. He activated the blade, coiled his legs and then sprang forward. He brought the blade up, stabbing it upwards until it stuck out of the armor on its head.

Badger withdrew the blade and leapt off. The worm fell forward with a gurgle, one of its spades propping up an arm. He turned around just in time to see the spikes explode diagonally across the other worm's body, right to the head. The worm's armor was just blackened, but the flesh was torn up. It let out a growl and charged.

Badger coiled his legs and lunged again. But this worm had a tactic; it pulled its body into the confines of the armor. Badger's weapon merely slid across the armor's surface, creating a bright red line. *This one's got more brains,* Badger thought. A noise to his left made him whip about and drive the blade into neck of a terref, it fell backwards without a sound.

Another terref appeared from the shadows, an identical blade clenched in its thick hand. "Demaw, fei!"

Badger leapt over the alien's slashing attack and swung his own blade in a downward curve. The terref's arm and blade fell to the ground; in turn, it fell to its knees and stared into Badger's eyes with cold remorse. With a single kick to the side of the head, Badger rendered the alien unconscious.

Henry had reloaded the Sticker and fired another barrage at the worm, which was now circling him, searching for a weakness. When the spikes exploded, Henry leapt over the worm as it lunged at him. Looking at the blacked flesh of the worm's face, he remarked, "What's it take to kill you?"

Badger had pried the unconscious alien's blade from its severed limb and held it in his other paw. He sidestepped until he was looking at the worm's plated back-armor. He sprung again at the worm, driving both blades up into its head. This time he actually cut through the helmet and went flying forward.

"That's two," Henry exclaimed as he drove the caddie of spikes into the face of a human. These spikes were designed like the crystals. Luckily, the spikes remained in the caddie when he withdrew them from the dead soldier. "Wish I knew what these things are called."

Badger withdrew his swords from a wooden crate that he had collided into and kicked dirt over the fire he had made. *I don't go flying about like this with my kukri,* he thought. He whirled about, slashing one blade across the chest of a terref and driving the other one through its midsection.

The Reach were losing against the overwhelming forces. PDCT units were all over the place, killing every Militant that stood. The aliens refused to be taken prisoner and fought to certain death. A few Marines had been killed, but they had made all the difference. The battle would be finished in less time than it started.

PDCT Corporal, Kruger had found himself forced to get onto the crates to get a clear view of the battle; his Liner was cocked and ready to deliver. The bullets punched through the armor of two Militants trying to sneak between the crates. He swiveled his view to find another target. A mole-worm in white armor that reminded him about the gray one in New Kunlun Shan; he didn't like this one either.

The worm was standing in front of a huge, bolted door, looking about, listening to the sounds of battle. A well-placed sabot-round just below the helmet practically disintegrated its head. It fell with a rumble.

Another round was already in the impulse chamber as Kruger searched for another hostile. But one had already found him. Kruger was shocked when a long, strong arm curled around his neck and a purple blade was projected right against his chin. Kruger barely had time for a gasp before the three-jawed beast twisted him around and drove the blade up through his chin and into his brain.

The beast deactivated the blade and lifted Kruger up by the throat. The black man's hands fell limply from the beast's forearm and his head fell back. The beast threw the PDCT off to the side and looked about the field. It blinked its bright blue eyes as it saw the others dieing. It looked to the door, looked back at the Marines and then activated the blade. With a soft hiss, the reptile fell forward off the crates, its sword thrust through its own gut.

The last worm had been killed by a sword piercing its heart. Badger deactivated the other sword, when he heard the last echoing shots of battle die away. It was all over now.

* * *

A rather dirty, grass-stained Marine who had been on Forerunner for nearly twenty years since he had enlisted, set a charge on the metal bolt that locked the door. He activated the electronic adhesives and pressed a variety of buttons and then pulled back a little bolt. He had everyone stand back a safe distance while he took a remote detonator from a pouch at his side and pressed the button.

The bolt slammed forward and the charges exploded in the Marine's intentional pattern. The way the charges exploded caused the bolt to break apart in three pieces. The door fell down onto the floor, exposing a long, winding tunnel.

"You, Specters," said Sergeant Alexander, looking at Badger and Henry, "you go first."

The companions obeyed wordlessly, moving swiftly down the tunnel. The tunnel was braced with large metal bars, mostly titanium and red lights were attached to each one. The tunnel just kept going, spiraling downwards, it almost seemed as though it continued forever.

And then, around one more bend, they found themselves in a structure, a metal hall of an unknown architecture. Every dimension of the hall was a work of art. It had an odd sort of brassy-orange color to it and seemed as though it had just been made. There was not a scratch on it anywhere. Shapes and figures graced the walls, depicting a story in such a way that, if they took the time, they would easily understand.

The hall led on straight, at a downward angle; ahead they could see a light. A shimmering blue light that rippled and pulsed. When they reached the end of the hall, they found themselves in a room. It was shaped like a cylinder from the floor to the ceiling; the ceiling was dome-like with a large hole in its center, from which crude stone could be seen.

The walls were made of the same alloy as the hall, only here they sensed intelligence; the Specters could feel it. The room was abuzz with information and memory. Lights flew in the air, moving about as phantoms, lighting the entire room. Badger watched one wearily as it stopped in front of him and transformed into his likeness, stripped of armor, and then moved off to join the others.

The floor of the room dipped in the center, where a gray ring in the architecture hummed melodiously. In the center of the ring was holographic panel, a blue circle rimmed with red. But the Specters' attention was taken away from these things when they realized what was scattered about the floor; countless dead bodies.

Reach, Chinese and ragged looking people that they had used to excavate the room. Upon being informed that they wouldn't be able to deliver the object directly to the ship, the Reach and Chinese had set about killing the workers and then killing themselves so that they wouldn't be taken prisoner. This had happened just prior to the Specters reaching the room; they had not been able to activate the panel.

"Lovely," said Henry, bending over the limp form of a woman who had a cauterized wound across her back. He took off his helmet and let his head fall into his hands. "These monsters, if I get the chance…"

"You will," said Warren, "and very soon. But first, I need one of you to activate the panel. And put your helmet back on, I'd like to watch."

"Sorry," Henry said into the helmet's sender. He put it back on and noticed that Badger was already at the panel.

Badger watched as the panel lowered itself to his shoulder height; this was incredible. He put out a paw and touched the hologram's center and was shocked to find out it was solid.

With a sigh, like that of someone who's been asleep for a long time, the ring, spanning nearly one hundred feet in diameter, rose out of the ground. All eyes in the room watched as it rose higher and higher. The inner rim of the ring was a bright viridian that grew in intensity until there was a straight beam from the roof to the floor where Badger stood. The ring continued to rise until it had reached the middle point of the room and then it continued to hover there, as if waiting for something.

"Now what?" a Marine asked.

There was a sudden hum and then the phantom lights dropped onto the floor and conformed into a single point of light that began to take on shape. The Soldiers had to cover their faces from the bright light; one of the Marines commented that he could see the bones in his hand. After a moment the light passed away and everyone uncovered their faces.

There before them was an odd creature, standing erect on two legs with two arms and wearing some sort of formfitting clothing made of constantly moving lines. The creature seemed to be made of a strange, silvery gold, with purple pentagons moving across its smooth features. It had a head somewhere between a ferret and a ocelot with large, green eyes that were surrounded by amethyst lakes, tiny sparkles of light flashed like stars in those eyes, and it had five long tails that seemed more like lethal blades.

"Stay back," said Alexander, fixing his sights upon the creature.

It looked about for a moment and then its eyes changed to blue with sideways ovals in them, they glistened like pure pools of liquid sapphires. It addressed Alexander in a melodious, silky voice. "First Sergeant Alexander McClain, pleasure to meet you, your data is most interesting. I was not aware that things fallen into such a state of decline since the Great Schism."

"How do you know my name?" asked Alexander, lowering his weapon, but still keeping a wary eye upon the creature.

"Martyr Abel translates all enciphers," said the creature holding up a finger. He then walked in a hunched over way to Rookie.

Rookie leaned back as the creature, standing almost as tall as he did, leaned forward keeping its face close to his screen. When the creature spoke, he could see two rows of sharp obsidian-colored teeth. He swallowed hard and raised a hand; he didn't want the creature to read him.

"You are different to read," said the creature and then he added with a whisper only Rookie could hear, "Worry not, sir, for secrets are always safe with me."

"Get away from him," Alexander commanded.

The creature backed away, shifting its weight heavily from side to side. It looked back at the sergeant and smiled. "I mean no harm, for it seems customs are very different these days."

"Who are you?" asked Henry, trying to be friendly.

"Did I not say?" the creature asked, cocking its head. "I am Martyr Abel, the custodian and caretaker of Sixth Entity. The ring, this chamber, have been my home for uncountable ages, it is good to be awakened. Awakened by… you?"

The creature pointed a long, pointed finger at Badger. It dropped to all fours, and rushed up to Badger, using its tail to touch him and looked him all over. It leaned it head closer and sniffed, it smiled, seeming to enjoy the smell.

"What are you doing?" Henry demanded, raising the barrel of his rifle a little.

"Oh… nothing," said Martyr Abel, "I'm just fascinated by him, what would you say he is?"

"A Genetic Modular," said Henry, "the best known."

"Ah," Martyr Abel said, he purred secretively and stood up to his full height. "How could I have missed that core of data? Badger, my, what a charming name."

Badger didn't know what to do when the creature curled its tails underneath his helmet and slid it softly across the armor, leaving behind almost microscopic scratches. He watched as Martyr Abel turned around and stepped under the ring.

"So you have been sent to retrieve Sixth Entity? How pleasant, much better than what these Reach of Tyranny fools were attempting. I would have killed them all, if only it weren't against my nature."

"You're not one of the Reach of Nimrod?" asked Henry, stepping forward.

"Of course not," said Martyr Abel, "Nimrod, a god? Don't make me laugh. He was a tyrant, what he said we all followed. Forgive me, but it's wonderful to see him not here."

"Wasn't Nimrod a hunter?" inquired John, hefting his rifle and chuckling. "Kruger likes to be called Nimrod, he fancies himself a great hunter."

"Hunter: one who hunts," Martyr Abel translated, "one that seeks prey, one that captures, one that subdues, one who rules through fear. That is your mighty hunter."

John was taken aback. He lowered his rifle and looked about awkwardly. "Well looks like I'm gonna have to inform Kruger…"

"That should be past tense," said Martyr Abel, "I am very sorry but your friend, I detect by the sergeant's data, is dead. Please accept my most sincere condolences."

John almost collapsed. He looked at Alexander, who looked back at him and nodded sadly; he raised a hand, dangling from it was Kruger's dog-tags. John fell upon his knees silently and looked at the floor. Everyone around him moved away to give him room to mourn.

"Would you mind not listening to our data?" Alexander shouted at Martyr Abel.

"Forgive me," said Martyr Abel, closing his eyes and taking a deep breath. "I shall remain silent until you have this thing removed from here."

"Good," said Alexander, beckoning Rookie over to his side. He spoke briefly with him. "Don't say anything to John for a while, he and Kruger were very close; I'm not sure what reaction this will cause, but be prepared."

"Specters," said Warren, doing a bad job of hiding the amazement in his voice. "Get to the *Traveler*, you have a new mission; we've located the Reach ship in a place called whisper valley. Leave Martyr Abel and the ring to us. You'll need all the rest you can get."

"Roger that," said Henry. He turned to Badger and patted him between the ears. "Com'on boy, let's get some food and rest. We can leave this weirdness to the others."

Chapter 28

Moonlighting

Warren was glad that the Specters were finally able to get some proper sleep; they would be moving out in a few hours. He surveyed the reddening sky; the sun was starting to set. He then turned his attention back to the problem at hand. The base had been mostly cleaned up of the bodies while several military engineers were applying the last of the explosives to open the ceiling of the underground structure.

Several VTOLs hovered nearby with cables and hooks to pull up the ring. The base was abuzz with military activity; lights and machines were up and running and vehicles moved supplies to and from VTOL landing-zones. Warren was curious as to where the whale-like craft was; it was nowhere in sight.

"Sir," said a Marine, getting Warren's attention by tapping him on the shoulder. "We are ready to blow the ceiling."

"Good," said the Hispanic as Sarah clung to his right arm. "I've wanted to watch a big explosion for a long while."

"Blow it," said Warren.

The explosions went off like sonic waves directly into the ground, sending low tremors about in a small radius. Dirt and sod were blown high into the air and a large funnel began to form, pouring dirt into the unknown structure, almost sucking one of the small buildings in with it. Within moments, an extremely deep, crater had been formed above the lit room.

The VTOLs flew in low over the hole and soldiers began to rappel down the cables to the ring. Several moments went by and then the VTOLs got the signal to lift; a green flare. The soldiers stopped their work to watch the VTOLs lift the object out of the crater. Dirt fell off as it drifted up with the cables; the odd caretaker was suspended in the center of the ring, remaining silent. Soldiers stared at the ring, glowing with a bluish radiance. The VTOLs raised the cables and piloted the ring into one of the *Traveler*'s hangars and then lowered it down onto the middle of the deck.

Captain Khan and several PDCTs watched as the soldiers that had attached the cables undid the hooks and leapt off. The VTOLs pulled the cables in the rest of the way as the ring made a loud *bang* on the metal deck.

The captain watched as the caretaker looked about and then stepped out of the ring. Khan nodded in satisfaction at the work, trying not to show much astonishment at the two amazing factions. He turned to a warrant officer that was staring open-mouthed at the creature.

"Warrant officer," called Khan.

The warrant officer jumped to attention and saluted the captain. "Yes sir?"

"Bring me one of the ones they call Militants."

"It will be done sir," said the soldier, walking swiftly away.

"We'll see if he'll know anything about this," said Khan, taking a bullet-propelling pistol from his pocket. He then turned to the creature, which was sliding its claws upon the ring's surface.

The Militant the soldier brought back, with an escort of eight Marines, was a terref, very bedraggled with singed fur all over his body. His armor had been confiscated and his undergarments were very impractical. He fell to his knees when he was brought in front of the captain and lowered his head until it almost touched the deck.

"Kill me," the terref pleaded, "end my shame."

"Your English is very good," said Khan.

The terref made no reply.

"I assume you know about this ring," said Khan, slowly walking around the terref.

"It would do you no good to know," said the terref, tucking his tail in between his legs.

"I'll be the judge of that," said Khan, placing a cold hand onto the terref's neck. It shuddered. "Perhaps I can end your shame."

"Then kill me."

"In a less brutal fashion," Khan added.

"Then my soul goes to oblivion." The terref actually had tears rolling down his muzzle.

Khan stepped up next to the ring; the light began to swirl about his feet like fog. "Just tell me about this object and I'll consider ending your shame."

"You're lying," said the terref, looking directly at the captain's back, body shaking with both anger and grief. "You ISEN haven't the respect to fulfill such a desire."

"How much respect does it take to kill a pitiful wretch like you?" Khan demanded loudly.

The terref looked back down at the ground and became silent.

Khan turned around, knelt in front of the terref and forced his chin up so they were looking eye-to-eye. "You listen and you listen well, you and your buddies have murdered uncountable innocent people on this planet. You know this, don't you? That's why you are quiet; just tell me about this object. What is it?"

The terref turned his watery eyes to the ring and the caretaker and then closed them tightly. After a moment of silence, he began to sing a rather ominous dirge. The words, being translated into English, lost something in the translation.

Petals of black,

Remains and Ashes,

Falling from the skies,

The heavens erupting far above,

No passing of night into day,

Demons walked the upon her,

Tearing the darkness with darker light,

Falling as rocks from oblivion,

The demons led the weak onto her shore,

Moon was not to rise,

Not for all the grieving tears of blood,

Eyes of the storm,

Cold as the night,

Creating hate to bring forth the horrible dawn,

Left abandoned she perished,

We are left with a few choices in our grasp,

Do we know if the end draws near,

Do we have what it takes,

Searching our whole lives,

For a trace of forgotten glory,

Do we know what we are searching for?

Khan sighed and let the terref's head drop. "This is useless; take him back to his cell."

Khan stood up and began to walk off. The Marines were about to pull the terref up to his feet, when he yelled aloud, "it is a key."

"Leave him," Khan commanded swiftly. He stepped back over to the terref, kneeling again. "Please continue."

"I only follow orders," the terref said, trying to keep his eyes focused on Khan.

"Of course you do," Khan said reassuringly.

The terref began to sob, but kept a firm voice. "The song is both a lie and truth. The ring is one of twelve keys to open the Gate. Do not ask where the Gate is, no one but the Emperor and the hierarchs know. We are their instruments of reconciliation and justice; we obey, or die, thrust into oblivion."

"Do you know how to work the ring?" Khan inquired.

The terref lowered his head and heaved a sob. "I am but a lowly servant, I cannot even ask how."

"Do you know of anything that the ring can do?" asked Khan.

"I am broken of my brothers; my soul is but a whisper." The terref lowered his head until his nose touched the deck. "It is not known what true power and knowledge is possessed inside these artifacts, each one is different; I cannot tell you more."

Khan patted the bedraggled alien on the head and signaled the Marines to take him back. "Make sure he is kept separate from the others and give him something to eat."

"I shall not touch it," said the terref, standing to his feet.

"You'll have it anyway," said Khan, walking away to the edge of the hangar. He wasn't quite sure what to think of the alien, but a feeling of sadness loomed inside of him.

"I believe he hates his old connections," said Martyr Abel.

Khan jumped when he saw the creature standing next to him. He looked the strange caretaker over for a moment and then looked at the ring. He spoke in a stammer. "Do you know what else the ring does?"

Martyr Abel nodded, looking back at the ring, he chuckled. The blue radiance about the ring started to shift and conform until it was a gigantic globe of uncountable dots.

"In particular," said Martyr Abel, the dots began to conform into a single dot, which grew and shifted, becoming the Milky Way galaxy. The galaxy conformed again until it showed a planet, Forerunner. All over the planet's surface were the Reach of Nimrod ships, ISEN traitors and the cities, even aircraft could be seen. The globe was as large in circumference as the ring.

Everyone stared in absolute silence as the globe slowly rotated.

"What is it?" asked Khan, clasping his hands behind his back.

"An Echo Map," said Martyr Abel, "Everywhere you look is as it is now."

"How does it do that?" asked Khan, reaching out a hand and thrusting it into the hologram. "How far is its range?"

"Slip matter," Martyr Abel replied, "that which is between time and dark matter. Its range is to the end of the universe, it will show all the planets, habitable and otherwise. Use it as you like, destroy the Gate, make Nimrod's work a failure."

Khan nodded and laid a hand on the creature's shoulder. "Will do, sir, will do."

Martyr Abel took a deep breath and smiled, hissing through his teeth. "All his work shall be waste."

* * *

A PDCT's funeral wasn't very fancy, but it was considered to be among the most honoring. Armor cleaned and polished, a flag and ASP put into his hands, the PDCT would be laid inside the ship's engine and then was instantly atomized by high frequency radiation. Kruger's funeral had been held several hours after the base had been taken, the captain said the traditional burial prayer and then Kruger had been atomized.

The rest of Delta Hunter watched through the transparent-iron window at the empty place where Kruger had been. Each one was dressed in a green and blue, semi-armor, ceremonial uniform. PDCT ceremonial uniforms didn't come with hats, but each one wore his own helmet as a symbol of their duty.

John, who was the most crushed by the man's death, quietly whispered over and over again the prayer said by the captain.

"Death not so sweet for the living

In his left hand his country's flag ever still waving

Well they know him as all who serve should be

Brave to the end, all foes tremble before your grave

Those he loved he did save

Rest ever more at heaven's gate

Speak to the one who controlled your fate

Amen."

John pulled off his helmet and wiped the back of his hand across his nose, sniffing mournfully.

Alexander placed a hand about John's shoulders and patted him kindly. Alexander sighed sadly, he only had two remaining soldiers in his squad and he couldn't afford to lose them.

Rookie stayed back several feet from Alexander and John, they had been standing there for hours. Rookie, though he was tired of standing, dared not voice a request, for fear of triggering some sort of wrath. He too missed Kruger, he had been competitive, confident and the biggest thing out there, but these two had been with him the longest. Rookie instead worked with a datapad, an older kind with a second-dimensional screen.

He was suddenly caught off guard when a voice sounded over his radio.

"Ubyehgl aoh aowaoak, Ackory Jace? Ubyehgl aoh aowaoak, Ackory Jace?"

Rookie tried to keep his voice to a whisper, but it was hard because of all the excitement building up inside him.

"Ackory Jace s'ubehyebe," he said excitedly.

"Ackory Jace," replied the voice, sounding equally excited. "S'ersrsuwye aoh weg uweaocaoglez uhwyewaote."

A new voice came over the link. "Ackory Jace? Ubyehgl ueaog eaobzebz aowaoak? Ubyehgl rsao ehglyeh weg aowaoak?"

"Nockta-nockta," returned Rookie, looking about cautiously.

"Errsyegl?"

"Nyi," Rookie stated.

"Ewaogaor?" the voice persisted.

"Ehrset ewaogaor," Rookie sighed.

"Ehyeweaocuhjweg?"

"Ewaogaor," Rookie hissed pleasurably, trying to keep unnoticed.

"byeaorsclyeh yeaop. Shrone."

"Shrone!"

The link was disconnected and Rookie shut off his datapad and placed it into his pocket. As if it was their cue, John and Alexander turned around and signaled for Rookie to follow.

"Come on, Rookie," said Alexander, "I was just sent a wave saying we're going to be heading out with some Specters again tonight. We'd better get some rest."

"Okay," said Rookie, catching himself before accidentally speaking in a different language. He followed the other two out of the engine room; he managed to keep his excitement under control by remembering the funeral. He almost felt invincible now. Mainly youthful stupidity.

Chapter 29

"Whisper Valley"

The foreign moon was part way hidden behind a dark cloud and large bats flitted about to snatch insects out of the air. A wind picked up, blowing through the trees in the valley, the rock formations in the valley caused the wind to sound like a thousand whispers, thus the name. The wind was so strong and blew so often that every tree in the valley was knurled and twisted by its continuous force. This wind masked the ISEN VTOL's approach; the Cod was a thin craft, capable of holding only six soldiers, with no doors, allowing easy access and exit. It landed in a small clearing near the valley's surrounding cliffs.

Henry, Badger, Alexander, Rookie, John and a Marine sniper named Pedro leapt out of the VTOL. Henry signaled the pilot to leave, the single Halo-turret bobbed as the pilot nodded and then lifted off. Henry watched it until it disappeared over the edge of the valley, he lifted his Disputer, a compact weapon with a curled handle, forward horizontal grip and duel barrels; a shotgun underneath and a rifle on top.

On the way there, Pedro had informed them about the Reach's soldiers and their racial systems. Spriks were thrust to the back of the order, for no known reason other than being small, they wore the fans that theoretically enhanced the armor of the other soldiers, but there were other varieties of fans that performed other duties, the golden ones were suicide soldiers called Sporadics. Terrefs were designated as amphibious scouts and special forces, apparently trained for speed and precision to terrify enemies with screams and light-shows or kill from the shadows. The three-jawed beasts (called mights, simply because of their strength) main purpose in a battlefield was heavy-lifting and breaking-down barriers. Humans were given a tactical advantage, the spikes on their backs were all weapons, each one for a different purpose, and they could act as armories in the midst of battle. There were a couple other creatures from Settlement artwork that had not been spotted yet by the *Traveler*'s crew and forces, a near-feline race called cattran (derived from: cast and transpose) and a hulking race called orig (original) that were part of the invading forces. The cattran were said to do more aquatic and zero-gravity combat than land battles, but also seemed to work with construction. The orig were used for vehicular combat, but, when on the ground, were as terrifying as mad dogs. The Reach also used non-armored soldiers for light warfare, but these were rare do to the fact the Reach enjoyed fighting in the open for some sort of glory. Their ranking system seemed to be based upon how many they managed to kill. The lowest rank was a Lesser with yellow grotesque lights, on its face-like helmet. Next were the Confessors with silver stripe lights on a smoother helmet. Sages came next with green scowling lights, these were able to lead small groups of soldiers. The Militants with their tusked helmets and teal light with the ability to lead large forces into battle with extreme prejudice. Than two others that had not been seen yet, Elites with a white helmet that was adorned by glowing viridian symbols, they could control an entire ship. Finally there were the Grand Marshals, the rarest on the battlefield, with three purple symbols upon their golden, four-horned helmets; they commanded entire fleets. Some of the Reach were called honored and could utilize a variety of specialized weapons and equipment, such as the energy shields, crystal blades, or the gravity-controlling gauntlets. Than there were the Berserkers, the leather-masked soldiers that had attacked so insanely at the base. They had only three ranks, each one based on an intelligence through drug use system. The mouth masks were the sign of the Springers, deadly savages that would kill everything in their path, including their own. Those with a mask that covered the mouth and nose with the relief of eyes were Butchers; they were somewhat more controlled, venting their mindless wrath upon only the enemy. The mask that looked like a wildcat identified the Hoods, who utilized tactics and intelligent assault coordination in a combat situation. Every Berserker was given a drug that was instilled within the mask and was activated when it detected the hot breath of the user.

Pedro also told them about the Reach aircraft. The ones with the three extremities that could be used as legs were called Stalkers, usually flown by orig or sprik Sages. The teardrop-shaped craft were Seeps, used for troop deployment but were also deadly bombers and maneuverable fast-attack craft. The fighters with the egg-shaped chassis enclosed in the three prongs were called Skates, another troop deploying aircraft, but much faster and more maneuverable, with a high rate of energy fire. He didn't have much knowledge of anything else of the Reach, but he felt certain that this would be enough for the moment.

Due to the needed severity of the mission, the six soldiers had to have silencers attached to their weapons. These were specially engineered silencers that would leave the accuracy the same, probably even increased a little. Henry's silencer was specifically built for the Disputer, fitting over both barrels at the same time; also designed for Henry's SEAR loads.

Pedro knew the valley more than most others, having lived there for almost twenty years before the coming of the Reach. His knowledge of area was almost unsurpassed; he was the most logical choice to guide them through the area. The silencer for his rifle was different; the tip had a large integrated compensator.

The whispering wind seemed to be saying something and the sound of nocturnal creatures seemed to be answering. Large footsteps could be heard in the surrounding forest, but Pedro assured them that it wasn't anything dangerous.

"Probably just a herd of meuks," he said. Then his face took on an odd expression. "But they're wetland creatures; the Reach must be driving them away."

"Is this a bad sign in any way?" inquired Badger, a meaningful look in his eyes.

Henry had already explained about the neural AI, so no one was surprised.

Pedro nodded solemnly. "Meuks are favorite prey for filoens. Filoens are vicious indigenous creatures, very territorial."

"What do they look like?" asked Henry, as he watched a grove trees where he heard loud footsteps coming closer.

"Black skin," Pedro began, "each has a different pattern of creases on its face, claws like scythes, a huge tail and two tusks on both sides of the mouth. Anything built in this valley had to be made of metal or stone to keep them out. We might be in for some trouble."

"Great," commented Rookie, "we just had to lose Kruger; this would've been his element."

Alexander and John lowered their heads and wordlessly nodded in agreement. They both missed the large black man.

Henry stepped back a pace as a large creature stepped out of the grove, walking steadily towards them. It was completely hairless, save for its large feet, a row of long spikes ran down its back, its head was narrow with a noticeable under-bite and its small eyes seemed to see everything. It had a long tail that was split at the end, probably for grabbing branches that were out of reach. But what was really noticeable about it was the gigantic burn at the base of its neck.

As the creature, a meuk, came closer, everyone but Pedro stepped back further, until they were backed up against the cliff. The meuk stopped in front of Pedro and lowered its head until they both saw eye-to-eye. Pedro reached out a hand and touched the tan skin, the meuk emitted a low bugle and other meuks started to wander out of the trees.

One larger meuk, however, didn't seem to like Pedro touching its mate. It opened its mouth wide and let out a gargling growl. It began to lumber forward towards Pedro, pushing others out of its way.

Badger attached his Assault Rifle to his holster, dropped to all fours and ran at the charging meuk. Badger leapt and collided with the side of the beast's neck. While they had been sleeping, Badger's exoskeleton had had some extra work. The meuk bellowed in pain as it scrambled to keep its footing.

Badger growled menacingly at the now humbled beast. It turned around and walked away, periodically looking back at the small juggernaut. Badger stood back onto his hind legs and walked back to Henry.

"Thanks, dog," said Pedro as he watched the burnt meuk wander after its defeated mate. "That's not natural for them to do."

"What is natural?" inquired Rookie, watching the herd as it grazed in the field. A very small meuk remained by its parent, taking a mouthful of grass and then coughed it out, it was far too dry.

"A child could walk between one's legs and it would stand still," said Pedro, cautiously watching the herd. "We domesticated some, but those are dead now, I think. I doubt the Reach care about our work."

"Taste any good?" Henry asked as he started walking in the general direction of the valley's center with Badger at his side.

The others quickly followed, walking through the weary herd. The meuks gave them a wide berth. The animal's eyes all watched the group, suspiciously, waiting to see what they might do.

"Tastes very good," said Pedro, smiling broadly. "But it is not just their meat, their milk also is excellent."

Rookie tripped over a rock as he thought that over.

With the bright moon overhead, none of the soldiers had to use their night vision. Badger's natural night-vision allowed him to see about everything in front of him. He remained close to Henry; every inch of himself was alert, his ears twitched and he periodically sniffed the air. Every time a bush rustled he would turn and watch it until he was sure it wasn't a threat.

Odd creatures moved through the branches of the trees and crows cawed in the distance, calling others to a dead corpse they had found. Strange eyes glittered in the moonlight, seeking prey and the sight of the soldiers was promising. Small, nocturnal rodents scurried for cover before the soldiers' approach, ducking into burrows, or underneath rocks. Flowered moss clung to the trees, the tiny white flowers feeding upon the moonlight. Tiny creeks flowed from the tops of the cliffs, rushing along the ground towards the valley's central wetlands, where they had concluded was the ship's position.

"I hope we find this ship soon," muttered Rookie, watching a pair of glittering eyes disappear behind a tree.

A swarm of the floating jellyfish weaved through the overhead branches of a tree. Badger watched them carefully, making sure that none were turning purple. They only floated past, looking like hundreds of tiny torches.

"Don't worry about those ones," said Pedro, noticing Badger's expression. "If they land on you, that's different; it may be simple curiosity, but smash them. The Reach's transgenic pods will call in the Core and then you will have difficulty."

"He's killed one already," said Henry, smiling with pride.

"Really?" said Pedro, looking again at Badger. "It would appear there's something more to you than meets the eye. Even they fear their own creations; they thought they could control them, but they failed, now their transgenic pods kill whatever they find. Thankfully, there are not many."

"Why are they called pods?" Badger inquired.

"They are filled with hot gas," said Pedro, "except these new transgenic kind. The gas allows them to be weightless; their umbrellas allow them to move in any direction."

Badger suddenly froze and projected to everyone, "stop! Something's up ahead, use your radios. I'll take the point."

Everyone became silent and crouched low; it was then that they noticed how quiet it had gotten. The only noises were those that were far off in the distance. They pressed their weapons tight against their shoulders as they strained their ears to listen to what was up ahead. Alexander thought that he heard a crashing noise; he couldn't tell exactly where it came from, he would have to wait for the GEM's report.

* * *

Badger parted a bush with his free paw to see what was beyond it. There were just more trees, but there was a distinct, flickering light ahead and the sound of voices. His sure, silent step soon got him to the edge of the timberline, looking out at a small clearing. It was the Reach; they were working on a windmill.

The windmill's fan was shaped like a twisted horseshoe with a center post running through its and with a resilient-fabric net stretching form the twisted horseshoe to the center post. The windmill sat like a mast atop a metal and stone structure with a blue eagle-and-star symbol (ISEN's symbol) set above a dented, steel door. Nearly half a score of spricks and other soldiers, headed by a human Militant, stood outside the structure.

A large alien with a wedge-shaped head on thick stooped neck, an orig, was menacing a woman and her two young children, with a large weapon, while the woman's husband seemed to be forced to work with a sprik that had a fan of jagged blades. Standing near the two workers was a terref, a short, stocky being that gave glances and growls at the orig, as if he didn't like what he was doing.

Two spriks with fans of hooks were linking into the windmill's power storage with special gloves, sucking out the continuous energy and transferring it through the air with their fans to the ship. They just stood there, talking in their odd language; they even seemed to laugh on occasions. The fans had power jumping between them with powerful snapping noises.

Badger had seen enough. He projected into the radio, "there are eleven aliens and four civilians; they appear to be using a windmill to send power to the ship. The ship is out of sight, but it should be close by. Come in slowly, I might have missed a guard."

When the others arrived, Alexander whispered and signaled out their priorities. "Pedro, take care of the one menacing the family; Rookie and John, move out a bit and take care those spriks with the... hooks. You, Specters, I would suggest taking care of the rest of the guards, while I get rid of the Militant."

"We'll take that advice," said Henry, then he and Badger vanished into the foliage.

"That kind of special forces always gives me the shivers," muttered Alexander, marveling at how silent they were. "Pedro, should fire first."

Alexander placed his crosshairs on the Militant's chest and then waited for the distraction. He didn't have to wait long. The woman screamed when the orig's head split and it fell at her feet. The militant turned to see what had happened, he he too fell.

The Reach fell quickly while they were distracted by these sudden deaths. The terref Specialist was the last one killed; Pedro's bullet had shot straight through it. The man rushed to the defense of his family, who were practically crying.

"There is no need to be alarmed," reassured Alexander, stepping out of the timberline. "We've been sent here to find a ship."

The man smiled in relief and even laughed a little. He rushed up to the PDCT and shook his hand. "Thank you, thank you! We've been cut off from everyone else for the longest time."

"Were you mistreated in any way?" inquired Alexander, prying the man's hand away.

The woman suddenly fell to her knees and burst into a stronger fit of tears. "Yes," she wailed, "they beat Roger, to find his weapons. They even threatened to harm our children."

Roger took his wife by the hand and lifted her up to her feet. "Never mind that now Kara, take the children inside. Good! Now be sure to lock it."

"I would suggest you go with them," said Alexander, watching the man pick up a wool hat from the ground.

"Not if you knew what I know." Roger placed the hat on his head and took the weapon from the orig's grasp. It was SEAR firing, had a pistol stock and a large blade underneath the barrel. The Sear was placed on a magnetic rail that ran into a slot, just above the barrel.

"And just what do you know?" Badger inquired roughly, he didn't like the man's deliberate tardiness.

The man didn't even look up. "I know you're here for the ship, but from the looks of it, you've got a few days still. Also, I know where a prison facility is, it might be worth quite a lot to ISEN."

"Who's in it?" asked Alexander.

"Scientists," Roger simply said.

"Just?" said Henry.

"There wouldn't be any use in putting civilians into it. We're allowed to live here as long as we obey them. The scientists are kept there and they work. They're being forced to invent new equipment, basing it off of Reach and the Enterprise stuff."

"We're interested," said Warren, speaking so suddenly over the radio that the soldiers almost jumped.

"You've got yourself a deal," said Alexander. "But I think you should remain here."

"Not likely," said the man, stepping back a pace. "My son's in there and I've got something of my own, locked up somewhere safe, a complete record of the Reach."

"Blackmailer," muttered Alexander.

Chapter 30

"Contacted"

Warren was still waiting for the report from Victor, wanting to know the results of the blood re-exams as soon as possible. As he waited, he sipped coffee from a black ceramic cup and watched more news on the war raging throughout the planets.

A satellite image of a RSR (Renewed States of Russia) tank battalion blasting away a Chinese convoy off of a dessert on Grasp was on a holographic console right next the one that was waiting to receive the message. The Russian tanks were distinguished by their well-defined duel-barreled cannon with four halo-turrets on either side. Not known for their subtly, Warren was quite sure that the Russians would play a key part in the battles yet to come. Or perhaps, he feared, they would follow the Chinese's conversion.

Two rapid clicks told him a message had been received. With a smile, he set his cup onto the desk and looked on the computer screen. He was surprised when he saw that it wasn't from Victor; instead it was labeled: Searching for allies of virtuous skill? Underneath it was a strange red symbol.

Warren turned around and spoke to a young Marine that was standing close by.

"Soldier, go fetch the captain and tell him we need to talk."

Chapter 31

"The Containment Facility"

The facility had two floors, the first one had walls of stone and metal to keep filoens from breaking in, the second was made of simple, reinforced wood. The roof was simple, reinforced, insulated aluminum sheeting. The main door was made of thick type-65, a grayish, starship grade metal; it was bolted from behind with a steel bar.

With a snap and a muffled gasp, a Sage orig was dropped to the ground, its head twisted almost all the way around. Two large hands grabbed the orig by the legs and tossed it into a large bush. The attacker was almost invisible, save for an almost indiscernible, huge silhouette. The attacker picked up the orig's weapon and deposited it into a large pack on its back.

The figure peered through the darkness at the facility; he didn't like the Reach ever since they had come and had ruined everything. He and the others liked those that built the whirling antennas that fueled their machines and herded the meuks. He and the others liked helping fuel these strange creatures' machines by purposely flying at night and turning them really fast. These strange creatures had even given them a name: Banshees; he and the others liked the sound. But now the Reach invaded and enslaved them.

The others didn't want those they had come to secretly love to be treated like this, so they retaliated against this atrocity. The Banshees were a curious kind, loving their seclusion in the cold mountains and subterranean halls, but a prophecy foretold that this was all to change someday. The Banshees felt that the time of their secrecy was soon to end with the coming of the Reach.

The Banshee's large eyes absorbed and reflected the lights that hung about the facility. He wanted to break through the wooden portion and free everyone, but the fear of being seen stopped him. He missed flying up to windows and listening to the stories that those inside told, he understood a little of the mixed languages in the valley, but now the Reach had frightened the people.

A noise behind him made the Banshee start up the great cedar. Up in the branches, he did his best to see what it was. Some armored soldiers and a small animal that was used for domestic, or in this case, military purposes, were what caused the noise. The Banshee recognized the unarmored one. He had, more or less, stolen a book from his house several years ago. He lowered his alarm; surely the unarmored one hadn't also joined these horrors.

* * *

Roger had led them carefully through the forest, showing them hidden paths to evade detection equipment. On occasions he would point out rock formations and tell them that there were weapons hidden in them. Eventually, after almost an hour of detours and evasions, they had all arrived on a small rise within sight of the facility. Immediately, they all dropped to their stomachs and crawled forward until they could see everything.

"It's not very big," remarked Rookie.

"How many scientists did you think are in the valley?" asked Pedro.

Rookie fell silent, not sure how to answer that question.

"I smell something dead," Badger alerted the others.

"I'm sure there are a few dead scientists," Roger stammered, not sure who was speaking.

"It's nothing like that," said Badger, "I smell exposed bone and blood. It's not a human."

Roger looked at the soldiers; he was getting a little worried about his situation. "Who's talking?"

"That would be Badger," said Henry, "he's got a good nose."

"And who would that be?" persisted Roger.

"The dog," Henry exclaimed in a loud whisper.

"The dog?" asked Roger, looking at Badger, who was glancing about.

Badger swiveled his head around to look at the man and nodded, "neural technology and a theory."

Roger kept quiet and shivered. Neural technology was an old development, used for fighter pilots and domestic work, but for a GEM to speak, that was a little much.

"Henry?" Badger projected. "Should I find the source?"

"Sic it," said Henry.

Badger moved with silence on all fours, sniffing the air to pinpoint the smell's source. There was another strong smell in the area also, but he figured it was some Forerunner beast. He finally pinpointed the smell to the large bush near the great cedar. When he pulled aside the branches, he was alarmed at the sight of the orig.

"I found it!"

"What is it?" asked Henry.

"An orig," he answered, "Sage."

"Was something eating it?"

Badger let the branches fall back and shook his head. "No, something broke its neck, almost twisted in a full circle."

"Could be a filoen," said Pedro, putting his crosshairs on a solitary PDCT traitor. "I heard they kill their prey and leave it someplace until their hungry." The PDCT had landed in some ferns a couple yards away. The Marine swiveled his view to find another target. "Any tracks?"

Badger looked at the ground, there were some large tracks.

"Enormous ones," he projected.

"Filoen," Pedro remarked, he then pulled the trigger and watched as another lone guard was hidden in the undergrowth. "We'll have to be careful; they're the most dangerous creatures in the valley. The Reach was foolish to drive them from the wetlands."

"Agreed," muttered Roger, watching as yet another guard vanished.

"Do you think they're close by," Rookie asked, looking about worriedly.

Suddenly, there was a scream from the forest far to the right of the soldiers. After a moment, a couple of spriks came running out of the trees, crashing through the undergrowth, handguns held high as they rushed towards the facility. Crashing through the forest after them was an enormous black beast, four tusks, scythe-like claws and thick limbs, exactly as Pedro had described it. The filoen roared as it chased the spriks.

The other guards began to provide cover fire for the spriks. This only made the beast angrier. Within moments it was in the middle of the Reach and Chinese, slashing, smashing and even using its tail to knock its attackers away. The guards screamed in fear as the giant beast flayed about.

In an attempt to aid their comrades, the main door was pulled open and several Lessers and a Militant rushed out. They were going to try to get the others back inside, but they were cut down by the silenced weapons of the covert team. They made sure that the civilian didn't use his weapon, which might have attracted others.

"Go-go," said Alexander. "This could be our only chance."

The soldiers rushed across the open ground as fast as their legs could carry them, Badger and Henry made it first. While the others took care of other guards inside the room, Badger quickly closed and bolted the door by himself.

"I'm glad Kruger's prize was of some use," muttered John, referring to the fileon that Kruger would never be able to hunt, as he eliminated a Militant. Beside him, Roger was using the non-silenced rifle; it was amazingly inaccurate, the aluminum went everywhere.

The other guards outside the small, windowless room closed a second, smaller door and locked it. It had a red ring and eye symbol painted on it. There came shrieks and cries from beyond the door, the Reach were obviously well startled by their appearance.

"That'll do," said Alexander as he took the rifle away from the civilian, who was still pulling the trigger. "Forget shooting something that's bulletproof; leave it up to the battering ram. Badger, don't risk accidentally shooting the scientists, use the Photon Sword."

*   *   *

The Banshee was intrigued by these soldiers that fired weapons that didn't make any noise. This was a different science. The others were trying to duplicate the weapons he and others collected, but it was a long, tedious operation. He never fully understood why they didn't just expose themselves to these strange creatures, that way they could easily recreate these wonders. But he never questioned the point.

Tonight was different somehow, he didn't know if it was the prospect of more weapons, or the silent soldiers. He felt it was more of the small animal, something about him drew him. Whatever it was, he stayed watching, the building, giving the filoen's battle periodic glances. He wanted to deliver the weapons to the others, but he couldn't leave, he was far too curious.

* * *

The metal door resembled a battered crescent, it laid on the ground a few yards from where it had been hinged. Not wanting to break his helmet, Badger had used his shoulder and the Photon Sword, which left a clean cut along the middle of the door. The door had killed a couple Chinese Marines on the other side, crushing in their ribs and skulls.

Badger finished off the last of the soldiers on the first step of the staircase that led to the top floor. He deactivated the purple blade and let the hooded terref fall backwards, stepping aside as the alien slid down to the floor, its head propped up by the last step at an unpleasant angle.

The scientists were contained behind force fields on either side of the room. Each one had a single generator that projected it from the wall-to-wall. They were cheering and beating their fists on the fields; extremely happy for their rescuer. They also called out, saying: "Let us out," or "The generators, destroy them," one even shouted out, "upstairs, you must stop them."

Badger quickly used his Photon Sword to pierce each generator through the top. Sparks flew into the air as the force fields blinked and then shut off completely. The scientists were free; they quickly picked up the weapons of the dead.

"Hoorah for ISEN," shouted one, raising a fist into the air.

"Thank goodness they finely sent you all," said a black lady, reaching out a hand towards the sergeant. "We were beginning to think that the solar system had been captured."

"Earth and Mars are still under multi-nation control," said Alexander, "thanks to these Specters."

Henry blushed behind the screen as the lady practically hugged him. "Er, yeh, thank you… ma'am? I've a job to do."

"Sorry," she exclaimed as she let go of him. Her face suddenly turned pale and she pointed towards the stairs, "up there, you have to stop them. Eric made a weapon, something powerful, their bringing in a convoy to take it back to their ship."

"Eric?" shouted Roger, "my son's up there? What'd 'e build?"

"A laser," the woman said.

Lasers were nothing new, but the way the lady was talking, Eric had made a breakthrough of some kind. The soldiers began to mount the stairs, taking them four at a time, Roger lagged well behind. Upstairs they found, three Militants and nearly a score of Grunts. One of the soldiers was a human, Elite. The white helmet and viridian symbols were even more elegant than they imagined.

In one of the Elite's hands was a large weapon, there was a rise at the front that sported a slanted computer screen displaying various diagnostics and a zoom-in display. The handle was near the front and had a thumbhole, with a curve on the stock to keep it comfortable on the Elite's shoulder. In the Elite's other arm was a young man in a dirty, wool jacket and jeans, pulling at the arm that was about his throat.

"Eric," shouted Roger, trying to dash forward, Rookie and John restrained him.

"I would not attempt such," said the Elite. "I am Yoak Jar, Elite of the *Path of Honor;* I do not wish to kill. Stand there and you may live. Let us take this weak one and his honor and the other to my ship, I give you allowance to go unharmed."

"What other have you got?" asked Henry, keeping his Disputer trained on the Elite.

Yoak Jar made two clicks with his tongue against the roof of his mouth and another Militant came around a corner. The soldiers stepped back in surprise at what the Militant had. The Militant, a might, was holding an ASP to the skull of a struggling terref wearing the tattered rags of what used to be a fine cloth and several tarnished gold rings about her neck. The terref showed spirit as it lashed at its restrainer with its tail and letting out high-pitched barks.

"Who's he?" asked Alexander, looking at the Elite.

"She," the Elite corrected. "She is the daughter of the Shilan emperor; she is leverage to our cause."

"What cause?" demanded Roger, looking despairingly at his son.

"To take what you have robbed us of and all the others to unlock the Gate to the other realm," said the Elite accusingly. "You may have the ring for a while, but we shall take it. Now leave, I don't desire to kill."

"Don't do it," said the young man, "I've heard them, they'll kill millions."

"I don't desire much to kill either," said Henry, stepping forward a couple paces, Badger again at his side. "But it comes with the job and I will not allow you to take any one of your items."

The Elite lowered his head and sighed sadly. "Respected, but this" –he pointed the weapon Henry- "has much more power. Sorry we could not get know each other, but I have tradition to uphold."

Several things happened at once: Badger sprung at the Elite as something large and black burst through a wall, grabbed the Elite and smashed through the other wall; Eric fell to the floor gasping as the laser went off and blew off most of the facility's roof; the female terref finally freed herself from the might's grasp and bit out his throat; Badger collided with a Sage sprik instead of Yoak Jar; then lastly, the Elite's body fell to the floor from the sky, shortly followed by it's severed head. The sprik had not survived the impact. Roger rushed to his son's side as the vengeful female terref began to fight the other Reach while the soldiers quickly eliminated everyone else.

It was hard to tell which shocked everyone the most, the laser's destruction, the female terref, who was equally surprised, or the black creature that had saved them all. The female terref picked up an ASP from a dead body, shot several splinters into the skulls of the dead and wandered over to her rescuers, who were gazing about at the destruction. She wiped the blood from about her mouth and spat out the pieces of unpleasant flesh. The other scientists had come upstairs after the noise had died; they gazed about at the marvelous destruction and much of the wood was even on fire.

Ashes drifted to the ground like hot snow, tiny embers swirled about in the slightest breeze like millions of fireflies. Everything was quiet, save for the heavy breathing of the terref, who was unaccustomed to both blood and killing. She was wearing a blue garment with steely plates on the chest and shoulders with a flap of cloth curved about her waist and draped about her knees. She stood a good head taller then everyone else and was very graceful in her movement.

"Glad to see that she's alright," said the black lady, holding out a hand to the female terref.

"You most kind," returned the terref in a pleasant voice, accepting the hand in a firm grip with her own thick, furry hand. "I did not expect to be rescued."

"Not to appear ignorant of… friendlies, but we didn't know we had any allies," said Alexander.

"Return me to my parents and we can work an agreement," the terref said, tossing the ASP to the side. "Though," she started, "I am most curious… what were that?"

"Was," corrected the black lady, giving the Elite's head a vicious kick, sending it across the room, leaving behind a crimson trail

Henry glanced at what little remained of the roof and most of the walls, save a small portion in the back; it was like they were on a platform. He shuddered at the thought of what the laser might have done to him and the others. He gave the terref a glance and then picked up the laser and handed it over to Eric. "Don't drop it."

Eric managed a smile as he took the weapon. "Don't worry; just have ISEN take it from me, I don't want to build anymore weapons."

"You won't have to," said Roger, "I'm going to try and get you and the rest of the family a trip to Earth."

Rookie had been looking up at the sky; he wiped the hot ashes from his screen. He suddenly noticed a large shadow moving amazingly fast across the sky, it was almost impossible to make out any recognizable details. He pointed it out, though no one noticed, "anyone know what that was?"

"It could've been a Banshee," suggested Eric.

"Don't be ridiculous," scoffed the black lady, "that's just a ridiculous legend."

"No it's not," Eric said firmly, "I saw one once... when it took my father's bible."

"You didn't tell me this," said Roger, giving his son an odd look.

"Would you have believed me?" asked Eric.

Roger nodded. "Yes! I would have."

"A little late now, it's probably read it several times."

"Excuse me for interrupting this family conversation," said Henry, twisting Roger around so they were face-to-face, "The document, please."

Roger reached into a pocket and pulled out a datapad. "Everything I've documented and a program."

"What program?" asked Henry, crouching down to Badger's level so they could both examine the datapad. It was a simple, slip-resistant grip, crystal screen and chip slot.

"Would you all like to know what the aliens are saying?"

Every teammate and scientist stared at Roger.

"How do you mean?" asked Henry.

"I'm not just a wind farmer." Roger pulled out what resembled a small crowbar that had a little purple light on one end. "If you allow me to upload this program on your helmets it will allow you to understand everything they're saying and even decrypt transmissions."

"How'd you make that?" Rookie asked.

"I used to work for the Enterprise's Ninth Section."

Everyone was stunned. The Ninth Section was one of the most top-secret facilities in the international counsel's business. For this man to just say that he worked there was putting him under threat of international law.

"You do realize what you just said?" said Henry, stepping up to the man.

Roger smiled and raised the rod. "You want the program?"

"No one heard a word he said," said Warren.

"Alright," said Henry. He was about to take off his helmet, but Roger stopped him.

Henry watched and Roger pointed the light towards the screen, almost every muscle in his body told him to duck, but he stood still. A beam of purple static shot from the light and hit the screen. The light of the impact point was intense; Henry was forced to close his eyes.

"There, finished."

Henry opened his eyes and looked at his HUD, nothing was damaged. "Are you sure it worked?"

"Absolutely," said Roger, turning towards Alexander.

Henry turned to the female terref. "Can you speak the Reach's language?"

She nodded and said, "Ih."

Henry heard it as "yes", but he didn't know she had spoken it. "Good, so can you say something in it so I can test this out?"

"I did," she said, giving him a look.

"I thought you said yes," said Henry.

"No, I didn't say yes, well, er, yes I did say yes, but I said… ooohh." The female terref covered her muzzle with her hands, feeling very much confused now.

Chapter 32

"A Glitch"

Badger was the last one to have his helmet uploaded with the program. But, unlike the others who had been uploaded, he somehow felt as though there was something different going on inside his helmet. The memory that his suit had absorbed in China may have had something to do with it; he didn't openly express it. Conflicting programs happened occasionally but they eventually reached a compromise; it happened to him once in Nigeria.

In Nigeria he had been hacking and uploading information from a terrorist computer. His helmet's programs and the terrorist's programs weren't cooperating with each other, as a result, his HUD became a little fuzzy and his identification program was malfunctioning with the shimmer. But after a while his own programs had won out over the terrorist's. When they had gotten back to REPEL, Eternal Force, REPEL's integrated AI system, removed the terrorist programs, causing his entire HUD to concoct a virus. Eternal Force then had to infiltrate the helmet himself and reprogram it all.

This conflict would soon go away. He watched as portions of his HUD bent and blinked, but always returned to their original positions. He ignored the malfunctions and reached up, took the datapad from Henry and turned it on. After cycling through various programs and documents, he came across one that read: LOAD DRIVE. He accessed it and the information, interestingly, was projected up from the screen as a hologram.

The soldiers gathered around and viewed the hologram. The scientists and the female terref showed very little interest in the datapad, obviously due to their long exposure to the Reach's cruelty. The hologram displayed pictures with identifying words under them.

The first images were diagrams of Reach weaponry.

DATA RECORDING: 3 MINUTES 23 SECONDS:

(Metaphysics) the Reach of Nimrod generally use self-energized weapons known as meta-physics. Metaphysics is an advanced stage of smart energy polymers that, when shaped properly will fire concentrated bolts of energy. Each weapon is completely solid; when the energy is depleted, the weapon is made useless. The only way to recharge the polymer is to melt down the depleted weapon and then reconstruct it. The Reach of Nimrod has also developed a taste for ISEN aluminum loads, because they can fire many times more projectiles and can be easily reloaded. Their own projectile weapons use the same smart polymer, but are shaped to propel their explosive spikes and crystals. The alloys used in these weapons are unknown due to the fact that these cannot be depleted.

The image changed to show diagrams of odd vehicles, one of which the Specters recognized as the one they saw at the base

(Vehicles) the Reach of Nimrod are not very concerned with the production of vehicles; their factories are capable of building a thousand light reconnaissance vehicles in a single day. Their aircraft are designed to look like sea creatures, having something to do with their religion and are held up by either rotary equipment or anti-gravity devices. These non-conventional aerodynamic designs allow the aircraft to perform immeasurable stunts that could not be achieved with anything Enterprise has ever made. Their ground vehicles are held up by anti-gravity devices and can use a reverse-gravity field that sends them into a rapid boost. For all main aerodynamics and weight purposes, they are well superior to that of Enterprise.

The image changed to show a diagram of a Reach ship.

(Reefs) the Reach of Nimrod's vessels are referred to as Reefs. The insect appearance is believed to be for intimidation, some think that it has more of a religious meaning. Instead of hangars, the Reefs have specially shaped portholes on the outside for the hundreds and, in the cases of the gigantic Divinity-class Reefs, thousands of interstellar and near atmospheric craft they utilize. They use a process of super-fast travel they call Manipulation; it's much faster than wormholes and much safer and more reliable. The Chinese and Reach are trying to combine the two travel forces to achieve faster and much safer routes.

Now the image was that of a mole-worm in four varieties, the gray, gold, white and a purple with one spade and a kind of pliable tubular weapon that ran along its entire arm.

(Kismets) these altered mole-worms are one of the Reach's greatest biological near-robotic soldiers. The grays are called Clout Kismets; they have superior performance-enhancing armor compared to their brothers; there are extremely few of them, as the armor is laborious to make. The gold are called Sluice Kismets; they carry a low yield performance-enhancing armor with swords instead of spades, and are usually employed to clear buildings or to act as guards. Strangely, their armor makes their back spikes grow longer which requires maintenance by clipping the spikes so they won't catch. The whites are Chic Kismets; their white armor is more yielding then the gold; they are more intelligent and able to learn how to eliminate something during the duration of a fight.

The purples, known as Dragon Kismets, are by far the most dangerous of the Reach's near-robotic soldiers. Most of one arm is removed for the purpose of attaching the biometric fire cannon and the other is tipped with three claw-like hooks; they carry no back armor which would only slow them down and their cannons can melt metal and turn bodies to ashes in seconds.

The image changed again to show picture of a large three-jawed reptile, heavily armored in iridescent black armor with a diamond-shaped, split crest on the back of its helmet.

(Zealots) there is only one kind of Zealot, the three-jawed reptiles known as Kul'hura, or Rippers. They appear to be born for the purpose of being forced to grow to twelve feet tall and have a form of BINAN surgery done to increase their molecular density to a state of amazing, natural strength with bones that won't easily break. There is only one per Grand Marshal it seems, and, if the Grand Marshal dies, so do they. Their armor is extremely light, non-enhancing, for their strength is more than sufficient. They carry long Photon Swords, Personal Stickers, and, occasionally, energy shields.

END OF RECORDING: 0 SECONDS.

"There's more on there," said Roger, smiling broadly, "you just have to find a computer that'll get you past all the hidden codes."

"I'd hate to meet a Zealot or a Kismet on a dark night," said Rookie, laughing nervously.

Badger turned off the datapad and handed it back to Henry, who took it and slid it into a pocket. Badger hefted his rifle and looked out at the forest. The smoke made everything appear wavy, in shapes, strange unidentifiable shapes. But then, one became familiar, it was like a terref form. Then he realized the truth… it wasn't smoke.

It was too late for anyone to react, much less call out an alarm. Within moments each one of the soldiers had a Photon Sword held against his throat and the scientist were surrounded by a group of Lessers that had deactivated their void-signatures. Badger was held in the air, a Sage holding him more by the underside of his helmet than his throat, a Photon Sword pricking his protected neck.

The Grand Marshal of the group soon appeared, a Zealot leaping up after him carrying what Roger had documented as a Personal Sticker; it was as big around as an oak trunk and was bristling with the spikes.

"Too bad ISEN warrior," said the Grand Marshal, "but to fight fear you have to face it."

"It was just a statement, you didn't have to bring him," said

Rookie, looking from the Zealot to the sword.

"The clan of Pure Collect, with the aid of a Zealot, was sent here to retrieve an item of extreme value." The Grand Marshal looked about and Badger could hear the faintest suggestion of a chuckle. "We were supposed to meet Yoak Jar, but"- he knelt down and picked up the Elite's head- "it would appear he won't be joining us for the return journey."

"You don't seem all that disappointed," said Henry, calmly pulling at the arm that held the sword against his throat. That was odd, it wasn't the exoskeleton, the Lesser was allowing him to pull away the sword.

"Why should I?" inquired the Grand Marshal, tapping the tip of his tail against the Zealot's leg so it would stop shuffling and miss stepping on it. "My clan is of the Select, only the Select can become the Holy Troops and the Jar clan is not of the Select. Weep for a brother, not an enemy."

"He's on your side," Henry pointed out. He was surprised that he had actually gotten the Lesser's sword to point at the ground.

"Not anymore," said the Grand Marshal. He made a clicking noise and the rest of the clan released the teammates and left off surrounding the others.

"I don't understand," said Henry, looking about at the Reach soldiers.

"I had to keep up appearances in case any of the others were left," said the Grand Marshal. "But, as we figured from our aerial view, everyone else is dead. The Pure Collect has been severed from the Reach; the last cords are now cut. You would have come here for the vessel, would you not?"

Henry pushed past a Lesser and stood in front of the Grand Marshal. "Yes and are you insinuating something?"

"I ask you to say differently, I don't understand that."

"Are you telling us that you're going to help?" Henry said, purposefully making every syllable long.

The Grand Marshal lifted his head in acknowledgment. "If you and your enhanced pet are as efficient as I observed during your skirmish at the base, we cannot fail."

Henry raised a fist in the Grand Marshal's face, causing the Zealot to growl deeply. "You get one thing straight, he is not an enhanced pet, his name is Badger, get it right."

The Grand Marshal backed away and bowed politely. "I meant no offense, but when fighting in the nearby city, we've procured a number of them to send back to our families as pets. Whenever we find one, we catch it, unless its military, then we just eliminate it. A sad pity really, their minds are nothing but tools, weapons."

Badger felt as though his chest had been stabbed. The Grand

Marshal was right; it seemed his only purpose in existence was to fight. He quickly controlled the emotion; he couldn't let it hinder his duty.

"Yeh," said Henry, "but if you so much as have one of your soldiers point a sword at him again I'll kill you."

"It would appear we're going to have some difficulty then."

"What do you mean," Henry demanded.

"Because," said the Grand Marshal, "For us to get you to our ship and take the information you want from it, we have to make you look like captives."

Henry gave the Grand Marshal a strange look. "How do you know our mission?" he demanded.

The teammates looked about at the Holy Troops, not so sure what was happening now. Even some of the Holy Troops acted as if they were confused. Apparently the Grand Marshal was keeping secrets from everyone.

The Grand Marshal reached up his hands and pulled off his helmet, his face was grayed with age and one eye rolled about uncontrollably. "Because your kernul told me about it and your positions; I see that he is trustworthy, so now you must trust me."

"Warren," Henry shouted, "you've got some heavy explaining to do."

"Not really," remarked Warren, "you wouldn't have trusted me if

I told you. Now, go with the Converts and get to your objective."

"But…"

"No time," said Warren, "The *Traveler* is leaving back for Mars now. An alien invasion fleet is appearing at this moment; you're all going to have to find a way off. Good luck."

The words LINK TERMINATED appeared on the teammates' HUDs and then vanished. The Grand Marshal replaced the helmet and nodded. "All is not lost, you can still find what you came for and then we can find you a way off."

A thunderous noise made everyone look up. The alien ships broke through the atmosphere and seemed to be blotting out the stars. The class of ship was only determined by size and slight differences in design and color. They moved across the sky, scattering about. Four, however, were converging towards one place over the valley's surrounding hills.

"Where are they going?" asked Rookie, watching the four.

"To your city of New Greenwich," said the Grand Marshal, "They are being sent to finish the resistance."

"What resistance?" Henry asked. "Why don't you just bomb the city?"

"Our religion," said the Grand Marshal. He looked up at the sky and hissed violently. A rather large transportation craft with the appearance of a six-finned whale appeared above the facility.

"I was wondering where that thing went," said Henry.

A blue-white beam made up of static particles was lowered from its center. The Grand Marshal gestured for the female terref to step into it, "After you, princess."

The female terref was raised into the craft and the rest of the teammates and Converts followed. Henry, Badger and the Grand Marshal were the last to go. The Grand Marshal rose into the craft while Badger waited for Henry.

Henry looked at the scientists and sighed. "I'm sorry, but you're no longer our priority, we'll try to resolve this mess, maybe we can get rid of them."

"Wait," said Eric, grabbing Henry's arm as he turned to leave. He handed over the laser and smiled. "Send them all to the hottest place in Hell. I'm calling this the Marine Laser."

Oh no, Badger thought to himself, as he stepped into the beam. The virus on his HUD was still blinking and bending, but now it was turning purple; even the identifying shimmers were purple and he hadn't activated them. *This is going to be a bad night.*

Chapter 33

"One Problem after Another"

The Banshee was flying as fast as he could, beating his wings as hard through the sky; he had just shown himself, for however short a time, but it was enough. He had betrayed the trust of the others, the punishment in his culture was banishment. They would find out. But he no longer cared.

He had saved the lives of these strange creatures and he loved them. He would follow them to protect them and even, perhaps, show himself to them. But first, he would return to the mountains to retrieve a weapon. He no longer cared for the tradition of secrecy. The oppressors of these strange creatures would pay this night.

* * *

"We'll arrive at the ship in only a few moments," said the pilot, a Sage.

"I didn't realize how large this thing was," said Henry, he watched as the Zealot paced about, stooping a little.

"The Minor Giant is an exceptional craft for both speed and maneuverability," said the Grand Marshal, handing a metallic canteen towards the female terref, who took it gratefully.

"I notice that you're not using a canteen made of a skull," remarked Henry. "Why is that?"

"Because it is both unethical and worthless," said the Grand

Marshal. "They're also too fragile."

"True, we've been smashing everyone we could find," said Henry, wiping a spot off his screen.

"Forget about the skulls," Rookie cried, "I want to know why the colonel didn't tell us about you helping us. Can you explain? Tell us."

"I wasn't aware that he hadn't told you," dismissed the Grand Marshal.

Rookie walked up and grabbed the Grand Marshal, lifting him off of his seat and into the air. "You're lying, you're conspiring or something and it's a trap, isn't it?"

"I can assure you it isn't a trap, GEN fool."

Everyone jumped and Rookie dropped the Grand Marshal back onto his feet. The ghostlike image of a orig had appeared on everyone's screen, another Grand Marshal in full armor. He was sitting in a throne that hovered a little above the floor.

"I am the Grand Marshal of the fleet of Nimrod's Hand; you stubborn colonialists refuse to give into the greater power of the Reach, now we've been summoned to subdue you. But for you traitors, you shall not be subdued, you shall be hung by your own sinew before the eyes of your children and your blood shall be drained for your wives to drink as shame for your treachery. And you" -the orig's voice became softer, almost playful- "little GEN warrior who hasn't yet fought against a real enemy. The Chinese and this advance group are nothing compared to what we hold inside of our vessels. Where is the Emperor's right?"

"There's no GE…" started Alexander, but Rookie cut him off.

"I'll take it to the grave, you shall never find it," Rookie was actually clawing at his screen. "Search for eternity, but you can't ever have it. True, I'm not too accustomed to combat, but I will take down as many of your followers as God allows."

"Christians and their Christ," mocked the Grand Marshal, "when we find your key and when we have opened the Gate, you will see where your Christ stands."

"Right there to close it," returned Rookie, balling his hands into fists.

"Pity your verminous union had to come, lead by the Demon; we would have had the universe by now if it weren't for him. But there is no such warrior anymore; the next time we shall watch those who oppose us burn with sacred fire."

"You're not going to stop us, the next time it shall be the Gate that burns, glassed by the weapons of the GEN," Rookie growled in return.

The Marshal growled and turned to look at someone that wasn't on the visual-ghost display. "Prepare the gravity bomb, you shall not have the information you seek."

The Marshal vanished from the HUD and everyone looked towards the cockpit and its one-way metallic armor screen. They saw the first, vague sightings of the Reach craft; it was nestled deep into a depression in the valley. Then there was a bright flash and a wavy beam of viridian light shot from the underside of one the operational spacecrafts, completely crushing the derelict vessel like a pancake. Purple and blue fumes plumed into the air, fires clung to trees and devoured them hungrily.

"Very efficient," said Henry, staggering to his feet and sitting back down on the seat.

"I'll find us something even more efficient in a second," said Alexander, grabbing Rookie and shoving him against a wall so he could look at him face-to-face. "First of all, who are you really? Second, you'd better be working with us or I'll kill you for the deaths of the rest my unit."

"I'm Lieutenant Ackory Jace, of the Galactic Encounter Navy," said the frightened PDCT. "I'm most definitely with you; my superiors sent me away to hide one of the Reach's keys. I arrived by random teleport, just before the Reach could apprehend me. I found myself on Mars and hid the key where I could retrieve it when I got my bearings on the planet. But, when I got back it was gone. I joined ISEN as a means to search for it. I doubt I'll ever see it again."

Alexander was quiet; he backed away from the young soldier and collapsed onto a seat. He looked at the floor for the longest time and then looked up at the lieutenant. "Then… what are your orders in this, lieutenant?"

"You're my sergeant," said Rookie, stepping forward and placing a hand on Alexander's shoulder. "I'm following your orders, not until I can get back to the GEN can I regain my rank."

"We already have orders," Henry stated as he walked up behind the pilot. "Get us to New Greenwich, there might be some sort of transport we can get a hold of there."

"Perhaps we can commandeer one of the Marshal's interstellar fighter craft," suggested the Grand Marshal.

"Why not an entire ship?" put in John sarcastically.

"What about the Chinese?" Rookie pied up.

"Let's figure this out as we go," said Henry watching as the pilot navigated towards where the four stationary Reach ships had positioned themselves stationary. "This is going to take quite a while."

That depends on you how much faith you have, Badger thought to himself, tapping his screen as if it could correct the conflict.

Chapter 34

"The Gauntlet"

Over the edge of the valley the occupants of the craft could see the city; New Greenwich was dark and lifeless. Bright flashes of light from conflict could be seen even at their great distance. The Reach craft were hovering above the city, motionless, small, dark shapes flew about the vessels. The red streaks of missiles could be seen being launched into the sky, but the Reach had missile avoidance and elimination systems that almost always knocked them away.

Using their zoom-vision, the teammates got a good look at the Reach's land vehicles. If the vehicles weren't walking, they were using anti-gravity systems for lift and to propel themselves across the ground. The vehicles were dull, non-reflective colors ranging from gray to black. The vehicles had no lighting systems, suggesting an integrated night-vision simulator. Wrecked ISEN and civilian vehicles were strewn about the roads, burnt and broken ruins of failures.

"We do not pride ourselves on what you are seeing," said the Grand Marshal, placing a sidearm version of the Sticker, known as a Wasp, in the female terref's hands it was hoop-shaped and iridescent brown. The Grand Marshal took another one for himself. "The Pure Collect only followed the orders they had been given. What is past is past, we can only establish the future of the universe."

"I only hope we don't get shot down," said Henry, switching back to normal vision.

"Don't worry," said the pilot, "I shall deploy you all, the princess and the Grand Marshal and Zealot upon the nearest landing station. My other brothers and I shall seek our fight elsewhere."

"I'll stay here," said Pedro, "I won't be much good inside."

"Very well," said Alexander.

*   *   *

The first landing pad they came to was on the edge of the city, a large chunk of it was missing. Turrets lacking ammunition and power had been left by ISEN and were positioned around the edges, looking forlorn and rejected. The building itself looked like a lifeless husks, but they could all feel the life that was in it.

The Grand Marshal signaled for the craft to leave. He then looked about the group for a reasonable leader. His eyes fell up the unranked human.

"You," he said, pointing at Henry, "I sense you to be more capable than I am to lead."

"You're very misled," Henry smiled, "but, Badger and I'll see what we can do."

Badger swept his tail across the ground agitatedly at the sight of the building's entryway. Everything had been moving far too fast throughout the entire time they were on Forerunner. They had fought the Chinese, made contact with an alien threat, found an ancient key and were now practically abandoned on the planet. In the few years he had been a Specter GEM operative he had never had such a choppy assignment.

The entrance to the building was made with two, large transparent doors with the image of a green turtle imprinted in the center. Past the doors they saw that it was a restaurant and by the crystal display cases that contained ancient samurai and ninja equipment it had been a Japanese restaurant. Silverware and dishes were scattered about, tables were overturned and rotting food was everywhere.

"Charming," said Alexander, prodding at a lump of something that was covered in green fuzz. "I wonder how long it's been since anyone's been 'ere."

"Not too long," said Henry, indicating a trail of footprints that had been left when an alien had carelessly stepped on a fuzzy lump. "I'm no expert with food trails, but I'd say that those were made just an hour ago."

"Your humor is strange," the Grand Marshal remarked as he examined a display case that contained samurai armor. "I wonder why the Reach didn't take these treasures, hmmm."

The Zealot was curious about the eatery and he walked until he arrived at a balcony. The balcony overlooked another area of similar panic. Only down below there was a fishpond filled with odd, purple fish with pincer like mouths. He leaned over the rail to get a better look.

"Fei, Fei, Fei!"

A sprik suddenly appeared from beneath the balcony and stabbed at the Zealot with a sickle-shaped knife. The knife merely glanced off. The sprik cried out as the Zealot grabbed him by the throat.

The Zealot merely squeezed the sprik's neck, crushing every bone in it. He tossed it into the pond and growled in outrage, "Filthy weaklings!"

The fish wasted no time in nibbling at the sprik's exposed flesh. After such a long time eating each other, the fish were glad to have something new. The taste of blood was very savory.

"So that's what fei means," said John, watching as the Zealot wandered over to the Grand Marshal. "Kill."

The female terref was wide-eyed after the sudden appearance of the sprik. She pointed the Wasp at everything that might possibly hide a hostile.

"Rookie," said Alexander, "see to her, you are now her personal bodyguard."

"Yes sir," said Rookie.

Badger climbed on top of a round column with the engraved image of crow clutching a dragon in its claws. He swept his eyes about;

the appearance of the sprik had made him more cautious. He took a quick sniff at the air and immediately gagged. The smell of rotting food almost overpowered everything else. But there was something in it, something that wasn't on the floor.

Badger, quite slowly, looked up and immediately projected caution to the others, "on the ceiling."

"Huh? What? Uh-oh," Alexander inhaled.

Everyone looked up to see that the ceiling was covered in sleeping spriks, who apparently slept upside-down with all four limbs clutched to the ceiling. Unwittingly they had stumbled upon a resting militia group. Each sprik was armed.

"We have stumbled upon a hive," said the Grand Marshal. "We should leave."

"I have forgotten they slept like that," the female terref whispered to Rookie.

"Uh… they're not going to be asleep very long," said Henry.

spriks, trying to be silent, were climbing over the balcony, still a little drowsy. Each one had its weapon ready. Upon noticing that they had been spotted, they all began to shout, "Traitors, kill, kill."

"Not good," said John, picking off a couple with his rifle.

"Now the whole hive is awakened," cried the Grand Marshal.

spriks began to drop to the floor, some accidentally landed on each other. They began shouted and firing, rushing at the enemy in their thick forces. Their numbers kept swelling until the floor was no longer visible.

The team quickly found an escape route, an elevator that was large enough to hold two trucks. But still, the Zealot had to duck low to avoid the roof. The Wasps weren't explosive like the larger versions, the spikes merely fragmented into sharp shards with little pops. The return fire from the squad was more devastating than that of the spriks', who were too tired to shoot straight. Before the elevator closed, the Grand Marshal took a thick disc, about the size of his hand-paw and threw it into the room.

"Ah, that stings," John complained as four spikes fragmented in his left arm. The spikes barely pierced the skin, but their residing energy was painful.

"It shall end," said the Grand Marshal, breaking a couple crystals on his chest before they turned to gas.

"I guess we got the worst of it," said Alexander, seeing that the Specters and female terref hadn't been touched.

"Good work, Rookie, you kept her safe."

"No problem," said Rookie, brushing some shards from his shoulder. He had managed to block all the projectiles that could have harmed the female terref, who he slightly knew by reputation.

"There will be a problem soon," said the Grand Marshal.

"The entire building's probably alerted by now," said Henry.

"Not that," said the Grand Marshal.

"Then what?" asked Henry, looking at the terref.

There was a sudden explosion that rocked and jerked the elevator, sending everyone onto the floor. The rumbling and shaking continued and the sound of splitting stone, metal and wood was heard loud and clear. The elevator suddenly began to drop very fast, plummeting downwards like a bomb.

"Zealot," said the Grand Marshal, "if you please, our mission isn't to die."

The Zealot grunted and activated its photon Sword. The blade was black and shaped like a long tear-drop with a dark purple shimmer about the edges and the two cover-knuckle blades didn't touch each other until the tip. He stabbed it into the wall, one hand braced on the ceiling to steady him; the elevator quickly began to slow its descent. A high-pitched creaking noise resounded about the small chamber as the blade cleaving through the metal and stone.

After a short while, the elevator came to a near stop, still slowly descending as the hot blade cut through the shaft walls. Everyone rose to their feet, moaning a little and dusting themselves off.

"What was that?" asked Henry, looking up.

"A Calamity charge," said the Grand Marshal, "the hive is destroyed, there is nothing left alive that may pursue us."

"Yeh, but now the entire building is alerted to us," said Henry.

"This may work for us," said the Grand Marshal, "should the ISEN see us killing their enemy, they will know we aren't to be feared."

"You have a slight point," said Henry. He turned to Badger and pointed towards the doors. "Find out what floor we're on."

Badger leapt forward, smashing the doors open to reveal they were halfway between floors. He landed in a hall on all fours, turned around and wagged his tail to show them it was alright.

Henry came next and then the PDCTs, followed by the Grand Marshal. Rookie and John aided the princess out of the elevator and then bid the Zealot to come. The zealot, in one swift movement, deactivated the sword and the elevator began to fall. He was out just when the opening was just large enough for him to fit through, and he rolled to leap back up to his feet.

"Impressive," said John. He turned back to hall full of rooms ahead. "But, heroes, we still have to find transportation."

"Let's not be too hasty," said Henry, "I'll activate my heartbeat detector."

The group began to move again, walking cautiously through the halls. The Specters took the lead and the Zealot took the back.

For his size, the Zealot was actually very quiet in his movements. His enormous feet treaded soft on the ground, something not easily done with hard-edge armored footwear. He was almost bent double in the hall, holding his Sticker out before him.

The Zealot only used the sword for up-close conflicts. It didn't occur to him that a straight hallway was considered close-range until the Grand Marshal pointed this out. Very stiffly, he attached his Sticker to his back and activated his sword. The blade was so extensive that the Zealot had to hold it high above everyone's head to keep from harming them.

Henry stopped suddenly when a heartbeat large enough for a hostile appeared on his detector. Actually, there were three hearts, each one too large to be human. Henry held up a hand for a halt and pointed to the wall that the hearts were beating behind.

"Just use the laser," John suggested.

"I'm not about ready to bring the entire building down on top of us," returned Henry. He crouched down and placed a hand on Badger's neck. "There are three of them, past that wall, get 'em."

Badger was off like a shot; he broke through the wall and found that he had surprised three orig Militants. Each of the origs had a handheld Sticker and a short stave with a blunt blade that was rimmed with energy emitters, behind the blade was a green crystal that glowed in the light.

Badger wasted no time in dodging the three lethal staves, which cracked the ceramic-fiber floor like powered hammers. Badger fired several rounds into one's chest and then used its stave to knock another out a window. The last one he jammed his kukri into its collar and twisted it to sever anything that would allow it to call out an alarm.

The final orig fell to the floor with a gurgling gasp. Badger wiped his knife on a cushion that was inside the room and attached one of the staves to his holster. Stepping out of the room, he nodded in conformation that the room was cleared of any threats.

Chapter 35

"It Was Quiet at First"

"It is a pity that I could not have gone in there," growled the Zealot, tightening his grip on the sword handle.

"There shall be more glory ahead," the Grand Marshal said, nodding admiringly at the GEM. "There is a little more fight in this one than the others."

"Should be," said Henry, "he's the best GEM in REPEL's Specter teams."

"It is fortunate that you were assigned such a tool," commended the Grand Marshal.

"I bought him," said Henry, "he wasn't assigned."

"Where then could you purchase such?"

"A farm," said Henry.

"Forget the market industry," said Alexander, "we've still got to find a transport."

"And perhaps we'd better hurry," urged John. A feeling was creeping over him that something had gone wrong.

Badger twitched his ears; he could hear footsteps, above and below. He let out a low growl and looked up at the ceiling, raising his rifle also.

"We're going to need something faster than a luxury elevator," said John. He looked at the ceiling, but he couldn't hear what Badger was hearing, but he was sure that there were plenty of hostiles coming.

"Now what are we going to do?" asked Rookie, keeping close to the female terref.

"Running might be advisable," said Henry. "Zealot, Grand Marshal and sergeant, in the back; John and Rookie, guard her, good. Badger and I'll take the point, now run."

Badger switched his rifle for the stave, thinking it would work better for the closeness of the halls. He quickened his pace so that he would be far ahead of everyone else and could eliminate the bulk of hostiles in their path. He flew down a staircase and knocked away a couple of spriks that were heading up, they died without a sound.

The stave's dull blade killed everything it came in solid contact with. Armor cracked and fell apart, bones shattered and blood splattered the walls and floor. Badger brought down everything, the stave was an extension of his arm and it cleaved away everything in his path.

A Militant had a Photon Sword and leapt at the small juggernaut. His helmet and shards of armor flew in various directions as he himself was spiked to the ground. Badger lifted the stave in time to deflect several high-explosive spikes from a large Sticker.

The launcher, a Lesser, ducked to let the spikes fly overhead, but this only allowed Badger to blow him to the side. He let out a rattle as air escaped from his dead lungs and he slid down the wall leaving a red trail.

Badger smashed in the face of a sprik with the end of the stave and then charged down another flight of stairs, killing the Reach as they tried to head up. spriks flew everywhere and the heavier races knocked down those who were behind them as they were blown away by the powerful stave.

*   *   *

The Zealot had placed himself at the very back of the group so that he could use his black sword to strike down any that got too close. The Grand Marshal and Alexander killed the others at range, mostly they were Lessers, but there were some Sages and Militants mixed in. The Zealot slashed a Militant in half while the Grand Marshal and Sergeant killed the shouting Lessers.

"You will all see the price you must pay for the Emperor's leadership," said the Grand Marshal, shooting several spikes into the masses.

"Dumb wall climbin' freaks," shouted Alexander, firing nonstop at the sprik hordes.

"Here's the stairs," Henry shouted back to the others. "Don't trip over the bodies."

Henry leapt over a dead Confessor and wound up landing at the bottom of the stairs. He waited until the others caught up.

"I wish I had a dog like that," said John looking about in amazement at the destruction.

"Wouldn't anyone?" chuckled Henry.

"We shall be over run by these weaklings if we do not do something to stop them," growled the Grand Marshal.

Thinking it was a command the Zealot took his sword and struck thrice at the ceiling. Then, he slid his claws into the red-hot crack he had made and pulled down. A square block fell from the ceiling and the zealot wedged in it tightly on the staircase.

"That should hold them."

"Very commendable," said the Grand Marshal, nodding at the Zealot.

Henry struck a might in the face; it and others were coming out of a door at the bottom of another staircase. "How many are there in this building?"

"Enough to capture or kill those that resist Nimrod," said the Grand Marshal.

"That's… encouraging," said the female terref, shooting a few spikes at an orig.

*   *   *

A couple of Confessors went flying when Badger hit them with the stave.

The Reach's melee weapons were devastating and were even more so when used against them. Badger flew down two more staircases, dashing the hostiles that got in his way and found himself in the lobby of the skyscraper.

In the lobby there were dozens of soldiers. One soldier in particular, staring out the transparent doorway at some other combat going on outside, stood between four Militants with elegant spikes on their armor; each was holding a stave. The observing soldier was an orig, bigger than the others Badger had seen, he wore graceful black and red plates of armor with a fan-like crest on the front of his helmet.

Badger quickly tossed a firefly into the room and covered his eyes. When he uncovered his eyes he saw the Reach staggering about, except for the regal figure and his guards. Badger launched himself at a group of spriks and sent them flying with one sweep of the stave.

"Arraugh," the regal figure shouted loudly and took two Wasps from his hips. "Tool of ISEN, die like all those who oppose us."

The four bodyguards rushed at Badger, hefting their staves high. The bodyguards were all origs and they swung their staves about in perfect, coordinated forms. Their performance-enhancing armor gave a modest boost to their abilities.

Badger avoided the bodyguards while he caused mass havoc among the still blinded aliens. A Lesser went flying through the doorway and onto the street, knocking over a Militant and a couple Sages. Next he hit a table that was stacked high with treasures that the Reach had found and would later divide.

The treasures and pieces of the table flew everywhere, injuring or killing those they came in contact with. A couple Grunts slipped upon hundreds of pearls and gems and went skidding, across the floor towards Badger. Badger sent them back where they had come from and also to where they were going.

A bodyguard leapt at Badger, swinging his stave. Badger leapt over the lethal melee weapon and smashed the orig's head in, making a depression on the floor.

The next bodyguard charged Badger, swinging the stave in a blinding figure-eight. Badger somersaulted over him, smashing his own stave against its back. Badger landed in front of the third and knocked its legs out from under it then smashed the stave's blade into his chest.

The last bodyguard rushed at the GEM, but then the side of his helmet was suddenly dented in and his brain was shattered by a shot from Henry's Disrupter.

"Don't ever think you can attack Badger."

Badger barked thankfully and whipped about to send an aluminum chair flying at a might Elite. The others made short work of the rest of the Reach and then Henry used the Marine Laser to eliminate the others outside. The laser blasted a deep trench in the flexcrete, making it glow orange with intense heat.

"Glad you didn't use that inside," John remarked nervously.

The Zealot was the one to charge forward and pierce his sword through the leader's midsection, twisting and jiggling the Photon Blade. The Zealot removed the blade and then began hacking vengefully at the dead form.

"Alright," said a voice from outside, "we can see you, step out slowly. We won't shoot, we just want to be sure who you are and I'm sending some Marines to you."

"Well, at least we made contact," said Henry, attaching the laser to his holster.

Chapter 36

"A Violent Argument"

"Alright," said a sergeant, a dirty black man with several burns and scars on the right side of his face. He was trying to stop the Marines, who he had sent to "escort" the newcomers, from molesting them.

"That's enough," he shouted. "There's no need for that. Point that rifle at the ground, Marine. Do you think you're in the army or somethin'."

"A little on edge?" Henry asked.

"Well," said the sergeant holding out a hand, "glad to hear you're not Chinese. But… who are the other three?"

Henry took the hand and shook it firmly. "They're… traitors, didn't like the pay or publicity they were getting."

"A Zealot and a Grand Marshal," commended the sergeant, "it's hard enough to kill them, much less turn them to your cause."

"It may not be as hard as you think," rumbled the Zealot, "the Reach is in an age of doubt. It is only the fear of Nimrod that holds the others back."

"Yeah-yeah and everything else about your religion that threatens everyone," dismissed the sergeant.

"You're very rude," the Zealot growled.

"Welcome to the Marines."

"Sir," one Marine piped up, "I don't think we can trust them, we don't even know who they are. We should dispose of 'em."

"Back off," growled the sergeant, "the Reach don't kill each other like these were doing. But I agree, we don't know who they are, start sounding off."

"Henry Mindell United States Specter F-38A and this is Badger, F-38B."

"First Sergeant, Alexander McClain, 106-3742, ISEN PDCT."

"Private, John, 106-4765, ISEN PDCT."

"Rookie, a little between ranks and ID numbers at the moment."

"Fine," said the sergeant, giving Rookie an odd look. "Now who's the alien out of uniform?"

"That is your devoted ally, if she survives long enough for us to return her to her family," said Rookie. "Her father is emperor of Shilan, a nation neutral to the Reach."

The sergeant gave Rookie another odd look before turning to Henry. "How does a Specter find himself here?"

"Classified," said Henry.

"Your kind of Special Forces gives me the chills," muttered the sergeant.

"That's the basic idea, we walk in, something's missing," said Henry. "And, not to press something upon you, but... we've missed our flight and have been ordered to get back to Mars. Do you know where a ship is?"

The sergeant looked up and pointed.

"Something less hostile and on the ground?" Henry pressed, not at all impressed.

"I've heard a lot of the same stories," said the Sergeant, turning away. "We've got a security bunker a short way from here, why don't you collect some gear and… aaaahhh."

Henry had grabbed the sergeant about the neck from behind and held his knife against his throat. "You listen to me; I've been infiltrating China, running through forests full of killer jellyfish and fighting the Reach for days. I don't really care how much you've heard this story before, because you're going to listen to this one. We've been ordered to get back to Mars, now, where's a ship?"

The rest of the squad was leveling their weapons at the Marines that were now positioning their weapons on them. The Zealot was the most intimidating; his sword raised high and ready to strike. They were all at a standoff.

"First of all," said the Sergeant, grunting and tugging at the arm, "why would I tell you where one is?"

"Because we both know what the Reach can do," returned Henry, releasing the sergeant and sheathing his knife. "Now, be polite and tell us if you know where a ship is."

The sergeant rubbed his throat for a minute and then gestured for his team to lower their weapons. He looked about at the squad and sighed. "Fine, but first, you have to do something for us."

Henry suppressed a yell in his throat. "Like what?"

"I know where a ship is, but the Reach has us blocked into the city. There are three missile pods around the north section of the city, the Reach and Chinese have deactivated them. If you can clear the roads and reactivate those pods I'll take you to the ship."

"Sounds fair enough," said Henry. "How long has the Reach had this city in such bad shape?"

"For three weeks," said the sergeant, "every since they cut us off from the wind farms. As soon as those pods are up we can evacuate the entire city."

"Figures," said Henry. "We're going to need something fast, preferably four-wheel turning."

"We've a truck you can use."

"Technical?"

"Civilian!"

"What type?"

"Malingerer-36, an older model," the sergeant said with an apologetic shrug.

"That's my model," Henry said jovially.

"Then you're welcome to it," said a Marine, "I'll call it in for you."

In a couple moments, a streamlined, yellow truck with a halo-turret attached atop of the hood, came rolling in, sliding to a smooth stop. Four Marines got out of the truck and watched in amazement as the Zealot took the turret and the Grand Marshal took up a position behind him.

"Mine had a shorter bed," Henry remarked.

The PDCTs got in the truck-bed with the aliens and the Specters took the inside.

"Be sure to keep her safe," said Henry, nodding towards the female terref, then he added, "Where can I find you when the pods have been activated?"

"You'll find me at one of the pods," said the sergeant. "If you activate them it'll take more then a thousand Kismets to deactivate them again."

Chapter 37

"Drive Slowly, We're Reloading"

"I'm not so sure that the sergeant has much faith in us," said Rookie, mostly to himself.

"He's known too many disappointments in this hell to think we could do any different," said Alexander.

"He could've at least been a little more encouraging," Rookie remarked.

"That he could've," agreed Alexander watching the buildings and streets for hostiles.

As Henry turned down a street, he glanced at the dashboard's compass to be sure they were heading in the right direction. He had been sure to leave the headlights off and use his night-vision, but he didn't think that mattered much. The burning rubble and wrecks lined the streets; it was very much like New Kunlun Shun. He made a skillful swerve around two corners then curved around the wreckage of a MATO.

Badger held back from the window, expecting that at any moment hostile projectiles would be firing in. The barrel of his rifle stuck a little out of the side window, his ears twitched as air rushed through the side window and blew his fur about. His training had made the tickling sensation a minor nuisance.

REPEL's genetic modular training programs were extensively for deprogramming young minds to REPEL's desire. After the deprogramming, when extensive tests in hardship and endurance were completed, they went on to augmentation. Some of their tendons and joints had to be completely restructured for human flexibility and strength; some couldn't handle it. The percentage that survived, seven of ten, were taken to the neural programs that would test them for AAP (Acceleration in Ability Pathways).

AAP was one of the most significant portions of the program. GEMs were given various trials while their brains were being scanned. After this, many were sent off as guards, being considered failures, but those that could manage the trials were sent to different training zones to practice these new skills. Badger had been the only GEM to not have to go through the augmentation and he excelled all others in his trials. Amazingly, he was the only GEM in REPEL's records to ever receive the highest marks in every test, including math and written vocabulary.

But, against all programming, which inferred that he was to answer only to the team's overseer, he would gladly neglect it for Henry. They had not been able to fully deprogram him; even Colonel Warren knew this and he felt that someday Badger would depart from REPEL forever. An unknown origin was enough to set most everyone at REPEL on edge, wondering about something they knew nothing of.

Ping! Ping! Splat!

Two spikes from a Heavy Sticker glanced off the windshield and an energy bolt splattered its residue across the lower half. The street began to fill with the disorienting lights of the Reach's soldiers.

The Zealot pulled back the trigger and swept the halo-turret wildly from side-to-side. He howled aloud as he saw the lights drop, or even turn to run. He kept his head low and felt SEAR glance off his tall crest.

The PDCTs and the Grand Marshal took out the remnants of the hostiles as they flew past. One might had the courage enough to take a leap and grab hold of the wall of the bed. The Grand Marshal began punching the reptile's face, but then swung his Wasp, the spikes tearing open its face. It fell onto the road with a painful shriek.

"Ouch," John remarked aloud.

Henry swerved the truck to smash a Militant and two Confessor spriks and then practically ran over a barricade. The truck almost flipped, but the occupants shifted their weight to one side to steady it again. There wasn't any need for stealth anymore, Henry turned on the headlights, levered them up so they would shine into the enemy eyes.

Several spriks covered their eyes from the bright headlights and were both shot and ran over. A orig with an Energy Stave swung at the vehicle, missed by fractions and sent a terref and sprik flying.

"Filthy soldiers," the orig shouted after the vehicle, raising his stave high.

John dropped the orig with two shots. "That's right, filthy, crazy and proud of it."

"I should have been angry," said the Grand Marshal, giving John a sideways glance. "Why smile about such a thing?"

"Because," said John, looking back, "it's all true."

Henry skidded about a corner and leaned back, shouting out loud when he saw a bulky, hovering tank ahead. The tank was made of a scaly gray metal, gracefully designed in every feature, even the duel barrels were works of art. There was an elegant canard with a propulsion unit on either side of the tank. The two barrels were more like rotating tripods, centered with a purple energy emitter. On the front of the tank were two halo-turrets, looking very out of place.

"Whoa," shouted Henry, maneuvering to avoid a purple beam of energy and the turrets' hot aluminum. "I wasn't expecting that."

"Flee," shouted the Zealot, "it is useless to assault a Tithe with these perforating weapons."

"I doubt that," said Henry, passing the Marine Laser to Badger. "I'm going to turn us around now, be sure it's completely obliterated."

"Yes, Henry," projected Badger, taking the weapon and grasping it against his shoulder; the laser was just as long as he was tall. He leaned himself out the window, grabbing the roof with his left paw, crushing the metal into a perfect grip.

Henry made a rather unbalanced turn and raced towards the revolving tank. The halo-turrets were still firing, even though they were at too much of an angle to hit the truck. Henry was driving so that he would run behind the Tithe.

Badger watched his crosshairs, centering them at the tank's great middle. He squeezed the trigger and the beam smashed into the tank, blowing off the armor shell. The halo-turrets were inactive now, merely twitching and jerking while spitting sparks, one of the barrels was missing. But it wasn't finished off.

"That thing must be three times as strong as flexcrete," Henry exclaimed.

Badger slipped back in through the window. "I believe it's running out of power."

"Well you did blow off a huge junk of it," said Henry, turning around so Badger could get another shot off.

"I was talking about the laser."

Badger pointed to the integrated computer, there was a blue bar with a short bit of red blinking on its edge. Above the bar were Reach of Nimrod symbols, no interpretation was needed.

"Recharge battery, eh?" Henry remarked dryly. "I just know that kid did this on purpose."

Badger leaned out the window again, aiming at the Tithe; he pulled the trigger and drained the last of the energy. The beam struck the Tithe just as it fired its remaining barrel. The remaining armored chassis exploded into several large pieces, one of which flipped about like a fish, its anti-gravity device still operating. One extremely hardy piece of the gray metal flew through the air and smashed against Badger's helmet.

Badger let out a loud yelp, he had hardly felt the glancing blow, but the surprise was enough. He shot back into the truck and ascertained what was missing. The helmet's entire screen was gone, along with the top, his ears stung a little from the ear-slots being ripped away so fast. Other than that, he was fine.

"You okay?" Henry shouted, glancing Badger over animatedly. "Cm'on, answer me."

"My ears sting a little," Badger projected dryly. "I didn't get hurt, it was only a glance."

"Thank you, thank you," Henry prayed softly as he watched the road ahead. "If... when we get back to Mars, I'm going to demand a vacation for the both of us. Even with this alien threat, we both need a break."

"Not a good time to discuss trips," projected Badger, dropping the laser onto the floor. He nodded towards the road ahead; purple-blue lights had appeared ahead, moving rapidly.

"Wonderful," remarked Henry, denting the dashboard with a fist. "What kind of vehicles are these?"

Badger was glad of one thing; his HUD wasn't bothering him anymore. But now he had to use the iron-sights of all the weapons; this he didn't like. He was the only one to see the vehicles naturally. They were scaly gray and anti-gravity like the tank but were much smaller and not as bulky; gracefully designed with short-finlike balance canards on either side. The fronts of the vehicles were split like pincers, each end had a double-barreled energy cannon.

The vehicles were two-seaters, side-by-side and were driven by Militants. The controls to these vehicles were two orbs fit into the dashboard, one for the cannons. The pilot used both hands to maneuver the craft while operating the cannons.

The Zealot was already firing the turret at the hostile craft. Badger leaned out of the window, gun blazing and wind blowing full force into his face. He could hardly suppress the smile on his face as the wind whipped his fur and ears about.

The halo-turret tore off a chunk of one of the vehicles as it passed by, firing its energy cannons. Pink fumes poured forth from the gash, until it crystallized to seal it. The rider had been killed and the pilot had several nicks in his armor from glances.

"What are these?" asked John, shooting at a pilot and ducking to avoid flying energy.

"Shepherds," said Rookie, "built specifically for urban combat, but are still lethal in the open. Due to the speed they can be manufactured, the Reach hasn't attempted to give the pilots ophthalmic helmets."

"How fast can they be built?" John asked, firing some more until he saw the pilot fall off.

"Just a few seconds," said Rookie. "They're actually hollow inside, the gas that leaks out of them is what in English might be called intelligent memory-guard. It crystallizes in air. They use it in many of their craft; it's like an eternal battery and gas computer."

"That's interesting," said John dropping to the bed as several energy bolts flew at him. They instead hit the Zealot, splattering across the back of his armor.

"It burns," grumbled the Zealot, taking up his Sticker and returning fire upon the Shepherds.

"All will die," he shouted, ignoring other bolts that splattered on his armor.

"I can't believe this guy," John muttered to Rookie.

"We're going to be dead in a minute if something doesn't happen," projected Badger. He looked in one of the mirrors, watching the vehicles carefully. Already he could tell that the energy was quickly taking the truck apart.

Henry wasn't listening; he was too busy maneuvering to avoid the bolts of energy and block the hostiles' path. He knew something had to be done soon, but he wasn't at all sure what it was. It wasn't until Badger opened his door that Henry could be distracted.

"Huh? What are you…?"

Badger didn't hear the rest; he had leapt out the door with his stave in paw. A Shepherd, rushed straight for him, he leapt in the air and landed on the front of the Shepherd, smiling broadly at the terrified Militants.

Badger swung the stave, ridding the Shepherd of its two Militants. He dropped into the seat and brushed away the blood in his eyes. He was able to see ahead of the craft due to a monitor, it didn't have a wide range of view (it was used only for heavy fire situations) but it was better than standing. After a moment, he had figured out the controls and went tearing after the others.

Chapter 38

"Reunion Road"

The Shepherds had thinner armor in the back, making them easy and pitiful targets for Badger. The pink fumes crystallized in the air and panels blew open; the Militants couldn't take the energy pounding that the Zealot was taking. There was no safe place for the Militants to move along the road; they either got blown up by the Zealot or were burnt by Badger.

One ducked off down another street, the Militant slightly wounded by energy. He sped off down the road not daring to look back for fear of seeing the other Shepherd in pursuit. He was the only one to get away.

"Way to go Tall Dwarf," Henry shouted enthusiastically. He watched in admiration as Badger pulled ahead of the truck with the Shepherd, providing a kind of defensive barrier.

Badger contacted Henry through whatever remained of his radio, "Henry, how much more damage can the truck sustain?"

Henry had to listen hard; the connection was so full of static. "Ah, not much, we had better reach one of those pods soon and we should hope for another vehicle."

"Maybe I should have a look ahead."

"Ah! Yeah! That would nice, go on ahead. Just be careful."

"No promises," projected Badger, pressing the maneuver orb to jump the Shepherd into a rapid boost. The alien craft was amazingly maneuverable at this speed. Badger found this out when he came upon a downhill slope that was littered with abandoned or destroyed civilian vehicles. Without bothering to end the boost, Badger swerved skillfully about the vehicles.

"Wise guy," Henry muttered.

Badger's ears were pressed back by the wind and the wind tunnel created by the seat caused his tail to flap about like a streamer. He narrowed his eyes against the wind in search of any signs of the Reach or one of the missile pods. In a few minutes, he unwittingly came upon both.

He turned a corner and let out a yelp of surprise when a gigantic energy shield bubble loomed up before him. Inside was a score of Reach soldiers, mostly Confessors and Lessers with a Sage. There were also two Tithes inside the shield, hovering about menacingly to guard the tall missile pod. A couple of sprik Specialists were working on the missile's programming, not having much success.

"I've found one of the pods," projected Badger, as the Shepherd crashed into the shield. "Ow! There's some sort of energy shield around it, this Shepherd won't go through."

"We'll be there in a few seconds, try to find someway of shutting it off."

"Whatever you say, sir," projected Badger, taking few shots at the shield. *Nope, that won't work, uh-oh.* The energy splattering across the shield had alerted the Reach to his presence.

The Reach moved to protect two hook-fanned spriks and the Tithes placed themselves on either side of the missile pod. The soldiers were able to stick the muzzles of their weapons through the shield to stay safe while applying fire on the Shepherd. The shield clung about the weapons like a sticky resin.

If that's all I have to do, thought Badger as he grabbed his rifle. He coiled his legs and sprang high into the air, he slipped through the shield and it clung to him for a moment then returned to normal. Badger landed on the ground and started spraying aluminum about the area.

"It's interesting," projected Badger, "you have to walk through it, it doesn't let vehicles in."

"I think I got that," returned Henry. "We'll be there in a moment."

Badger didn't care where the aluminum was directed at this moment, just as long as it was towards a hostile. He zigzagged and rolled about to avoid fire while firing. The Tithes fired periodic shots at him, mainly with their turrets, which were energy instead of the other's salvaged ISEN ware.

The Sage, an orig with a yellow crow painted on his right

shoulder plate, shouted out commands to his troops while trying to get a shot off at Badger with his handheld Sticker. He quickly reloaded the caddy to fire another barrage at Badger, firing in bursts for easy control.

"Kill the tool of these unheedful rebels, or I shall carve your flesh from your bones."

A sprik fired off a couple energy bolts before it retreated back into its hiding place. A Lesser took out his Photon Sword and leapt at Badger. But with a flick of his paw, Badger sent the dead Lesser flying with the stave. Then, as quick as a flash, Badger was somewhere else, crushing flexcrete and killing the enemy. Then, Badger thought he saw what might be the shield generator and smashed it like a pancake with his stave, sending pink gas into the air.

The Sage had never seen such speed delivered by anything. The fire from the Tithes would not be enough to stop the unstoppable force who had built himself up into a rampage. The Sage backed away as Badger started for him, he emptied the handheld's caddy in a desperate attempt to stop the beast.

Badger rushed at the Sage until he saw headlights come around the corner; he leapt to the side and let Henry smash the Sage with the truck. He barked joyously to see they had finally arrived. But this was short-lived.

Both Tithes fired both cannons at the truck; the occupants dove out as all four beams impacted upon the damaged truck. The truck exploded in a torrent of crimson flames and blue sparks. Pieces landed about the road and the Tithes moved forward, firing their small turrets.

A tire landed next to Badger as he watched the tanks. They no longer had the laser and there was little they had that might stop the tanks. He looked down at the stave and then at one of the tanks. He let out a growl and loud bark as he leapt at the gray vehicle.

The Zealot had activated his sword and lunged at the other tank. He landed in front of the cannons and began slashing with all his might at the double-lid of the cockpit. He stabbed, hacked, kicked and even punched at the hard armor until the lid caved in. Then, with a great growl, he lifted the pilot up out of the tank and threw him at the ground. He dropped onto the pilot and stabbed the sword in up to its basket hilt.

Badger had managed to stop the other tank much faster, with five great slams onto the lid; he broke the armor, killed the pilot and snapped the stave in two with the force of the blow. He threw out the pilot and dropped onto the ground, barking and growling approvingly at the swift work.

"Nice," said Alexander, looking at the still operable tanks.

"Ouch," said John, wiping at a burn on his chest. It hadn't gone through his armor, but the heat from the energy had been transferred to his skin.

"Let's get this thing reactivated," urged Henry, stepping up to the missile pod's computer. He worked at it for a moment, pressing buttons and lightly kicking the independent generator. Suddenly there was a vibrant grating noise and the top of the missile pod began to move.

Henry stepped back with the others and watched as the pod fired its missiles up at the closest Reach ship. The missiles streaked into the sky like fireflies and burst apart against the armor.

"A beautiful sight," said Alexander, "you Specters do know what you're doing."

"We have to," Henry said plainly.

Badger looked away from the alien vessel and towards the wreckage of the truck. He saw something familiar underneath what used to be the hood. He flicked the hood away and lifted the laser off the ground; it was only blackened by the explosion, no damage at was done to it.

Henry chuckled as he accepted the laser from Badger. "That kid knows how to make something last."

"To fire that powerful a beam it would have to," remarked the Grand Marshal, looking from tank to tank. "We have a slight problem with transportation."

"The Shepherd's in fine condition," projected Badger.

Grand Marshal heard but didn't notice. "That will be for the capable one and his tool."

"We can wait here for the Marines to come," said Alexander.

"No," the Zealot rumbled, "I cannot fit into a Tithe; I was bred and enhanced for walking, I shall remain here."

"Then you shall come," said the Grand Marshal, pointing at Rookie. "The GEN knows how to control our work."

"Sergeant?" asked Rookie.

"Go ahead, liar," said Alexander with a chuckle. "Be sure you survive."

"Fool some people for about five years and you're branded for life," muttered Rookie as he climbed into the cockpit.

The controls of the tank were simple, a crescent to move, a sensor-enhanced all-around screen that allowed the pilot to just turn his head to turn the weapons and two buttons above the pad for firing. The only drawback to the Tithes was that the cockpits no longer had the protective lids. But, with or without the extra protection, the Tithes moved steady forward along the road.

"It's a pity we had to lose the truck," said Henry, "it was nice while it was recognizable."

"You got one at home," projected badger as he started the Shepherd after the tanks.

"Yeah," shrugged Henry, "but it's such a thrill to abuse a vehicle that's not yours."

* * *

A group of bedraggled and terrified civilians, many covered in untreated wounds, were made to march along the street with the Reach prodding them along, none too gently. The armed guard consisted of an orig with the black and red armor, four elegant terref Militants with staves and several sprik Lessers. They were going to meet up with a Minor Giant that would take the civilians to be workers at Chinese facilities.

One of the spriks, carrying a Heavy Sticker, lagged casually behind. He was going to be pulled out with the civilians for a few days of rest with the Chinese and he was looking forward to it. This was his first time fighting, he enjoyed the slaughter, but the risk he had to take for the thrill was tiring.

A simple, red-hot metal rod through his skull ended all his hopes forever. The metal rod glanced off the ground and stuck into a building where it slowly cooled. None of the others soldiers or captives had noticed.

The Banshee had managed to procure a crossbow, based off the design and method used by the ISEN guerillas. He had switched his satchel out for a quiver full of the lethal rods and, with the grainy holographic scope, he couldn't miss. Of course, any piece of metal would do for the crossbows, but the rods were far more accurate and not to be spent stupidly.

He watched sadly as the progression was led further along the street, he couldn't risk a shot that might alert the others. He looked about for another target. He soon spotted one on a building a couple hundred yards away with his excellent binocular vision. It was a terref with a large tubular weapon that resembled a stag beetle with three stubby green mandibles. The weapon was a high-explosive weapon devised by both the Reach and Chinese, known as the Type-1 Paste Launcher, or the Painter, as the Reach's enemies called it. It was a new design of biometric weapon, firing balls of air-intolerant bacteria that, when on impact with an object, explodes with a temperature of nearly 1000 degrees.

The Banshee had seen the Chinese use it a few times; he had seen ISEN loyalists and Rebels have their flesh burnt to scraps of charcoal. The Banshee let out a low growl and placed an aluminum can that he had picked up off the ground onto the rail. He sighted in on the terref's head and fired.

The aluminum can melted with the friction into a flying sheet of liquid metal, leaving behind both vapor and distortion. The terref, a Sage, never felt a thing; his crushed head flew off through the air while his body remained standing for a few short moments and then fell backwards.

The Banshee growled appreciatively, though slightly unsettled by the sight of the disembodied head dropping out of sight. He was no longer interested in retrieving weapons for the others, they could hide themselves for as long as they wanted and they could gather their own research too. Mirchlaen spread his wings and with a single downward blast, had crossed the street to another building. He loaded another can onto the rail.

He was about to fire the can at the convoy's leader, known as a Skull, when a sound distracted him. He turned and looked down the street to see two Tithes and a Shepherd. He swiveled his upper body and started to take aim at the vehicles. He lowered the crossbow and used his own sight when he saw what was in it. The dog, missing half his helmet and one of the human soldiers; they had escaped.

The Banshee sighted in on the Tithes to see if he could spot the other soldiers. He saw another human and a Reach Grand Marshal. This was confusing. The Banshee pondered a moment before coming to the conclusion that the Grand Marshal was a traitor. Noting the appearance, or lack of the Tithes' lids, they were obviously commandeered forcefully.

The Banshee let out a joyful grunt and turned back to the Skull and fired the can at his back. It instead curved a bit and struck his shoulder, tearing it off and twisting him so fast that his spine was snapped. The others began to yell and scatter about, searching for the attacker while keeping the civilians in place.

*   *   *

"Something happened ahead," the Grand Marshal spoke over the radio.

"Please clarify that," Henry yelled over the sound of six Reach aircraft flying overhead. The aircraft were teardrop shaped with the back end split like a claw; the ships were just beginning to deploy them as missiles were becoming a concern.

"I am reading my broth… the Reach's signals within a short distance of my placing, up ahead on the road, they are calling for help and a sniper is attacking them."

"Anything else?" asked Henry.

"They have civilian prisoners," finished the Grand Marshal. "We are at your command, capable one, what are your orders."

"My name is Henry," said Henry, "I have no rank; me and Badger are special operatives who are trying to get off this planet."

"Very well then," said the Grand Marshal.

"Good," said Henry, "now let's go free some civilians."

"Time for some target practice," said Rookie, rotating the turrets.

"Pull us ahead, Badger," said Henry, pressing his rifle stock against his shoulder.

"With absolute obedience," Badger said with an excited bark. He pressed the orb and the Shepherd burst forward. The voice entered his head again.

"Remain strong; you will live to do wonders that shall never pass from your cup."

Like all the other times, his memory was immediately erased of the voice.

Upon reaching the sight of the panic, the Reach thought they were there to help and three rushed towards the oncoming Shepherd. Badger merely ran them over and commenced firing the energy bolts at the others.

Chapter 39

"The Banshee"

"About time you showed up," said Alexander as Marines started to fill up the area around the missile pod.

A couple of large vehicles with guns drove up beside the turret to give support from Reach aircraft with their heavy anti-air guns (HAAG). The guns were large and shaped like tuning forks, each side bearing three bullet-propelling barrels. The bullets were high-explosive and semi armor piercing for penetration and delayed detonation inside of the aircraft. For extra stability, the vehicles deployed hard spikes into the ground to keep from moving.

"I wasn't exactly expecting you to activate it," said the sergeant, examining the turret with a broad smile.

"You should expect nothing less then a result," growled the Zealot, pressing a fist at the sergeant, who backed away nervously.

"Lower those weapons men," said the sergeant as the Marines raised their weapons in defense. "Our large friend is just pointing out something."

The Zealot growled and turned away.

"You wouldn't happen to have another spare vehicle, would you?" Alexander asked.

"What happened to the other one?" asked the sergeant.

"I think you're standing on its ashes."

"Am I standing on the others' ashes also?" asked the sergeant looking about in disgust.

"No, they left in a couple of tanks and a Shepherd," said Alexander giving the sergeant a sideways glance.

"They're trying to find the next one?"

John and Alexander nodded.

"If you promise not to lose it, I'll give you a Cat Buggy and a Prowler escort." The sergeant let out a sigh as though he had already been informed that the vehicles were destroyed.

The Cat Buggy was a heavy troop carrier, with seating for eight Marines and one gunner on the back. The vehicle was in reasonably good condition, had a few burn marks and a crack on the hood, but it would suit their purpose. Two Marines got onto the Prowler and several others piled into the buggy. The Zealot pulled off the Marine that had taken the gunner's position and took command of it.

"Didn't wanna go anyway," muttered the Marine.

"I've got a bad feeling about this," said the sergeant as he watched the two vehicles disappear around a corner.

*   *   *

"Thank you, thank you, thank you," a bearded old man said to Henry, grasping his armored hand in a pitiful grip.

"You're welcome," said Henry, chuckling nervously as the civilians began to crowd around the Shepherd and Tithes. "Does anyone know where we can find a couple military missile pods?"

"Yes, close by," said the man pointing in a direction that was obscured by a building. "They're both located at the water park, but the Chinese are guarding them."

"Shouldn't be too difficult," said Henry. "They'll die like anyone else. What defenses do they have?"

"I don't know," said the man, lowering his head.

Henry placed a hand on his shoulder and gave it a soft squeeze. "You've told us enough already, thank you. Now, if you'll all get out of the way."

The civilians ran to the sides of the streets, to let the soldiers pass. Badger was just starting the vehicle forward when a humongous creature landed on the center of the street. The Specters were startled as the civilians screamed at the sight of the creature.

It stood a good head taller than the Zealot, covered in black scales and wore a metallic-looking armor vest with a ratty mesh of green and brown fabric about the collar. It had two wings of immense size and bat-like distinction, but there was something odd about them. Its head resembled a mixture between a cat and salamander with a bony crest that ran flush with the flat-top skull and its eyes were set near the front of its face, feline and milky-blue. It had a long, flattish tail used for maneuvering in flight and it held a gigantic crossbow in its large paws.

Badger's paw rested atop of the weapon orb, not knowing whether or not to fire at the beast. He stared into the creature's face and saw no hostility, just fear, determination and curiosity. "Should I fire?"

"Plase dun't," said the creature, folding its wings tight against its back and striding towards the Shepherd. "I broke throwe the walls to save you all."

"Oh," said Henry, remembering what Major Tac had told him. "We're actually very grateful."

The Creature's face was a blank.

Henry looked about as he thought of what to say. "You didn't have to come all of a sudden and scare off the civilians."

"Apologizes." said the creature. "But I tire of hiding with others and just observe you kind at night. I am a Banshee."

"You would be," said Henry, glad that the creature was stepping backwards, away from him.

The creature cocked its head to the side. "I dun't understand."

"And you wouldn't want to," said Henry.

"As amazed as I am with this creature," said the Grand Marshal, sticking his head out of the Tithe's lid, "we should already employ its services and get on to the water park."

"Filthy invader," growled the Banshee.

"Granted," Henry said, "But he's right. Do you know where the water park is?"

The Banshee shook his head. "Have not ben here."

"Then let's head in that direction," said Henry, indicating the where the man had pointed. "Why don't you get onto the rooftops?"

Without a further word or expression, the Banshee took off into the air, beating his powerful wings until he was atop the roof and building. He slung the crossbow over his shoulder and began to lope along the roof until he reached the edge and then he would spread his wings and glide to the next building. He repeated this process several times until he reached a building that overlooked a circular area of ground with trees that surrounded a large pool.

About the pool were the Chinese and several spriks patrolling the area, weapons ready and eyes weary. There were also a few Kismets, two Sluices and two Dragon Kismets. The Sluice Kismets' spikes were extremely long on their backs, standing out like small saplings. The Dragon Kismets were slower in movement than their golden counterparts, stalking about, shifting their weight from side to side.

There were no vehicles, but some halo-turrets had been set up. A couple small fires had been lit and some of the soldiers stood about them with their helmets removed. Some were laughing at jokes and others were eating foods or drinking intoxicating liquids. Other than the Reach aircraft flying overhead, the Chinese thought that the night was fairly quiet and would remain so.

The Banshee, of course, had another idea than letting them enjoy the night. Again, dismissing the rods, he searched until he had found several large pieces of metal to place on the rail at once. He didn't even bother with the sight; he merely pointed the crossbow at a group of soldiers and pulled the trigger.

The Chinese were startled by the sudden deaths of four of their comrades and a three severely wounded. They hefted up their weapons and moved for cover. What the Banshee had failed to see was that several of the soldiers had Paste Launchers. After he had fired a second shot, the Chinese knew where he was and fired the biometric weapons at the rooftop. Several shot over the roof, but those that had hit the building exploded in loud crimson flashes.

The Banshee merely stood there, the flames were nothing to him; his flesh could resist the hot magma that loomed underneath the mountains. Banshees did not live above ground; they lived underground, near the molten lakes. The mountains were the only known way in or out of their subterranean home. He let out a hissing laugh at the pitiful assault.

Chapter 40

"Shadows and Enlightenment"

Pedro was feeling rather uneasy inside the Minor Giant with the Pure Collect. Even though he was sitting apart from them, he could feel their eyes curiously roving over him and his equipment. Though he was very much frightened of what the Reach could do, he felt that these terrefs were more frightened of what he could do. They didn't get too close to him, mostly because his hand was resting on the handle of his rifle.

The Elite, having sat opposite Pedro for the longest time, finally broke the silence that had reined over the Minor Giant's interior for over an hour. "What is it you colonists base your weapons upon?"

Pedro nearly jumped with the suddenness of the question. He stuttered for a moment before answering. "Magnetism, we use magnetism to launch our projectiles."

"Intriguing," said the Elite, handing Pedro a heavy Sticker. "We base our weapons upon energy and gravity. By redirecting and amassing greater force through manipulation, we could destroy entire cities with a planet's own gravity. Or, by using a contradicting energy force we can launch these spikes great distances."

"Nice," said Pedro, stroking a finger over the razor-sharp tips of the Sticker's spikes. "I bet it would make a good slicer too."

"I have gutted a few of your meuks with such spikes," the Elite said proudly.

"Wish you wouldn't," said Pedro. "They're very gentle creatures and you're making them untrusting towards colonists."

"But they taste so divine," said the Elite. A couple Lessers chuckled and nodded.

"I agree," said Pedro, "but I saw one with a large burn on its neck and then its mate tried to attack me."

"The vessel's engines and the Reach did that." The Elite had said "Reach" as if it was now a curse.

"You don't like the Reach?"

"Why else would we have left?" growled a Lesser. "They're evil and uphold little honor, many of our brothers' lives have been wasted with the orders of the Reach."

"The Pure Collect, part of us, have separated ourselves from the rest, no longer wanting to follow the Emperor and counselors," growled the Elite. "We swore upon all that lives that we would see the Reach fall and the Gate broken."

"What is this Gate?" asked Pedro, trying to see if the soldiers were more open now. They all started to activate their swords.

The Elite had activated two swords, both pointed towards the ground, burning into the floor. "The Gate," he snarled, "is a giant artifact, only the hierarchs and the Emperor know where: it is the first of thirteen artifacts, one of which you have uncovered. The smaller artifacts are the keys to activate the Gate. The Reach has all but two and, unless your vessel has it aboard, all but one. The last is a small object, able to fit upon one of my fingers, but the GEN warrior you have has that one, hidden or somehow destroyed I hope."

"What happens when all the keys are in place?" Pedro wasn't sure he wanted to hear the answer.

"Then the Gate shall open and the Reach can pass into the heavens," the Elite said as he deactivated his swords and sat down. "Then... and only then can the Emperor amass an army large enough to conquer the entire universe."

"Who is the Emperor?" Pedro asked, watching a couple Lessers that were seething with rage and shaking their swords.

"No one but the Emperor and High Priest know," said the Elite, "he is the one that formed the Reach after the discovery of EVE, a great shrine, until the Demaw race, the universe's deliverers, destroyed it before he could harvest all the knowledge needed to rule."

Pedro was about to ask another question when the terref in the cockpit shouted back. "Enough stories, I spy a prize before us."

The Elite got up and shoved the two Lessers back into their seats on his way to the cockpit. He let out a gurgling laugh and gestured for

Pedro to come. When Pedro was beside him, he pointed out a landing pad on top of a smaller building. On it were four blue-and-green beetle-like aircraft that were standing upon six legs that acted as landing gear and for walking, while a large energy weapon, similar to Major Tac's sonic weapon, was placed just below the cockpit.

"What are those?" asked Pedro, leaning in close to the screen.

"Scarabs," said the Elite. "We will need them, let us purify the area."

"As you desire," said the pilot.

The pilot brought the Minor Giant in close to the landing pad before firing the craft's weapon systems at the Reach and Chinese that were on the ground. The craft's weapon system, as the Elite explained to Pedro, was gravity based. The gravitational energy beams were the same color as the gravity bombs, but these were flat like paper and made a grating sound with every shot, they could even curve to follow a hostile.

Pedro watched in horrified fascination as hostiles, upon being hit with the gravity beams, were crushed or knocked flat, dead. A couple of soldiers were blown against the next building. It didn't take long for the pilot to eliminate every last hostile on the pad, leaving the Scarabs free for the taking.

The pilot brought the craft over the pad and opened the hatch for the others to get out. "Shall I follow?"

The Elite nodded. "We may need a carrier for reinforcements, if we can find any in this labyrinth."

"Very well, brother," said the pilot, reversing the beam.

"Come with me, Marine," said the Elite, "I shall need a secondary gunner."

"Why me?" asked Pedro, not exactly thrilled with the idea of flying with an alien.

"Because I like you," said the Elite.

The six other Converts had dropped down to the ground with the Elite and Pedro and they quickly rushed to get into the Scarabs. The way they got into the craft was to pull a lever beside the cockpit, which would make the cockpit split open like a Venus flytrap. Each Scarab had two cockpits, one at the nose for the pilot and one on the back for the secondary gunner, both had to lie on their stomachs.

The Elite crawled into the front and waited until Pedro was securely inside the other. "The controls are very simple Marine, you need merely to look upon a target to hit it and you must press the orb before you to strike."

Pedro was surprised with the cockpit, from the inside it was completely transparent. He laughed quietly as he watched the other Scarab's fold up their legs and lift off the ground with what was probably an anti-gravity energy. "This is nice."

The orb was a floating, bright purple hologram that hovered several inches from his face. He reached out and touched it. A gravity beam shot out and struck a building, smashing a small crater in the flexcrete.

"Careful," exclaimed the Elite, "there is little use for no self control."

"Sorry," Pedro muttered.

The Elite ignored Pedro's apology and lifted the Scarab up off the ground. The Scarab, though it didn't look like it, was very fast and maneuverable in the city. The Elite made sure that they were all flying below the rooftops, away from the threat of fighters.

"I've never seen a Reach craft like this before," said Pedro.

"It is a new craft, made by the Chinese," said the Elite, "using both our technologies to create these small war machines."

"Do you know where you're going?" asked Pedro.

"Yes," said the Elite. "Out of this city; there is a building out there. If there is but a single ship left on this planet it shall be there."

"But what about the others," Pedro demanded.

"The Grand Marshal is concerned for our honor; he desires to get as many of you out of this city where they can fight as he can. He didn't tell the others because they would have gone immediately to fulfill their objective. The Grand Marshal and your Kernul knew, but they're no longer worried about this world, because it shall fall, the more that can fight may keep the Reach occupied. We will wait for them at the building."

Pedro remained silent. Everything that had happened tonight had had a shadow over it. He had been fighting the Reach for a month, now he was joined with a group of them. He had no idea what to think, but he felt that he knew one thing; he would never leave Forerunner.

*   *   *

The Banshee, not wanting his crossbow to get destroyed, had devised a way to avoid the Paste Launchers and still eliminate the Chinese soldiers. He would fire one salvo of metal fragments he collected and then fly to another building at a random position around the water park and then fire again. But the metal was so inaccurate, some even disintegrated without hitting anything, that he was hardly doing any damage at all.

It was only with the arrival of the vehicles that the tide turned against the Chinese. Both energy and SEAR was fired from the Shepherd, while the Tithes fired all their weapons. The Chinese couldn't even use their Paste Launchers in the confusion.

The Banshee slung the crossbow over his shoulder and dropped towards the ground like a streaking missile. The wind thrummed around his body as he plummeted downwards. He hit the ground on all fours with a loud *bang* and then he opened his mouth and released two contradictory gases from his cheeks, they connected and ignited.

Badger and Henry watched in dumb silence as the Banshee spewed forth the hot flames about the crowds of Chinese. Major Tac hadn't been lying. The Chinese ran about screaming and leaping into the water to dowse the flames, but that couldn't save them. The Banshee leapt in after them, biting, clawing and thrashing.

The Banshee arose back out of the water after he had killed the last hostile, leaving the water dark crimson with blood. A Dragon Kismet fired its flame upon him, but it did nothing. He rushed forward, dodging a blow from the hooks and bit off the worm's head. The body fell to the ground like a sack of flour; he turned to search for another.

Badger had leapt out of the Shepherd and rushed at a Sluice Kismet, rolling to avoid the two blades that whistled through the air. He grabbed a panel of the armor and swung himself up and onto its shoulder, using his kukri thrust into its neck as a brace, he activated the Photon Sword and stabbed it up through the worm's helmet, the point glittered in the dim light. He leapt off to avoid a blast of fire from the other Dragon Kismet, which torched the Sluice like it was made of oil.

The Banshee, fire still clinging to its body, came up behind the Dragon Kismet and used its claws to tear out its back. It thrust its arms up into its body and into the head. He felt around until he found the brain. He promptly tore it out and tossed it into the pool.

The other sluice leapt at the Banshee, arms raised high for a killing strike, but two blasts from Rookie's Tithe blew it back. The final mole-worm lay upon the ground, its armor blown apart and burned, there was practically nothing left of its flesh.

"Glad you had fun," said Henry.

* * *

It was nearly dawn when the other two PDCTs arrived with the group of Marines in the Cat Buggy. The missile-pods were still firing at the Reach vessels and now the damage could be seen. Thin lines of fumes poured forth around them. The Marines started to set up a perimeter, taking up the Paste Launchers and halo-turrets, for the defense of the pods.

The sergeant arrived a while later with a larger force and the female terref. He walked up to Henry with a belittled smile on his face and held out his hand.

Henry took it and shook it firmly.

"I didn't think you could do it," said the sergeant.

"That was very apparent," said Henry, removing his helmet and smiling broadly. His hair resembled a rat's nest and his face glistened with sweat. "Now… where's this ship."

"Just twenty miles outside the city," answered the Grand Marshal.

Henry was taken aback. "You knew?"

The Grand Marshal nodded.

"And you had us risk the solar system by not taking us to it?"

"The solar system would be at more risk if you didn't," said the Grand Marshal climbing into the Cat Buggy. "Warriors are always needed. I believe you and your tool should get in also and whoever else desires to come. The city is lost and the planet shall soon follow."

Henry sighed climbed into a seat, a short ways apart from the Grand Marshal. Badger sat down beside him and whimpered in consideration to Henry's troubles. Henry reached a hand over and stroked Badger's ears. "Yeah, you're a good boy, Badger."

"The ship will only fit a few," said the sergeant. "The entire city is being evacuated, I sent out the call. We'll be here to guard the pods for only two hours and then we're leaving as well. The best of luck to you all, I hope you can end this."

"My clan shall meet us there," said the Grand Marshal, "hopefully with more than the Minor Giant."

Henry looked about as Marines and armed civilians climbed into a multitude of vehicles. He looked up towards the two PDCT soldiers, John and Alexander and nodded when the Cat Buggy was full. "Let's get out of this place."

Henry put his helmet back on and slid his fingers over the back of his rifle. Next to him he heard Badger project, "I want to kill them all."

"Glad to hear it," he said.

No one asked, but they were rather surprised when the large catlike reptile climbed on top of the Cat Buggy. It was a rather ominous sight, since it was loading a rod onto a giant crossbow without strings.

Chapter 41

"Exodus"

Vehicles sent up a mist as they drove over the wet roads, outside New Greenwich. Those that looked back could hardly see the city due to the mist; mostly they saw the ships and fighters that were flying about and the missiles as they struck the vessels. Hostile vehicles, such as Prowlers and Shepherds were being encountered, but the people had more fire power.

"I got one," a Marine would occasionally shout out after killing a Reach soldier.

A MATO had been encountered once along the road, but it wasn't able to do much damage because the people just blew right past it. A few soldiers and civilians had taken some shots at it, but the bullets or splinters just glanced off.

"Shouldn't be too much further," said Henry as he shot a sprik Specialist that was running along the side of the road.

"Definitely not," said a Marine next to him. He looked up at the Banshee and then nudged Henry. "What is that thing?"

"It's a Banshee," said Henry.

"They're just a myth," said the Marine.

"Tell that to him," said Henry.

A Militant dropped with a hole through his chest from a rod. The

Banshee growled triumphantly as he loaded another. He fired this one at a Prowler. The Prowler and its riders erupted into flames.

"Lethal guy ain't he," said the Marine.

"You should smell his breath," said Henry as he shot at a sprik.

Vehicles started to break off from the large group, heading off the road, or down roads that cut away from the main group. No one had any idea where they were going, but it didn't matter, just as long as they got away from the city.

Badger could feel his stimulants wearing off, but his adrenalin was far surpassing it now. His amber eyes roved over the road and roadside, as he looked energetically for targets; mostly they were low ranking spriks, but there were plenty of officers.

"Scarabs," someone shouted.

Suddenly the grating sound of gravity beams was heard coming from the side of the road. The soldiers began to turn their fire upon half a dozen of the insectile craft. A Technical was sent somersaulting when a sonic beam hit its side.

The Marine watched as the living occupants crawled out from underneath the technical and waited for another to stop and pick them up.

"They were lucky," said the Marine.

"Luck had nothing to do with that," said Henry.

"Are you about to launch into a religious talk?" said the Marine as he rolled his eyes. "Forget it; I don't want to hear it."

"What if that was you," Henry asked as he took a couple shots at the Scarabs.

"Well it wasn't," said the Marine, also firing.

The Banshee launched a rod at one of the Scarabs, it missed. He quickly loaded another one and fired it at the Scarab's nose. The rod stuck deep, piercing the face of the pilot. The Scarab quickly spun out of control and crashed into the ground, sending up smoke, sparks and mist.

"I hate those things," said the Marine. "The Chinese made them for their new friends, they're like a VTOL and MATO in one."

Badger didn't care what or who made them, he wanted to break them. The chassis of the Scarabs wasn't impenetrable; he could see holes made by an Assault Rifle SEAR in the armor. He waited until one was coming at an angle so that he could shoot where the cockpit was most likely placed and pulled the trigger. By the time the Scarab was nearly ten yards away he could see that the nose was covered in holes. It crashed on the other side of the Cat Buggy.

A Technical and all it occupants were smashed by a sonic beam and two civilian cars went flying by another. The cars were flipped back up onto their wheels and the bruised occupants hurried to get back on the road. Three gravity beams demolished one.

The Zealot took down one of the Scarabs with the turret and

pierced several holes in another. He had to be careful to not hit the Banshee.

Badger and Henry fired upon a Shepherd that tried to use this opportunity to get in close. It was torn apart by the Zealot and the two Specters and several others Marines. The crystallizing pink fumes flew into the air and the Shepherd crashed into the front of another Cat Buggy, which just knocked it aside like it was nothing.

Badger was suddenly surprised when the Banshee reached down and took the sword from his belt. The Banshee launched himself into the air with his wings spread wide. The sword was like a dagger to him, he could only hold it with two claws. He then slashed the sword across the nose of a Scarab, slicing the pilot in half.

The Scarab crashed into a truck, killing most of the occupants. A single soldier staggered up and was pulled into another vehicle by his comrades.

"Here come some more," shouted John, "and they've got a Minor Giant too."

Several Marines started to fire at the new Scarabs, but when they saw the new Scarabs firing upon the remaining two of the first group, they halted and watched. The last two hostile Scarabs broke apart and fell to the ground, killing a Militant upon a Shepherd.

"Hi," Pedro's voice came over the radio. "Are we too late?"

"No," laughed Henry, "you're just in time."

"I'm glad we found you," said Pedro, "I was beginning to think that we'd have to leave without you."

"We would have done no such thing," said the Elite.

"Your honor is pure," said the Grand Marshal. "Let us lay aside our differences and purge ourselves of this world."

Badger barked triumphantly and shot a sprik off of a Prowler. He had slightly wondered where the other terrefs and Pedro had been.

"What is that?" asked Pedro.

Henry already knew what Pedro meant. "That is a Banshee, the one that saved us at the prison facility."

"I knew they were real," said Pedro.

The four Scarabs flew over the convoy, shooting sonic and gravity beams at the hostiles, which were beginning to grow uncertain. Some of the Holy Troops began to flee. But the officers that stayed made sure that those under them stayed as well, but it was only a matter of time before they too would run.

"See how they quake in fear," growled the Grand Marshal. "If they were of any honor they would stand and die for the Emperor."

"Better for us," muttered the Marine.

The Grand Marshal growled menacingly at the Marine. "Quiet!"

"I-I think this is it," John shouted back.

Those within hearing range, or those that had already spotted it, looked at the building that loomed up before them. The building was shaped like an irregular triangle, the longest portions being the thickest. A sign on the road read: CARLSON BOTANICAL GARDEN. There was a large covered parking lot that led straight inside the building and exotic trees lined either side.

"I'm not so sure," Henry shouted back.

"This is it," barked the Grand Marshal. "Take us inside and we shall firsthand see this vessel."

"How would you know it's in there?" Henry demanded.

"The Pure Collect was sent to investigate it," the Grand Marshal returned with a chuckle. "The thickest portion, for a reason yet unknown, disguises a ship for emergency evacuation."

"Anybody in there?" asked the Marine.

"Civilian workers of the plants," the Grand Marshal shrugged. "There may be some room for them in the vessel."

"That's kind of cold, don't you think?" said the Marine.

The Grand Marshal gave him a poisonous stare. "Those that can't fight are captive, those that do fight suffer. Those that suffer must free the captive; the captive cannot free those that suffer."

"I didn't understand a word he said," the Marine whispered to another that was behind him. The other Marine nodded in agreement.

Badger looked at the building; he twitched his nose and ears suspiciously. Something wasn't right, perhaps it was the look of it, it looked deserted and the Grand Marshal had said there were civilian workers, but he couldn't see a single one. Also, the Reach of Nimrod were nowhere in sight, not a single vehicle or soldier was in sight, they had even disappeared from the road. He quickly made this known by snarling menacingly in the building's direction. A few of the ISEN and civilian vehicles remained with them, while the others had split off.

Henry noticed the disappearance of the Reach also. "Have any idea where your friends are, Grand Marshal?"

"They would not be friends," the Grand Marshal barked. "But I have faith you are asking if our foes are close by. I most certainly say they are."

"Inside," said Henry.

"Perhaps," said the Grand Marshal, "but one can never tell."

A radio signal was quickly sent through to every vehicle and Marine, telling them to remain alert once stopped. A quick decision was made for the PDCTs, Specters and Converts to go in first; this was unanimously appraised by everyone but the forgoers.

"Here we go again," said Rookie, climbing out of a well-damaged Technical.

The Banshee tried to follow, but was told to stay because it would be too large to fight in the halls. The Banshee let out an indignant growl and sat down on the flexcrete parking lot, he was given a wide berth by everyone else. He hated being left behind, even by those he hardly knew, or hardly knew him.

The female terref, who was also given a wide berth, hesitantly came up to the Banshee and placed a hand upon one of his great wings. She recoiled when the Banshee flinched to her touch; they stared at each other for the longest moment and then the Banshee twitched an ear and returned to his original position. The female terref smiled and stroked his wing softly.

The Banshee let out an indiscreet croon. "Feel gude."

"I am most glad," returned the terref. "I am Princess Tan-Jhin Tafbar, of Shilan."

"I Mirchlaen," the Banshee returned. "You are kind."

Nearby Pedro watched the pair with an odd look. "Looks like a scene from <u>Saint George and the Dragon</u>," he muttered.

*   *   *

Inside the building, the group looked about for anything that would at least give them an indication of some sort of life. But the place seemed hollow and lifeless, every step they took echoed about the halls. There was, however, a single clue, a smell, only detected by the Converts, the zealot and Badger.

"What is this foul stench?" the Elite demanded into thin air.

The Grand Marshal activated his sword and held it out with his Sticker. "I do not know, but I have smelled it before. Be wary, there may be chemical deposits."

"Perhaps it is these plants," said the Zealot, grabbing a few vines that were trailing on the floor. The vines were covered in tiny red flowers and they immediately twisted about the Zealot's wrist. The Zealot was about to sever the vines with his sword, but the vines, seemingly intelligent enough to know he wasn't soil, released him and dropped to the floor.

"Curious," said the Zealot as he watched the vines writhe on the floor until they found a spot of moist soil a Lesser had brought in. "Most curious."

The soldiers passed by the plant to investigate further inside, behind them another few vines crept over the floor until they found something to wrap around. The vines had wrapped themselves about a solid object that created a slight distortion as it yanked away from their grip. The invisible spectator gave off a low hiss and quietly followed the group around a corner that led to a few rooms and a wide staircase.

"Is this your smell," asked Rookie, pointing with his rifle into a room with several dead bodies in it.

The bodies didn't need to be examined close to tell what had killed them. They were civilians, with long, burnt, slash marks running over their bodies. There were blood smears on the walls and one of the civilians, a chubby man with a horrified look frozen forever on his face, was hanging upside down by his left foot.

"The stench of death fills these rooms," the Grand Marshal snarled. "But this is not the source of the smell."

"Well," said John, walking backwards, in the direction they had come, "I'll go outside and get us some hellll…!"

The soldiers turned to see John lifted high into the air by the blade of a Photon Sword with a semi-invisible user. With a sigh, John was let slide off the blade to the floor. The blade's owner then became visible and all saw an Elite Ripper.

"So you are the stench," growled a Lesser, "chameleon residue."

"You have come too late to save them, or the vessel. Nimrod, god of construction, has voiced his desire for the cities of this planet and I am here to fulfill his will."

Then, as if produced out of thin air, other hostiles began to appear everywhere. Each one had a sword and an ISEN Assault Rifle. They began to crowd around the soldiers, weapons raised menacingly.

"What is his desire?" demanded the Grand Marshal, taking a bold step towards the Elite.

"That they are all broken to the ground," the Elite laughed.

"Heresy to the very belief," shouted the Grand Marshal, lunging forward and driving his sword through the Elite's face. "You fools shall then burn with them."

The Convert Elite activated both his swords and drove them through the chests of two Lessers. "Be along your ways, I shall handle these."

The Grand Marshal deflected one Militant's sword while kicking another in the stomach. "We shall both handle these. All others get to the ship, get off this planet."

"What about everyone outside?" Alexander demanded.

"Land for them to enter," said the Grand Marshal, as he punched a Militant's screen.

"No time to waste," said Rookie, running up the stairs. "Let's go now."

The others, after taking a few quick shots, ran after rookie, killing other enemies that got in their way.

*   *   *

The soldiers outside had already heard the fighting, but they weren't able to go and help, a new problem had arisen for them. A small Reach of Nimrod Reef had come into the atmosphere and was dropping vehicles about the building. One vehicle that fell crashed into the Minor Giant, destroying both; the fragments were equally lethal. Fortunately, the

Converts had cleared out of the Minor Giant beforehand.

"What's happening," demanded a civilian, shooting at a Sage that was leaping over a Technical.

Pedro smashed in the front of one Lesser's helmet with the butt of his rifle, killing it instantly. He turned and shot another through the stomach; the projectile passed through and killed another that had just come around the corner of a Cat Buggy. "Where did you all suddenly come from?"

A Militant climbed over a noncombatant vehicle and used an Assault Rifle to kill three Marines and then smashed another skull with a vicious kick. He stepped over the dead bodies and walked towards a terrified civilian that had dropped his weapon. He gave out a rumbling laugh and activated his sword and lunged forward.

A mighty hand of lethal claws caught the Militant by the stomach and slammed the Militant onto its back. The Banshee, keeping a protective wing about the princess and with his hand pinning the Militant to the ground, opened his mouth and torched the Reach soldier.

"How... pleasant," said the female terref, smiling nervously.

"I find notting pleasant abot burnt flesh," said the Banshee, giving her a quizzical look.

"Sorry," she said.

·The Banshee suddenly whipped out with his tail, knocking back two other hostiles. His large eyes roved over the combat. Pods were still dropping from the ship, bringing in more soldiers; Scarabs and Minor Giants were coming also. The Minor Giants were dropping scores of spriks, many of which were the suicidal Sporadics. The Banshee growled menacingly and held the female terref closer to his body, he knew she was important.

He spat out a large fireball, consuming three spriks, one of which was a Sporadic that blew up. He watched as the soldiers and civilians that were supposed to be on a ship leaving for another world were killing and being killed by those they were trying to escape. The Reach, mostly mights and terrefs, with a scattering of humans and origs, were larger than most of the people and their armor made them stronger. This battle was already lost.

A sword had cut out the load in Pedro's rifle and now he used it as a bludgeon, gripping it by the barrel and swinging it about. An orig Confessor was knocked back a pace when hit by the rifle, but he caught the next swing and grabbed Pedro about the neck with his huge hand and then used its claws to punch through his eyes and into his brain. Surprising, Pedro wasn't dead yet, he took out his knife and drove it up under the Militants helmet, up into his brain. Blood splattered on both the inside and outside of the helmet. Pedro and the orig fell dead, Pedro with a hole through his head from a sprik's ASP.

* * *

The sound of automatic fire echoed about the halls, as the soldiers ran. Reach were appearing from everywhere, using swords or rifles, but it didn't really matter, the Converts and their allies were having a terrific run of blessings. Even Badger, void of his HUD, was milling about the halls, using his kukri and Photon Sword. enemies were left behind, dead or severally wounded.

After several twists, stairways and dead ends, they finally arrived at the ship. It wasn't a large ship, but it was large enough. Made to look like part of the garden, plants of every variety were decoratively placed about it, making it difficult to tell that it was ship. Behind several large leaves was the hidden control panel and an incredibly thick crystal screen was fused over it.

"Wonderful," moaned Henry, trying to pry the covering away.

"I find this not as pleasant," remarked a Confessor.

"That's not what I meant," hissed Henry. At that moment he heard footsteps running through the hall. He and the others whirled about; they were relieved when they saw the Grand Marshal and Elite.

"A vessel has come here," yelled the Grand Marshal.

"We can see it," said Rookie, placing a hand upon the ship's view screen. He watched as the final few pods fell to the ground and watched the flashes of energy.

"We've wasted everything," said Henry, sending a plant down the hall with a swat of his hand. "If you had just taken us here everything would have been fine."

The Grand Marshal remained silent for a moment before changing the subject. "Not so or important any longer, we must leave now."

"We can't," shouted Henry, "the controls are fused with this dumb crystal."

The Grand Marshal looked over the panel and growled. "Then everything is lost."

Badger removed the remains of his helmet and stepped up to the panel; he felt the crystal and thought for a moment. The image of the broken canister on the core he had killed flashed into his mind. He had no idea how he howled like that, but he had a feeling he was about to find out.

Everyone started at the sound of the piercing howl and watched in amazement as the tiny crystal fragments chimed on the floor like little bells. Badger looked about at everyone else, smiling modestly.

"I forgot about that," said Henry as he walked over to the controls. He slid his hand over them to ensure they were completely uncovered. "We're good to go."

"Allow me to handle this vehicle," said the Grand Marshal.

"Can you?" Henry asked, trying to keep the edge out of his voice.

"The Chinese are very hospitable to their allies," returned the Grand Marshal, removing his helmet and pushing the plants aside to sit on the stand. He looked at the controls for a long moment.

"Is this anything like ISEN ships?" asked Alexander.

"I shall manage," said the Grand Marshal.

The ship gave a groan and then a grating noise announced the ship's detachment from the garden. A door, well hidden by some vines, shut as they all grabbed hold of something as the ship started to move.

"Wait," said Rookie, "we can't leave; the princess is still down there."

"What can we do?" asked Alexander.

"How slow can this go?" Badger projected.

Again, none of the Converts noticed.

"I feel I know your reasoning," said the Grand Marshal, "I dare not stop, but perhaps that winged beast has a mind to take a few with him."

"Find a way to open the doors," said Henry.

The ship was now fully removed from the building. It was box-shaped with a trapezoid bow. The Grand Marshal curved its flight to fly underneath the Reach ship and made sure to go as slow as was safely possible.

"Found it," shouted Rookie as he opened the doors with a lever he found behind a feathery fern. He pulled back the lever and the doors slid open with a groan.

Two Lessers and a Sage went to the doors to see if they could assist in any way. They looked down at the battlefield. The Reach had already won and the Reach were just going around and giving no quarter to the wounded. Barely a handful of Marines, the Banshee and the princess were all that remained. In the distance, the Reach Reefs were pummeling the city with gravity bombs, leveling the great buildings.

*   *   *

The Banshee was swinging at all the hostiles while guarding the female terref, who was doing damage of her own with a semi-automatic biometric rifle. The Banshee was cut in several places, but nothing serious, his tough scales and armor protected him from most of what was thrown at him.

A Confessor rushed up with a sword, the female terref killed him with several shots. A orig with a Sticker fired at the Banshee; he was burnt to a crisp by his target. A Marine fell onto his back after a might punched him in the chest, he killed the might with his rifle and then kicked away a sprik, but was then stabbed through the chest by an Elite. A sprik Sage crept up behind one Marine and stabbed a thin metal spike up his spine, killing him instantly, a Militant human spat in demeaning anger at the sprik.

The Banshee ducked as a Technical flew at him, it missed him by a fraction. He spewed forth his final fireball (the gases had been depleted) and he curled about the female terref, sensing the end was inevitable. But then a noise touched his ears, he looked up and saw a box-shaped ship flying towards him, he used his binocular vision to look past the screen.

With a triumphant hiss, the Banshee grabbed the female terref with a forepaw, spread his wings and took flight. He flew low over the battle field and grabbed two Marines that were in bad spots. The Marines struggled until they discovered what had them. The Banshee flapped as hard as he could towards the ship, he knew they were coming to save them. He glided alongside the craft until he saw the doorway; the young PDCT and Converts were gesturing for them to hurry with their arms.

The Banshee caught a piece of the ship with a free hand and noticed with great horror; the opening was too small to fit him. But he swung himself up so that he could toss the princess and Marines in. Then, with a despairing roar, he spread his wings and glided back to the ground.

"Wormhole now…!"

"But what of those on the ground?" the Grand Marshal asked, standing up. "Nay, you and the others must go, but the Pure Collect have still a debt to pay for our work."

The Converts, one by one, started to leap out of the ship, landing lightly upon the ground below. They were a destructive force upon landing, almost nothing could stand in their way. The Zealot himself, more accustomed to large spaces, hacked at everything within range of his sword.

"They're all going to die anyway," shouted Henry, "if they don't get sucked in it'll be better than being killed by the Reach."

"Not if you climb high enough," said the Grand Marshal. "Fortune and the Christian God be with you."

"And I may have vengeance to reap" said the Elite, "that Pedro and I were friends."

The Elite was the last to go, when he landed, he stabbed a Grunt through the back, cackling maliciously. "Come to the vengeance of the Pure Collect, none shall oppose us again. There is no honor left in your pact, join us or fail."

Rookie, Alexander and Badger shut the door and then rushed to grab hold of something.

"Grab tight," shouted Henry, he yanked a switch marked: FORE-INSTRUCTED VORTEX.

The craft vanished into the vortex, which sucked in a couple Reach aircraft behind it. There was nothing to be seen, it was as if the ship had never been there.

* * *

The Banshee and the Grand Marshal stood over two prone figures; one was the dead Marine: Pedro and the other was the Elite, breathing in a watery rasp, sobbing for breath with several holes in his chest. The Grand Marshal had removed his helmet, kneeling over the Elite, tears rolled down his cheeks.

"I am sorry, father," said the Elite, "I have failed you."

"You could never fail me," said the Grand Marshal. He reached down and squeezed his son's hand.

"But I killed so few of these," the Elite gasped.

"You need not kill anymore," said the Grand Marshal, "your sons are doing well and they shall live, my grandchildren."

The Elite let out another gasp, harder and more painful then the others. Blood trickled out his mouth. "The pain, father, it is great. Do not let my children be shamed, let my wife know how I died. I died avenging my friend. I don't even know his family name."

"Your wife was blessed to know you," wept the Grand Marshal. "Your honor is true."

"Do not let them capture me," the Elite growled, "my mate must not be shamed."

"As you desire," said the Grand Marshal, "heaven's gates are open for you."

Without further words, the Grand Marshal activated his sword and plunged it into his son's heart. His son gave a final gasp and then his head lulled to the side, a smile upon his face. The Banshee retreated a few paces, unsure of what the terref might do next.

The Grand Marshal let out a reverberating roar, lifting his head to the sky and raising his arms. He stood up and kicked his helmet away. He removed the sword and approached the scared Banshee.

"I shall not kill you," said the terref, "for I need you and you need me. Take me up to the Reef and together we shall make them pay for everything. Were it that cheap of a payment."

Chapter 42

"Home Sweet Home, If Only"

ISEN's *Galilee* awaited docking on United States Orbital Defense Station (ODS) Gamma while the *USS Lewis* was being refitted with extra magazines. No one was saying much, but Captain Whittington, *Galilee*'s commander, felt that something big was getting ready to happen. It couldn't be the Chinese; that news was too old and the Chinese forces in the solar system were diminishing fast. ISEN had recovered several of their lost ships, but were still missing several that were last known to be exploring uncharted regions of space.

Whittington was an old man who had thick, white sideburns and more then one internal organ replaced during his service. He was always glad to return to Mars, he was born and raised there; he especially enjoyed visiting his family in the Central East Equatorial Region, part of Germany's diplomacy sector.

"What's taking so long?" Whittington had been waiting for two hours to dock, but it seemed that the *Lewis* was also having some maintenance done. He looked down at the bridge's computer, situated over a large walkway lined with computers and officers, examining his report that he was soon to turn in.

A door slid open behind him and footsteps were coming close. Whittington didn't have look to know who it was, it would be Seaman Miranda Chatsworth; a young woman with a bad demeanor around everyone.

"Set the coffee where I can reach it," Whittington mumbled as he closed the report. He watched in distaste as Miranda purposely put it just within reach of his hand. He snatched it up and took a long sip and almost gagged.

"What's in this?" he demanded.

"Just what you ordered," said Miranda with a blank stare.

"This is nothing of the kind of what I drink," shouted Whittington, rising from his chair. "What did you do?"

"I did nothing," said Miranda, "It was those incompetent civilian cooks."

"Those cooks have been with the *Galilee* for nearly ten years," growled the captain. "They're more competent than some of this crew I could mention."

Miranda stuck out her tongue when the captain turned around, "Obviously not."

"Sugar," Whittington shouted, having found the answer. "You put sugar in this, I can't have sugar."

"What's the difference between that and honey?" Miranda rolled her eyes as Whittington shoved the cup into her hands, spilling some on the floor and her uniform.

"Just take this back and return with my coffee. And when you get back you're going to clean that up, then clean your uniform and then you will be confined to quarters for the next twenty-four hours."

Miranda turned around rolled her eyes while muttering. "For a German you sure talk like an Englishman."

"For your education," began Whittington, stopping Miranda in her tracks, "English is the international trade language; some countries just want to skip speaking two languages."

"Whatever," Miranda mumbled under her breath as she walked out.

The Captain was all too overjoyed when the door closed behind the seaman. He sat back down in his chair and quickly looked up Miranda's file. He grunted when he saw all the dozens of bad marks on her, many of which were placed by him. He quickly wrote up another as he waited.

"As soon as I get back to headquarters I'm going to have her put back on that supply freighter."

"You could just give her a dishonorable discharge."

Whittington looked up to see Commander Long, a lifelong friend. Commander Long had a shallow face, wiry red hair and one of his ears had an electronic chip on it to regain the hearing lost during a malfunction with the on-deck cannons. They quickly saluted each other.

"That's what she wants," said Whittington, "but I won't allow it. Either she finishes her term or gets a dishonorable discharge somewhere else. Nothing's too bad for her."

"She won't be back for a while," said the commander, rubbing his damaged ear.

"Every moment is like heaven," laughed Whittington, leaning back in his chair and closing Miranda's file. "Do you have something to report? Or, do you just want to talk about something."

"Something to report," said the commander, handing over a datapad. "The *Traveler*'s back and it's brought a rather bizarre cargo with it."

Whittington's eyes widened as he examined the report. "Top secret until the real threat arrives?"

The commander nodded. "We're the only ones aboard the *Galilee* that know."

"Keep it that way," said Whittington, handing the datapad back. "Ah, here's my coffee… I hope."

"Black with honey," groaned Miranda, handing the cup over.

Suddenly, the ship gave a lurch, sending the crew staggering and the coffee flying onto Whittington's uniform. Miranda and the commander fell to the floor, but the captain managed to steady himself with his chair.

"Hitler," he cursed. "What was that?"

"Sir!" shouted an ensign. "A ship has just come out a wormhole one hundred yards off our stern. There's seems to be two other derelict ships floating behind it."

"Is it the Chinese?" demanded Whittington, looking out the bridge's humongous view ports.

"No sir," said another officer, "unidentified, derelict and drifting."

"Engage tractor beams," said Whittington, pull in that ship and garbage. Ready four units of PDCTs in the marked hangar, this could be a trap."

"Yes sir!"

Whittington turned to look at Miranda; her face was white with horror at the sight of the captain's uniform.

"This just isn't your day," smirked Whittington.

*   *   *

The passengers inside the derelict vessel let out great groans as they stretched their aching limbs. Badger was the least effected, having pressed his back against the door as the ship went into a jump. Alexander and Rookie dug themselves out from under a cascade of plants, dirt and broken pots.

"Let's never do that again without following ISEN safety

procedures," Alexander groaned, sitting up.

Rookie groaned and took off his helmet. "I think ISEN should try and find a safer way of manipulating space."

"Is the GEN's any better?" asked Alexander.

"Everything is manipulated, a slipstream, though much slower, is actually no more than drifting."

"Sounds heavenly," muttered Henry, pushing himself off the floor.

"What do you know about heaven?" asked Alexander.

"Better then the alternative," Henry groaned.

"That's true," said Alexander, sitting down on a mound of soft dirt.

Henry lifted Badger up onto his hind paws. "Oh, I kept forgetting to ask private, or lieutenant, are you a Christian?"

"Yes," said Rookie, "since I was six, or was it five."

"How can that be?" asked Henry.

Rookie noted that both Henry's and Badger's expressions were the same. He shrugged. "Who knows, supposedly a group of Voyagers, a religious group that believed in knowledge, is thought to have brought it from Earth."

"How did you get to Mars again?" asked Alexander, standing up and helping Rookie to his feet.

"Random teleport, a Nimrod artifact that will unpredictably send those who enter to any habitable world," Rookie said.

"Where did the GEN find this artifact?"

"It was something left over from EVE," said Rookie.

"And what of the final key?" asked Henry. "Where have you hidden it?"

"The GEN already hid it," said Rookie, "I merely placed it where it would be safe."

"What's that supposed to mean?" asked Alexander.

"I can't even tell my superior officers," said Rookie.

"Enough chatting," a Marine piped up as he stiffly stood up. "Let's figure out where we are."

"Agreed," said Henry, walking back to the control panel. "Can anyone see anything through this?"

"Impossible," said the princess, "the screen is completed fogged."

"Obviously," said Henry, wiping the screen with his gloves. Through the clean area, he could see two ships and an ODS. He began to laugh and Badger barked once jovially.

"It's Mars," shouted Henry, "we've made it."

"Derelict ship," a voice came over a speaker above the control panel. "Is anyone there? This is ISEN *Galilee,* we're going to pull you aboard, remain calm. Can anyone aboard contact us?"

After fumbling about on the control panel, Henry found the communications switch to talk to the *Galilee*.

"ISEN ship, this is Henry Mindell, United States Specter F-38A, please inform REPEL that their Agents have returned from Forerunner. We've got other survivors with us, Forerunner has been lost; we are the only one's to have escaped."

"I'm sorry to hear that," was the reply. "The ISEN ship, *Traveler*, has already returned to Mars, fully intact. But Captain Whittington requests an explanation why two comet rounds were missing. Can you explain?"

"Not yet," said Henry.

"I understand," said another voice, an older, more commanding voice. "I've been informed about the… encounter and need no other details. How many of you are there? Does anyone need medical attention of any kind?"

"I imagine so," said Henry, looking about the interior of the ship. "But I and my partner have to get back to REPEL as soon as possible to fill out our reports."

"You shall have my personal transport," said the voice, which everyone guessed to be that of the Captain. "The others shall be deployed to the ODS when the *Galilee* docks for professional medical attention. Please remain seated; your ship's going to jerk a little."

Everyone dropped to the deck. The Marines were heard to say, "This bad," or "just wonderful," even, "if only he knew." The ship jerked hard, sending more plants and dirt across the floor and over the bodies.

"That wasn't so bad," said Rookie, removing his arms from about his face.

The *Galilee*'s tractor beam lowered the little ship and all the space debris into the hangar. The PDCTs that were sent into the hangar as guards looked at the debris in fascination and disgust. The other ships were lowered onto the floor and hot blasts of steam smacked all three vessels to defrost them. The PDCTs slowly approached the ship; one banged his hand on the door.

"You're inside the hangar, come on out."

The PDCTs stood back when the door opened and the PDCTs, Marines, Specters and an alien stepped out. They were all very filthy and bedraggled looking, the Marines were limping slowly. Mostly the PDCTs stared at the alien; she was breathing deeply and rubbing her face.

"It's so nice to be aboard a good ship again," a Marine cried out, actually dropping to his knees and praying.

"I'm sure," said one of the PDCTs. "You there, Sergeant Alexander."

"Yes?" asked Alexander. He quickly added "Sir," and threw a salute when he saw the other's rank. It was a colonel.

"Mind explaining this disaster and this… alien?"

"Can't I just file a report, sir?" asked Alexander. "I've been through a lot in the last twenty-four hours."

"How about a quick basic?" the colonel asked.

Alexander sighed. "There's an alien religious faction called the Reach of Nimrod, they're trying to open something called the Gate. This terref is with us, she's a princess of a country that may side with us if we return her home. The Chinese and Reach have joined together to try and conquer the universe, now Forerunner is being bombed to oblivion."

"Too much information," said the colonel, looking over the debris and survivors.

*   *   *

Whittington had arrived into the hangar just when the other two ships were opened; the occupants were dead, frozen solid. The colonel had already informed him about the little craft's occupants, giving him a visual display, so the captain didn't look surprised when the door opened and he was looking at the debris and alien.

"Welcome," Whittington said, trying to sound cheery. "We don't have very comfortable commendations, but we'll do what we can do to help you all recover. I've already informed ISEN and the Allies that Forerunner's been lost. God help us all with this new threat on the horizon."

"I'm sure he will," said Henry.

Whittington looked at the Specter curiously. "Have I seen you somewhere before?"

Henry shrugged. "You probably saw a lot of faces during the Mauritanian War."

"Ah, yes. Those were brutal times."

"Let's not talk about them," said Henry.

"With pleasure," said Whittington, trying to suppress horrifying images of the war out of his mind. "How much damage have you and your partner sustained?"

"Just a few bruises and burns," said Henry. "We'll just need some coolant and restoration patches. We really should leave soon."

"I'll have a medic attend you on the way," said Whittington. Then he had a thought as he looked about thoughtfully. "Where's your partner? I thought you said there were two of you."

Henry looked about as well. He saw Badger examining one of the Reach aircraft. "There he is, the white GEM with the stripe."

Whittington nodded. "If I'm not mistaken, that's Badger. You're Henry Mindell?"

"Yes sir," said Henry his face betraying no emotion. "Badger, come here."

Whittington signaled for a seaman to come. "This seaman will take you to my transport; a medic will be waiting there for you."

"Thank you," said Henry, starting to follow the seaman when he remembered something. "Wait a minute, do you see that alien in the fancy blue clothes?"

Whittington looked over the crowd and nodded when he saw her. "They seem rather ruined, but yes."

"Sher father's a very important person, possibly friendly, please treat her respectfully."

The Specters didn't wait around to hear if Whittington had anymore questions, they followed the seaman to the transport. The transport was located at the bow of the ship, several meters below the comet-guns; it was torpedo-shaped with a transparent doorway in the back. Inside was the medic, a stern-looking Mexican with a thick accent and rough hands. The pilot was given clearance to detach and soon the Specters were streaking into the Martian atmosphere towards REPEL. To the Specters, things were finally going right.

Chapter 43

"Call Me Dave"

The transport, known as a Prawn, activated its landing gear, three hydraulic legs that bent softly under the Prawn's weight. The pilot had already received clearance to land upon one of REPEL's landing pads; four miniature combustion engines slowed the Prawn's decent and its passengers looked eagerly out the transparent rear doors.

The patches felt good on both of the Specters' skins. The patches were stretchable pieces of soft, sticky, moist fabric which released the medication that was absorbed by the skin, quickly healing bruises, burns, or minor cuts. They were also cool and comfortable to the touch.

"This is it," said Henry, rubbing Badger's ears. "Too bad you lost the VED portion of your helmet, buddy, now Warren will only get half of the visual report."

Badger let out a dismissive noise.

"Yeah," said Henry, "it would just be another perspective of the same thing."

The Prawn's rear doors opened with a hiss.

"Time to get out," said the pilot, getting ready to take off again.

"Thanks for the ride," said Henry as he and Badger stepped out.

"And my mom said it would be a thankless job," muttered the pilot, closing the doors.

Henry and Badger stepped back and watched as the Prawn slowly lifted off the ground. The legs folded back against the Prawn's body and then the main engines, three that were located about the doors, ignited and the craft zipped away with a roar.

"You know," said Henry, "sometimes I think it takes a special kind of man to just step onto the deck of a spaceship."

"I agree," projected Badger, remembering everything that had been happening.

"And neither of you will step into one for a while."

Both Specters whirled around to see the familiar face of Warren. The colonel was accompanied by two Marines.

"Hello, sir," said Henry, removing his helmet and let it hang by his side. "I would like to request…"

"A vacation," Warren finished for him.

Henry pressed his lips together, tilted his head and nodded. "Absolutely, when you see what we've been through you will agree…"

"I don't need to see it," said Warren, "I have a mission for you, a mission only you two can handle."

"What?" Henry cried. "What could possibly be more important than what we've already done?"

"Another asset to the Reach of Nimrod," said Warren.

"Can it wait a couple days?" asked Henry.

Warren shook his head.

"But we're both tired," Henry groaned. Badger remained silent, though he felt in favor of a vacation.

"Exactly why in two hours you'll be on a first-class, all expenses paid, trip to New Seattle."

"What?" Henry asked; his face had twisted into a shocked expression. Even Badger's eyes had widened a little.

"That's right," said Warren, a smile on his face. "Come inside, change back into your civilian clothes and I'll explain your mission while we eat. But first, I'll need the neural AI and the information that the wind farmer gave you."

Suddenly realizing how hungry they were, both Specters were quick to hand over the equipment and follow Warren into REPEL. Inside they quickly went to the shower room; the walls were lined with labeled lockers and racks of light firearms. Henry, though wanting to eat as soon as possible, found it increasingly difficult to take a quick, warm shower. Even Badger taking a GEM bath (a moisturizing fabric with stiff follicles that both combed and injected soaps and shampoos onto his fur while rinsing him at the same time on which he merely had to roll) found it hard to stop. Badger promptly leapt out and turned off the bath when he heard

Henry get out of the shower. He stood in front of the dryer, a vent that dried his fur while at the same time keeping it flat against his body instead of it spreading in all directions. He put his red collar on, the license was a thick circle of aluminum with his name engraved in large letters; he'd had it since he was a puppy. Henry stepped around a corner, zipping his brown wool coat up half way for ventilation and stuffing a bit of tobacco into his elegant pipe.

"Looks like your ready to eat, boy," Henry said with a smile.

Badger gave him a half-smile and a low bark.

"I take that as yes."

Henry, with Badger trotting beside him, walked through the halls lighting his pipe and sucking deeply. Smoking his pipe always enhanced his appetite and the smell was very was spicy like peppers and sweet like almonds. Even Badger enjoyed the smell of the smoke, as was apparent by the amount he sniffed the air.

* * *

Lunch was a modest spreading of sandwiches and tea for Henry, Warren, Victor and a young boy. Badger had a bowl of dry dog-food and water while Samuel was on the table with Victor spooning tuna into his mouth. Badger had always liked Samuel and Victor, in fact, he had always liked cats, specially Samuel. Whenever Samuel and Victor were around there was a pleasant atmosphere about the area. The lunch was held in Warren's private office. Both Henry and Badger, between mouthfuls of food, glanced at the boy and Warren, waiting for an explanation.

After a few minutes, it became apparent that Warren expected to be asked.

"Alright, already," said Henry, putting down his sandwich. "What's the mission and who's he?"

"I thought you would never ask," said Warren.

Badger had finished his dog-food and stood up to rest his forepaws onto the tabletop, sniffing the boy curiously. He recoiled slightly when the boy touched him between the ears to pet him. He let out a grunt-like whine and sat down by Henry, waiting for the explanation.

"This boy is Dave Hudson," said Warren, "son of Professor Hagen Hudson. I believe you've heard of him."

"Who hasn't?" remarked Henry.

"The Professor has been kidnapped," said Warren; he watched as Henry jerked in surprise. "An important person like that's disappearance is not to be dismissed."

"So you want us to find him?" asked Henry, taking another bite of his sandwich.

"No," said Warren, "we already know where he is."

"So its rescue mission," said Henry.

"Partially," said Warren.

Badger heard a patter of soft paws and turned to see Samuel walking along the edge of the table towards him. He smiled stood up so Samuel could climb down his back and onto the floor. He dropped back to a seated position and watched as Samuel rubbed against his legs and then curled up in front of him, drifting into a fitful sleep. He stroked Samuel, softly sliding his blunt claws across the bare, mottled skin.

"What do you mean partially?" Henry didn't like the sound of this.

"He's been captured by a rather radical colleague of mine," said Warren. "During the Mauritanian war we both worked in a military facility to research combat biometrics. My colleague made a very important discovery, he tried to sell it to the Mauritanians, a Specter team was sent to kill him and retrieve the research."

"And they never made it," Henry finished for Warren.

Warren nodded slowly. "We found their bodies and another that resembled my colleague, Nordahl Wildenvey. We figured he was dead and his research with him. But now I've found him again."

"So he didn't get a chance to sell it to the Mauritanians?" asked Henry, glancing at the boy.

"They never got it," said Warren, "and nobody ever knew what he had discovered. Now he's resurfaced in New Seattle and he's got Mr. Hudson and now he needs his son as leverage."

"And the mission?" asked Henry.

"Eliminate him and retrieve Hagen, alive," said Warren. "Dr. Nordahl Wildenvey is a competitor of a corporation called Reach; both their companies have suddenly taken an interest in the Chinese and Mr. Hudson."

"What about the Reach Corporation?" Henry asked.

"I've already sent a Specter team there," said Warren, "any team could handle that."

Henry was taken aback. "Are you saying that…?"

"Dr. Nordahl Wildenvey is extremely dangerous," said Warren. "We'll give you updates as you go, we're still finding things."

"Well, Mr. Hudson," said Henry, giving the boy a little smile, "I guess you're going to be reunited with your father soon."

"Call me Dave," said Dave, smiling back.

"What ever you say," said Henry. He turned back to Warren. "How are we going to travel to New Seattle?"

"First," said Warren, standing up and walking to a desk to take two slips of paper from a drawer. "You're a wealthy man in the computer industry; you'll arrive at the airport via civilian VTOL. At the airport you go find the *Ghost of Enlightenment*, an airship; your luggage is already waiting in your rooms."

Badger stopped stroking his friend for a moment and stared up at

Henry with wide eyes. He could hardly believe it. Samuel whimpered and twisted and he started stroking him again.

"Glad we don't have to pack," said Henry.

"When you arrive in New Seattle, you'll be given a suitcase with the means of eliminating Wildenvey. Mindell, there may be a chance that you may have to perform more than one assassination as the Reach could have already infiltrated. Not the corporation Reach."

"I didn't think so," muttered Henry, wringing his hands together. "Where can we find him?"

Warren handed over the slips, the tickets, "At Biotech, a company that's a close second to Program."

"What happens after we finish the job?" asked Henry, putting the tickets into a pocket.

"You can have a vacation until the threat, the Reach of Nimrod arrives."

"Sounds good to me," said Henry, reaching down and scratching Badger's neck.

"We'll inform you of anything else along the way," said Warren. "Have a nice trip."

*   *   *

The *Ghost of Enlightenment*'s design was based off of the dirigibles of old; its exterior skin was made of a silvery material and the interior was filled with billions of conductive tubes filled with non-flammable gas that lifted the craft when heated. The propulsion systems on the craft were similar to that of the Prawn's, but were much slower, making for a comfortable, lengthy ride. The *Ghost of Enlightenment,* Henry thought it an redundant name, was built on the interior like a mansion, straight up to the top of the craft where several elegant rooms were placed to give special guests a more enjoyable ride.

Henry was actually very pleased to discover that he was on the list of special guests and a stewardess in a crimson uniform with a blue hat showed them to their room. The room was wonderfully decorated with a two beds, one being a kind of basket for Badger; there was even a tray of cold shreg salad and a pastry dish. Also there were three different bags of dry dog food Badger had never laid eyes on before.

Henry hung his coat on a wall peg and sat down on the bed, it was exceedingly comfortable. He remained quiet for a moment while thinking about what he should do next.

"To bad this isn't going to last," said Henry, watching as Badger inspected his own bed. The GEM also seemed very impressed with the furniture, he circled the bed for a moment; no matter where he turned there was no altering in the consistency.

Henry laughed aloud.

A knock came at the door and a friendly voice called out.

"Mr. Mindell, I've brought an activity sheet for you, we forgot to put one in your room before you arrived."

Henry reluctantly got off the bed and opened the door. "Thank you."

The man outside the room was wearing a white suit with an elegant blue, knitted vest. In one hand was a green piece of folded paper and in the other was a silenced ASP.

"Compliments of Dr. Wildenvey," the man said with a smile.

Chapter 44

"A Tale of Two Companies"

Hagen was once again locked into the large chair, his legs covered in scars from the previous interrogation. His resolution was solid after this past week of cruel treatment, he still had kept his mouth closed to his research. He had lied a few times, but the doctor only used more painful techniques after the lies were discovered. All he could do was scream.

Nordahl wasn't in the room yet and Sekou had already left, he was completely alone. He sighed bitterly as his head sank onto his chest, trying to think of things other than the torture. He thought of his son Dave, but that reminded him of when his wife died; he had never told Dave how she died. She had been murdered in their house, stabbed to death by a man looking for some of his papers.

Canine had been built after the murder; he had painstakingly made every piece of software and armor plating. But there was a secret installment he hoped never to have to tell anyone. Canine's was partially sentient, Hagen had zip-cloned his wife's brain a day before the funeral, this kept her neural basis intact. He used a special biological extractor to conform the wavelengths of the dying brain into Canine's chassis. Canine was, in fact, for most practical purposes, Dave's mother, but had never been issued the program to use the neurological data.

He tried to stop thinking about it, but the images of his wife's limp form and Canine kept popping into his head. He began to sob uncontrollably, tears rolling down his shallow cheeks and onto his filthy clothes.

"You look like someone that 'as a lot of sorrow."

Hagen felt his face grow hot and a scowl creased his face. "Are you here finally, Wildenvey?"

"You misunderstand, I'm not the doctor, but 'e'll be 'ere in a minute."

The voice didn't belong to Nordahl, in fact, it was female and with an edge of compassion to it. "Who are you?"

The chair rocked as something leapt onto the back, of it and scrambled up to the top. Hagen tilted his head back, but he couldn't see anything.

"You poor man," the voice said pityingly, "I wouldn't trade places with you for anything."

Hagen shrugged as best he could. "Thanks for the encouragement."

"Do forgive me for my bluntness, but it's true, even with 'is wonder drug I probably wouldn't last a minute."

"Where are you?"

"On the back of the chair, I was clawing loud enough, don't you think?" the voice seemed rather perturbed and sad. "Are your screams blowing out your eardrums?"

"Then… what are you? Why don't you show yourself?" Hagen tried again to catch a glimpse of his visitor.

The voice sighed wearily. "The Norwegian doesn't permit that I show myself, please forgive me, to his guests."

"And why is that?" asked Hagen, grateful for the company and compassion.

"I haven't the smokiest," the voice said dismissively, "I don't question 'im, I just do or die."

"Then why do you work for him?"

"I like to eat," the voice said. "You know the idea."

Hagen nodded solemnly. "I see your point."

The voice chuckled and more clawing sounds were heard on the back of the chair.

"Don't go," pleaded Hagen.

"I was just finding better foo… claw-holds. There! Anything you'd like to know Mister Hudson?"

"Where am I?" Hagen asked hopefully.

"I'm not permitted to say that," the voice said apologetically. "But I can tell you that you're far away from Forge and your son."

Hagen's heart leapt for joy. "Dave escaped?"

"Yeah, well we would've 'ad 'im if not for the Reach corporation. They fouled up everything, trying to get the boy. But, thanks to 'is guardian they weren't able to catch 'im. 'E's at REPEL now."

"Good," Hagen sighed happily, "they got to him in time."

"Dumb Reach terrorists," muttered the voice, "all for the profit they could make from the external powers."

"External powers?" inquired Hagen.

"Ah… it would be difficult to explain at this moment, but, believe me, you'll see them soon enough."

"Can you tell me anything?" Hagen's curiosity had been peaked.

"No," the voice said bluntly. "Oh well, the Reach 'as failed and let's 'ope that gets them out of the picture, they can't even buy proper VTOLs."

"Is that such a bad thing?" asked Hagen.

"Not for your son," the voice chuckled, then turned into a weary sigh. "After that entire night I spent staking out your 'ouse and examining those security systems, all to waste, it was 'arder to get out than in."

"What?" Hagen demanded with a great shout.

The voice let out a cry and the owner fell to the floor.

"You staked out my house so they could grab my son?" he began to struggle with the restraints. "You… you… go away, leave me."

The visitor climbed back up the back of the chair and began to speak in a silky voice. "Okay-okay, calm down, I didn't want to do it, I like children, I didn't want to see 'im 'urt, but, it's like I said, I like to eat. You don't know what I went through before Dr. Wildenvey gave me this job. Please, try to understand."

Hagen softened when he detected a sob in the voice. He took a deep breath and sighed wearily. "Alright... but tell me... what did you go through?"

The voice suddenly became jaded. "No! You don't need to know that, no one has a right to know that."

"You seem upset," Hagen pointed out.

"What makes you think that? The universe is corrupt... you're... you're just mistaken," she spoke slowly. "I'll leave you now, I can 'ear the doctor coming and I don't like to 'ear the same pleas over and over again."

"Fine, then just for you I'll come up with some new ones," said Hagen, trying to cheer her up.

"That's not what I meant," the voice said now openly sobbing.

"Are you all right," Hagen inquired kindly.

"Why would you care?" they voice said with a heave. "No one cares... they didn't and I'll become like them."

"Oh, Mr. Hudson, it appears that you've met Alder," said the sadistic voice of Nordahl. "Quite charming, isn't she? I suggest you run along now, the professor and I, are going to have another talk."

The unseen speaker dropped onto the floor and spoke in a forcibly controlled voice. "Thank you again for the vending machines; they've been a big help."

"Don't mention it," said Nordahl, his voice calm and persuasive.

The door was heard to open, announcing the visitor's departure. The doctor walked around the chair until he was in full view of Hagen, making a great show of opening the box again. He pulled out the syringe of bacteria.

"Wait," said Hagen.

The doctor, syringe held high, turned to face Hagen with a smile, he leaned against the box as he asked. "Do you wish to tell me your research?"

"No," Hagen said resolutely.

"Then you're wasting my…"

"I wanted to ask you about your competitor, the Reach Corporation," said Hagen.

The Doctor's face lit up and he replaced the syringe into the box. He delighted in subjects that interested him, especially when they involved him. He closed the box and sat upon it, stroking his chin thoughtfully.

"Well, to start with, our employers, whom you'll meet soon enough, are very demanding. They issued a demand for soldiers, a biologically superior soldier, soldiers for a war to end all wars. You see, the Reach Corporation is absolutely void of any imagination whatsoever and want their warriors to be made from simple beasts they've imported from other planets. How ridiculous. I, however, have imagination and the intellect to do just what I want to; my warriors are made from what you Americans call scratch. I'll put it simply, BINAN warriors made piece by piece, made superior in strength and speed, due to an internal musculoskeletal structure I've created. I have fifty physically disabled men and women just waiting to have their consciousnesses shifted into these creations.

"But...I'm missing one thing; a way to control them; I need what you have discovered. And I'm more than prepared to work on your internal organs to find your secret. Rest assured, when we get your boy, I'll have no mercy upon him, then for a change of pace, you can watch and listen as your son has this same torture performed upon him. But, if you were to tell me now, I'll leave the boy alone and you can both share in my glory. My employers are honorable, but they don't know me, they want the universe, but I've a plan to take it from them. You could have everything you've ever wanted, working for me. I'll even keep it a secret about your son's guardian, about what this... Canine really is. How does that suit you?"

"How do you know about that?" Hagen demanded, eyes

widening.

"I know many things," Nordahl smiled cheerfully. "Now, I even know about your secret research. You'd be able to link minds with another creature, that you would call a bond for a different type of war. I could use this to control my creations. They do have a few glitches; I've tested a few and for the first thirty-two hours, they are crazy."

Now it was Hagen's turn to smile. "You know much, but you still haven't grasped a fraction of what I've found. Your low-tech creations, as you've perfectly described them, could never stand up against what I've discovered."

Nordahl leapt up angrily and tore open the lid of the box. "After all this time of torture, you know what I'm capable of and you dare insult my work. You're going to regret every word."

"Never," Hagen calmly returned.

"We'll see how bold you are," Nordahl laughed maniacally, "while I'm removing and replacing your stomach."

"You're not going to break me," Hagen hissed.

"I don't really care today," Nordahl shouted, lunging forward with the syringe and scalpel.

Chapter 45

"New Reformation"

A natural reflex, Henry jumped aside, the man fired and missed, Henry grabbed his hand yanked it forward and then slammed the door on the man's wrist, snapping it clean. The man shrieked and dropped the ASP; Henry, still holding the hand, pulled the man inside, kicked him in his midsection, making him keel over and then brought his knee up into his face. All this happened in the blink of an eye. The next thing the man knew was that Badger had all four paws on his chest and was snarling ferociously in his face.

Henry knelt over the man, a fist raised to strike at the first sign of trouble. "Who sent you?"

The man, other than moaning, remained silent, staring back at Henry with cold eyes.

"You nose is already broken," Henry spat contemptuously, "ready for some broken teeth?"

The man grinned and spat blood into Henry's face. "Dr. Wildenvey, I already told you that."

Henry wiped away the blood yanked at the man's hair, making him squeal. "Who told you I'd be here?"

The man remained silent.

Henry smacked him across the face, splattering blood across the stainless carpet. "Who told you? Do you want me to blow off your kneecaps?"

"I'm not going to betray aaahhh."

Henry rubbed the back of his hand tenderly; he needed to come up with some other form of interrogation. He grabbed the man's broken wrist and began to twist it. "Ready to tell me now, because, you see, I could keep this up all day."

The man shrieked as he felt his broken joint move everywhere. "Alder," he began to shout, "Alder, Alder told me, she got into REPEL's mainframe, stop, please."

"Who's Alder?" Henry demanded, squeezing the injury.

"I don't know," said the man, "I've never seen her, she's close to the Norwegian, close to, aahh, Dr. Wildenvey. Find the Norwegian and you've found her, please stop."

Henry threw the man's arm back onto the ground and patted his cheek gently. "Glad to know you've got no great sense of loyalty. Ah, I believe security is coming; come on Badger, let's make it look right."

Alerted by screams and several calls, four members of the security staff arrived shortly at Henry's room. They saw the man on the ground, clutching his wrist, the ASP on the ground and a traumatized

Henry holding back a very protective GEM.

"What happened, sir?" asked a young blonde-haired lady, eyeing the gun and Henry's bloody hand.

"He... he told me he was here to deliver an activity sheet," said Henry, shaking his head bewilderedly, "When I opened the door he was holding a gun on me. I-I don't know what happened afterward, the next thing I know is that he's on the ground and I'm pulling Badger off of him."

"Try to remain calm," said the lady, "can you tell us anything at all? Like... what did he want?"

"I think he said something about a program," said Henry, wiping a hand across his forehead. "I think he might've been sent by a competitor of mine, he wanted one of my programs."

"I think that'll be enough," said the lady, smiling and shutting off a small recording device on her wrist. "We won't have to bother you about this anymore. Please, head to the bridge, the captain will see you and we'll clean up this mess."

"Okay," Henry said, standing up off the bed and pulling Badger around the assailant, who was being pulled to his feet. Badger let out two barks before disappearing around the corner with Henry.

The lady rolled her eyes. "Rich people."

As soon as they were out of earshot, Henry let go of Badger's collar and patted him affectionately on the head. "You're not a bad actor, did you know that?"

Badger grunted dismissively.

"No, I mean it. After this whole thing is cleared up, you could retire and make movies." Henry laughed and sped up a little.

*   *   *

The whole incident had been cleared up without much having to be said. The man was taken off the airship to the police and Henry was given a well-rehearsed apology by the airship's captain for the inconvenience. Back at the room the blood had been wiped away, the bed remade and a written apology, copied many times, had been placed at the foot of the bed.

Henry tossed the note into the waste bin next to the bed. "I'm going to contact Warren. Do you know where my portable is?"

Badger put a paw into Henry's pocket and pulled out the oval piece of fabric.

"How do you do that?" asked Henry. Badger always seemed to know where everything was.

Badger tried to reply, but then remembered that the neural AI had been removed from his ear. He figured he'd been born with the ability, ever since he could remember he could count, read, solve problems of various kinds and remember small details.

Henry placed the fabric onto his wrist and activated the electronic adhesive. Then he pressed a small pad in the center; a holographic screen with an overtop keyboard appeared.

Badger heard footsteps in the hall; he dropped to all fours, spreading his legs in a firm, defensive stance. The footsteps passed on by. But, he remained vigilant, growling lowly.

"Don't worry," said Henry, giving Badger a sympathetic glance. He was about to link into REPEL's memory field, when he noticed the green piece of paper on the dresser, next to it was a blue piece of paper with the word, ACTIVITIES, written on it. He picked it up and opened it, there was something written on it in a language he didn't know.

The portable had downloaded software that could translate words, written or typed. By simply moving the holographic screen in front of the paper, Henry could see it translated into English. He read it aloud.

"Dear Mr. Mindell, if you're reading this it means you're alive. Just to show you what you're up against, again, I've left a mark on the back of this paper, hold it up to the light and you will see. You will be contacted again before you arrive in New Seattle. Have a pleasant trip. Sincerely: Dr. Wildenvey."

"At least we know he's friendly," mocked Henry as he looked at Badger who was giving him a queer look. "I was kidding."

Badger inclined his head and returned to watching the door.

Henry held the paper up to the overhead light. "What's it written in, invisible ink? Mere child…"

Henry froze at what he saw. A portion of the paper had been purposely faded by acid to show a circle surrounding a large swastika. The hooked X quickly brought visions of Mauritania back to Henry's mind; he crushed the paper in his hand and quickly set to contacting Warren.

"Mindell?" said Warren, a visual display appearing. "Why are you contacting me?"

"I've just had an attempt on my life," said Henry.

"Nordahl?" asked Warren, his brow furrowing.

"No, one of his henchmen," Henry said sarcastically. "I persuaded the assassin to tell me how he knew I was here and he told about someone named Alder."

"Alder?" said Warren, "no one in intelligence told any of us about this."

"Apparently not," said Henry. "And I found something to make this situation even worse."

"And what's that?" asked Warren.

"The Nazis are trying to rise again."

"They all scattered after Mauritania," said Warren, not sounding surprised. "It's quite possible that Nordahl got into their circle."

"I believe the right word is probable," said Henry, trying to regain his mixed thoughts of Mauritania and the problem at hand.

"Calm down Henry," said Warren.

"You were in Mauritania," Henry said loudly, "how can you possibly tell anyone to calm down?"

"How did you get this information on Nordahl?" Warren almost shouted.

Henry held up the crumpled piece of paper. "His assassin left his calling card, saying I'd be contacted again before we landed."

"It's a good thing REPEL packed your suitcases then," said Warren, "you'll find everything you need in the small one."

Henry casually took a small, gray suitcase from under the bed and opened it. Inside was a miniature automatic weapon; four cryogenic containers that contained the organic ammo were lined on the back side. Underneath the weapon was a thin metal spike.

"Were you expecting this?"

"No," said Warren, "but I was concerned about when you landed."

"Thanks for the concern," said Henry, fitting a canister into the weapon's cavity. "This ought to work fine, providing they're not wearing armor."

"I've got an update for you on Nordahl," said Warren.

Henry watched the screen as he slipped the weapon into his

pocket.

"The wave was a little scrambled, but we managed to confirm two other disposable targets for you. Managers of Biotech, which are suspected Nazis evacuates from Mauritania. Be positive that you kill them. But, it's gotten complicated. They've got mercenaries in and around the building; we'd prefer that you be selective with them."

"Prefer?" asked Henry.

"Most don't even know who they're working for." Warren turned to his left and waved a hand dismissively at somebody off focus. "Also, there seems to have been a gap in security measures in REPEL's systems and in national security."

"Alder?" inquired Henry.

Warren nodded. "Alder is probably a program or an AI system in Biotech, if so, it will need to be captured or eliminated. We'd prefer if you captured it."

"You've got a lot of preferences," said Henry.

"We'll need a lot if help if the national security gap is compromised."

"What happened?"

"It appears that Alder managed to sneak in someone or some people, possibly Chinese or Reach."

Henry thought back to the image of the city being bombarded.

"Let's pray it's the Chinese."

"That's your job," said Warren.

"Come on," said Henry, "surely you've got some curiosity."

"Of course I do," said Warren, not meeting Henry's gaze.

"Most don't admit that."

"Just stick to the mission, Mindell," said Warren. "On arrival in new Seattle you'll be given more needed equipment."

"Now you're on edge," smirked Henry.

"Our last update is that the princess and a GEN soldier are on their way to Red Haven. After your brief mission you'll be taken to Red Haven as well for the piloting of the *Kitty Hawk*. Make sure at least one of you gets back."

Warren broke the link and Henry shut off the screen, but left the portable on his wrist. He turned to Badger and smiled broadly. "He's coming around."

*   *   *

His comrade had failed and he wasn't so certain that he would succeed either, but the Norwegian's orders were not to be disobeyed. The man's hands were covered in white silk gloves and he wore a ring on the outside, silver with a three, nearly microscopic emeralds inlaid into it, etched atop every emerald was a red swastika and Reach cathead.

The man opened a small suitcase, inside were his clothes. Taking a stiff, blue jacket from the suitcase, he quickly started to remove certain threads, each one metal. After removing the threads, he twisted them all together until they formed a short rod. He then took a small cylinder from his pocket; it had a socket at one end and a button on the other, he fit the rod into the socket and pressed the button.

With loud pops and snaps, the tip turned red-hot and sparks jumped out. The man let go of the button and waited for the tip to cool down, then he put it into his pocket. The principle of the weapon was simple, the metal threads would spread out after sent into the body and the voltage emitted from the socket would be enough to break bones with muscular convulsions. He quietly stepped out of the room.

Chapter 46

"Some Fun"

Knowing the meaning of the phrase "safety in numbers", Henry left his room to mingle with the other passengers aboard the *Ghost of Enlightenment*. The day was still young and the airship was floating high above the ground at a leisurely pace. Henry and Badger toured the craft; they had never been in an airship before and Badger was eyeing everybody with suspicion. Guests were wandering about, women wearing exotic furs and men wearing fine suits. Everyone eyed Henry and Badger as if they were aliens as the two of them weren't dressed as everybody else. The guests that had pets, had them decorated in the most ridiculous and hard to describe fashions. The airship wasn't all that large, but it was big enough to hold its two hundred passengers and workers. Near the front of the airship there was the dining room and a game room where guests could swim in a pool, play cards, or have bowling matches. But it was the top of the ship that took the brunt of the Specters' attention, an immense, transparent dome observation deck.

From space they could see the entire planet, but this was something much more. From space they were in perfect safety, but aboard the airship, they had a terrifyingly incredible view of land and sea for leagues around.

"This is incredible," said Henry, pressing a hand against the crystal.

Eyes wide, Badger pressed his forepaws against the barrier, wagging his tail and looking about everywhere, trying to take in everything at once. But then, he remembered the note. *What am I doing?* He thought. He quickly turned around to watch the guests.

Henry saw this and sighed. "You really should learn to relax a little, Badger; no one'll attack in front of all these people."

Badger remained vigilant, eyes probing everywhere for possible threats. He didn't make any violent sounds, not knowing the stability of the people, he remained firmly placed.

Henry shook his head and began to walk along the wall, he heard Badger following. "There are times when I wish I'd never signed you into REPEL. You were quite a playful one when you were a puppy, do you remember?"

Badger snorted. Of course he remembered, he could remember just about everything, except where he was from, before he was on that farm. But those old memories had no place, did they? He shook his head to keep on the subject; he didn't like the conflict that happened with his memories.

Badger couldn't help, though, to recall an event that happened just before his enrollment. Although Badger had only spent a year there, he could remember the exact layout of the apartment he and Henry lived in. It had one room, with a small kitchen in the far left corner, an enormous adjusting-density window (a conductive crystal window that could be shaded from clear to dark with a small switch) opposite the doorway and a small bathroom. It had been furnished with a flotilla (a bed that was suspended in midair by magnets), a bookcase filled with old books, a carving of a wolf atop a small table on which sat an ultra sight.

He had been left there alone while Henry was off buying more bullets for his pistol; he was almost out. Badger knew that it would be a long time before Henry returned; he always liked to examine all the weapons at the store. He had been patiently lying on the flotilla, looking out the window, counting air taxis and then he rolled onto his back and watched the door, thoughtfully kicking his hind paws.

His eyes landed on the ultra sight (or US), it was shaped like an old CD, Henry had a few of those antiquities, he listened to them quite often, but Badger didn't have his master's taste in rock music. There was a crystalline fixture atop of the US; he leapt onto the table and pressed the top, a selection of shows appeared above the table; he pressed a random one and found himself in a western scene.

He quickly leapt back onto the bed and watched the show. Guns were going off everywhere. And there were several slow motion scenes where he actually tried to catch the bullets. He even dropped off the bed and walked around the table to get a different view, the background shifted with his movement. He leapt aside when several horses rushed at him.

He got hungry and looked about for the open bag of dog food. It was atop of the kitchen counter. Not to be deterred from his desire to eat, he quickly thought up a plan.

He went to Henry's bookcase and started to pull out books with his forepaws, stacking them into steps. It took nearly ten minutes to get the books to the correct height but it had been worth it. He pushed over the bag and nosed his way into it and began to eat his fill.

Henry, for some unexplainable reason had come home early this time. He opened the door and let out a yell when a large cowboy shot at him. He quickly realized it was the US and turned it off, all the while looking about for the culprit. Then he saw the stack of books leading up like steps to the counter and the tail sticking out of the bag. He dropped the box of bullets in amazement.

Upon hearing the crash and rattle of the bullets, Badger backed out of the bag, head tilted in puzzlement. Upon seeing Henry, his face broke into a smile and he performed a joyful back flip. He rushed down the makeshift staircase and sat down at Henry's feet, tail wagging happily.

Badger was brought back down to Mars when he felt hot air in his left ear. He turned his head to see a small, long-furred dog with a ridiculous bow between its ears sniffing him. He rose onto his hind legs, ears back and teeth bared; he barked warningly. The pathetic little animal ran off in search of its owner.

"What cruel and unusual treatment," said Henry, watching as the little dog disappear into the crowd. "Its owner ought to be ashamed."

Agreed, Badger thought, again watching the crowd with his amber eyes.

* * *

Badger and Henry had participated in some of the *Ghost of Enlightenment*'s offered recreation, mainly in the pool, swimming in a warmed pool that was meant for guests and their pets. Badger still kept a close watch on everyone, but, for Henry's sake he tried to enjoy the water, which he did, but avoided letting it go to his head. He kept close to Henry and far from everyone else. After swimming, they returned to their room where they promptly washed themselves; the bathroom even had a GEM bath. After they were cleaned and dried, Henry went on to play a game of cards, wearing a fine brown suit he found in another one of the suitcases that had been packed for him. Badger remained vigilant at his side, license nicely polished to keep up appearances, watching other people in the game room. Around Henry's table was a wealthy Texas wind farmer on a business trip, a proper-speaking Russian core miner and a successful young gambler from Orinoco (an international mining and research city orbiting around Jupiter), the gambler wore a white suit with a ring on the outside of his white gloves.

"I shall bid two hundred credits," the Russian said, placing four little red chips in the center of the table.

It was a friendly game of Flip (a popular game where Jokers made a hand worthless), no real money was being laid out. The young gambler, however, was trying to instigate a riot with the outrageous bets he placed.

"I'll raise two thousand," the gambler said, placing out two white chips.

"That's preposterous," said the Texan, clenching a fist and pounding it on the table. He was a heavyset man, with a creased face that reddened with anger.

"You could back out," the gambler prodded, giving the Texan a smug smile.

"No... no," the Texan said firmly, "I've never quit before, I concede."

The gambler smiled as the Texan placed down several chips.

"I'll raise you all, four thousand," said Henry, sliding several chips with his index finger to the center pot.

"This is crazy," said the Russian, "you are most certainly bluffing."

Henry lowered his hand to show Badger. "Am I bluffing, boy?"

Badger gave him a cockeyed stare; he didn't know the first thing about the game.

Henry returned his hands to the top of the table. "He doesn't think I'm bluffing."

"Like an enhanced pet can read," the gambler remarked.

Wouldn't he be surprised, Badger thought, rolling his eyes towards the ceiling with a smug expression.

"Oh, you might be surprised," said Henry, smiling broadly.

"I think I've seen that dog somewhere," said the Texan glancing over the edge of the table.

"Probably," said Henry, "there was an entire production of his type; he's just one among hundreds."

That hurt. Even though Badger knew Henry was lying, he didn't see a reason why he had to be so convincing with that. He shook his head and looked about.

"Probably," said the Texan, looking back at his cards and sighing deeply. "I prefer regular dogs myself, border collies. I don't think that you can really improve on what's natural.

Badger lifted one side of his mouth to expose his teeth, a scowl creased onto his face. He let out an indignant sound and twitched his ears.

"I wouldn't exactly say that," said Henry.

"Who cares," said the gambler, "I'll raise you again, two thousand."

"I am out," said the Russian, placing his cards facedown on the table. "This is crazy; I am going to the dining room."

"Suite yourself," said the gambler, smiling roguishly. "Anybody care to make another wager, or you could just back out."

"I don't have that much left," said the Texan, laying his cards down and pushing himself away from the table and walking away to a bar that was close by.

"Well then," said the gambler, winking at Henry, "it's just you and me."

"Yep," said Henry pressing out several chips to raise the wager.

The gambler, unused to a game going on like this, swallowed nervously. "You think you have a good hand?"

Henry shrugged and leaned back in his chair. "Do you have a good hand?"

"Ah," said the gambler, placing both palms on the table and tapping his fingers on the felt cloth. "What say we just push all the chips into the center? You know, just take a chance; see who really had a good hand."

"Fine by me," Henry said as he calmly pushed all his chips into the center.

"Forget it," said the gambler, showing his cards, "you win."

Henry looked down and saw a Joker in the hand. He smiled broadly. "Are you sure?"

The gambler nodded and sighed. "Any other day I'd have tried to bluff my way through it, but I was getting bored. It's eight AM, I'm starving."

"Well then," said Henry, taking a card out and flipping it around for the gambler to see.

The gambler laughed and took the card as he stood up. He flicked the Joker back onto the table and shrugged. "Oh well, it's about time I found someone who was a better bluffer then me."

Henry stood up and shook the gambler's hand, the one with the ring on the outside of the glove. He looked back at the pot and laughed. "I wish we were betting real money, I'd be rich."

"I thought you already were," the gambler said.

"Richer," Henry corrected himself in a tone that made it sound like a joke.

The gambler, Henry and Badger walked together to the dining room; a circular room with an immense crystal chandelier and a band playing stringed instruments. Being designated only for the special guests, there were only a few, large tables made of rosewood with soft, pink, stainless linen tablecloths. Ornamental displays made of wax fruit, roses, bleeding hearts, blue tulips and large leaves of a tropical tree sat as centerpieces to the tables. Cushioned chairs were arranged about the tables and three waiters promptly pulled back three of them for the guests to sit on.

Badger looked at the waiter that was holding a chair and staring at him. He swept his eyes about without moving his head looking if possibly the waiter was waiting for someone else. He let out a whimper to show he didn't understand.

The waiter turned to Henry and the gambler. "Which one of you owns this dog?"

"I do," said Henry, with a nod, "is something the matter."

"Yes," said the waiter, nodding at Badger, "please inform him that here on the *Ghost of Enlightenment* the pets are to sit at a table for their meals," the waiter looked back at Henry, "with the exception of your own room."

"Appears he heard you loud and clear," said Henry, smiling broadly.

The waiter was surprised to see Badger, somewhat awkwardly, sitting on the chair and shuffling his paws nervously. "Very good, there."

Badger remained on the chair as it was pushed in and tried to watch as the waiter tied a bib about his neck. He wore a disconcerting look on his face and he looked pleadingly at Henry.

"You look like you were born for gracious living," Henry said with a chuckle.

The gambler guffawed loudly at the stare Badger was giving Henry. "I don't think he thinks it's funny."

"Sorry," Henry said apologetically.

Badger shrugged and placed his front paws atop the table, looking about thoughtfully. A menu edged with golden scroll-work was suddenly thrust in front of his nose. Instead of words, like the ones that were similarly put in front of Henry and the gambler, this one, that the waiter opened up for him, had pictures. Completely unsure of what to do, Badger pressed a claw against the picture of what looked like a crown made of shrimp and a chunky kind of meat that was held together by a white glaze.

After Henry and the gambler had ordered their meals, all three menus were taken away in one smooth motion. All three watched as the waiters walked away to the kitchen, which was completely exposed for the guests to watch the cooks, if they wanted.

"Very efficient," said the gambler, "I've never been on one of these dirigibles before, but believe me, I think I might like to come again. This kind of attention you won't find in any luxury hotel in Orinoco."

"I think we know that," said Henry patting Badger's neck. "I'm just glad that the meal comes with the ticket, or else I'll eat dog-food."

Badger gave an indignant snort.

Chapter 47

"Return of the Hindenburg"

A few people joined the three companions at the tab; an elderly man with his wife and two daughters. Each daughter wore a pink dress, lined with sable fur and one of them had a small black and yellow cat that she set upon the tabletop.

Badger watched the cat as it curiously wandered towards him. He lowered his head and sniffed its face a few times before sitting back and waiting for his meal. He recoiled in shock when the cat's owner reached out and scratched his chin with her long fingernails.

"He doesn't like to be scratched?" the woman asked, looking between Henry and the gambler.

"He's not used to other people," said Henry, giving Badger a nudge.

"Not out much?" the woman asked, giving Badger a pitying look.

"More than you'd think," said Henry. "But he doesn't really socialize."

"At least he doesn't attack cats," said the woman, stroking her pet when it returned.

"He likes cats," said Henry, "he may have been raised by one himself."

Not wanting to draw attention, Badger slid his eyes towards Henry and discreetly shook his head. Henry was carrying on about being a rich computer expert too far.

"Oh, by the way," said the elderly man, "my name is Ben Marceline, founder and owner of Marceline Construction and I would like to discuss a business proposition with you."

"Sorry," Henry said quickly, "but I've already got an agreement with Program."

"Oh," said the man, shifting his eyes to the tablecloth, "well, I can always find someone else."

"Thanks anyway," Henry said around a forced smile.

"Well," said the man, "you win some, you lose some."

"You're telling me," Henry muttered.

"What was that?" asked Ben.

"I said: if it has to be," Henry said, leaning back when a hot plate with a large, peppered steak was set in front of him. "This looks good, thank you sir."

"The finest East Raindrench calves for these steaks; properly tenderized and then basted in kelp extract, with several secret spices," said the waiter with a broad smile. "How is to your taste?"

Henry found that the steak was so tender that the fork severed a small piece like it was butter. His eyes brightened and a smile lit up his face. "Excellent, send the chef my compliments."

Badger couldn't stop his mouth from watering when the aroma of the hot seafood dish arrived. Steam wafted up from the meal like smoke from a campfire. He breathed deeply through his nose and grabbed a silver fork that lay on a linen napkin next to the plate and stuck it into the dish. He rolled the morsel about in his mouth and found it amazingly delicious; he had never tasted anything like it before. He swallowed and let out a small bark of appreciation.

"That looks good," said Henry, eyeing Badger's meal. He stopped a waiter and pointed at Badger's quickly diminishing food. "What is that?"

"Lower Wreath, a Region 49 Australian dish, made from Crystal Bay oysters, held together with a salt krill and seaweed paste and topped by Scroll Sea shrimp, suited for the pallet of both humans and animals."

"Well, hope he enjoys it," said Henry, returning to his steak.

"By the way he's inhaling it, I'd say he's not going to let a scrap get away from him," said the gambler, rubbing his hands together when he turned to his lobster dinner.

The meal was the most enjoyable thing either Specter ever had, and at the end of his meal Badger unashamedly licked his plate clean. He then wiped his lips with a linen napkin and took a drink from a silver bowl of water. He smiled broadly, tongue hanging out the side of his mouth, panting appreciatively.

Henry savored every bite of his steak; it had a wonderful salty flavor, thick with pepper. He talked more business, which he knew nothing of, with the elderly man, while the gambler conversed with the man's daughters. They whiled away nearly two hours at that table. The band had stopped playing and another band replaced it, this time they were playing soft brass.

Badger watched the little cat walk about the table; he gave a small smile when it started playing with the flower display. He then shifted his eyes up to the crystal chandelier; the light flitted about like millions of fireflies. Then the sound of footsteps behind him made him turn, his suspicious gaze fell upon a waiter carrying a piece of paper.

"Excuse me sir."

Henry turned around and accepted the paper. "Thank you."

"What's it say?" asked the gambler, leaving off talking to one of the daughters and leaning towards Henry to look at the note.

Henry read it aloud, "Henry Mindell, I request your appearance on the observation deck, bring your pet, but no one else, your career depends upon it."

"What does this mean?" asked the gambler; he looked across form Henry and saw that Badger was leaning closely as well. "Does that dog listen in on everything?"

Henry and Badger gave the gambler a queer look.

"Sorry," said the gambler, sitting up straight and taking a sip form his glass.

"I guess we'd better go," said Henry, getting up from the table and bidding everyone a goodnight.

The stairway to the observation deck was a short distance from the dining room and the two Specters started to climb. When they were halfway up to the observation room, the sound of pounding feet behind them made them turn; running up the stairs was the gambler, holding an ASP.

"Stop right there, Specters," said the gambler, leveling the ASP at Henry.

"Wonderful," Henry muttered. "So you're the second assassin?"

"No," said the gambler, striding calmly up to them. He leaned up close to Henry, glancing at the snarling Badger. "The colonel sent me; I've been stranded in Orinoco ever since the Mauritanian war and this is my first job."

"Glad to hear it," said Henry, pushing the ASP away from his chest. "But would you mind…?"

The gambler moved the ASP back against Henry's chest. "I've been assigned by the colonel to be a double agent, working for the second assassin. Now… please act as angry and perturbed as you possibly can."

"Easier to do than to say," Henry remarked, placing his hands on his head and walking up the stairs, Badger in front of him, doing a good job of snarling maliciously.

Once reaching the top of the staircase, the Specters saw the back of a sturdily built figure in a white suit, white hat and white gloves with a ring worn on the outside. His hands were clenched behind his back and when he turned, his appearance made Henry's blood turn cold.

"Shall I apologize to you again, Mr. Mindell?" asked the captain of the *Ghost of Enlightenment*, smiling cruelly.

"I always did hate officers," Henry moaned, walking forcibly up to the captain.

The gambler and the captain threw a quick Nazi salute to each other, the gambler somewhat reluctantly. The captain turned again to Henry, kicking Badger sharply in the chest. He was unnerved when Badger was unmoved.

"Very interesting… It would appear that the Norwegian will be minus two assassins. But, before I kill you, tell me, why would you stoop so low as to do such a lowly act as stabbing someone in the back?"

"The front is just the same," Henry said with a smile, "a calm knowledge that the world has one less maggot."

"Charming," said the captain, reaching into a pocket and pulled out a rod composed of thin wires. "This is going to be fun. Please close the all the entrances, I'd hate for the guests to hear."

The gambler quickly closed the entrances, large double doors. He quickly locked them; the locks were circular bars that were locked with a twist. He kept the ASP trained on Henry as he walked back to the captain.

"Now," said the captain, drawing back his hand to strike, "I did enjoy interrogating during the war."

Without awaiting an order, Badger sprung at the captain, knocking him backwards and barked loudly.

"Die you... aaah."

The captain screamed in pain when Henry too was upon him, keeping his arm down on the ground by stomping on it. The gambler rushed over to them and took the rod from the captain's hand.

"Well," shrugged the gambler, "you could have at least waited for some information."

Suddenly all three operatives felt the cold metal of gun barrels pressed against their backs. They turned around and saw five soldiers wearing jet black uniforms and each with a biometric sub-rifle.

"This was going to be fun," said the captain, shoving Badger off of him and standing up to his feet. "But I guess I'll just have you all shot."

"I should have thought," said the gambler with a dismissive smile.

Henry noticed that one of the soldiers was the lady security guard, "Nice to see you again."

"Pity isn't it?" she returned, "I would have liked to see some of your programs."

"I'm just aluminum, biometrics and knives," said Henry, "and Badger is just loyal, with a fabulous singing voice that could break glass."

"What?" the lady asked.

Badger didn't ask; he stood upon his hind paws, leapt high into the air and howled as loud as he possibly could. The transparent material cracked like a spiderweb and Badger could feel the terrible strain in his lungs, it felt like someone was stabbing his throat. But he kept it up, it felt like an eternity, but everything really happened in a split second.

Several shots were quickly fired randomly, but an enormous vacuum created by the hole sucked everyone out into empty space. The operatives managed to grab some of the anchor cables (used to keep the airship stable upon the ground) and the captain and one of the soldiers grabbed two others.

"Warren should be so lucky," Henry muttered as he looked at the abyss below.

Close by, Badger nodded in agreement as he wrapped all four limbs about the cable. *What a way to ruin a vacation.*

Chapter 48

"The Reality of Day Five"

Martyr Abel looked about REPEL's central lab, called the Chamber. Like everything else in the Beehive, it was hexagonal shaped and lit by computer screens. Martyr Abel's mind was greater than any computer, and he deciphered the codes, languages and dialects within moments. In the room with him was only Victor and Samuel, and held in Victor's hands was the orb that Badger had found in the fighter. Martyr Abel had told them that the orb was something important for their research of the Day Five project.

The orb was open, and Samuel watched it with immense curiosity, the tip of his tail flicking about shakily. Martyr Abel and Sixth Entity had been taken to REPEL by Enterprise's orders; due to the reality of the threat they couldn't let the Reach capture either one of them.

Datapads were strewn atop of a cleared table; many of them were from the slide-rail station Badger and Henry captured. In the center of the table was the holographic display of an old ISEN simulation space station, named Eden; it had been abandoned for nearly one hundred years. A perfect place for Day Five to begin.

Eden was cone-shaped and nearly a mile in length; long

communication pylons and solar panels encircled it. On the display were four American ships, from which interstellar ships went back and fourth with supplies for five hundred workers that were toiling ceaselessly to install a prototype Slip-Drive Capacitor into the newly placed distortion engines. Martyr Abel had been very obstinate with giving out information and technologies, but had conceded to give them the means to travel into slip space. Going into slip space was traveling faster than wormholes, circling Mars endlessly until the occupants had aged nearly fourteen years while those outside slip space had aged just a few minutes. But slip space matter was a funny thing, if one was to apply dark matter into a contained atmosphere; the aging process could easily be controlled by a computer. Martyr Abel, Victor and Samuel would remain at a single age while their fifty subjects in the Day Five project aged from birth to fourteen years.

Martyr Abel held up a datapad and looked it over carefully. "It is odd that you must use these for your army; and each one made atom by atom."

"It's called BINAN," said Victor, placing a datapad into an aluminum crate. "We've got everything we need now for the Day Five project. Once the final neural readouts come up we'll get aboard Eden and begin the process."

Samuel leapt onto the tabletop, stumbling a little and wandered over to the holographic display of Eden. He worked at the keyboard for a moment and then watched as the display zoomed in on the engines. It was at ten percent completion. This would take a long time. He purred once and curled up with his chin resting upon one of the datapads.

"If only you had better knowledge of medicine," Martyr Abel remarked, reaching out and sliding a claw softly along Samuel's side. "It would be most interesting to hear what he could tell."

Samuel lifted his head and purred appreciatively at that.

"Samuel's been my best companion for nearly ten years," said Victor with a smile, "I'm sure he could tell everyone a lot of things."

"But he shall not become as the Day Five subjects," said Martyr Abel, handing a datapad to Victor.

"Thank you. No, he won't be; but I think he's more human," said Victor keeping in context with Samuel's thoughts.

"He is all human," said Martyr Abel, "he has the brain of one, but he's separate from you."

"I know that," said Victor, grabbing another couple of datapads.

"The Day Five subjects shall be just as human," said Martyr Abel.

"What?" asked Victor, coming to a stop when he was closing the lid of the crate.

Samuel gave Martyr a long, hard stare, very curious as to what he meant.

Martyr Abel put it simply. "Because I will make them so. As

Nimrod did with what you call the alien invaders, I shall conform them as clones to souls of men."

"How can you do that?" Victor asked, taking a step towards Martyr Abel and reaching out a hand.

"If I could teach an ant how to make wormholes, the universe would be destroyed within the passing of a year," said Martyr Abel, grabbing another, empty crate and setting it upon the table. "Let us continue with packing and leave the souls to me, there are very few qualified to wield this knowledge with me."

Chapter 49

"End Mission, Begin Game"

The air was very thin at that altitude and all the survivors knew they had to act fast or they would pass out and fall into the abyss. The Nazis, now relieved of weapons, started to climb the cables, which whipped about in the wind that whistled about the exterior of the airship. The operatives began to climb also, straining their limbs and kicking their feet to find a foothold. A loose cable was suddenly buffeted towards the survivors like a bullwhip; it cracked in the air and wrapped itself about the Nazi soldier's waist and then whipped back, pulling his screaming figure away like a serpent with a mouse.

The four remaining survivors watched in horror as the cable was pulled loose from the airship and the soldier fell, screaming and clawing at the air. He was quickly lost to sight in the black abyss, swallowed up by the thick darkness.

"I... don't suppose... this could get worse," said the gambler, panting heavily for air.

"Don't look down," shouted Henry, "just take deep breaths and climb. Jesus, help us."

Henry glanced over at the captain.

"Most of us," he quickly added.

"I like your dog's… voice," the gambler shouted.

"Thank you," Henry shouted back. "He's the most sophisticated GEM known."

"Never thought I'd see the real Badger," said the gambler, pulling as fast as he could, his muscles felt like they were being burnt to a crisp.

Badger, using all four limbs in a push-pull motion, was actually moving up the cable faster than the others, but he stopped a great deal to keep an eye on Henry, who was getting weaker by the moment. He would not allow Henry to fall, his loyalty was invincible.

"It won't matter if you survive this," snarled the captain, kicking for a foothold. "The Norwegian will hunt you down; you will live in fear for the rest of your lives."

Badger groaned in annoyance and continued to climb.

"The Reach will come and we shall rule the universe together," shouted the captain, "everyone who does not join will be killed; man, woman and child."

"Seriously," said the gambler, "he's… eergh, ah, getting annoying."

"Fine then," said Henry, reaching into his pocket and taking out the biometric pistol. His vision was starting to cloud from the lack of oxygen and pressure. His arm was shaky and the first three biometric projectiles missed. He clenched the cable in both hands when the wind started to blow him about; he heard Badger let out an urgent bark. When the wind calmed down, he held out the pistol again, steadying it against the side of the airship. He fired several shots in succession; the captain soundlessly let go of the cable and fell.

The operatives watched as the captain disappeared. Henry breathed heavily, the lack of oxygen was too much now, his arm fell and he felt his other hand start to slip from about the cable. He closed his eyes when his head began to swim and then everything went blank.

The next thing Henry knew was that the gambler was slapping his face and calling his name. Then something wet was sliding across his right cheek. Through his closed eyes lids he could see bright, reddish light and something warm was wrapped about him. He began to get a grip upon reality and found that he was in his room, in the bed and sunlight was shining through the window.

"What happened?' he moaned, sitting up and rubbing his eyes.

"You almost fell to your death," said the gambler, handing him a crystal glass of water. "Eh, eh, don't drink too much or you'll get sick. It was the luckiest thing I ever saw, as you fell, your leg got tangled up in a cable, so after we reached the top, we managed to pull you up also."

Henry rubbed his eyes and saw Badger lying next to him, his amber eyes filled with concern, but a joyful smile was fixed upon his face.

He smiled when Badger licked his cheek again.

"Okay-okay," he said, "I'm glad you're alright too."

"How did it happen your dog achieved this lung capacity?" the gambler asked opening one of the dog food bags, pouring the contents into a bowl and placing it next to Badger.

"That's classified," said Henry, "and I'm still wondering, myself."

"Well, we managed to lock the observation deck down after we exited, and with me carrying you on my shoulders, managed to get you to your room without being spotted. I found some restoration patches in your suitcase and your leg is as good as new. Now, I hope you don't get into too much more trouble, I'd like to have a pleasant evening with one of Ben Marceline's daughters and not have to tangle with Nazis again."

Henry smiled and laid his head back down on the soft pillows. "I hope I don't need you again, I'd like to enjoy the rest of trip. By the way, what time is it?"

The gambler looked at a clock that was set above the door. "9:21. Care to join me for some breakfast, or are going to order room service?"

"I'll order room service, thank you," said Henry looking about for a link.

"Oh," said the gambler pressing a button on the side of the bed.

A hologram popped up in front of Henry, first it showed the

picture of a red seagull and then changed to the face of lady with a forced smile.

"Good morning, Mr. Mindell," she said, "how are you this morning?"

Henry rolled his eyes. "You can lose the smile; we both know you really don't care."

"Right," said the lady, shifting her eyes to the side but still held the smile. "But it is company policy."

"I'm just calling room service," said Henry. "I would like some toast, eggs and bacon, and a pitcher of tea. And I'd like to know when we'll arrive at New Seattle."

"By tomorrow, sir," said the lady, managing to keep the smile. "But expect to be delayed; there's been an accident, the captain and several members of the security staff were in the observation room when the window was broken open. As a result, the observation deck is off limits for the remainder of the voyage."

"How awful," Henry said convincingly.

"Your breakfast shall arrive in a moment," said the lady, "have a good day."

The hologram shut off and then the computer on his wrist projected the face of Colonel Warren.

"How are we feeling today, Henry?" the colonel asked

sympathetically.

"My leg is a little sore, but I'll be fine," said Henry, returning the smile.

"I hope you appreciate the fact that I didn't inform you about the assistance, but we couldn't risk anyone listening in."

"I suppose I should thank you," said Henry, "and I am. But, could you do me a favor?"

"Anything," Warren said hurriedly.

Henry was silent for a moment, Warren seemed all too eager to please. "I was going to ask if you could inform the police not to detain me at the airport when we land."

"That was already done," said Warren. "I can't have you two slowed down for any reason. This mission is far too vital."

The face disappeared and Henry looked at Badger, who was looking at him with his eyes cocked and head twisted to the side a little. "Warren's acting a little generous. I hope that's not suggesting that this is a suicide mission."

* * *

After collecting their luggage from the conveyer drones, Henry and Badger walked calmly past the police that were questioning the other guests of the *Ghost of Enlightenment*. He threw a casual wave to the gambler, who was standing next to one of the elderly man's daughters; he waved back with a smile. Badger heard the gambler say, "good luck."

The remaining time they had had upon the airship was very relaxing, mostly for Henry, Badger was still very high strung. Henry watched as Badger turned and snarled at the sound of a bell, the last assassination attempt had done it. Badger seemed more machine now than ever.

Badger twitched his ears at every sound and let out an almost inaudible growl when someone walked close. His face bore a severe scowl and his eyes betrayed nothing other a serious resolve. He felt he would not rest easy until this Norwegian matter was resolved.

As they stepped out of the Airport and onto the covered curb, a man carrying a brown suitcase came up behind them and tapped Henry on the shoulder. Badger whirled about, paws firmly planted and partially baring his teeth. Henry turned about and saw the man hand out the suitcase.

"You left this back there sir."

Henry looked down at his arms and saw his only suitcases. He gave him a suspicious look. "Are you sure?"

The man nodded. "Absolutely, sir, now my family is waiting for me at the car, have a good day."

Before either Specter could say or do anything, the man set the suitcase on the ground and walked along the flexcrete sidewalk until he arrived at a green car. He opened a door and two kids rushed out to hug him. Then they climbed into the car and drove away.

Henry put down his suitcases and crouched down to grab the other one. But Badger let out a whine and placed his paw upon Henry outstretched arm. Henry watched as Badger shook his head worriedly.

"Is he afraid there's a bomb in there?"

Both Specters looked up to see a security guard, carrying an old-fashioned, explosive-launch shotgun. Beside him was a guard dog and behind him was a dowser. A dowser was a large, four-legged insect creature with a yellowish exoskeleton and two fuzzy pincers just in front of its compound eyes. Dowsers were BINAN creatures that were made for the purpose of a chemical agent they secreted to deplete radiation or biological hazards.

"I-I don't know," said Henry, "a man just walked up to me and handed it to me, I thought I only brought along two cases."

"Let Cork sniff it sir," said the man, snapping his fingers over the suitcase so the dog would step over and sniff it. After a moment, the dog walked back to guard's side and sat down. The man smiled and patted the dog on the head. "That's it then, you'll be just fine."

"Thank you," said Henry, "I guess I did bring three after all."

When the guard walked away, Henry laid the suitcase on its side and opened it a short ways. Inside was a tripod, a miniature mounted turret with a laser-based sensor attached underneath and a large cylinder of SEAR. He flipped it over and saw a metallic backpack-like object and something wrapped in black cloth.

"Praise the Lord," said Henry, closing the suitcase, "he hasn't let us down yet."

They quickly hailed a taxi and drove away from the airport into New Seattle. New Seattle was partially built over water and its towering skyscrapers were so intimidating that one felt compelled to just stare. Some buildings were connected by scores of transparent tubes known as skyways that allowed quick and easy travel from home to work. Domestic robots continuously cleaned the streets and hundreds of sports cars zipped about everywhere. Street venders set up shop at the curbs and waited for customers all day.

"Is there any buildings about the area that are larger than Biotech?" Henry asked the driver.

"Yes," said the driver, a tough black woman with a scar across her lips from a contact with a gang. "Slot and Cruise, a department store, they've got a great observation deck where you can see the entire city. But why would you want to see Biotech? It just a crackerbox and everyone knows that it's security is high latch."

"I'm a contractor," Henry made up quickly, "I need to see it in person to get my bearings."

"Whatever you say," said the woman, "but, other than starting over completely, you're not going to do much for the looks of it. As I said before, it's only a high latch crackerbox."

"I'll be the judge of that," said Henry, "I'm sure I can change it a little."

*   *   *

Henry and Badger stepped out of the department store's elevator and looked about the rooftop. There were nearly twenty civilians who were sitting on chairs, looking through binoculars at the city, purchasing items from venders and generally relaxing. Henry set the suitcases onto the ground and waved his hands over his head, calling out to get people's attention. Badger helped by barking.

"Excuse me," said Henry, "we've received word of a possible bomb threat up here, please do not panic and do not alert anyone else. We just need you all to leave calmly, it's probably nothing serious."

At first everyone just stared at them, then, in a calm, very quick way, everyone began to crowd into the elevator. The operatives made sure everyone was off before examining the full contents of the new suitcase. He took out the turret and the pack, unwrapped the object from the cloth; it was Badger's neural AI. He attached it to Badger's ear and turned back to the case. Underneath where the pack had been was some folded, black cloth. Underneath the cloth were their knives and two ASPs.

"Looks like a full kit," said Henry, unfolding the cloth. They were ultra thin uniforms. He removed his suit and put on his uniform, then tossed the other to Badger who did the same.

The uniforms were built for stealth, but the ASPs didn't have silencers. The uniforms had a kind of hood with a piece that could be stretched across their mouths to muffle their breathing and protect them from toxic fumes. The HUD of each uniform was a hologram project in front of their faces, which could only be seen from their perspective. The uniforms zipped up along the chest and were moderate performance enhancers, built in gloves and foot-shaped shoes provided extra comfort and mobility.

They both walked around the top of the store until they spotted Biotech. As the cabdriver had said, it was shaped like a cracker box. Its roof was over two hundred feet below, three large satellite dishes sat on top and every window was darkly tinted, giving it an abnormal appearance. Red holographic signs appeared on each of the four sides, reading: BIOTECH INDUSTRIES.

"Looks like its going to be a long drop," Henry remarked.

"Not long enough," Badger projected.

"You enjoy structural jumps?"

Badger nodded. "I like wind."

Henry put the pack on and shoved the ASP and knife through a band that was about his waist. After this he pulled the cloth piece over his mouth and called to Badger. Badger leapt up onto Henry back, gripping the pack tightly. He set up the turret; the tripod's legs automatically drilled themselves into the flexcrete wall. He inserted the SEAR and then climbed upon the wall. He reached back and grabbed two handles that were on the corners of the pack.

Badger tightened his grip, closed his eyes and felt Henry take a deep breath; then he felt Henry leap out into the empty air. He opened his eyes and grinned when he saw they were plummeting downwards. He loved this part of a structural jump.

Henry yanked on the handles and two wings made of a gray, conductive fabric shot out each side. The wings caught the air like parachutes and the Specters began to slowly circle down towards Biotech. Henry voice activated the turret and used his HUD to target half of the windows on the upper floors.

"Fire," he said.

The turret fired and swiveled at an incredible rate, the molten aluminum shattering the windows into countless crystal fragments.

"Cease fire," Henry said when he was confident that there were enough broken windows. He reached his hands up behind him and grabbed the wings, folding them back so that they would descend rapidly. When he was level with Biotech's roof, he released the wings and glided in fast towards the broken windows.

They came to a sudden landing four floors down from the roof. Badger leapt off of Henry and Henry pushed the handles back into the pack, causing the wings to draw back in. Inside the room were several wide-eyed people, standing against the far wall, staring at the broken windows and the two Specters. Henry stood up and addressed them in a calm tone.

"It would wise if you started evacuating the premises. But first, where are your managers?"

"Never mind that," Warren said, coming over the uniform's integrated link. "We've already located them; the closest one to your position is on the floor above, testing room fifty-two. The other is in the lobby. But we haven't been able to pinpoint Nordahl. But we've spotted the professor; he's on an elevator heading down with a bodyguard."

"I love technology," said Henry, looking at a display that appeared in the center of his HUD; an x-ray view of Biotech. The Managers and the professor were highlighted in red.

"We're on it."

The civilians had already run out of the room and the sound of pounding footsteps were heard out in the hall.

"We may have to wait a minute," said Henry, "Badger, see if you can find something useful."

Badger quickly came up with a long length of cord.

"That'll work," said Henry, taking the cord. He walked to the broken window and looked up, "I might be able to throw you up there with this. What do you say?"

"It should work," Badger projected, taking an end of the cord and tying it about his waist.

Henry planted his legs firmly and reached out a hand; Badger grabbed the hand in both forepaws and curled up into a ball. With a great grunt, Henry swung Badger up; Badger caught the edge of the next floor with his paws and quickly pulled himself up.

It was a small office space, holographic computer screens were set upon a couple desks and two dead civilians lay close by the window. Badger quickly hid the bodies behind a large plant so that Henry wouldn't see them. After he was satisfied that Henry wouldn't see the collateral damage, he tied the rope to one of the desks and called Henry up.

Henry climbed up the cord and looked about the room, overlooking the blood on the floor. He was about to go over and open the door, but then he spotted something flashing on one of the screens. He touched the flashing box on the screen with his index finger; it opened a brief message, which he read aloud.

"The Norwegian requests your appearance in the sub-level with the Reach leaders. The final act in the Homunculus project is to commence within the hour. The professor is already on his way, but the Norwegian feels that he still will not talk. Alder in and now out."

"That confirms it," said Warren, "Alder is defiantly not an AI, she must be a person."

"Or thing," Badger projected.

"Take care of the Managers quickly, then find the sub-level, eliminate Nordahl and be sure to stop his project," said Warren, in a darkening tone.

"Don't worry, we'll take care of it all," said Henry, opening the door and looking out into the hall; it was deserted.

"Warning, all personnel evacuate the building, terrorist attack in progress on upper levels," loudspeakers were blaring out.

"At least our cover isn't blown," said Henry, running hurriedly through the hall, searching for the room.

Badger was right behind Henry, running on all fours while matching Henry's pace. His ears caught the sound of footsteps close by; he turned his head and saw three figures with guns running around a corner. The mercenaries were doing their job.

The mercenaries' weapons fired bullets; the bullets practically exploding anything they hit. They gave chase and fired at the Specters.

Badger whipped around and shot the legs of each mercenary with his ASP. The mercenaries fell wounded and yelling to the floor, gripping their disabled legs. Badger nodded in satisfaction and started after Henry again.

"Thank you," said Henry rounding a corner, the doors were marked and the numbers were rising into the forties.

Another mercenary appeared around a corner and again Badger shot his legs before he could get a shot off. The loudspeakers kept on blaring on about a terrorist attack, so much so that Badger shot several of them.

When they reached room fifty-two Henry shot the handle off and kicked it open. Inside were two overturned desks, barricades for five mercenaries and the manager, a wiry man in a blue overcoat.

"Kill them all," commanded Warren.

Without question or hesitation, the Specters liberally shot up the room, breaking canisters of chemicals which started a fire, shot through the desks, killing those on the other side. The manager was severely wounded, crawling on his back, away from the two operatives, even to the point of partially crawling into the flames.

Henry and Badger finished him off with several shots.

"Good work," Warren commended, "now get to the lobby as fast as you can, the second Manger is leaving."

"Ready for another structural jump?" asked Henry, stepping out of the room.

"Completely," Badger projected with a bark.

"Move it Specters," Warren urged.

Chapter 50

"The Homunculus"

Police and SWAT teams had arrived at Biotech and were starting to press inside; there was some discussion as to the jobs of the mercenaries and law enforcement in this predicament. Everyone was shocked and enormously surprised when a human and a GEM in black uniforms landed on the street, shot a man through the head and rushed inside before anyone with a weapon could react.

Inside, Henry and Badger managed to get into an open elevator. Henry quickly hit the button marked: SUB-LEVEL, the doors closed just before a rain of projectiles reached them. Henry and Badger sagged against a wall, breathing heavily and laughing a little; Badger busily scratched his left ear.

"That'll give you something to tell your grandchildren about," said Henry. "Whew, let's never do that again."

"Hurry, the both of you!" Warren was shouting now.

"What's wrong?" asked Henry, shaking his head to relieve himself of the sudden daze.

"A Reach of Nimrod ship, or Reef, has just arrived; it's three times bigger than any ship we've got. Great! Two Chinese ships have just appeared behi… never mind, it appears there's an entire invasion fleet, converging on every planet in the solar system. Finish the mission and get to Red Haven, we have everything to lose."

Henry let out a moan and sagged further. "Why does it have to happen on such nice days?"

"*Kitty Hawk* will be waiting for you until midnight," said Warren, a clinking noise in the background. "If we don't see you within five minutes of midnight, we'll use another pilot. But I can be sure that you won't… uh oh."

"What now?" asked Henry, "is the galaxy captured?"

"No, there appears to be a distress signal coming from the sub-level. Our equipment can't see through the ground, something's gone wrong, hopefully that means Nordahl has been killed for you. You'll be our eyes down there. Try to get the professor out safe."

"Will do," said Henry, getting up quickly when the elevator came to a complete stop.

The doors slid open and both operatives yelped in surprise when a dead mercenary fell face down on the floor. They stepped up close and looked at several large wounds in the man's back, like something had clawed him to death. One wound was on the back of his neck, almost cutting it off.

Both Specters' heart skipped a beat when an eerie howl arose from the flexcrete halls of the sub-level. Gunfire was heard, screams and pleads sounded everywhere. Both Specters stepped cautiously out, knowing they were up against a something completely new.

"I do not like this, Henry," Badger projected.

*   *   *

Canine, for some unknown reason, was acting a little strange, moving around on all fours or rolling about like a ball. All along repeating the phrase: "will, won't, he is trustworthy, but is it okay? Will he do right? Or shall he do wrong?"

Dave watched his guardian with great fascination; he was standing and twisting about to watch Canine's odd spectacle. Victor, Samuel and Warren were in the room also, Warren was watching the Specters movements through their HUD's integrated camera.

Samuel was watching Canine from Victor's right shoulder, managing to keep his shaky limbs planted. His eyes slid about, keeping easy track of Canine's movements. His ears twitched a little as thoughts raced through his partial mind. It was rather entertaining in a strange way. But there was also something very uniform in the droids behavior.

Victor had been watching the Specters' movements along with Warren; he was mystified and curious about what had happened in the sub-level. As he watched, he felt Samuel shift on his shoulder and nestle his cold nose into his ear and start to whisper. Samuel didn't really whisper, but had managed to create a way to exhale and inhale in ways that made meaningful sounds.

Victor turned about and looked at Canine and then strode over and gripped her chassis. "Please halt and explain, Canine, because we're curious. What are you trying to say?"

Canine unfolded herself from the ball she had rolled into and stared at Victor. After a moment she turned to Dave. "Your father gave me something and then he told me to give it to someone I could trust."

Victor watched as Canine turned back to him and stretched out an arm and then an almost imperceptible compartment opened, revealing a small disc. Victor reached out his hand towards the disc, but then Samuel ran along his arm and picked the disc up gently in his mouth and then ran back up to his shoulder.

"I can trust you both," Canine projected. "Use it to our advantage."

Victor stood back up and held his hand under Samuel's head, Samuel immediately dropped the disc. Victor thanked Canine and turned to Warren, who was still watching the screen.

"Sir," said Victor, "we now have the professor's research."

Warren quickly turned around and looked at the disc with raised eyebrows. "Well done, where was it?"

"Canine had it," said Victor, gesturing towards the droid with a smile.

"Then get them both to Red Haven," said Warren. "The professor is still a priority. Let's hope what's on the disc is something you can use."

"Yes sir," Victor said, exchanging satisfied looks with Samuel.

"If what our intelligence thought Mr. Hudson had is on that disc, and since Martyr Abel won't tell us anything, we can start D-5."

"I'll begin processing this as soon as possible."

"With this invasion fleet, we'll need to initiate it as soon as possible. Send the disc to the lab… now."

"Yes sir," said Victor.

Dave and Canine watched as Victor and Samuel left the room in a hurry. Dave looked at Warren, who had turned back to the screen again. "What's D-5, sir?"

Warren didn't even glance at Dave. "That's classified until it's in action. When it's in action it'll be unstoppable; unless we were wrong about your father's research."

"I hope dad's alright," said Dave.

"Don't worry," Warren said kindly, "these are the best in the business. They've never failed… yet."

"I heard that last word," Canine projected with a hiss.

*   *   *

The sub-level was a catacomb of rounded halls that twisted in a uniformed manner; ceramic maps were placed at every corner. The lighting of the halls was a red tube-light that ran along the ceiling, giving the halls an eerie gleam. There were dozens of rooms with circular, metallic doors adorned by yellow lights in the center that opened when touched. The rooms were mostly laboratories, but there were some bunkers and surveillance rooms. Other than dead bodies and the strange howls, the halls were completely void of movement.

"When I signed up, it wasn't to be in eerie sub-levels with mercenaries that are clawed to death and just thrown all over the place," said Henry.

"Enough sarcasm," said Warren. "You have two more passengers waiting for you at Red Haven. The kid's droid just gave us a disc and it's been confirmed that it's the professor's research, we will now be able to jumpstart start project D-5 on Eden."

"Genesis one all over again," Henry remarked.

"Part of it, anyway," said Warren.

"Well let's just say that it… what was that?"

"What?"

"Quiet, listen," said Henry.

Badger was frozen stiff as he concentrated his ears onto a sound that was coming from behind a damaged door up ahead. Fumes issued out from the two rattling doors that shifted on their tracks. Inside they could hear someone moaning and as they listened they could also hear him talking.

"Can you hear what he's saying Badger?" asked Henry, striding silently up to the door.

Badger nodded and caught up with Henry after taking a quick look about the hall. "He's talking to himself, like he's another person, something's scared him to insanity and he's talking about shooting himself."

"Then we'd better hurry," said Henry arriving at the door and pressing his fingers into the crack and pulled. The door wouldn't budge.

"Wanna give a paw, Badger?"

Badger fit his claws into the other side of the door and pulled opposite of Henry. Both Specters were amazed at how the doors now slid open easily. The doors opened to reveal a room with chemicals on the floor releasing the fumes, several dead mercenaries and an incoherent mercenary with his pistol aimed at his head.

Henry rushed over and snatched the pistol away and then kicked the mercenary over. He pressed his foot down onto the mercenary's chest and instructed Badger to guard the door.

"What happened here?"

The mercenary looked up at him as if he hadn't even seen him until he spoke.

"What happened here?" Henry asked again, emphasizing each word by applying more pressure upon the man's chest.

"The Norwegian is mad," said the mercenary, "crazy, he turned those friendly, disabilitied people into monsters. I thought I was guarding a project that would help them. I gotta go, no sense staying here, they're everywhere… everywhere? Give me my pistol and I'll send my head everywhere. There's fifty of them, hee-hee, big, huge… claws, such terrible eyes, I'd kill them all, but I'm a coward. I hope the others get out, but not me, no way, I'm not going anywhere, I need my pistol. You're looking for the doctor, right?"

Henry nodded. "Yes and we're also searching for Alder and the professor."

"Alder, sweet Alder," said the mercenary. "The adopted daughter of the Norwegian, I'm not so sure she likes him and I'm not so sure he likes her. What a perfect match. Now those aliens he brought down here should've been the clue, a clue to run, but we were too fixed on the Homunculus; but then they woke up. If you want to find them you'll have to go to the teleportation room, yes, that's where you need to go. It's close by, I'd join you, but I've got to blow my brains out. May I have my pistol?"

"Where's the teleportation room?" Henry asked, he felt pity for the mercenary, who was utterly transfixed with terror.

"It's not on the maps, but if you go to the teleportation room, you'll see a door directly ahead. The Homunculus have large teeth, kill them all, they're strong and fast, there's only fifty, nothing we can't handle, I don't believe me either. Can I have my pistol?"

"How about not?" said Henry.

"That's fine then," said the mercenary, smiling pleasantly, "I'll just find another way to kill myself before the Homunculus get me and eat me alive."

"Forget that," said Henry, handing the pistol back to the mercenary, "just do it after we leave."

"No problem," said the mercenary, sitting up and placing the barrel of his pistol against his right temple. "Do have a good day or night, I don't know what time it is and suddenly, I don't think I care."

It felt good to leave that room; behind them they heard a shot, followed by the mercenary saying, "missed," and then a second shot, followed by silence.

"I'm glad to leave that room," Henry muttered.

"He was definitely not prepared for what happened," Badger projected.

"Warren?" asked Henry. "Have you found anything else about Alder?"

"Yes, I was just about to tell you about her extracurricular activities."

"Alright then, tell us."

"She's got several counts of minor extortion, nothing serious, no pictures and she donates large amounts of money to children's hospitals, orphanages and foster homes. She also owns several small ice cream shops, has made and sold several very advanced programs, one of which REPEL owns. Isn't that interesting? She might know exactly what we're doing. And yet…"

"And yet it doesn't appear she wants to," said Henry.

"Exactly," said Warren. "Maybe she's on our side; she could be a lot of help. She also has hacked into our national security, I'm surprised no one spotted it until now, possibly to allow in several Nazis and these Reach ambassadors."

"Sounds like she doesn't know who to trust," said Henry, performing a shoulder roll to get around a corner and leaping up. Nothing was there.

"You said something similar to that when you first heard about the Reach of Nimrod," said Warren, "so you might be right this time too."

"People who are uncertain are usually dangerous," said Henry.

"Someone who gives to children's hospitals and orphanages?" Warren said shrewdly.

"You may have a point," said Henry. "But let's not forget -Whoa!

What is that thing?"

Suddenly, an enormous beast, twice as large as any human, completely hairless with tan skin, came tearing around a corner. It was like an enormous warrior of Anubis, the Egyptian god of the underworld, its eyes were red as blood and its claws were like short scythes, its teeth were like ivory and its body was as covered in stiff muscles and sinew like iron cords. It shrieked and charged at the Specters.

Badger and Henry peppered its body with molten aluminum, but it kept coming as though the projectile were merely annoying stings. Both Specters dove to the sides and let the beast crash past. The beast smacked into a wall, but it then shook its head and charged right back at the Specters. They fired wildly at it with the same effects.

"What is this thing?" Henry demanded.

"A Homunculus," said Warren, "shouldn't that be obvious?"

"Alright," said Henry, "do you have any idea on how to kill it?"

"Not a clue," Warren said dully. "But why not try and aim for the head."

"That's a little hard at the moment," said Henry, diving to the side again.

"I can't give you any help," said Warren, "but... SWAT teams are coming down; perhaps they can distract some of them."

"You've got a wonderful sense of humor," Henry said hollowly.

"Got him," said Badger, after dropping the Homunculus with several headshots.

The Specters had little time to celebrate; more Homunculus were starting to appear. They ran as fast as they could, shooting wildly about, spraying and praying as they went. The Homunculus were wildly clawing at the flexcrete floor and each other to get at the Specters, some were even leaping over the backs of others to try and get ahead.

"Its times like these I wonder why I became a Specter," said Henry.

"Never a dull moment," Badger projected, running backwards for a moment to get off several good shots, one of which was lethal.

"I hope the teleportation room is close by," said Henry, "we can't keep these things at bay forever."

Badger's eyes widened in joy when he saw a dead mercenary ahead and next to the dead mercenary was an SMG and a satchel of ammo. He snatched up both while they ran past the body and tossed them to Henry.

"Use these."

"Thanks," said Henry, turning around firing the bullets into the ranks of Homunculus.

The Homunculus weren't able to handle the bullets, but the bullets mainly had a blow-back effect. Instead of piercing their hides, the bullets only caused the Homunculus to be knocked back a few steps. Other than that, the bullets were practically useless. But, after a few magazines had been used, the Homunculus gave up the chase and ran off elsewhere.

"I think an Assault Rifle would do much better," said Henry.

"We weren't figuring on this," said Warren.

"Obviously," Henry commented.

"Henry," Badger projected, "I think I've found the teleportation room."

Chapter 51

"The Vending Machines"

The door, clearly marked TELEPORTATION ROOM in bold letters, was different from all the others in the fact that it was diamond-shaped. Two lights were situated in the center, needing two hands at once to open it. Henry pressed them both and the doors opened to a wide, circular room. Like the mercenary had said, right across from them was another door, same as the first. But the room was curious. In the center were several holographic computer screens and keyboards, which were hovering above the ground and all along the walls were capsules and crystal tubes. The tubes had been smashed open from the inside; the Homunculus had originated from this room.

"Before proceeding into the next room," said Warren, "get the data from the computers and check the capsules."

Once they entered the room, the doors closed behind them. Henry went to check the capsules, while Badger stuck his right paw into the screens, absorbing the memory into his suit which then transferred it to REPEL. The computer displayed a white bar that was slowly turning red and above it were the words: DATA CLONING.

Henry stepped over to one of the capsules and removed a

magnetic panel from the front, the capsule stood higher than him and when he opened it he nearly jumped. Inside was a young women, void of an arm and the lower halves of her legs, a strange green gel was pasted on her bare scalp; attached to the gel was a cable. Henry traced the cable outside of the capsule and saw that it linked into the broken tube to the right of the capsule. He closed the capsule up and went to open the others. In each was another disabled person, all young; in total there were twenty-five men and twenty-five women. He could tell each one was dead.

When he opened the last one, he didn't even look at the occupant; he stretched out his right arm and touched the face of the young man. "Jesus, I pray you never let him know who he once was, amen."

He closed up the capsule and stepped back solemnly.

"You're a very emotional person," said Warren, "we've talked about this before."

"We've never talked about murder, genocide and… this, this goes beyond murder and they've robbed these people of all they were. And all they could have been."

"Eyes on the mission, Specter, the cloning is almost complete," Warren said to distract Henry.

Henry reloaded the SMG's magazine and stepped up to the second door. He waited for Badger; as soon as it opened he was going to kill everything that wasn't retrievable.

"Done," Badger projected, withdrawing his paw from the screen. He dropped to all fours and rushed to Henry's side. He stood up again and took out both his weapons. His kukri was held out along the barrel of his ASP like a wicked bayonet; action was the only thing on his mind.

Henry slammed two fists into the lights, one of which held his SMG, and the doors slid open, bright blue and white light flooded in from the last room. The Specters were forced to cover their eyes for a moment and when they looked again they saw several light-rimmed silhouettes, standing in the wavy blue and white lights. One figure was instantly distinguishable, a Grand Marshal terref. The others were anybody's guess, but at the feet of one was an animal and from the smell, Badger knew who it was.

"That's the GEM that the Hispanic had," Badger projected.

"Had is right," said a voice (it was impossible to tell who had said it) "I had one of my men slit his throat to get it."

"You never told me that," said a female voice, sounding extremely shocked.

"Enough," said Henry, "we're here for the professor and Alder; I'll pay you in lead and aluminum."

"From the looks of it you'll never be able to find them," said the voice again. "Unless of course you try and shoot us all."

"I'll go for your legs then," said Henry, pulling the trigger and shooting bullets around into light.

The voice laughed and the Specters watched, dumbfounded, as the bullets, still moving, were moving at a slug's pace after exiting the barrel. The occupants of the room, except for the GEM and one man, wiped the bullets away before they impacted. The one man let them hit him, the bullets merely dropped to the floor.

"Only something organic can move anything fast in here," said the voice again. "We are about to teleport to the Reach of Nimrod fleet and there is nothing you can do to stop us now. The professor is the one who didn't move to stop the bullets; he's wishing he was dead at this moment. He still hasn't told us anything, but rest assured I'll be able to recreate a better version of these Homunculus."

"Noooo," Henry shouted, throwing the gun at the alien, who staggered back a step, and then he took out his knife and dove into the light.

"No, Henry," Warren shouted. "Don't go in there."

But it was too late; Henry was atop of someone, someone huge, with great strength. They tussled about, for a moment, but then the Grand Marshal came up and struck Henry on the head. Everything went dark and Henry fell limp.

Badger leapt forward towards the teleport, but the grand Marshal whirled about and dealt him a vicious kick to his stomach, he went sprawling across the floor. Everything was beginning to swim, he barely managed to prop himself up onto his forepaws. He stared at the light, unable to move.

One of the figures, probably the professor, tried to jump out of the teleport, but he was caught by the collar by the Grand Marshal and the GEM had grabbed the heel of his shoe. The professor kicked, sending the GEM out of the teleport and into the other room, where she tried to scramble back up to her feet.

Badger watched in horror as the large figure picked up Henry's knife and was prepared to stab the prone figure, but the one Badger guessed was Nordahl stayed his hand. Badger heard a scrambling noise to his left; he turned to see the blurry, double figure of the GEM, running back to the teleport. Badger turned to try and see Henry, but all he caught was a glimpse. The large figure was holding Henry up by the hood, the professor was struggling to break away from the Grand Marshal and then the blue and white light lifted like an elevator. Everyone but he and the GEM was gone. He collapsed breathing hard, trying to refocus his mind onto what was going on. He thought he heard Warren's voice, but then there was another one, female, the words were jumbled and it was all too confusing for him to understand. He moaned and tired to curl up, but something had him by the muzzle and was even staring into his face.

After a moment, he shook his head vigorously and everything

started to come back into focus. The first thing he saw was the feline GEM, she was talking to him, but with Warren talking also, he couldn't understand a word. He scrambled up to his paws and barked as loud as he could. That silenced them.

Badger sat back down onto the floor and looked from the GEM to the empty room. Then he turned back to the GEM, who was staring back at him with wide eyes; in her eyes he could see himself, he was alone. For the first time in his life, he didn't know what to do, Henry was gone. He looked about and whimpered a little, but then he remembered something and he turned, snarling angrily at the GEM.

"For some unnatural reason you're talking," he projected, "but I don't care, you're Alder, aren't you?"

The GEM nodded, but remained silent, looking away from Badger's eyes. Badger noticed she was wearing a black suit with yellow shoulder pads, a blue swastika was in the center of her chest.

"You know where Henry is, don't you?"

The GEM shook her head.

Badger raced forward slammed her back against a wall and barked aggressively. "You are lying."

"Okay-okay," said the GEM, "I do know where he is, but I don't know where that is."

"What is?"

"The Gate," said the GEM, "they talked about going to the Gate. I don't know what that is, please don't kill me."

Badger released her and dropped back down to all fours. "I can't, my superiors have emphasized that too much." he turned his attention to the teleportation system.

"You will not take her into the teleport to go after Henry," Warren growled, "you're going to Red Haven."

"And what if I don't listen?" Badger projected.

"What?" Warren sounded greatly taken aback, Badger had never contradicted a single order before. He quickly stated his reasoning, "because there are more important things to be done. The *Kitty Hawk* needs a pilot and you're the only one left who can do it."

Badger looked into the empty room and then at the computers, he probably couldn't follow anyway. "What time is it?"

"About seventeen until the cryo-bomb goes off," said Alder.

"What?" Badger projected, staring at the GEM as if just noticing her.

"The doctor installed a cryogenic bomb to go off in case of emergency, which would only go off twenty minutes after the teleport moved him and select others to a safe location. That way he could return at any time to get rid any intruders and then thaw his allies. But he doesn't plan on ever returning now. Now if you don't mind, I'd like to leave."

Badger looked about the room; he spotted his weapons and picked them up. "Talking animals, what else?"

"Hellooo," said Alder, "you're the one talking with a piece of fabric attached to his ear. And we've only got sixteen minutes now."

"That's more than enough time to reach the elevators," said Badger.

"Won't work," said Alder, "that's another fail-safe option; the elevators will stop working so that no intruder gets away."

"Are you saying there's no way out?" Badger started to look about urgently, he had to get out so he could find Henry.

"Yes, there's another way out," said Alder, "and it'll take us both. But even if we do get out of here, there's not a much better chance out on the surface."

"Why?" Badger projected leaping up and hitting both the lights on the door. He looked about the hall and then signaled for Alder to come with his ASP.

"Thank you for moving," Alder said, her voice dripping with sarcasm. "He's got something scheduled in time with the cryo-bomb, a mega drop of ten thousand genetically altered creatures. And that's just for this city. Go right."

Badger turned about and stared the GEM in the face. "How about you lead the way," he projected.

"No problem," she said, slinking around him on all fours, "I think you have a good point."

"Never mind that," Badger projected with a growl, "just make sure you keep on moving, I can hear the Homunculus."

"Can you handle them?"

Badger gave her low bark. "Quiet, you're going to lead them to us. Until I find Henry, nothing is going to stop me; I'll destroy every ship they have if that's what it takes."

"What did you do? Swallow a dictionary?" asked Alder.

"Quiet," Badger projected while listening to the sound of heavy claws scraping over the flexcrete. The Homunculus were close by and they sounded very agitated. Their constant sniffing and growling made Badger's blood turn cold and his neck-fur stood on end.

"Ah, good," said Alder, "I found one."

Badger suddenly realized that he had stopped right behind Alder, who was staring at a capsule, a much smaller version of the ones in the teleportation room. Set in front of the magnetic panel was a holographic screen, which Alder worked with, the screen displayed various charts and words at such rapidity that Badger couldn't read them, but Alder seemed to be able to.

"What's this for?" Badger asked.

"You'll see in a minute," said Alder, digging her claws around the edge of the panel and pulling it open. "I need to do something before we can 'ead into the escape route. Stay 'ere and 'old off those 'Omunculus until I get back."

"Back from what?" asked Badger, cocking his head and twisting his ears.

"You'll find out," said Alder, closing the panel, there was a low hum and the capsule began to rattle.

Wonderful, Badger thought. He braced his hind legs and held both weapons out, the ASP out front and the knife held high. He could smell the Homunculus; they had a distinct, musty smell about them, like rancid water. He snarled viciously when one appeared, walking calmly around the corner, it spotted him and snarled back.

Another snarl came from behind Badger, he turned his head to see another one coming from the opposite direction. He looked back to the first one and saw that two others had joined it. He turned so that his back was to the capsule and he could see the Homunculus converging from both directions. He tapped lightly on the capsule with his kukri.

"Take your time in there," he projected.

The Homunculus lunged forward, mouths open, teeth dripping with blood and saliva. Badger let out a bark and charged towards the larger group, knife held high. When he came to the closest Homunculus, he dodged to the side to avoid its mouth, then dug his claws into the side of its neck and stabbed the kukri deep into the jugular vein. He gave the knife a twist and leapt off, ready for the next three.

The dead Homunculus kicked its legs convulsively, twisting in circles.

Chapter 52

"Don't Look Back"

Badger leapt up and stabbed his Kukri deep into the shoulder of another Homunculus, hanging on and riding as the Homunculus ran about in circles, trying to throw him off. Badger tore at the beast's leg with his hind paws and then utilized his ASP to shoot at its head. The beast seemed to have regained enough sanity to feel the pain, it howled loudly and Badger shot at the back and side of its thick skull.

One shot finally reached its brain and the beast let out a yip, dropping to the floor and rolling about after death. Badger had been thrown off and his kukri was still lodged in the Homunculus' shoulder. He rolled out of the way of another Homunculus' claws and leapt up onto his hind paws, shooting at the others.

One Homunculus made a leap for Badger; Badger leapt aside and peppered its side with aluminum. The Homunculus whirled about and opened its mouth wide. Badger lunged forward and stuck his ASP and foreleg into its mouth, firing three shots up into the brain. He quickly pulled his foreleg back when its mouth snapped shut.

"Try and keep your legs, Badger," Warren said, "a one-armed pilot isn't worth too much."

"Sorry," Badger projected, diving to the side as the last Homunculus dove at him.

When he leapt up, the Homunculus swung at him with the back of its claws, knocking him into the body of the Homunculus that had his kukri. His ASP had flown out of his paw on impact. The Homunculus coiled its legs and leapt at the GEM.

Badger reached up and yanked the kukri out of the shoulder, slashing it through the Homunculus' lower jaw and throat in one movement. Blood splattered all over the place and the Homunculus released a long blast of hot, rancid breath.

Badger managed to wriggle out from under the dead Homunculus' head, partially using his kukri as a spike to stab into the other Homunculus, pulling himself forward. After releasing himself from the heavy weight, he lay on his back on the floor, taking deep breaths to slow down his heart. After a moment, he got up, wiped his knife upon one of the bodies and retrieved the ASP.

He leaned his back against the capsule and tapped it. "You can come out now."

At first there was no reply, but then, something inside began to move around. Then the panel opened and a soaking wet scrap of life fell out; shook a little and turned to Badger.

Badger let out a shocked bark and aimed his ASP.

"Calm down," the thing said, "It's me, Alder."

Badger lowered the ASP and leaned close to the wet thing, it wasn't the GEM, but it was wearing the same suit. "What did you do?"

"Something that's needed to do certain things," said Alder, using her claws to comb her fur. After a moment she showed herself to be a mongoose, still dripping wet, a different voice, but the same mannerisms.

"That wasn't a clear answer," Badger projected.

"Ooh, curious are we?" Alder said without looking at Badger. "I shifted my consciousness from that GEM to this mongoose. Okay, let's get going, we've only got like ten minutes. That's right, follow me. My consciousness was shifted into the mongoose in a cryogenic storage room somewhere else in the building; funny, the doctor never told me where. I 'ad to thaw out quickly, that's why I'm so wet. I've secured a number of GEM forms, but I suppose the doctor isn't very choosey about 'ow 'e gets them for me. I'd like to get my teeth about 'is throat and... that's blood that I'd savor."

"Isn't he your father?" Badger projected, getting alongside Alder, looking and tilting his head at her.

"In-law," Alder corrected, sounding relieved at that fact. "Being part of his experiments seemed better than what I had going before. Childhood prodigy and my…"

Badger noted how Alder's voice trailed off and she looked away;

Badger sniffed and inquired, "What did you have going before?"

Alder suddenly whirled on him, slashing at him with her claws and snapping with her teeth. "You will not ask that again, or I won't show you the way out and we can spend eternity here as a couple of ice sculptures."

Badger had been forced sideways against a wall by Alder's sudden fury, his eyes were wide and his ears were pressed back in shock. He nodded to show he agreed. He stayed rooted to the spot until Alder moved a few yards away and then he regained himself and ran up alongside her again.

"Ready to brave the claws again?" asked Alder.

"The Homunculus aren't that tough," Badger projected with a glance at Alder.

"I was talking about me," Alder said.

"You're not so tough either, I just wasn't expecting you to suddenly attack," Badger projected with a glare. "But, the next time you do that, I'm going to break your left hind leg."

Alder stepped to the side to get away from Badger and shivered. "I was kind of 'oping I was in the custody of a gentleman."

"No such luck."

A howl sounded close by and then several screeches erupted out of the darkness somewhere behind them.

Badger and Alder began to run now, their paws pounding hard on the flexcrete. Alder turned around a corner and slipped on a puddle of blood next to a dead mercenary. She quickly scrambled to all fours, but then Badger grabbed her and tossed her onto his shoulders.

"You're too slow, hang on," he projected, racing forward on all fours. "Just tell me where to go."

"All right," Alder shouted, digging her claws into Badger's uniform. "Forward. Right! Keep going, there's just a few more turns. Look out for the cable."

Badger dropped and slid backward on his side underneath an enormous cable that had somehow been dislodged from the flexcrete ceiling.

"Nice," said Alder. "Don't throw me off. Go left! Go down the second 'all on the right."

Badger leapt over a dead Homunculus and nearly got his feet tangled in the strap of a mercenary's SMG. A broken door was leaning out, Badger moved around it, but the slight wind he was making had upset its balance and it fell at him. Alder screamed and he leapt to the side, avoiding the door by fractions. He ducked down Alder's prescribed hall and saw that a chemical laboratory had been opened; flames and smoke poured from it. When he rushed by, something exploded and flames shot out across the hall, the chemical fire clung to everything, turning the hall into a burning tube.

"Why are these Homunculuses insane?"

"It's said only Homunculus. It's simple really," panted Alder, looking back at the flaming hall. "One more left and then I'll tell you when to stop. The doctor formed them all, one atom at a time, but he neglected the brain a little, never fully appreciated it."

Badger turned left, noticing that the side to the right was squared and covered in maintenance tubes. Also there was the noise of rushing water on the other side, sloshing about at a leisurely pace.

"My mistake," said Alder, "the other direction, the tubes should be on your left."

Badger growled and came to a skidding stop. He got traction with his claws and raced in the opposite direction he had been going.

"Anyway," Alder continued her narrative. "It never crossed his mind about how much the surface area of the brain matters. The brains were simply rounded, no neural connections and so when the volunteers had their consciousnesses shifted into the 'Omunculus, they went crazy because of the pain. Their brains are creasing and folding at an incredible rate, in other words, they've got severe 'eadaches. Stop 'ere."

Badger came to another skidding halt. Alder leapt off his shoulders and approached one of the pipes, on it was a yellow BINAN symbol. Badger stood upon his hind legs and took out his weapons; he could hear Homunculus close by. But he kept one eye on Alder.

Alder placed a paw upon the symbol; a green line appeared, stretching from both sides of the pipe, then breaking in the center. The piece of pipe pushed itself out and the green line split to expose a compartment.

"I'll just be a second," Alder said, crawling into the pipe. The compartment closed up and looked as if it had never been there.

"She had better not be lying to you," said Warren. "That might just have been her escape route."

"We'll just have to wait and see," Badger projected, watching a Homunculus shadow crawl around a corner. "What's on the other side of these pipes?"

"The city sewers," said Warren, "if that's your escape route then you'd better be careful, there are sharks in there."

The Homunculus was now completely around the corner, its drooling lips opened wide to expose its teeth. It unleashed a low growl and sprang towards Badger. Halfway to Badger, it rose onto its hind legs and clenched its paws like fists.

Badger let out a snarl and fired at it. To his amazement, the Homunculus dropped dead after only a few shots in the chest. He didn't have time to wonder as more and more Homunculus were appearing, these too were falling dead as easily as the first.

"It might be that their brains are no longer as deformed," said Warren, "the relief of the pain is now allowing them to relax their muscles a little. That means their muscles are no longer providing an armor against the projectiles."

This is good news, Badger thought, dropping two others with five shots. But Homunculus were still pressing into the hall. Badger was finding it extremely difficult to keep turning and firing, the Homunculus were just coming far too fast.

Suddenly, there was an explosive noise from inside the pipe Alder had crawled into, the panel flew open and bolts of purple electricity shot out in all directions. Badger wasn't touched, but the Homunculus caught the full brunt. Those that weren't dead were on fire, running away, howling and shrieking.

"Are you coming?"

Badger whirled about to see a small, square opening in the pipes, water gushed from two of them. He dove through the opening, landing in waist-deep water. Quickly he got to his hind paws and coughed out the saltwater. He turned and watched as the opening closed up again with the same green lines.

"I was worried for a moment there," Badger projected.

"You should still be," said Alder, she appeared from behind a vertical tube; she was in the cat form again. "The cryo-bomb will go off in thirty seconds and freeze everything inside and outside."

"Then let's get out of here," Badger projected, putting away his weapons and running, Alder was close behind. "Why are you that form again?"

"Because to open that panel, one form has to die," said Alder, grabbing hold of Badger right foreleg. "I waited a moment for this one to thaw before I applied the rapid transferal. That mongoose is nothing but ashes now. Also, this form seems to bother you."

"You have no idea." Badger groaned and leapt over a piece of discarded metal. "Why did you want to get rid of the mongoose?"

"It's the only form that can open that panel," said Alder, practically letting Badger drag her, "more security precautions."

Badger was finding the water to be getting deeper. He looked about urgently for something to get upon, for he could hear something large moving in the water ahead. But there was nothing, not even a box.

"Get on my shoulders," Badger projected.

Alder obeyed wordlessly, very glad to get out of the water. She used two claws to pull a weed off of her hind paw and toss it away. She rested one paw on Badger's head and watched attentively to what he was doing, all the while looking back to see the effects of the cryo-bomb.

Badger took a deep breath and ducked his head underwater; he heard Alder give a muffled cry and dig her claws into his fur. He looked about through the murky depths until he spotted movement, a large, torpedo-shaped creature was moving in a zigzag formation towards them. He took out his ASP again and held it out straight, waiting to see what the creature would do next, all the while he moved towards it, the water ever deepening.

After a few moments, the beast got close enough for Badger to identify the species. It was a bull shark; its pale eyes seemed to hypnotically stare off into space. Badger knew he had to fight. He raised his ASP and fired three shots, all three hit the shark, provoking it to charge forward. Then it all happened at once.

Badger dove to the side, the shark's fin clipped his stomach a little and then the cryo-bomb went off. The entire sub-level and everything in it was frozen instantly, several pipes burst when the water froze. The freezing cold turned much of the water outside to ice and the shark died after going into shock from the sudden cold and then pierced its brain on a protruding spike of ice.

Badger lifted his head above the surface and took a deep, shaky breath; the sudden shift in temperature hadn't sent him into shock, but it took the air out of him. He put the ASP away and swam off through the sewer as fast as he could. He whimpered uncontrollably against the cold as he stroked his forelegs and kicked with his back legs as fast as he could to warm up again.

Alder was on the brink of shock, barely holding onto Badger's uniform with her claws. She tried to talk, to tell Badger to hold onto her, but all she could manage was a quivery huff. She breathed heavily and moved to see if she could lie down between Badger's shoulders. But the movement sent a violent pain throughout her entire system; her voice was choked in her throat. When she finally managed to gasp it out, her legs gave way and she plopped face first into the icy water.

Chapter 53

"Cross External Powers"

Professor Hagen Hudson applied a wet rag to the back of his patient's head. He had already wiped away the dried blood and cleansed the wound with supplies the Reach had issued him, the alien had hit him pretty hard. They were in a cell aboard a ship, a uniquely angled cell, illuminated by a ring-shaped hologram in every corner. The door to the cell was comprised of dozens of horizontal blue bars, each opened opposite the direction of the one below and above. The Reach of Nimrod had just put them into the cell and left them; leaving two terref Militant's behind to guard them. In the cell directly across the hall were several bedraggled soldiers, who were setting up crude dominoes they had made from bits of equipment they had been left with.

The Militants mainly ignored the professor and his patient; they were more intrigued by the soldiers and their game. This gave the professor some privacy to check his patient's uniform for any pieces of equipment that might be useful, but the aliens had already removed anything that could be used as a threat.

Hagen's heart leapt for joy when his patient started to move and moan. He pressed the rag harder onto the bruise and his patient let out a louder moan, getting the Militants' attention. Hagen was overjoyed when his patient reached up and snatched the rag away.

"What are you trying to do? Kill me," the man groaned.

"You really should lie down," said Hagen, trying to hold the man down. But holding the man down was like trying to hold back an avalanche with water. The man got up enough to sit down and looked at the professor, he seemed to have no idea what had happened.

"Where am I?" the man asked, rubbing the back of his head tenderly.

"You are upon the *Appraised Transgression,*" one of the Militants said, "for some reason the Doctor requested that you were important for the professor."

"I met some of your friends on Forerunner," Henry said, regaining awareness; he hid his feelings behind a mask of hatred. "The Pure Collect sends you both a message."

The Militants leapt back when Henry spat at them. Then they just stared at him as if they couldn't believe what he had just done. They looked at each other and then back at the man. They backed up another step and watched.

"They seem shocked," said Henry, turning back the professor. "I'm Henry Mindell of the United States Specters, I was sent to rescue you and kill Nordahl… seems as though I made a mistake."

"An idiotic one," Hagen said as kindly as possible. "But, at least I've got some company. Hopefully he won't work with you too."

"What do you mean?" asked Henry.

Hagen lifted his shirt to show large scars on his stomach. "He loves his work."

Henry stared at the scars, his face turning to pity. "Just be glad your son is safe."

"Dave?" Hagen almost shouted, he let his shirt drop. "They haven't got 'im?"

"No," said Henry shaking his head. "If Badger's still alive he'll get him off planet to a safer location."

"I hope so," said Hagen, "I would have to tell Nordahl everything, or else Dave would go through what I've gone through and I can't let that happen."

"Good, then let's remind you of what it feels like to be motivated."

The prisoners turned to see Nordahl standing outside the bars with the Mauritanian. As soon as he saw the symbol about the Mauritanian's eye, Henry felt his blood grow hot, but he remained silent; he could wait.

The doctor gestured for the Militants to open the bars and when this happened, he and the Mauritanian stepped in. The Mauritanian shoved Henry aside and grabbed the professor by the collar of the shirt.

Henry took this opportunity to pounce upon the Mauritanian's back and jerked so that he let go of Hagen. The Mauritanian tried to shake Henry off, but Henry had too strong a grip. The Militant's moved to assist Sekou. Henry started to choke the man with his left arm and then grabbed his chin with his right. With a quick pull and a sickly snap, the Mauritanian fell dead with his neck broken.

The Militants clubbed Henry unconscious and tossed him into a corner. Hagen made several pleas for Henry's life, to which Nordahl listened.

"Don't worry, professor," said Nordahl, laying a hand on the pleading man's shoulder. "You need someone to keep you from going insane. You two, drag that worthless carcass out of here and be sure to bring some food to that one when he wakes up. I can see we're all going to get along fine."

One Militant dragged the body out of the room while the other closed the bars. The bars closed with a metallic *clang*. Henry was left alone in the cell, with the soldiers across the way pressing themselves against the bars to see the dead form of the Mauritanian being dragged away. "That guy's got some attitude," said one of them.

Chapter 54

"Filled Cheeks"

Badger had removed his uniform and wrapped it about Alder, he held her tight against his chest (he was swimming on his back) with his left foreleg while his other pulled him forward. He could feel Alder shiver, she hadn't contracted hypothermia, that much Badger could tell, but she had fallen into shock, she needed to be taken outside. The water was warmer where he was swimming now and he kept an eye out for other predators.

Plants growing out of the cracked ceiling dripped water, the droplets hitting the water below resounded about the sewer with eerie echoes. Floating plant life drifted along, wrapping about any stationary object they came in contact with; Badger constantly had to untangle his limbs from long strands. Small sea creatures swam about, shrimp and schools of small fish dodged around Badger as he searched for an escape route. Underneath the surface, crabs scuttled about, picking at dead fish and plant life. A large eel shot out of a tube and grabbed one of the crabs and then ducked back inside.

Badger didn't know how long he had been swimming, it seemed like hours. Alder had his uniform, so he couldn't check the time on his HUD. All the time he was down there, he was hearing noises from above, rumblings and the sound of large objects smashing into the flexcrete streets.

Alder moaned a little and curled up tighter on Badger's chest. She wasn't' shivering as much now and her breathing was growing more rapid.

Come on, Badger thought, *There's got to be a way out of here somewhere.* He punched the side of the sewer and growled. It seemed as though this would never end.

And then a light up ahead caught his attention, it was coming from about the next corner; he moved his limbs harder. Around the corner was a dead end with a ledge, and on the ledge was a ladder leading up to an opening to the surface.

Badger barked for joy and prayed thanks. He quickly pulled himself onto the ledge and then scrambled up the ladder with Alder still held against his chest. He was now out in the open above ground, and the most unpleasant sight was there to greet him.

High above New Seattle was a gigantic Reef, titanium colored with red along the edges. Skates and Seeps zipped overhead in perfect formations, but there weren't any Scarabs or landing crafts. The reason was soon clear.

A sleek needle-shaped object, released from underneath a Skate, flashed down and smashed into the flexcrete just few yards in front of Badger. Badger stared at it for a moment, then the sides of the object dropped off and several black creatures crawled out.

They were large crabs, spiny backs and four legs with sharp tips. But these crabs didn't have mandibles; instead they had three jaws, rimmed on the inside with spikes, sharp enough to tear flesh.

Badger held out his ASP, it had been kept inside the confines of his uniform, as he felt his fur stand on end. He backed up and the crabs slowly crawled towards him. He growled menacingly, although he knew it wouldn't mean a thing to them.

The closest crab literally leapt at Badger, legs spread wide and mouth opened. Its body split in half with a single shot of SEAR.

Badger barked loudly and fired at the other crabs, which were charging him. He blasted one in half and kicked another to the side. They were like ants, swarming at a single target.

Badger fired until all the crabs were dead. He took a deep breath and then let out a yelp when two other needles smashed into the ground.

He didn't wait around to see what came out of them; instead he ran and ducked into the nearest building. It was a little blue structure, set between two apartment buildings. He slammed the door shut and looked about.

It was completely lifeless, several chairs were overturned and one table had an apron laying on it. There was a large counter with a holographic sign underneath it, displaying all the wares. A ceiling-fan was still spinning and soothing music was playing in the background.

Badger unwrapped Alder from his uniform and wrapped the dry apron about her. She let out a sigh of relief and lay still on the chair where Badger had set her. Badger put his uniform back on then checked the time. He still had about seven hours till midnight.

He climbed atop of a table and looked out the window; the streets were void of people and the crabs were scuttling all over the ground. Several of the crabs crawled down the sewer opening. Badger looked about the building again and began to notice some things.

It was an ice cream parlor. There were several vending machines behind the blue and white speckled counter; on the counter was crystal computer screen. Next to the screen was a crystal box with metal seams, half full of money and marked with a sticker: For St. Christine's school for the mentally retarded. Above the door on the inside was a golden plaque with a poem written on it.

> No small gift is wasted
>
> That is given to those who haven't tasted
>
> The wonders of life as we
>
> But have yet to find a gracious life
>
> Given from us to them
>
> In my eyes the innocent are a gem

Not deserving of strife

A parent's refusal may end a dream

But let them have a future

From us who love Ice cream!

(Alder)

Badger looked back down at the bundled up form of Alder, this was one of her shops. When he looked back out the window, a crab was on the glass, trying to bite its way through. He leaped back and fired one shot through the window, destroying the crab.

He breathed heavily and then leaned his back against the counter and then slid down until he was sitting with his forelegs draped at his sides. The excitement of the day was too much and the loss of Henry was coming back to him. He curled his tail up onto his lap and began to stroke it.

"Badger," said Warren.

Badger gave him a grunt.

"Forget about finding a way out of the city, we'll send a Mosquito to pick you up. We'll designate the LZ on your HUD; until the LZ is designated, stay where you are. I'll start up the link again when we find one."

"Good luck," Badger projected, still stroking his tail.

"Be back ASAP," Warren said.

Badger sighed and lowered his head, a whimper escaping from his throat. His ears drooped forward, almost covering his eyes, he sniffed, remaining silent and still. He could hear the Reach aircraft flying overhead and the rumbling of the Reef's engines. He didn't know what to do.

Alder's eyes fluttered and then remained open. She squirmed her way out of the apron and shook vigorously. After several deep breaths, she stretched until her back popped like a telescope. It took her a little while to realize where she was and what had happened. She spotted Badger, he wasn't moving.

"Hey, Sniff," she called. "Are you dead?

Badger looked up at her and then back down at his tail. "Sit down, they'll be calling soon and we'll get out of this city."

Alder sat down upon chair and stared at Badger. "You've seen the crabs?"

Badger nodded. He inclined his head towards the window, indicating the hole he had shot in it. He then returned to looking at his tail while prodding at his lips with his tongue.

Alder shook her head when she saw the hole. "Pity, this place was doing really nice. Ooh, when I see the doctor again, I'm gonna…"

Alder didn't finish, she hissed and scraped her claws on the wall.

Badger looked up at her again and twitched his left ear at the noise she was making. He groaned. "Will you stop that? We've got enough to worry about."

"Look," said Alder, leaping onto the floor and trotting up to Badger until their noses were practically touching. "I'm tired of that piece of fabric speaking your mind for you. Open your mouth and talk for crying out loud."

"I can't talk," Badger projected, cocking his head.

"Yes you can," Alder shouted. "If you're thinking in English, you can speak in it. It's the international trade language."

"I'm a GEM," Badger projected with a growl, pressing his head forward so that Alder would back up. "You've had biological surgery done on your forms to allow you to speak, I haven't."

"I've 'ad absolutely no surgeries," Alder said firmly, pressing Badger's head back by pressing hers forward. "Now talk or I'll rip your ear off."

"You're in no position to be making demands," Badger projected, whipping out his kukri and pressing the tip against her chest.

Alder ignored the knife and scowled at Badger. "You're just thick 'eaded, not the smokiest idea of what's 'appening. Do you know who you are?"

Badger nodded. "I am Badger, the most advanced GEM in the world."

"That's what everybody says," said Alder, "I looked at your profile."

"So you have been watching us," Badger projected.

"Of course I 'ave, it's what I do. But I never told or gave anything to Nordahl, I 'ate that pig. I just want to be 'appy and you're in the way of 'appiness."

Badger looked from side to side, kukri still held out, but his face was a blank. "Say that again, please."

"With pleasure," said Alder, rolling her eyes and sitting down. "'Ow old are you?"

Badger was taken aback. "You're not asking…"

"I asked you a question," Alder shouted, "now be courteous and answer."

Badger lowered the kukri. "I've been with REPEL for nearly four years."

"So you're about five then," said Alder, "five years old and already a genius."

"Wait a minute," Badger projected, shaking his head rapidly, not grasping what she was hinting at. "What are you…?"

"What are you're skills, Badger," Alder asked in a much calmer, more collective voice.

Badger stared at Alder, eyes cocked; he still didn't know what she was saying. "I've qualified in every test for every kind of work station. I could be a lab assistant right now."

"Ah," said Alder, looking towards the hole in the window. "And so you're modest too. No... I mean it. According to your profile you excelled in everything that only 'umans can supposedly do. Doesn't that make you think you're something special?"

"All it means is that I can think well in combat," Badger projected, sheathing the kukri.

"If you can do all that, why can't you talk?" Alder gave Badger a sideways look and a charming half smile.

"Because I don't think it's possible."

"And 'ow long have you thought this way?"

Badger sighed and looked out the window. "Ever since I was a puppy. My mother and siblings couldn't talk so I figured I couldn't either."

"Better all the time," Alder said. "Let me tell you something, Badger. I am only three years old and I can work with computers like someone who is ten times older than I am. I'm just asking you to talk with your mouth, give it a try, Sniff; I'll get us something to eat."

"Stop right there," Badger projected with a bark. He leapt up and aimed his ASP at Alder.

Alder had leapt upon the counter and was making her way

towards the vending machines. "Oh, will you relax. I'm just getting us some ice cream, I'll keep talking and making noise, you'll know I'm here. And start talking."

Badger sighed and sat back down with all four paws on the floor. He heard Alder humming and he also heard the sound of dishes clinking together. He thought for a moment over what Alder had been saying and then he took a deep breath and exhaled. He closed his eyes, lifted his head and tried to copy the sounds in his head.

"Ly alr you interastid in mey?" he asked. He heard Alder laugh and he rolled his eyes. *Why didn't I think of this before?,* he thought angrily. But he also felt a great surprise, he had actually said something, it was terribly pronounced and clumsy, but he had said something. Though his voice sounded like a teenager, he wasn't sure if this was good.

"Why 'ave you stopped?" Alder demanded. There was a soft hissing noise as the machines were being activated.

Badger asked the question again, feeling good that the sounds were becoming much easier now, "why alr you... interestered in mey?"

"Try it one more time, please," said Alder. "I'm almost done."

Badger took a deep breath and tried it again. "Why are you interested in me?"

"Very good," said Alder, sounding very pleased and excited.

"Just answer the question," Badger Projected.

Alder appeared back upon the counter, she was bearing an aluminum foam cup filled with a pinkish colored ice cream. She dropped upon the floor and set it down, "This is mine. Now try and use those brains of yours and not talk with your stupid ear."

"Forget abot the AI," Badger said, "just answer my quethion."

Alder leapt upon the counter and disappeared without saying a word, she returned a moment later with another aluminum foam cup, this one full of chocolate ice cream. She set in front of Badger and smiled. "All boys love chocolate."

Badger backed away from the cup. "Chocolate will kull me."

"No it won't," said Alder, taking a lick at her own. "I love shrimp."

"I can't have ice cream anyway," Badger projected, "why would you think…"

"Enough," Alder shrieked, leaping Badger's head and pulling at his ear. "Get rid of that thing."

Badger shook her off and snarled. "I'm trying to stay alive. Now answer my question."

"No," Alder said defiantly. "Not until you get rid of that thing, or start talking properly."

Badger reached up and deactivated the electronic adhesive and tucked the neural AI into the collar of his uniform. "Are you happy now?"

"Very," said Alder. "Now, first of all… nah, forget a long explanation, I'll go straight to the point. Me and you… we're kind of the same. We're both aliens 'ere."

For some reason, Badger had no idea what came over him, but he found himself rolling on the floor, yipping jovially, his equivalent of a laugh. His tail wagged quickly and he only stopped for a few moments when he was out of breath.

"I'm serious," Alder said, giving Badger a severe look. "We're not supposed to be here on earth. We're from elsewhere."

Badger was still yipping.

"If you don't mind, I can tell you something," Alder shouted. "Thank you. Stop smiling, what I'm about to say is going to deliver a blow."

Badger managed to lose his smile and regain his serious composure.

"Well, first of all, my real form is exactly what you are," said Alder, looking Badger over. "Except I didn't have as large a head and I have reddish fur. And, as I said before, I'm only three years old. Our species has an ability, when were abandoned or abused at a very young age, to develop our brains really fast. That's why we're both like this, your qualified as an adult at age fourteen, you're only five and I'm only three. Our bodies won't grow anymore, which is natural, but we're both forced prodigies."

Badger looked at her and then back at the chocolate ice cream. She spoke very believably, but he still wasn't sure. "I'll need mor proof."

"Look at your reflection in the window, Badger," said Alder, inclining her head.

Badger stepped over to the window and looked at his reflection. It seemed fine to him, his fur was filthy, but that was natural. He looked back at Alder and shook his head to show he didn't understand.

"Look at your cheeks," said Alder, "notice anything?"

"No," said Badger.

Alder sighed and leapt up next to Badger and placed her front paws on both cheeks. "I can both see and feel it, they're still round with baby fat. Look again."

Badger looked into the window again, and reaching up a paw he rubbed his cheek slowly. After a moment he had to admit, Alder was right. He nodded to let her know he understood.

"If you were a GEM, or regular dog, you would have lost it all in your first year," said Alder, stroking Badger's neck. "Now, you need to know, everyone has been wrong about you. And all I have to do is show you some baby fat and you look about ready to jump in front of a train. You should be happy."

"Henry," Badger said. "I have to find Henry."

"You're not focusing, Sniff," Alder said, giving Badger a shake. "You don't have to find anything or anyone."

Badger whirled on her, whipping out his kukri pricking her stomach with the tip. "I happen to have a sense of loyalty. I may just be an aliun… alien, but I'm a dog when it comes to loyalty, I need Henry. And, at this moment, it seems that he may need me."

Alder smacked the blade aside; snatched away Badger's ASP and aimed it at Badger. "That's it, I've had it. Your loyalty means nothing, if you don't look out for yourself your going to fail. Now don't follow me."

"Are you mad?" Badger demanded, starting to circle Alder.

"No, I'm furious," Alder cried, taking several steps towards Badger, "now back up and don't follow me."

"Alright-alright, you win," said Badger, cringing as the ASP was pointed as his face. "You can go. Look out!"

Alder whipped around. Nothing was there. The next thing she knew was that Badger had grabbed her by the nape of the neck and then threw her against the counter. She hit it with a whimper and the ASP dropped from her paws. Before she could retrieve it, Badger had her pinned to the ground, one paw on her hip and the other on her neck. She whimpered and squirmed in a vain attempt to get away.

Badger scowled at her and pressed hard. "Are we going to have any more problems?"

Alder shook her head and smiled nervously, "oh, no-no-no, definitely not, especially since I'm probably paralyzed."

When he let her up, Alder was anything but paralyzed. She rubbed her neck and groaned. "You seem to be really attached to Henry."

"He's my master," said Badger, picking up the cup and licking the ice cream. His tongue seemed to explode with flavor, he had never tasted something so delicious and in fact he couldn't stop licking it until it was all gone. By the time he was finished, there wasn't a speck of the delicious cream left in the cup.

"Master? This is America," said Alder, going back to her ice cream and moving away several paces. "You're sentient, so you should be free."

"I don't care," said Badger.

"Well, maybe you should," said Alder, "Do you really think he'll want you if you go up to him and say: 'Henry, I am an alien'?"

"Yes," said Badger, "I know him better than anyone, other than… whoa."

Smash!

A huge spider-like beast broke in through the window, also smashing the wall. It had a crustacean appearance to it, a hard dark-blue, smooth shell, six hoofed legs and a round chassis with a single large eye on its face, just below the eyes were two mandibles. It let out a warbling bellow and kicked the tables and chairs aside.

"It's a Shade," Alder shouted, diving behind the counter.

Badger fired a few shots at its chassis, but its hard shell was far too thick. It's eye seemed to be the only weak point, but the creature utilized a translucent eyelid to shield its soft eye. He leapt over the counter with Alder.

"Time to leave," he said. "Let's go."

"No way am I doing this," Alder shrieked, clawing at Badger's uniform. "It's suicide."

Badger leapt back over the counter and dodged through the Shade's legs, almost getting crushed twice and then he was out on the street. The Shade was in hot pursuit. Badger, with Alder tucked under a foreleg, fired back at the beast hitting it at times, but nothing that did any damage.

"Badger, where are you going?" Warren demanded. "I told you to stay where…"

Badger turned around to show the Shade to Warren.

"Never mind," said Warren. "The LZ is to be at the New Seattle railway station, get there, I'm uploading the position into your HUD now."

"Good," said Badger.

"Is something wrong with our connection?" asked Warren, "you sound a little funny."

"I'm talking without the AI," said Badger, firing a few more shots.

"What?"

"Long story short," said Badger shrugging, "I'm an alien."

"You can explain later," said Warren, "just get back to the station, with Alder."

Chapter 55

"Time to Leave"

Badger dodged to the side when the Shade made a leap at him, it hit the ground with a sprawling crash and then scrambled back to its hooves. Badger fired wildly, not even looking at the Shade, knowing that it would be useless to do so, he might trip over something if he did. The station was close by; he could see it on his HUD. The beast kept warbling and Alder kept on shrieking and clawing at his uniform.

The Shade was another creation of Nordahl's; it was dropped by the Seeps as a heavy infantry unit. If something presented a threat to its creators, it would immediately try to kill it. It had spotted Badger's weapons and assumed defense for its masters. Its incredible strength allowed it to smash through brick walls and overturn vehicles with relative ease.

A roar ripped through the sky overhead and a formation of Skates flew overhead, each one dropped a needle. Most of the needles hit the rooftops, but three of them glanced off of a wall and stuck into the ground. These opened to release the crabs. The crabs actually had a noise that they were making, a kind of throaty, high-pitched growl, usually when they leapt. Their spiky legs clicked on the flexcrete and scratched gouges into the carapaces of the others.

Badger didn't have time to avoid the crabs, he just bulled right through them, firing wildly into their masses. He ran over the crabs' backs, not doing much damage and blew them in half with molten aluminum. The crabs leapt at him, but he managed to shake most of them off. Those he couldn't shake off he ran with until he was out of their masses.

Once away from the rest, he dropped Alder and threw the others away into the crowd. When he did this, he noticed that the Shade had stopped; it was attacking the crabs, which in turn attacked it.

He watched in horrified fascination as the crabs swarmed over the Shade until they were like a second shell. After several moments of struggling, the Shade let out a low warble and collapsed onto the ground, the crabs had killed it. Badger listened to a terrible cracking noise and then the crabs lifted part of the Shades' chassis and deposited it in the street. The crabs crammed forward to get their fill of the Shade's flesh.

"Now I'm even more concerned," said Alder, looking between Badger and the crabs, "you seem to like this."

"It's completely disgusting," said Badger, "Let's go."

Adler tried to leave, but Badger grabbed and tucked her back under his foreleg, and started in the correct direction. Alder sighed wearily and went limp. "Why bother?"

"Good question," said Badger.

With a roar of an engine and a rush of wind, a SWAT Technical came around a corner, a man in the back firing a turret at the mass of crabs. In just a few seconds, the crabs were turned into smoldering chunks of flesh. The driver saw the two GEMs, he thought it was odd that the cat was tucked under the dog's foreleg, but he opened the door and signaled them to get in.

"Are you two lost? Get in; we'll take you somewhere where you'll be needed."

"No," said Badger, "you'll take us to the train station and you won't ask questions."

The SWAT team stared wide-eyed at Badger, unsure of what to do. They watched as Badger climbed into the bed and sat down.

"What are you waiting for?" asked Badger. "I'm a United States Specter and you will take me to the station now."

The team member on the passenger side looked out the windshield and shrugged. "Better do as he says, with what we've seen today I wouldn't doubt a few aliens being in our government."

The driver shut his door and nodded. "We'd better; I'd hate to argue with a talking dog."

"Yeah," said the other. "I'm just glad that we just cleared the way we're heading now."

The Technical started to move off, the gunner gave the two one last look and returned to his work. He couldn't stop from glancing at the two GEMs though. He pressed his feet firmly onto the bed of the Technical and swiveled the turret about.

Badger let Alder go and she grudgingly sat down beside him, watching the gunner. "You've never seen anything like these have you?"

The man stared at the cat. After what seemed an eternity he spoke in a hoarse voice. "Oh, come on, this is a little much, a talking cat and dog. I want to wake up from this dream."

Alder extended her claws and slashed the man's leg. She smiled at her work, watching the man reach down and rub his leg tenderly. "You sure don't feel like a dream."

"And neither do you," the man said. "You really need to be declawed."

Alder extended her claws and swiped again, but Badger caught her paw before she caught the man.

"That's cruelty," she said huffily

"Okay-okay," the man said, "just don't do that again."

"Fine by me," said Alder, licking her paw thoughtfully. "Just be sure you watch your mouth, I'm very sensitive you know."

"I think I have that figured out," said the man.

Then there came a loud warble from above and the gunner

swiveled the turret onto a building; a Shade was running down the wall. Not knowing whether or not civilians might be injured if he fired, he radioed headquarters and asked permission. It was granted.

The Shade, its body being pelted by countless aluminum projectiles, leapt from the wall and landed in the street, giving chase to the Technical. Like an enraged spider chasing a large beetle, the Shade ran with no intention of stopping until it had caught its prey. It warbled and slammed its legs upon the ground, moving at a rapid pace.

Badger knew it would be useless to try and assist the gunner with his ASP, but his body was rigid and he stood upon his paws, the left front held off the ground. His amber eyes were fixed upon the Shade and its graceful movements. He felt Alder lean against him and shiver; she was greatly frightened of the aberration.

Alder didn't have long to worry though, the gunner brought it down right when it had caught up to the trucks rear bumper. Alder, a little hesitantly, hugged the man's right leg and purred.

"Thank you, sir," she said. "And I apologize for cutting you."

"Yeah, well," said the man looking down at her, "I apologize for suggesting that you be declawed."

Alder let go of the man's leg sat back down next to Badger, who gave her an odd look. "You seem very grateful for someone so jaded."

"And your talking pretty good for someone who just started about ten minutes ago," said Alder, looking at the sides of the street. "I don't believe this."

"I don't believe it either," said the gunner, "I'm not telling anyone about this."

"Good," said Badger.

The driver rounded another corner and the streets here were more populated. Police and SWAT teams were taking up positions behind barricades and in windows; a tent had been set up as a field hospital and civilians stood or sat about, talking to each other and the law enforcement units. Alder spotted a little girl, her face was smeared with mud and a bloody bandage was wrapped about her arm.

A tear came to Alder's eye and a hiss escaped her throat. She turned to Badger. "I'm not going to run anymore, but only on one condition, you take me with you to find Henry, don't give me to anyone else. I'm going to tear out the doctor's throat."

Badger raised his brow in surprise. "You seem so sure that Henry will be with the doctor."

"Of course he will be," said Alder, looking away, looking towards the sides of the street. "Don't ever let go of hope, your Henry's alive and he does need you."

"This is very different from what you were saying earlier," said Badger, narrowing his eyes suspiciously at Alder.

"This is weird," said the gunner, looking at the two.

"If you give up hope, then I've no hope to kill the doctor," said Alder.

"Isn't that a little harsh?" asked the gunner.

"You're not part of this conversation," Alder hissed.

"Sorry."

"And what makes you think I would want you to come with me," said Badger.

"Because," said Alder with a mysterious smile. "You don't know if I know where the doctor is, but I can assure you, I know something."

"What?" Badger demanded.

"Oh, but first, we have to find something," said Alder. "It'll be worth your while."

Badger looked at the truck bed and sighed. "I don't know if I'll be able to take you with me."

"Just ask the colonel," said Alder, flicking the tip of her tail about.

Badger paused a moment. Alder seemed to know a lot, but she might also be lying to try and escape to kill the doctor on her own. "I doubt I can trust you."

"What have you got to lose," Alder persisted, then she added, "other than Henry."

Badger let out a whine. "Warren. I'd like to ask permission to take Alder along with me."

There was silence for a long time, but then Warren's voice came over the link. "Badger, permission granted."

"What?"

Warren sighed and said it again. "Permission granted, Badger. You're cleared to take Alder along with you in the *Kitty Hawk*. And, I thought I was crazy before, but now I'm sure of it, the GEN soldier here has confirmed it; he brought you here, Badger. You are the key he talked about. And Victor has just spotted something that we missed before."

"What?" Badger asked, glancing at Alder. She had told the truth; he also felt relieved that the ice cream wouldn't kill him.

"You've been starving to death for the last four years," said Warren. "Dog food, shall we say, hasn't provided you with anything your body really needs. When you get back to Red Haven, you're to be given a nutrition shot before you take off."

"Lovely," said Badger, looking down at his forepaws.

"I didn't think it hurt," said Warren.

"It doesn't," said Badger. "But, if what you're saying is true, I'm malnourished, not at my full strength."

"That appears to be the case," said Warren. "And you should be able to use your crystal-shattering howl to a much greater extent."

"Well, I'll see you at Red Haven then." Then Badger felt the Technical slow dramatically. "Why are we stopping?"

Badger and Alder leaned over out the side of the Technical and saw a roadblock; a couple of police officers were stopping the vehicle with raised hands. The police officers refused to let them past, noting that area was off limits to everyone now. The driver, unable to come up with a suitable excuse why he had to go through and not betray the talking animals, told the officer that someone in the back had orders. The officer walked around to the bed and addressed the gunner.

"It's not me," said the gunner, he inclined his head towards the two GEMs.

"Are you crazy?" said the officer, glancing at the animals.

"No he's not," said Badger.

The officer jumped.

"I'm Badger, United States Specter, how many times do I have to say that today? I've been ordered past this point, to get to the train station where I'll be picked up."

The officer took a pistol from his belt and aimed it at Badger. "Hold it right there. You idiots, they're probably a part of this invasion of alien freaks. I'll take them from here; you go back to where you were going."

Faster than the eye could follow, Badger whipped out his ASP, shot the pistol out of the officer's hand, leapt upon the officer's chest and held the pistol right between his eyes. He barked savagely and growled.

"In the past week, I've been shot at, knocked out, trapped and dropped from outside the atmosphere. Today I lost a very dear friend and that cat is coming with me and we're going past your stupid roadblock to the train station. I've the authority and right to kill you for interfering in matters that are vital to the survival of the universe... don't tempt me!"

"A Specter you say," said the officer, smiling nervously. "I suppose that if you weren't on our side you'd have killed me already."

"Now he's starting to show some gray matter," muttered Alder.

"Are you going to let us through?" Badger asked, pressing the barrel harder against the man's nose.

"Let them pass," said the officer.

"Good."

Badger leapt off the officer and back onto the truck bed. He sat down and put the ASP away. Alder smiled at Badger, her smile almost seemed admiring, but Badger dismissed this as her trying to be motivating to her own cause.

The officer signaled for them to be let through the roadblock, which was made of several flexcrete blocks; the blocks had shorts spikes on either side so that when something hit them they would grind into the ground and stop large vehicles. He picked up his pistol, it fell apart in his hand; he dropped the pieces and searched about for another one. He watched as the Technical turned around a corner as he did this.

"What else does our government have?"

*　　*　　*

"The train station is ahead," said the gunner, taking random shots at swarms of crabs that were on the streets. In the distance, Shades could be seen crawling up the sides of buildings and then smashing in through the windows.

Several screams issued from the surrounding buildings and a couple of people ran out of doors with crab swarms right behind them. The gunner managed to eliminate the crabs, providing the civilians with a safe path, but as he was finishing off several stragglers, he let out a gasp and fell sideways with three green spikes lodged in his back.

Alder screamed loudly when the man rolled over the edge and was caught underneath a tire. She tried to hide her face in her paws, but Badger was pulling on her paws and shouting, to both her and the driver.

"Don't stop this truck, there's nothing you can do for him now. Oh stop it Alder, we are going to have to operate that turret, I can't reach it. I said don't stop, I'll shoot you. Come on get on my shoulders. What is that thing?"

Alder climbed up Badger's shoulders and grabbed the handle of the turret. She looked about until she saw what Badger was talking about, she screamed again and swiveled the turret, kicking Badger's head as if it would make him sidestep faster. She pulled the trigger and shouted the name of the creature; the vibration of the turret almost unsettled her from her perch and numbed her shoulders.

"It's a Shadoooow! Tell them to speed up."

"We're going as fast as we can," said the driver, who had just seen the beast. "Kill it already."

The Shadow was an enormous creature, dwarfing the Technical. It looked like a spider, but it had an outer shell, brown and black striped with six eyes and four jaws (which looked like spikes), just above the jaws were two huge fangs. Short knobs ran down the centers of its separate shells and its feet were covered in short, spiny hairs that allowed it climb buildings with ease.

The Shadow's eight long legs allowed it to walk between buildings without touching the ground. It had just crawled over an apartment building when it saw the Technical, its partial computer mind designated it as hostile to its creators. There was a cavity beside each eye and each was full of hardened mucous. By compressing natural gases inside its head, it shot three of the spike-shaped mucous projectiles at the dangerous gunner. It then began to walk between the buildings, chasing the vehicle.

"Die already," Alder shrieked, "I hate you, die."

The beast fired two other spikes, but because it was moving, it didn't have a steady aim. One shot missed completely and the other glanced off the roof of the truck, leaving behind a large scratch. The Shadow let out a deep, throaty rumble and opened its jaws wide, each tooth dripping with yellowish saliva.

Badger felt useless, Alder was doing all the firing and he was just holding her steady. Her hind paws dug deep at his uniform, her claws almost pricking his skin. He grunted as he tried to keep standing up when the Technical quickly rounded a corner.

"How far away is the station?" Alder shouted.

"Just a few more turns," said the driver. "We won't stop, but you can jump off and we'll try to lure it away."

"What else could you do," Alder shouted, "this truck's the biggest thing on the road."

"That's not very comforting," the passenger said to the driver.

The Shadow charged at the Technical and swung out one of its legs, trying to grab the truck, but the driver swerved to the side and avoided it. It let out another rumble and charged full ahead.

Badger noticed that the beast wasn't very surefooted; it was kind of clumsy, more than once it almost stepped on its own feet. He shouted to the driver. "Turn around and run past it."

"What? But I thought you wanted to…"

"Just do it."

The driver turned the wheel and the car slid until it was facing in the direction it had come and raced forward. The Shadow struck out at it and turned to give chase again. When it was only half turn around, Badger told the driver to turn around again. The driver didn't say anything this time, he only whirled the truck around raced onward. He dodged a couple of the legs and looked in the rear-view display on the windshield's HUD.

The Shadow tried to turn back and give chase, but its legs got tangled together and it fell to the ground with a great crash and a rush of wind. It let out a rumble and slowly moved its legs to change its position upon the ground. By the time it got back up, the truck was well gone. It crawled up the side of a building and wandered off to look for more targets.

* * *

"Here's the train station," the driver shouted back, "prepare to jump."

"What?" shouted Alder, "but it's not following us anymore."

"There's a distress signal up ahead," the driver said, "we have to get there and we can't afford to stop."

"Well, I'm not jumping," said Alder, crossing her forepaws and toppling backwards off of Badger, "its suicide and I… augh."

Badger grabbed her by the scruff of the neck and leapt off. He rolled to spread the impact, Alder was tucked against his stomach. He let her go and she gave him a severe scowl, which seemed rather comical with her messed up fur, but Badger didn't laugh.

"There," he said, "you didn't have to jump."

"You're a scream," she growled.

Chapter 56

"A Dangerous Affair"

The train station had already been evacuated before they went inside. All trains were gone except one that had been smashed by a Shadow dropped by a Reef and it landed wrong. Crabs were crawling all over the place, a few were picking the remaining flesh from the bones of some people, but Badger managed to keep them at bay until they reached a staircase that led to the roof. The staircase had a door, which he shut, keeping the crabs out and those that were already on the stairs were no big matter. Upon reaching the roof, which was made of crystal, they sat down and waited, watching the city.

They could see several Shadows crawling upon the buildings and the Reach aircraft that had dropped the Shades and crab needles. The sound of sirens drifted through the air and smoke rose over the city like great pillars. Police aircraft were quickly eliminated by the Reach, exploding in bright flashes of light. Orbital Defense Stations pummeled at the Reefs, but more could be seen in the distance, over the sea and elsewhere over the city. But the Reach of Nimrod was prepared for the great guns and their shields stayed the destroying projectiles. Stalkers, dropped from the Reefs outside the city, were flying out over the forests and sea. Ships in the harbor were being sunk and naval artillery eliminated quickly. A great column of smoke billowed up from where the airport once stood and two Shadows crawled away over the buildings. The Reach was swiftly subduing the city.

The Mosquito, surprisingly, had made it through the Reach's defenses, Badger and Alder got aboard. The VTOL flew swiftly away from the city, carrying its passengers across the sea, avoiding the Reefs. Badger and Alder watched as the city grew smaller in the distance, a large, dark cloud was rolling over it; it would rain soon. Great flashes announced the presence of lightning. At a long distance it appeared to be a sad painting with no beauty about it.

It was night when they reached Red Haven and it was raining there as well. Red Haven was a circular building with a rounded top, smaller than REPEL. There was a small hangar on one side for a few VTOLs and three observation towers stood around it. It was made out of darkened flexcrete and an American flag flew high above it.

After landing, Badger was taken directly to a lab, Victor and Samuel were there and Badger was immediately given a nutrient shot. Afterwards, Badger removed his uniform and was given a pressurized flight suit. Alder was given another flight suit, made to her size from the visualization Badger had fed them. Victor patted Badger on the head and had him and Alder eat a MAM (moisture absorbing mat), a dry biscuit that expands inside the stomach after drinking water.

Badger handed the neural AI over to Victor and smiled, squeezing his wrist. "Thank you for everything Victor and you too Samuel."

Samuel sat up regally and smiled back.

"Just be sure you end this… and find Henry. He needs you and you are his only hope."

"I hope not," said Badger, "I'll be glad if anyone saves him, just as long as I can see him again."

Victor smiled and stroked Badger's ears. "Don't worry… I'm positive God is watching over you. Thanks Samuel. No offense, but I always thought you were weird."

Badger smiled, "I never would have thought, until… it's a little odd."

"I'll listen," Victor said encouragingly.

Alder sighed contentedly and rubbed her stomach as the MAM distended her a little. It felt good. She didn't care for the aftertaste, or the biscuit for that matter, but it was filling.

She listened to Badger explaining about the baby fat. She nodded in satisfaction as he explained perfectly, word-for-word.

Victor listened until Badger was finished, he held a hand under Badger's chin and lifted it. "You're Henry's boy, Badger, don't you ever lose that knowledge. Oh, look at the time, you have to go now, Warren has a covered Technical waiting in the hangar, it'll take you to the launch site."

"Good bye, Victor," said Badger, starting to leave.

"Good bye, Badger," said Victor, rubbing Samuel's chin softly.

"Make sure Day Five makes these Reach pay," said Badger.

Victor hesitated before answering. "Day Five is beyond our hopes; the Reach shall regret ever coming to the Milky Way. Because of information you found on Forerunner and Martyr Abel, who'll accompany me, it should be ready within fourteen years."

"Fourteen years?" Badger cried. "I don't think we have that time."

"That's just the thing," said Victor, "because of Martyr Abel; we've found a dimension of slip matter, according to him it speeds everything up. Fourteen years will pass for us but only a few minutes will pass in this dimension. We've taken an old ship and installed everything we'll need into it, including the ring. Everything is going to be fine when you return with Henry"

"I hope so," said Badger, nodding at Samuel and leaving the room.

Alder followed Badger on all fours; she gave Victor and Samuel a queer look and then turned and spoke to Badger. "What's up with 'im?"

"Them," Badger corrected.

"Well, what's up with schizophrenic?"

"The cat has the front part of Victor's brain," said Badger.

"What?" Alder almost shouted

Badger explained the story to her. Alder was enthralled with it, gasping at the description of Mauritanian cannibalism. When he was finished, Alder was amazed.

"That's incredible," she said. "I might go as far to say impossible, but it's happened. Oh and what's Day Five."

"That's classified," said Badger, giving her a stern look. "Don't ever ask that again."

"Fine, what's it to me?" said Alder.

"Nothing," said Badger.

"Let's just get to the *Kitty Hawk*," Alder said, walking faster.

*   *   *

The *Kitty Hawk* was situated a couple miles away from the base, in a clearing, covered in camouflage tarps. The covered Technical simply had a canopy over its back, where a few Marines sat with Badger and Alder. The rain sounded like drums upon the canopy, like a ceaseless drone. Alder complained a little, much to the Marines' amazement. The Marines had orders not to ask questions and they kept to the orders, not sure they'd like the answer.

The passengers for the voyage were sitting inside a tent, each in a pressurized flight suit. When Badger arrived, Warren announced the arrival of the pilot and they all stood up. The princess, Dave and Canine were perplexed at the sight of Badger and Alder.

The *Kitty Hawk* was then uncovered by a few Marines, it was a marvelous sight. Originally being designed for super-fast troop deployment, it had a large compartment underneath for a score of soldiers; the compartments were covered by transparent doors. There were two large wings bent forward at the back and the cockpit was set near the nose. The cockpit had two sections to it, one in front that would have been for Henry and the other was smaller for Badger. It was colored tan with orange edges and bright red letters spelling: *Kitty Hawk*.

"I like the name," said Alder.

"I chose it," said Badger.

"You did?" asked Alder, eyes wide.

"It was an accident," Badger shrugged, "they were discussing it and I knocked over a picture of the Wright brothers."

"Strange," said Alder. "Isn't that supposed to be one word?"

"I like cats," said badger, he noticed the look upon her face. "But don't get any ideas."

Alder returned to her other mask. "Well excuse me."

Warren got everyone's attention by clapping his hands together several times. He quickly explained the danger and safety measures of the craft.

"Everyone, this is a prototype portal craft, we were designing it for super-fast troop deployment. The first several met with disastrous ends, but that was because it overheated, but we've installed a cryogenic generator near the engines, that should cool it down enough. Now, to remain completely safe inside, do not touch the walls, as the metal is sure to heat up to an incredible point. Do not try to force open the doors, wait for Badger to open them. If he is unable to open them, there are several pressure-activated blasting caps along the lower rim of the doors; they must all be activated, after eight seconds they'll blow open the doors. We've used the echo-map we found on Forerunner to target a location, the princess's home world and she's helped us locate her home city. But there are no guarantees that you'll wind up there. The *Kitty Hawk*'s not perfect and may deploy you somewhere within a two hundred mile radius of the target location. All I can say now is good luck. You may get in."

Alder was about to get into the compartment with the others, but Badger caught her. "Oh no you don't, you're going into the cockpit with me."

"That may not be wise, Badger," said Warren.

"She's my only chance to find Henry, I need her," Badger growled. "I don't trust her, she could run off as soon as the doors open and then I'd lose my best chance."

"Do what you want," said Warren. "Just be sure that the *Kitty Hawk* is a success."

"Don't worry," said Badger, climbing up to the cockpit with the aid of a ladder. He pressed his paw against a pad next to the cockpit and the screen lifted, he and Alder climbed in.

Alder grudgingly sat in Henry's seat and curled up. "You really should learn to trust people more."

"You first," said Badger, closing the screen

A Marine removed the ladder and rushed to a Technical. Everyone watched as Badger closed the compartment's door and then started the craft's engine. The craft had only one engine, but three thrusters for vertical take off. The engine curved downward and the thrusters opened and then Badger turned hit the ignition. The thrusters and engine blasted out hot air and fumes, lifting the craft, slowly at first, but then making it climb faster.

"Excuse me," Alder said nervously, "but how dangerous, exactly, is a portal?"

"The physics suggest we should just disappear," said Badger, working with the craft's computer. "If this is true, then there will be no matter where we disappeared and matter must be everywhere. That's why we're flying; if we were still on the ground we would start a gigantic fire and disintegrate just about everything within a hundred yards."

Alder stood up and pressed her paws upon the screen, her eyes filled with fear. "I'm not sure I want to be on this flight."

"Far too late," Badger said.

"Wait, if you appear in the city, would you kill hundreds of people?" Alder demanded, staring straight at Badger. "Do you even care?"

"Of course I care," said Badger, that's why Warren had placed the coordinates for a mile above the city. But we may die still."

"What do you mean?"

Badger leaned back, his paw hovering over a blue circle on the computer. "No two masses can occupy the same space. We could be crushed by the air if we suddenly appear, or, the cryogenic generator doesn't cool the craft enough."

"But that thing releases the temperature of negative three hundred degrees," Alder said, her mouth agape.

"Do you know how the other prototypes were destroyed?"

Alder's mouth went dry and she sat down, looking out the frost-covered screen. She tried to swallow but couldn't, in fact, all she could do was shiver. She managed to let out a whine and closed her eyes tightly.

Badger dropped his paw, touching the blue circle. The next thing he knew was that there a great rumbling noise and that the cockpit was no longer covered in ice. It had warmed up considerably inside. He turned back to the controls and piloted the *Kitty Hawk* downwards.

Outside the screen he could see stars and an orange moon with a multicolored ring about it. This wasn't right, according to the computer it should have been broad daylight, but now it was night, even the computer was showing it as night. And the date was a week later. Day Five was already seven days in action. Much else could have happened since he was gone.

"You can open your eyes now," said Badger.

"That was it?" asked Alder, she looked about and then pressed her paws against the screen. "Ouch, that's hot."

"Warren said that would happen," Badger remarked.

"I thought the cryogenic instigator, or whatever, would cool it down enough."

"What books have you read?" asked Badger, pulling up a display that showed what lay beneath the *Kitty Hawk*. Down below were uncountable lights, vast amounts were moving, but the majority were stationary. It was a city, vast in proportion; it appeared Warren's theory was a little off. They were right on target.

"We have arrived," said Badger.

"I know," Alder said dreamily, it sounded as if she knew the place.

Badger was about to ask her if she knew the place, but the memory of her reaction in New Seattle to a similar question halted him.

Plus, someone was contacting him on the radio.

"Contacting the *Kitty Hawk*," said a voice, which caused Badger to go stiff, unsure how he was identified so quickly. "This is the Israeli *King David*, we've waited three days for your arrival. We're sending an escort for you to fly in with."

"Will do," Badger said, almost laughing. Warren had sent a ship after him. "Light them up and we'll be down ASAP."

"'Ebrew wasn't in your file," Alder commented with a thoughtful sound.

"What are you talking about. I never took that course," Badger said as he started a descent.

"That man just spoke in 'Ebrew," Alder said with a sigh. "You had to have heard that."

Badger paused, paw hovering over the computer screen. Words of a female seemed to seep into his head, *manipulative travel increases your power*. This time he remembered them. He ran a paw between and his ears in thought. Something had happened to his head.

Made in the USA
Charleston, SC
27 December 2013